D1330129

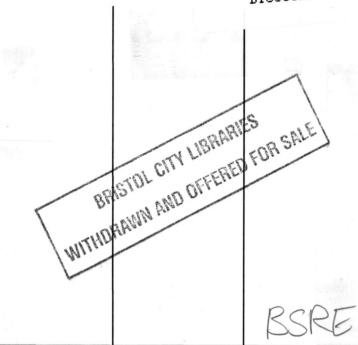

BRISTOL CITY LIBRARIES
WITHDRAWN AND OFFERED FOR SALE

BSRE

Please return/renew this item by the last date shown
on this label, or on your self-service receipt.

To renew this item, visit **www.librarieswest.org.uk**
or contact your library

Your borrower number and PIN are required.

Amazing opener and just gets better and better

Alex Knight is a British novelist who lives near Glasgow with his wife and three children.

Also by Alex Knight
Hunted

DARKNESS FALLS

ALEX KNIGHT

ORION

An Orion paperback
First published in Great Britain in 2021 by Orion Fiction,
an imprint of The Orion Publishing Group Ltd.,
Carmelite House, 50 Victoria Embankment
London EC4Y 0DZ

An Hachette UK Company

1 3 5 7 9 10 8 6 4 2

A CIP catalogue record for this book is
available from the British Library.

ISBN (Mass Market Paperback) 978 1 4091 9369 2
ISBN (eBook) 978 1 4091 9370 8

Typeset at The Spartan Press Ltd,
Lymington, Hants

Printed and bound in Great Britain by Clays Ltd,
Elcograf S.p.A.

MIX
Paper from
responsible sources
FSC® C104740

www.orionbooks.co.uk

To Luigi and Alison – thanks for everything

PART I

Thessaly

I

Thursday, February 4

Rain, beating down like it had always been raining, and always would be.

The windshield wipers struggled to keep up, even on their fastest setting. The reflections of the lane markers and the tail-lights of the truck ahead would become clear for the briefest instant, before being submerged again in a thick sheet of water. Melting into blurry, untrustworthy hints of themselves, shifted an inch this way or that, becoming unreal.

Thessaly risked taking her hand from the wheel for a second to rub her eyelids, one at a time. She didn't dare risk letting the road out of her sight for a second.

Impossibly, the downpour seemed to step up a pitch, and she saw the brake lights of the truck flash as the driver slowed down, facing the same visibility challenge. Thessaly braked a little harder than necessary, saw the needle drop to thirty, and then gradually eased the pedal down again to match the removal truck's forty-five miles an hour. *Rolling Movers*, the livery on the rear door had read, back when visibility had been good enough to make it out. Some family's earthly possessions making their slow way across America through the night. It was attractive.

The thought of a blank slate. Starting again somewhere completely new.

But for the moment, she had no choice but to head back home. She wished she could have stayed over in Reading, but she couldn't cancel the editorial meeting tomorrow morning. It had been a straight choice between going and driving back after the post-service get-together, or missing the funeral entirely. It had sounded like a good compromise a couple of days before, but the weather meant a three-hour drive was looking like extending to four or five hours, if the periodically readjusting ETA on her GPS was anything to go by. Barely halfway home, and she was already tired. So tired.

The day had taken more out of her than she had expected. Still, she was glad she had made the trip. Nate had been one of the best friends she had made in her time on the magazine. He had always been so much more full of life than any of the others. Always the first at the bar, always the first to suggest a beer on a Friday. If any of Nate's contemporaries had been asked to bet on his eventual cause of death – and Thessaly thought Nate would have enthusiastically approved of such a poor-taste suggestion – it would have been liver failure or alcohol poisoning. Suicide? She thought that would be the last thing anyone considered. Nate had always seemed so … together. Like a lot of her former colleagues, she had lost touch with him after *Inside NY* had finally shut down in 2017.

The sign for an exit flashed by. She had a momentary panic as she read 'Greenville', because that would have put her a couple hundred miles west of where she thought she was, but then she realized the sign had said 'Grenville'. Only one E. Also derived from 'green village', she supposed. Or perhaps just named after some long-dead British guy.

The removal truck was crawling now, down to thirty-five. If the rain didn't let up, she wouldn't make it back in time for the meeting in the morning. At this rate, she would get there sometime in late July.

A third light source suddenly appeared in the darkness. Up ahead and on the right-hand side, a red glow beyond the tail-lights of the truck.

The wipers swept the wash aside for another moment and she could see that it was a sign. A big red circle with some words beneath. It blurred again before she could read it.

A second of clarity. She saw that the circle was an 'O', and below it the word

OLYMPIA

And some smaller words beneath, which might have been 'All Nite'.

Blur. A third sweep would take her past the sign.

On the spur of the moment, she slowed and signaled, getting ready to take the turn when she could see it properly. She pulled into the almost-empty parking lot as the wipers cleared and the rest of the sign revealed itself.

OLYMPIA DINER
ALL NITE
FOOD * COFFEE * LIQUOR

At least two of those sounded like a very good idea.

There were only two other vehicles in the lot: a silver sedan and a black BMW SUV. Thessaly parked beside the BMW. She watched the road as the taillights of the removal truck slowly retreated from view. Her wipers were still on. Blur. Clear. Blur. Clear. Eventually the twin red points of light vanished. Perhaps the rain would stop while she took a break. It didn't seem likely, but her eyes needed a rest. She turned off the wipers and the engine and steeled herself for the run to the door of the diner.

She was drenched in the ten seconds it took her to get there.

She opened the door and stepped out of the February night chill and into the warmth, blinking in the bright light of the interior. A sign by the entrance said, *Please wait here to be seated*, so she did. She wiped the rainwater from her forehead and looked around. It was an old-fashioned diner, but not old-fashioned in the fashionable sense. It wasn't a Disney reproduction of some kind of 1950s ideal, with checkerboard floor tiles or chrome fittings or red leather upholstery, but all the basics were there. A stainless-steel lunch counter down one side, booths arranged along the opposite wall. A mix of fake vintage and humorous signs on the walls. *If My Music Is Too Loud, You're Too Old*. An old Coca Cola ad with two ladies in Victorian-looking bathing suits. She could smell coffee and hot oil.

There was only one other customer in the place. A middle-aged bald man in a worn gray suit, looking down at a notebook, a cleared plate to one side. He glanced up at Thessaly as she entered, his eyes squinting behind his glasses, then looked back down again. She thought that he looked tired, and not just because of the lateness of the hour.

Salesman, she decided. Was traveling salesman still a profession? Or another thing the internet had killed, like magazines. She thought about Nate again, and the others. She had been luckier than most, snagging her first book deal right before the final round of redundancies. But perhaps the universe owed her that luck.

A door behind the lunch counter opened and a waitress stepped out. She was young, with brown freckles and dark hair tied back in a ponytail with a yellow ribbon. She didn't greet Thessaly with a hello or a how can I help you, just raised her eyebrows expectantly.

'Just for one,' Thessaly said.

Her name tag said, *Kayla*. Kayla turned her gaze to the row of booths, thought about it for longer than seemed strictly necessary, and then gestured at the one closest to the bald man.

Thessaly noticed that there was a plate on the opposite side of his table. The remains of somebody's meal on it; bacon offcuts and an ignored pile of hash browns. She sat down with her back to the other booth.

She ordered a black coffee when Kayla came around, and glanced at the menu, quickly opting for French toast and bacon before she departed again. She shivered suddenly as a drop of icy rainwater dripped down the back of her neck. She ran her fingers through her hair to strain some of it out.

Leaning forward, she put her face in her hands, massaging her eyelids with her fingers. The urge to doze off was powerful. She didn't fight it too much. Better here than behind the wheel. Still well over a hundred miles to go.

She breathed through her nose and listened to the sound of the rain beating rhythmically off the roof, and then splashing into puddles at the side of the building. She listened to the hum of the coffee machine or the milkshake dispenser or whatever it was, behind the lunch counter. Underneath that, she heard the muffled sound of plates and skillets clattering and rattling in the kitchen.

'So are we done here? I guess I should tell you good luck.'

She started and opened her eyes before she realized the man in the next booth wasn't addressing her. She felt a bump through the back of her seat as someone sat down behind her and adjusted their position.

She blinked the tiredness out of her eyes and saw that the coffee she had ordered had already appeared. She must have been closer to sleep than she thought.

And then she heard something that made her wonder if she would ever sleep again. The voice of the person sitting opposite the bald man.

'You ever hear that old saying? Waiting for luck is like waiting for death.'

Thessaly felt an icy chill travel the length of her spine that was nothing to do with rainwater.

She knew that voice better than she knew her own mother's. She had been hearing it in her dreams for half a lifetime.

The voice of the man in the booth behind her belonged to a man named Casper Sturgis.

The man who had murdered her brother twenty years ago.

2

Waiting for luck is like waiting for death.

Thessaly straightened up in the booth seat like somebody had yanked her strings.

The words were as painfully familiar as the voice. Mitch's killer had told him it wasn't his lucky day. Then he had used those exact words before he pulled the trigger.

She didn't turn around. She stared straight ahead, at the vintage Coke poster on the far wall. It felt like she wasn't in the diner anymore. It was twenty years ago, and she was still in the Redlands Mall. She had never left Deadlands.

The guy who looked like a salesman was talking quietly. She couldn't make out individual words over the thump of her pulse in her head. And then she heard the voice again. Cold and deep. So deep that if she heard it on a song, she would assume the producer had looped in some kind of effect. Like the voice of a bad dream. Like the feeling of a partly healed wound being scratched at with ragged fingernails. She felt her head begin to swim, and the two Victorian ladies on the Coke poster looked like they were moving. She gripped the edge of the table and closed her eyes.

'You okay there?'

Kayla, the waitress, was examining her with a mildly

concerned expression. She was carrying Thessaly's order in her right hand. Her left was poised for action, as though she expected Thessaly to topple onto the floor at any moment.

'Fine,' she mouthed, but no sound came out. She cleared her throat. 'Maybe a glass of water?'

Kayla nodded and then looked up as one of the men in the other booth caught her eye. Had to be the bald man. The killer was facing the other direction.

'You fellas okay?'

'Just the check when you got a minute, thank you.'

Thessaly reached for her phone. It was lying face down on the table. When she turned it over and looked down at the screen, she was almost surprised to see the slender black mirror of a Samsung Galaxy, and not the chunky gray Nokia 3310 she had thought was pretty nifty back in 2001.

She risked glancing around. She could only see the back of his head. Dark blond hair with some gray. The collar of a plaid shirt.

Beyond where they were sitting, on the far wall of the diner, there was a neon arrow pointing toward the restrooms around the corner. She gripped the edge of the table and slid out. Her legs were unsteady as she moved quickly past the two men. She passed a mirror sign advertising Budweiser and her reflection told her why the waitress had seemed so concerned. She looked as though she was auditioning for a vampire movie.

When she had made it three booths down, she risked stopping and turning around. The two men were continuing their conversation, neither looking up.

She couldn't see the man on the other side of the table at first. The salesman's head got in the way. But then he shifted position to take his wallet out and she had a clear line of sight.

Dark blond hair. A dusting of stubble that had pinpricks of gray. A little fuller around the face and the chest than he had been twenty years ago. He was wearing a white t-shirt under a plaid shirt. He noticed Thessaly staring and glanced in her direction. She looked down quickly, pretending to examine her phone screen. When she stole another glance, he had looked away again and was talking to his companion.

Him.

It was him.

She went around the corner and stood outside the restrooms. Relieved to be out of the line of sight of the man in the seat, but not wanting to take her eyes off him. How long did she have? They had already asked for the check, and the waitress didn't have anything else to delay her other than Thessaly's glass of water.

She tapped the three numbers on her phone and held it to her ear.

'Nine-one-one emergency, which service do y—'

'Police.'

'Putting you through.'

The line wasn't great. Weather making the sound glitchy. She glanced around the corner and saw that the waitress had left the check on the table the two men were sitting at. The salesman was leaving cash.

'Pennsylvania State Police, are you reporting an emergency?'

'Yes. I mean ... I think so.'

'What is the nature of your emergency, ma'am?'

'I think I saw a murderer. I mean, I know I did. He's here now. His name is—'

'You're reporting a murder?'

'No, a murder*er*. The person who committed a murder.'

'Ma'am are you in danger at this moment? Where are you?'

'No, he doesn't know I'm here. His name is Casper Sturgis. He killed my brother, and I just saw him.'

'Somebody's hurt?'

She gripped the phone tighter and tried to speak slowly without raising her voice.

'No, he killed my brother twenty years ago.'

'Twenty years ago?'

'I think he's leaving. You need to send someone now.'

There was a long pause, and Thessaly wondered if the dispatcher was going to admonish her for wasting police time. Too late, she realized she shouldn't have been specific. Send a cop. Any reason. She could explain when they got here.

'What's your location?'

'Can't you tell from my phone? I'm at some diner on the seventy-eight.'

'The location I'm getting is no good. Looks like you're somewhere in Northampton County, but I can't see specifically.'

Her mind went blank for a second. What the hell was this place called again? Something about sports? No – the Olympics. Olympia. 'I'm at the Olympia diner on the seventy-eight eastbound. Please hurry.'

She looked out again and saw that the two men were already leaving.

'Sit tight, ma'am. We'll have somebody with you in about fifteen minutes.'

Thessaly hung up and looked around the corner. The booth was empty, the door at the exit slowly swinging shut. By the time the cops got there, they would both be long gone. She made the decision in a second and headed for the door. If she could get a license plate, she would have something to give them.

She hurried outside and saw that she was too late. The silver sedan at the far side of the lot had started up, its headlights bright in her eyes. It started moving out and turned right onto the highway. She saw the red light of the diner sign reflect off the driver's glasses for a split second. The salesman.

The BMW followed it out, turning in the opposite direction, crossing over to the westbound side.

Thessaly ran for her own car. She had left her jacket in the booth inside, and she was soaked to the skin by the time she got into the driver's seat. She pulled out of the space and accelerated out of the lot, sending a shower of muddy rainwater over the windshield as she bumped in and out of a big pothole at the exit. She turned into the westbound lane and pushed the pedal down as far as she dared. The needle climbed above seventy before she was rewarded with the sight of taillights ahead of her. She switched the wipers to full and risked going a little faster, feeling the wind buffet her as the rain poured down like she was in a car wash.

She was gaining. Soon she would be close enough to read the BMW's license plate. And then the other car seemed to widen the gap a little. Did he know he was being followed? Had he noticed her coming out of the diner right after he did?

She gritted her teeth and pressed the pedal all the way to the floor. The needle jumped over eighty and kept rising. This was insane. She never drove this fast on a cloudless summer's day in the middle of nowhere. She was closing the gap though, the other car slowing a little as the road began to climb. Almost there. She could make out the contrast between the white plate and the blue numbers now. Another two seconds and—

A truck appeared over the crest of the hill in the opposite lane, full brights on. She braked and squinted as she tried to keep her car in the lane. The truck dimmed his lights and blew past her with a thunder of eighteen wheels. She opened her eyes fully again, but it was too late. The other car had disappeared over the crest of the hill and the needle had dropped to forty. She floored it again, the transmission taking its time to shift and the engine complaining as she tried to accelerate uphill.

She crested the hill, wondering how much the gap would have widened, and saw ... nothing.

Just blackness ahead, the strip down the center of the road the only feature she could make out. The other car had vanished. The highway curved around and she hoped it would straighten out and she would see a set of taillights, but there was nothing.

She passed a sign.

Grenville ¼

He had to have taken the turn for Grenville. There was no place else to go. The GPS map showed a straight road ahead. This exit was the only one for miles.

She slowed and took the exit.

3

Thessaly pulled into the parking lot of the Olympia diner thirty minutes later. She took a sharp breath when she saw the gray patrol car parked in the very same space she had occupied earlier. In all of the excitement of trying to follow Sturgis, she had completely forgotten she had called the police.

Grenville had been a dark maze of buildings with unlit windows. It felt like it had no center. If the BMW really had taken that turn, it could have been anywhere. The car could have been any of the dozens parked in the driveways that she drove past. Challenging in daylight, impossible at night during a rainstorm. There was nothing to do but go back and retrieve her jacket.

She parked next to the patrol car and steeled herself again for the run to the door. When she made it inside, soaked to the skin once again and shaking, the waitress from earlier looked up at the doorway and pointed an accusing finger at her.

'That's her, Officer.'

There were two uniformed state troopers at the lunch counter, both men. Cups of coffee in front of them. Raindrops beaded on the waterproof canvas of their jackets. One was older: late fifties, gray-white hair and a mustache. The other had blond hair and green eyes and looked ridiculously young to be in any kind of position of authority. What was it they said, about the policemen looking younger?

'Hi,' Thessaly said, giving an apologetic smile. 'You came.'

'You're the one who made the nine-one-one call, ma'am?' the older of the two men asked.

'That's right, my name is Thessaly Hanlon.'

'I'm Trooper Fetterman, this is Trooper Reed,' he said. Fetterman had hooded eyes that made him look like he was on the point of dropping off. 'Says here you got…' he stopped to consult a notebook in front of him, rather unnecessarily. '…a murder. Is that correct?' He finished by taking a moment to look around the surroundings, remarkable as they were only for the lack of murder.

'It was a bad line. I saw someone. The man who killed my brother Mitch, years ago.'

Fetterman glanced briefly at his partner and the waitress, then back at Thessaly. 'You saw him in here?'

'Yes. She saw him too.'

Fetterman looked at Kayla expectantly.

'There were two guys here when she came in. I guess she's talking about them?'

'One of them, yes. Casper Sturgis. The blond man with the plaid shirt.'

Fetterman looked at Thessaly, then Kayla.

Kayla shrugged. 'I don't know what you want. Yeah there was a guy in a plaid shirt and a guy in a suit. They ordered coffee, pancakes, paid cash. We don't require names and ID.'

'Do you have any security cameras?' Fetterman asked.

'Covering the register, not the seats.'

'Thank you.' Fetterman's gaze switched from Kayla to Thessaly. He indicated the stool next to him. 'Have a seat, Ms Hanlon.'

When she sat down, he scratched her name in his notebook and then put the pen down to massage his temple. 'Let's backtrack a little. Your brother was killed?'

'Murdered, yes.'

16

'I'm sorry for your loss. When did this happen?'

'Twenty years ago. In New Jersey.'

'In *Jersey*?' Reed interjected, as though Thessaly had said 'the surface of Mars' rather than the next state.

Fetterman held up a hand to silence his partner and shifted around on the stool so he was facing Thessaly, subtly distancing Reed and Kayla from their conversation.

'And this man…'

'Sturgis.'

'Sturgis murdered him?'

'Yes. I saw it happen. I was a witness.'

'When did he get out?'

It took Thessaly a moment to work out what he was asking. 'What? No. He didn't get out. He didn't go in. They never caught him.'

Fetterman raised his eyebrows and took another sip of his coffee. He turned to Reed for a second. Thessaly couldn't see his expression, but she expected it conveyed the sentiment 'this is gonna be a long night'.

He turned back to her. 'The local police investigated your brother's murder?'

'Yes. McKinley Hills PD. The detective who was primary on the case was Mick Hendricks. If you speak to him, he'll confirm everything.'

Fetterman held a hand up. 'I didn't suggest you were making this up, ma'am.'

She opened her mouth to say that maybe he hadn't *out loud*… and then decided this approach wouldn't get her anywhere she wanted to go. She bit her tongue and took a deep breath.

'We were… exploring. We went to see a dead mall.'

'A dead mall?' he repeated, saying each word carefully, as though neither was familiar.

'Yeah, you know. They call it urban exploring these days. A

17

closed-down mall, an abandoned place out in McKinley Hills. The Redlands Mall. Me and my brother Mitch and our friend, Lee. It was supposed to be deserted. We interrupted some kind of drug deal or something – they never worked out exactly what it was. I was hiding. I saw a man shoot my brother, my friend Lee, and the guy he was there to meet.

'The police got there, but Mitch was dead. Lee survived. I told them everything. Gave them a description of the man, the car he was driving, everything.'

'They find him?'

She shook her head. 'No sign of him. It was a good description. I had a lot of time to look at him. To listen to his voice. I'm never going to forget him. They were looking for the vehicle right away. They never found it. Somehow he just disappeared.'

As she said that, she remembered hearing the sound of the engine fading to nothing as she knelt over her brother's body, fruitlessly searching for a pulse. From that moment, he had been gone. They both had; Sturgis and Mitch. She cleared her throat and tried to marshal the important details.

'They took Lee to the hospital and Mitch to the morgue. They drove me to the police station. These days I guess they'd have a counselor or something, but I'm glad they didn't. They just got straight into questioning me. They did a great job. Well, Hendricks did, anyway. He wanted to know everything: why we were there, how we got in, if we knew the two men. I think at first he thought we were mixed up in it. They got a sketch artist. They showed me mug shots. Nothing.'

'What about the other man who was killed?' Fetterman asked. He was interested now. Maybe he had accepted she wasn't making this stuff up.

She nodded. 'They moved on to him next. They identified him pretty easily. ID in his wallet. He was a used car dealer named John Ammerman. His wife had no idea he was there.

He had told her he was in Sacramento for a conference that day. They looked into his finances and found he had a lot of gambling debt, like two hundred grand.'

'I'm assuming he was mixed up with some criminal elements.'

'It seemed so. They found irregularities in his business's accounts, going back years. It hadn't been picked up on by the IRS, but once they knew there might be something there to look for, they found it. He had been laundering large sums of cash for a long time. Hendricks told me if they could work out who Ammerman was working for, it might lead them to the shooter.'

'And, since you have a name, I'm assuming that's what happened,' Fetterman said. 'Mob guy?'

'No. Not anybody they knew about locally, anyway. They looked into that at first. The man I had seen wasn't on their radar. Detective Hendricks cast the net wider. I went through more mugshots, and we found him.'

'A guy who looked like the shooter?'

She shook her head firmly. 'No. Not a guy who looked like him. It was him. Casper Sturgis.'

She could see the scene in her mind like it was five minutes ago. The cold interview room with the scarred wood table. The six color photographs laid out like playing cards. She remembered it had been the eyes that convinced her. That didn't make sense, of course. Back in the Redlands Mall, she had never been close enough to see his eyes. But when Detective Hendricks had flipped over the page in the book, the eyes had told her this was the one. Blue and empty, like the eyes of an intelligent animal. Wily, but without a soul. And then, widening her focus, the rest of the features had matched up perfectly. Dirty blond hair, the distinctive jawline.

She had asked who he was, after repeating three times that she was certain this was the man who had killed her brother.

'Hendricks said they would bring him in. But they didn't. He disappeared, and I guess sooner or later they stopped looking for him. And that was the end of it.'

As she said it, she knew that wasn't true. The truth was that it hadn't ended. In twenty years, she had thought about her brother and about the man who had taken him from her every single day.

There was no ending to the story.

Trooper Fetterman asked a few more questions and promised to make some inquiries, and to check out the register footage. She knew that would likely be futile, remembering Sturgis's friend leaving cash at the table. Before the two state troopers left, Fetterman suggested that Thessaly stop at a motel rather than continuing to drive through the storm. He even recommended one, ten miles along the road. Thessaly assured him she would think about it and thanked him.

'We'll be in touch if we can get a lead on this gentleman,' he told her as he left the Olympia. She liked to think he meant it, but she wasn't holding her breath.

4

It was after 6 a.m. by the time Thessaly made it to Buchanan and home. She collapsed into bed for a couple of hours' sleep and then dragged herself back out to shower and dress, leaving herself just enough time to drive to the train station.

The meeting was in the city, at the offices of her publisher in Midtown. Or, to be more accurate, her client's publisher. Her first novel had been picked up in a two-book deal for a pretty good advance, but the book hadn't sold, and the follow-up had done even worse, and so there had been no great clamor for a third or fourth book. After sending a few pitches around to no avail, her agent, Evan, had landed her a ghost job writing a memoir for a television actress, just to tide her over. That one had sold surprisingly well, leading to more ghost work. She was writing two a year now, and pretending to be other people was bringing in more money in a year than she would have made in three at her *Inside NY* salary. She told herself she would try writing another novel of her own sometime soon. Sometime Soon was always vaguely defined, but always After This.

The current project was fiction. She had signed a deal with Graystone, an imprint of one of the big five, to ghostwrite a basketball-themed mystery novel for Megan Adams, the sports reporter. Despite the two hours' sleep and the events of the previous night, she had managed to stay fully attentive in the meeting. The news they had given her wasn't great. They wanted to move up publication to summer, rather than fall, and would she be able to deliver in two weeks rather than at the end of April? She waited until they offered a bonus before telling them she could do it.

She could do it, couldn't she?

Riding down to street level in the elevator, the meeting and the daunting new deadline evaporated from her mind. Replaced with the more immediate memories of the previous night. Or, to be exact, the early morning.

Would the state police really look for Sturgis, or had Trooper Fetterman merely been humoring her, the way his partner clearly was? She decided it probably didn't matter either way. They had nothing to go on. Kayla, the waitress, had never seen either of the two men sitting in the booth behind Thessaly's before last night. They had paid cash, so there would be no credit card trail. Thessaly hadn't gotten a license plate, despite her best efforts. All she had was that Sturgis had been driving a black BMW SUV. After looking it up on the BMW website, she decided it was likely an X7 model.

She didn't even know for sure that the car had taken the Grenville exit. It would have been easy for her to misjudge distance in the dark. Perhaps Sturgis had just gotten so far ahead that its lights had been lost in the rain. And if he had turned off for Grenville, it didn't mean he had stopped there.

Nothing to go on. A chance encounter with the person who had taken her brother from her and sent her life on a different track, and she had blown it. Now that the meeting was out of the way, thinking about the missed opportunity made her feel tired and empty and … diminished, somehow. It was as though someone had stripped away every good thing she had managed to achieve, against the odds, over the last twenty years.

She caught the 4:14 on the Hudson Line from Grand Central,

taking a window seat and gratefully resting her head against the glass. She fell into a dreamless sleep somewhere after Harlem. When she heard the voice of the announcer say '...next stop,' she started awake so abruptly that she elbowed the man in the suit sitting next to her. She mumbled an apology as he frowned and looked back down at his book.

'What stop?' she asked.

The man in the suit didn't look up. 'Ossining.'

She sighed with relief and settled back into her seat. Another two stops still to go. She looked out of the window as the marina rolled by and then the buildings dropped away and the Hudson glinted in the winter sun. It made her think about summer sun, about twenty years ago.

The trip to the Redlands Mall had been Thessaly's idea. And so, when you came down to it, it had all been Thessaly's fault.

Post-graduation, she, her brother Mitch and his friend Lee had decided to go on a road trip to see Queens of the Stone Age play at the Convention Hall in Asbury Park, staying in a dive motel overnight, driving back home in the morning. It was Thessaly's first time at a concert, and she had loved it. 'The Lost Art of Keeping a Secret' was the highlight of the show. They had all drunk too much. There was a moment when Mitch had gone to the bar. The band started playing 'In the Fade'. Thessaly put her hand on Lee's arm, and then left it there. They looked at each other and she knew they were going to kiss, and she could see in his eyes that he knew it too.

They were leaning in when she saw Mitch out of the corner of her eye. Lee followed her gaze and flinched back. So obvious. Mitch had come back to borrow Lee's lighter, and knew exactly what he had interrupted.

None of them said anything, but she and Lee kept each other at arms' length the rest of the evening.

The unspoken tension in the car the next morning was the

reason she had been looking for a way to break up the return trip. Mitch was quieter than usual, when he wasn't making more-than-usually cutting jibes at Lee. Thessaly knew he wasn't going to be pleased with his best friend making a move on his twin sister. She thought it was the main reason nothing had happened between them over that long summer. She hadn't really wanted to dwell too long on her feelings for Lee, and up until that moment during 'In the Fade', she had no idea he reciprocated them.

Not that it would have been a good idea, even ignoring her brother's thoughts on the matter. She had been accepted into Princeton in the fall. Lee, and all of her other hometown preoccupations, would be in the rear-view mirror soon.

The detour to the Redlands Mall seemed like a good distraction. A way to break up what would otherwise have been a long, uncomfortable drive. Kevin Moretz, one of the harmless malingerers in the drama club, had told her and Mitch about it one day as they smoked out back behind the workshop. Or at least, he and Mitch were smoking. Thessaly had never started, a virtue of which she was quietly proud every time Mom made a meaningful comment about smelling smoke whenever Mitch walked into the room.

'It's sick, completely deserted. It's like fucking *Dawn of the Dead*, you gotta check it out.'

It had sounded fun.

She talked them into it. Mitch protested, said he just wanted to get back home. She could tell Lee was intrigued, but he pointedly stayed out of the discussion. Eventually, Mitch relented and detoured on the 280. The mall was a couple of miles outside the nearest town; the surface of the empty parking lot rutted and peppered with weeds. It already looked post-apocalyptic, even though the mall had been closed less than a year. Somebody had spray-painted the word *DEADLANDS* in red paint across one of the shutters over the main entrance. They found the busted-open fire door at the back of one of the units; a shoe store, going by the signage and the ankle-level mirrors.

Thessaly couldn't remember much of what they had seen after that. Just disconnected snapshots in her mind's eye. Shafts of sunlight stabbing down through a dirty glass ceiling, spearing dust particles in the main atrium. A nest of rats in a hole in the drywall in a sporting goods store. A sign shaped like a giant key dangling from a single length of chain, swaying in a faint breeze from somewhere else in the mall.

And then the muffled sound of a car engine outside, followed by the ratchet of a parking brake, followed by the piercing rattle of a roller shutter being thrown up. She remembered everything after that.

The train pulled to a stop at Buchanan. She gathered her coat and bag and navigated the way out, headed for the parking lot.

5

It was a little after five, but already getting dark when Thessaly parked her burgundy Subaru Legacy in the driveway of her home, a detached split-level house on a quiet street in Buchanan, New York. Sometimes when she parked, she paused for a moment and looked up at the house to think 'I didn't do so badly.' She had made the down payment on the house with the advance on the second ghost deal with Graystone, when she and Josh had been thinking about kids, and maybe a dog. The relationship didn't continue long enough for either. After the breakup, her friends were surprised that she stayed in the house. The place had three spacious bedrooms plus a master on the third level. It had an eat-in kitchen. It had what the brochure called 'cathedral ceilings'. It had a huge yard opening onto woodland. Surely it was too big for one person? It was. That was one of the reasons she liked it.

But today, she had just one thing in mind, and a moment of grateful reflection wasn't it.

She unlocked the door and tapped her fob against the alarm to deactivate it, then stepped inside, kicked off her shoes and called out to Alexa to turn on all the lights. After a pause, every room in the house lit up. Josh had been a gadget nerd, had made sure they had all the mod cons. She had been skeptical at first but had gotten used to the convenience. Using her phone to turn the heating on from thirty miles away meant she wasn't returning to a freezing house, for instance. And, though she never admitted it to Josh, it made her feel secure being able to turn all of the lights on at once when she was alone in the house. A good thing too, now that she was always alone in the house.

She walked through to the kitchen. The coral pink February sunset was lighting up the clouds above the treetops, casting a fiery glow through the double-height windows above the patio doors. She turned on the bean-to-cup coffee machine in the kitchen – *that* was her type of gadget – and went upstairs to the small bedroom she used as a study to turn on the computer while the coffee machine did its thing.

The study was her favorite room in the house. It had floor-to-ceiling bookshelves on three walls, a rug over the varnished floorboards, a green leather Chesterfield couch where she could curl up and read. Her desk was set up at the window, overlooking the street outside. The sky was fully dark on this side of the house already. The lights were all on in the Page house across the street. The kids were bouncing on the bed in the front bedroom. As she watched, the door opened and Lucy Page appeared, pointing her finger and remonstrating soundlessly with her daughters. They slunk off the bed and left the room, heads bowed.

Thessaly smiled and tapped her mouse to wake the screen. As it came to life, it lit up the framed photograph next to the monitor. The photograph had been there so long that she barely saw it anymore, but tonight, she let her eyes linger on it.

It had been taken in May of 2001, at an oyster bar in New Haven. Mom's birthday. In the picture were Thessaly, her mom and dad, and Mitch, all huddled around the too-small restaurant table. It wasn't a particularly good picture. Dad had red-eye from the flash, and Mitch had a spot of Tabasco on the sleeve of his shirt. But they were all smiling, and it was the last picture of them all together. There had been other photographs between then and now. Thessaly and her mom and dad, and then just with her mom, and then there had been no more at all. None of the pictures that followed had the same easy smiles, the same carefree look in the eyes.

Within five and a half years of that unremarkable family dinner, three out of the four of them were gone. She would give anything to be able to talk to any one of them right now.

Taking a deep breath, she shifted her gaze from the photograph to the screen. She saw that she had forgotten to close the Word file of the Megan Adams book when she had finished work before leaving for the funeral. That could have been a pain in the ass, had she managed to do any work between then and now. It would have meant having to resolve different versions of the document, but in this case, zero productivity had paid dividends. She saved and closed the file and opened up a browser window. Work would have to wait a little longer.

Casper Sturgis had never been very far from her mind, all these twenty years. This wouldn't be the first time she tried to find him on the internet. It wouldn't be the hundredth time. She had more than a dozen Google Alerts set up listing various search terms. She would receive an email if a new web page appeared that might be relevant. Thankfully, it was an unusual enough name not to throw up many false positives.

She had other alerts set up for when her brother's name appeared on unsolved murder websites. That had happened a lot in the first decade, but had died away to nothing now. The last hit had been a brief mention of the murders in an article on dead malls of America, maybe five or six years ago. There were many more lurid unsolved murders to be picked over and theorized about than Mitch's.

The trail wasn't so much cold as completely overtaken by the jungle. There was no trail, not anymore.

But now, for the first time, she knew the man who had killed her brother was still alive. And she knew that he had been eating in the Olympia Diner on I-78 at 2 o'clock that morning. And she knew that he was with another man, who drove a silver car. She understood it wasn't much to go on, as the pitying expression Trooper Fetterman had worn throughout their interview suggested, but it wasn't nothing. It was more than she had had for twenty years.

Thessaly Googled the diner first. It had a rudimentary website, proudly stating that the Olympia had been open since 1947. There wasn't much to the site. A few interior pictures and a downloadable menu.

She looked up the town next. Grenville had a population of twenty-six thousand. The Wikipedia page took up less than the height of the screen. Its most notable former residents were a minor-league baseball coach and an actress who had been a recurring guest star on *General Hospital*.

The Google map showed an orderly grid of streets fanning out for a couple of miles on either side of the main road through town. Two rivers split the town before intersecting. The street layout north of the intersection point looked older, more organic. Pins identified places of interest like the bus station and the library and the Baptist church and the 7-Eleven. She switched to satellite view and spent a minute or two scrolling over the roofs of family homes in wide yards.

She heard a low buzzing noise from elsewhere in the house and it took her a second to remember she had left her phone by the coffee machine. She hurried back down to the kitchen and picked it up. Private number. She answered with a wary hello. There was a long pause and then,

'Is that Ms ... Theresa Hanlon?'

'Thessaly,' she corrected, guessing that the speaker was attempting to decipher a handwritten note.

'Thessaly, okay.' There was a pause and somehow, she could tell the speaker was writing her name down more clearly. 'This is Detective Tyler, McKinley Hills Police Department.'

Her pulse quickened. She hadn't expected a callback this quickly. 'Yes?'

'You called for Detective Hendricks.'

'That's right, he was the primary on the investigation into my brother's murder. He used to call pretty regularly to let me know what he was looking into, but I guess it's been a while and ...'

'I'm afraid I have some bad news. Detective Hendricks passed two years ago.'

Thessaly took a deep breath. 'Oh. I'm sorry.' The man on the other end didn't respond, and she wondered if she was supposed to say anything else. She hadn't heard from Hendricks in a while, but it hadn't even crossed her mind to think anything had happened to him. 'Was he sick, or ...'

'Accidental firearms discharge.'

'Oh. I'm very sorry to hear that.' She knew enough to know what that meant. A last favor from the officers called to the scene to a brother-in-arms. A lot of cops die that way every year. Always accidental, never suicide.

'Yeah. Anyways, is there something we can help you with?'

She sighed. There had been one person in the world she knew for certain would be sympathetic to her story, who would back her up. Now she found that person hadn't been in the world for two years.

She went through the story anyway. A roadside diner in the middle of the night. A chance encounter. A missed opportunity. To his credit, Detective Tyler listened and sounded like he was writing some of it down. He asked a couple of questions. He mentioned that the Redlands Mall shootings were before his time, but that he knew of the case.

'I'll tell you what, I'll see if I can talk to someone over there. See if they know anyone matching this description. I gotta be honest with you, Thessaly ...'

'I know. It's a long shot.'

'Long shot's putting it mildly. But there's one good thing. A leopard doesn't change his spots. If this guy is still on the scene, chances are the local cops have him on their radar.'

Thessaly felt herself choking up a little and didn't know quite why. Sadness for Detective Hendricks, perhaps. A good man, perhaps worn down by too many unresolved cases like hers. Gratitude that one of his co-workers was taking her seriously, perhaps. She cleared her throat and thanked Detective Tyler.

After she had hung up, she looked down at the phone in her hand for a long time. She had been putting the call off. Making a whole list of things she had to check and find out before she did it. But she couldn't put it off any longer. If the situation was reversed, she would want to know.

The number wasn't saved in her phone. The number had been lost in the ether seven or eight upgrades ago, and she hadn't replaced it in her list of saved contacts, even though she could have done so at any time.

She couldn't begin to guess at any of her friends' phone numbers, or even the number of her local Chinese takeout place. Which, embarrassingly, was probably the single number she called most often. Now, there were perhaps a half dozen numbers she could remember off the top of her head, and none of them were in regular use. The landline of her childhood home. Her brother's cell number. Dan, the guy she dated for the first two years in college. And Lee.

She had changed her own number at least twice since 2001. There was a very good chance Lee would have done too. She would probably have to make more of an effort, if she really wanted to get ahold of him.

Most likely, the number would have been dead for years, or reassigned. She thought they did that when a number had been dormant long enough.

So what harm could it do?

She opened the keypad; the action unfamiliar, as opposed to scrolling back through recent calls. She dialed the number and her thumb hovered over the call button. She made herself tap it.

A pause, and then it rang. Not disconnected, then. Two rings. Three. Four.

Suddenly, her heart was in her mouth, and she wasn't sure why.

Please don't pick up. Please be—

The ring cut out and she took a sharp intake of breath as she heard a voice. But then she realized it was just the voicemail. The default recording for the cell network. No hint of who the number belonged to now. Straight and to the point: please leave your message after the tone.

The tone sounded, hurrying her into saying something. 'Hi, it's … it's Thessaly Hanlon. I just wanted to …'

To what? She hadn't thought this through at all. She cancelled the call. Relief. The strange anxiety subsided.

She put the phone in her pocket and went back upstairs to the study. Grenville in its entirety taking up the center of the monitor screen. She ran a finger along the vertical line of the road, along the path the black SUV would have traveled the other night.

6

Thessaly had a lot of time to plan out her day on the drive back down to Grenville the next day. Being honest with herself, she didn't think she had a very high chance of finding the man she was looking for. But maybe that didn't matter. Maybe going and looking was enough in itself. If she took what little information she had and explored every possibility leading off from that, then at least she could satisfy herself that she had done all she could. She wouldn't find herself lying awake at 3 a.m. in a year's time knowing it was definitely too late to do anything about it now.

Drake, her editor at Graystone, probably wouldn't be too happy if he knew she was spending her day driving to Pennsylvania when she was supposed to be chained to her computer finishing the book, but that was one of the advantages of her job: she could do it, or not, from anywhere.

The 287 wasn't too busy headed south, the traffic getting a little thicker as she joined the 78. The heaviest traffic this stretch would see would be early morning and early evening. Commuters yawning behind the wheel as they covered the monotonous miles between the office and the twin parking garage in their affordable commuter town. She took her eyes off the road and reached across to the passenger seat where her tablet was lying dormant. She tapped the screen to wake it, glancing down the Keep list she had made for the day ahead.

The first item was the easiest, and, thanks to a phone call before leaving, she was just in time to cross it off. Kayla's shift started at noon, and it was just gone eleven-thirty.

She pulled into the parking lot outside the Olympia ten minutes later and took the same spot she had used the other night. The big pothole at the entrance was still half-full of rainwater, though the local weather said the area had been dry for the last twenty-four hours. Thessaly had accumulated a lot of useless information like that about Grenville and its environs over the last couple of days. Take the Olympia itself. Opened in 1947, like the website said. In that time, it had had only two owners. The current owner was one Joseph P. Haim.

Daylight didn't improve the look of the Olympia. In the rain, she hadn't paused to take in the details of the exterior. Now she could see that it was a long building with white wood siding that looked like it had last been painted when Clinton was president. Wide, railroad-car-style windows extended from either side of the entrance, which jutted out as an enclosed porch. A thin streak of bird shit bisected the top curve of the unlit neon 'O' above the sign.

Inside, Thessaly was greeted at the wait-to-be-seated sign by a heavy-set redheaded guy in his twenties. He wore a white short-sleeve shirt with no nametag and had blue shadows under his eyes. He tried to seat her by the window, but she asked for a specific booth: the one Sturgis and the other man had occupied the other night. She could kill two birds with one stone by eating lunch while she waited for Kayla to get in.

'Welcome to the Olympia, I'm Hal, I'll be your waiter today. Get you something to drink while you look at the menu?'

'Yes please, I'll have coffee.' She smiled in a way that she hoped conveyed she was a good tipper. 'And I was wondering if I could ask if you've seen somebody I'm looking for?'

Hal blinked. Looked around the diner and then back to her, a confused look on his face.

'Like a customer,' she clarified. 'He might have been in recently.' She took a sheet protector containing all of the hard copies she had printed last night from her bag and slid the one with the blowup of Sturgis's face out of it. It was based on the original sketch that had been done from her description in 2001. The McKinley Hills PD had software that allowed them to digitally age facial composites the relevant time from when they were originally logged. Thessaly didn't know how accurate the software claimed to be, but from her sample size of one, it was a dead ringer for the man she had seen the other night.

'You a cop or something?' Hal asked, looking unsure.

'I'm just really interested in finding him,' Thessaly said, before leaning forward with a sheepish look on her face. 'It's a genealogy thing.'

'Oh.' He picked up the paper and stared at it. 'No, sorry. Not familiar. Our customers are usually just passing through. We don't really have regulars.' He put the picture down again. 'I'll give you a minute to look at the menu.'

She flipped the picture of Sturgis so that it was face-down on the table. 'I'll have the Olympia Cheese Steak,' Thessaly said, without opening the menu. She had already perused it on the website, and there hadn't been all that much to peruse. She needed something heavy that would mean she wouldn't have to stop to eat for the rest of the day.

The food arrived suspiciously quickly, laden with strips of steak and green peppers, and with home fries on the side. She was halfway through the sandwich, which tasted better than it looked, when she saw a battered blue Honda Civic turn into the parking lot, giving the pothole a wide berth. The driver parked in an employee space. A moment later, Kayla got out. 11:59 a.m.

She was dressed in the same uniform from the other night, but with a blue ribbon tying back her hair instead of a yellow one. She dropped her keys into her purse as she moved toward the door without any great urgency, pausing halfway between the car and the diner to tap something out on her phone. When she opened the door and saw Thessaly sitting in the booth, she did a double take. She shrugged her coat off and put it and her purse behind the counter, before coming over.

'You're back.'

Thessaly smiled and opened her mouth.

'No,' Kayla said before she could ask. 'He hasn't been back in. Sorry. Did the cops come up with anything?'

Thessaly shook her head. 'No.'

Kayla nodded, as though she had expected as much.

'I'd like to make a deal with you,' Thessaly said.

'You want me to let you know if he comes in again?'

Thessaly lifted the sheet protector. There was a hundred-dollar bill underneath it. She slid it across the table.

Kayla whistled. Glanced over her shoulder to check Hal wasn't watching. She lowered her voice. 'What's the catch?'

'No catch, just... some requirements.'

Kayla eyed the bill. Made no move to pick it up. Met Thessaly's gaze.

'Yeah?'

She took a sheet of folded notepaper from her pocket and handed it to Kayla. She took it and opened it.

'That's my cell, home number, and email address. If either of the two men from the other night come back, I'd like you to let me know the minute they come in. Doesn't matter what time of the day or night it is. I'll pay you another two hundred if you can help me track them down.'

'And you don't want them to know you're looking for them?'

'You got it,' Thessaly added. She turned over the picture of Sturgis and tapped it with her index finger. 'This guy in particular could be dangerous. Don't do anything out of the ordinary. Just serve him, and keep a close eye on him. Get a license plate for his car. If you can get a picture of him without being noticed, that would be perfect, but don't put yourself at risk.'

Kayla shrugged and put the folded note in her pocket, then swept up the hundred-dollar bill from the table like she was receiving a dealt card. 'Deal.'

7

The Grenville Police Department's building was in the corner plot of a business park on the eastern edge of town. Thessaly had passed by it the other night when looking for the black BMW. It was an anonymous one-story building, with exposed brick walls and a glass frontage.

Thessaly parked outside in one of the visitor spots and took her phone out to check the email Detective Tyler had sent after their brief call. It was short and to the point.

Hello
Det. Washington, Grenville PD. 1:30 p.m.

Thessaly got out of the car and took a deep breath. She had the document file in her hand, and she had prepared as if she was going for a job interview. Dark gray pant suit, light blue blouse, proper shoes. She hadn't felt the need to dress this formally for a long time.

She could see the reception area through the glass frontage as she approached. A high desk and a row of plastic-backed chairs arranged with their backs to the window. The automatic doors opened at her approach and the uniformed officer behind the desk looked up.

He was young-looking, with sky-blue eyes. Premature gray

at the sides of his buzz cut. The name tag on his navy blue overshirt said, *Lewis*. Thessaly told Officer Lewis she had an appointment with Detective Washington. She had to spell her name for him, as usual. He listened and then tapped at some keys on the keyboard. He paused and looked at the screen, and presumably was satisfied by what he saw there. He picked up the handset of his desk phone.

Thessaly looked around the reception area. There was no one else around. There was a door marked 'Private' at the far end, which she assumed led to the squad room. There was no handle on the door. She supposed it would have to be opened via a switch behind the desk. At the other end of the room was a large pot plant that had probably seen better days, and a bulletin board with various flyers and wanted sheets on it.

Officer Lewis began speaking to someone on the other end of the phone.

'Hi, you got a Thessaly Hanlon here to see you. Says she has an appointment?' He listened, then replaced the handset. He looked up at her. 'Take a seat.'

Thessaly took the nearest of the plastic chairs, which was even less comfortable than it looked. She wondered how Detective Washington would respond to her visit. Whether Detective Tyler had had to talk him into it, or if he had agreed of his own volition. She wondered how much Tyler had told him.

A minute later, she heard a muted electronic buzz as an automatic lock was disengaged and the door marked 'Private' opened and Thessaly saw that Washington was a she, not a he. Why on earth had she assumed the detective was a man? Perhaps because her experience with the police twenty years ago had involved talking to a parade of tired-looking male detectives in middle age, usually wearing crumpled suits.

Detective Washington didn't fit the bill on any of those counts.

She was in her mid-thirties, with her dark hair tied back. She was wearing a dark-gray pant suit over a plain white open neck blouse. She had a handful of papers in her left hand. The door was on a swing-shut, so she braced it open with her hip.

'Ms Hanlon?'

'That's me,' Thessaly said, getting up. 'Thank you for agreeing to meet with me.'

'Don't thank me yet,' Washington said, raising an eyebrow.

She held the door open for Thessaly and she entered a small office. Squad room seemed like too grand a term for it: just four desks arranged roughly toward each corner of the room. All of them were presently unoccupied, but from the assorted papers and stationery on each, all looked like they were in current use. Washington led the way to another door at the back which opened onto an interview room.

Thessaly hesitated at the door, eyeing the squat ten foot by ten box with off-white cinderblock walls, two chairs and a table. An interview room. It smelled a little musty, and she could see what looked like a patch of mold in one of the ceiling corners. It wasn't the décor that gave her pause. It was the size of the space. Enclosed. No other exits.

She swallowed and forced herself to step across the threshold.

'Relax,' Washington said, watching her reaction with amusement. 'I'm not getting the rubber hose and the phone book out just yet.' She waved a hand at the main office, just as one of the phones began to ring. 'Willis refuses to program his voicemail – in here we can ignore the ringing every five seconds.'

Thessaly sat down in the chair farthest from the door. The one the perps sat in, she guessed. To her surprise, it was a little more comfortable than the plastic chairs in reception.

'You want a glass of water or anything?' Washington asked.

'I'm fine.'

The detective sat down and opened her hands. 'So, what can we do for you?'

Thessaly put her documents on the table and rested her hand on top of the pile. 'How much did Detective Tyler tell you?'

Washington didn't answer for a moment. Maybe she wasn't used to being the one answering questions in this room.

'He told me his old partner investigated your brother's murder. I looked it up. You and another guy were witnesses. Two dead, one damn close. Looked like a drug deal gone wrong. Or maybe gone exactly as planned for one of the parties. They never caught the guy. No firm suspects. How am I doing?'

'You're doing very well,' Thessaly said. 'Except there was a suspect. Casper Sturgis.'

'Tyler mentioned the name. I ran it and we have nothing on our system. Which doesn't mean all that much. Grenville PD reluctantly joined the twenty-first century around ten years ago. Up until then, everything was still paper records. There's a digitization program, but . . .' she paused and eyed the spreading mold patch in the corner of the ceiling. 'There are a lot of programs, and they all require money.'

'He wasn't on McKinley Hills PD's radar either,' Thessaly said. 'Detective Hendricks – the one who was working the original case – he made the breakthrough. He found a stray thread and pulled it and got a name. He dug deeper and got a picture for the name, and he put it in front of me.'

'And you ID'd this . . . Sturgis as the shooter?'

'That's right. But he vanished. They had a last known address for him in Newark, but he was long gone. He never showed up anywhere after that.'

Washington nodded, a sympathetic look in her eyes. Maybe this wasn't the first similar story she had heard. 'I guess we were all a little less findable in those days,' she said. 'Easier to drop off the map completely.'

'That's what Hendricks said. Back then things weren't joined up as much. I kind of hoped that something would come up over the years, now that the net's tighter, but... nothing. Nothing at all.'

'Until you saw him, or think you did, the other night. That's what Tyler told me, anyway. Which is why you're here.'

'That's right.' Thessaly reached into her bag for the printout of the facial composite and placed it on the desk in front of Washington.

The detective took a long look at it. After what seemed like a century, she took a deep breath through her nostrils and shook her head. 'I'm sorry, he's not one of our local bad guys.'

'He won't be using his real name,' Thessaly said. She wanted to try and get a feel for how thorough the detective had been. She was encouraged by the fact she had even taken the meeting, but perhaps that was just professional courtesy to Tyler, and what she really wanted to do was give her a polite brush-off. 'Have you been working here for a while?'

Washington grinned. 'You got me, I'm new. I transferred from Philly two years ago. But, what you have to appreciate is, Grenville really isn't that big. We have our troublemakers, just like everywhere else, but you get to know them fast. And Tyler already gave me the basics on the man you're looking for, including this,' she said, gesturing at the picture. 'I didn't expect to find anything against the name, like you said. But I went back through arrest records for anything involving assault or robbery with a perp who matched the rough description. I went back fifteen years. Nothing jumped out. I went through unsolved cases. We have very few unsolved homicides in Grenville. Nothing that points to this guy.'

'Maybe he moved here recently. Or maybe he's deliberately stayed out of trouble.'

She sighed. 'If the man you saw the other night was really

who you thought he was, he's not on our naughty list. I'm afraid you've had a wasted trip.'

Thessaly caught herself shaking her head and stopped herself. She took a moment to think and said, 'Well, what about just … people? Not the usual suspects. You know of anyone who looks like this, fits the description?'

'White male, age forty-nine, six feet? Probably a couple thousand or so.' She gave an apologetic shrug. 'Okay I exaggerate, but not by much. Unless he's using the same name, or wearing a sign, this guy would not stand out in this town in any way.'

'That's what I was afraid of,' Thessaly said.

'Listen, I'll keep an eye out, okay? I'll show this around the other guys. Most everyone else has been here longer than the department has been in this building.'

'I appreciate it.'

Thessaly had hoped Sturgis would be known to the authorities, even if under a different name. Like Washington had said, they know the troublemakers. She was disappointed, but not surprised. She had expected this, and she had some other ideas about finding the man from the diner.

8

Thessaly got back into her car and headed toward downtown. Unlike the Olympia, Grenville looked much more welcoming in the daylight. A lot of trees, a lot of water. It would probably upgrade from comparatively welcoming to pretty in a couple of months.

Grenville was divided into thirds by a pair of rivers that met each other east of downtown. The older part of town was to the north, with buildings dating back to colonial times. Most of the commerce and residential streets were located to the south and west. Main Street Grenville had the feel common to many small American cities and towns: a place that had been built for far more trade than it now enjoyed. She had seen much worse-afflicted places, all in all. Businesses still open and trading included two coffee shops, some casual restaurants, a couple of bars, even a bookstore. The streets on the south side were laid out in a grid, the roads far wider than they needed to be, going by the sparse mid-afternoon traffic.

Thessaly still had no way to be certain that the BMW had even taken the exit for Grenville. If it had, she didn't know for sure that it had stopped in town. The first thing on her list was the most straightforward, but the most time-consuming. She cruised the streets looking for dark-colored BMW SUVs in parking lots and driveways. If only she had happened to glance at the license plate before she had entered the diner. Perhaps she would have recalled enough to be useful, even just a fragment.

After traveling the length of Main Street, she turned and headed back to the eastern edge of town and started driving the grid. Up and down, east to west, and then left to right, west to east. She saw Grenville in its entirety. Low-rise office buildings, a park with freshly painted railings and a duck pond. Large homes on generous plots with rose beds and water features. Tired-looking public housing, some of it as neatly kept as the homes in the more upscale streets, some with rusting automobiles in the front yards. She saw kids on bikes in the streets. A solitary police car, the cop in the passenger seat glancing at her as they passed by one another on 6th Street. She saw a workman on a ladder adjusting the wires on a telegraph pole. She saw two motels and an auto parts store and a county library and a boarded-up movie theater. She counted six BMW SUVs. Three of them a dark enough color to pass for the one the other night.

It was a long, laborious process, and after an hour, she didn't feel any farther forward. She had covered all of the main roads and many of the smaller, residential streets, but it would take her days even to check every driveway thoroughly. And what if the car was in a garage, or was someplace else when she checked the right house? She could try bars and restaurants, showing the picture to see if anybody recognized Sturgis, but to do it properly she would need to talk to a lot of people. The more people she talked to, the more likely it was that word might get back to Sturgis. No, frustrating as it was, she knew the best thing to do was wait and hope that Washington got back to her. Other than that, all she could do was drive the streets and hope she got lucky, seeing either Sturgis's vehicle or the man himself.

There was just too little to go on. His name hadn't shown up anywhere she could think to look. A reverse image search using the mugshot had struck out. All she had was a face and a model of car.

The warning light on her fuel gauge lit up, reminding her to fill up. She had filled the tank in Buchanan, but she had covered a lot of ground since then, much of it here in Grenville.

And then another light lit up in her head. Where's the one place that someone with a car will definitely go, and on a regular basis?

She called up the map on her phone. Six gas stations within Grenville proper. She couldn't ask everyone in town if they knew Sturgis, but it wouldn't make as many waves to ask a handful of gas station attendants.

The nearest place was a Sunoco on 25th Street. She paid for gas and asked the clerk if he could help. She was looking for somebody who might be a regular. Drove a black BMW SUV, probably an X7. She described Sturgis. He shook his head and said sorry, he was new.

She repeated the routine at the Marathon station on Industrial Drive and the UNI-MART on Ferry Street, buying soda and snacks in each instead of gas. She came up with a rationale for her inquiries; that he had left a wristwatch behind in the diner and she wanted to reunite him with it. Neither attendant had a memory of a regular matching Sturgis's description who drove a black SUV. She was beginning to lose heart when she pulled into the forecourt of the fourth station on her list, the Gulf at the corner of Northampton and 25th.

She took a bottle of water from the refrigerator. The guy at the register was in his early twenties. He wore a blue tennis shirt with the company logo on it and had thick-rimmed glasses and feathery dark hair. He put the payment through for her with a mumble of acknowledgment and looked back down at his magazine.

Thessaly leaned on the counter. It took him thirty seconds to register the fact that she hadn't moved. He looked up.

'Did you need anything else, ma'am?'

She went through the story.

He frowned, thinking. 'Black BMW SUV,' he repeated. 'You don't have a picture of him or anything?'

She hesitated. Having a composite image of the man who had lost a watch might strain the credibility of her story but, what the hell. She reached into her bag and withdrew the plastic document protector, sliding out the updated photofit.

He took it, giving her a questioning look.

She smiled sheepishly. 'I had some time on my hands. There's this website you can go onto and do your own photofit thing. Not as good as a real police one, but...' She paused as she saw something in his eyes. Recognition. 'It looks enough like him, I guess,' she continued. 'Does he look like anyone you might have seen over the weekend?'

'Lot of effort to return a watch.'

'I just think it's nice to pay it forward. If I had lost something, I would want them to find me.'

He was stroking his chin, thinking.

'It does look a little like...'

'Like who?'

'The guy who manages Atlantic, over on Maple.'

'Atlantic?'

'Auto parts.' His brow creased. 'What was his name?' He snapped his fingers a couple of times, trying to bring it back. His eyes were closed in concentration.

Casper Sturgis. She knew he was going to say it.

But then he didn't.

'Tony. Tony something. We send people over there when we don't have what they're looking for. Wiper blades or whatever.'

Thessaly opened her mouth to say that wasn't the name

47

of the man she was looking for, before she remembered that according to her story, she didn't know the name of the man she was looking for. The guy wasn't looking at her, though. He flipped the photofit of Sturgis over and started to draw a map on the back.

'It's on Maple,' he said again, turning the drawing around. He had labelled the streets. It looked pretty straightforward. He circled a start and end point. 'We're here, follow this road, left at the lights, another couple hundred yards, the store is here. There's a bank and a McDonald's across the street, you can't miss it.'

9

Thessaly looked down at the address and the crude map on the back of the picture.

Atlantic Auto Parts. 121 Maple Av. Tony.

Tony? She had been momentarily excited when the man behind the counter had seemed to recognize her picture, but her excitement had quickly dissipated when he remembered the name of the man he was thinking of. She flipped over the picture again and took another look at the composite.

The image was accurate, she knew it was. It looked like Sturgis when she had seen him the other night. But it was still just an approximation of a likeness. Like Detective Washington had said, it wasn't a description that would stand out. It could look like thousands of men across the country. Maybe even hundreds of thousands. It wasn't as though the face showed any unmistakable distinguishing features. He didn't have a crooked nose, or particularly bushy eyebrows, or a scar on his left cheek or anything useful like that.

She tried googling the name of the store and the town and 'Tony'. Nothing helpful. An image search just brought back pictures of the store exterior, and some auto parts stores with the same name in other towns. Occasional headshots of people

49

when she scrolled further down, but no one who looked anything like Casper Sturgis.

There was only one way to make sure. She would go to the auto parts store and see if she could find Tony Andrews. If nothing else, it would let her see if there was enough of a resemblance for him to be mistaken for Sturgis.

She followed the directions on the map and parked in the lot of the McDonald's across the road from the auto parts store. It was an unassuming building. A glass frontage, a blue sign wrapping around the building with *Atlantic Auto Parts* on it, a Hokusai wave cresting over the 'A'. She crossed the road and approached the entrance.

There were three cars parked out front. Nothing that could have been mistaken for a dark-colored BMW SUV. A VW van and a little Hyundai and a blue Honda Accord with a Tigger sun shade attached to the glass of one of the rear windows with a suction cup. It made Thessaly think of those Garfield stick-ons that were omnipresent in her childhood, and she wondered if anyone still had one of those.

She felt a weird trepidation before committing herself to walking through the door. For the past hour or so, she had been trying not to get too downhearted that her journey had yet to throw up a single usable lead. Now she felt herself wondering the opposite. What if, somehow, the guy in the store had identified the man she was looking for? What if he was actually in there? What would she say?

She wasn't worried about him recognizing her. He hadn't known she was there back in Redlands, which was the only reason she had escaped unscathed. She was more worried that her own reaction to him might give her away, let him know something was wrong. She didn't know how well she would be able to hold herself together if she came face to face with him.

She pushed the door open. A low buzz sounded as the sensor

on the door frame parted. The air inside smelled of rubber and the clean, varnish smell of synthetic oil. There was a high counter by the door, over which she could see the top of a computer monitor. Beyond it was an orderly array of floor-to-ceiling shelving, stocked with brake fluid and cans of oil and replacement wiper blades and wrapped air fresheners and a hundred other items. There was a sign offering a bulb fitting service. The store beyond was arranged into four aisles of six-foot shelving units, well stocked and with each aisle clearly labeled.

There was a door set into the wall next to the counter marked 'Private', and a little doorbell wired into the desk with a sign that said, 'Please ring for service.' Next to the button was a plastic business card holder with a few different cards in it. There were some focusing on specific services and products, and one that was personalized. Just the store logo and a name.

T. Andrews, Manager.

She took a sharp breath as she heard a voice behind her, relaxing when she registered that the voice belonged to a woman.

'Good afternoon, what can we do you for?'

She had appeared from one of the aisles. Maybe a little older than Thessaly, she was wearing a blue t-shirt and baseball cap matching the sign outside. Her dark hair was threaded through the back of the cap in a ponytail. She was smiling, ready to help. Perhaps she wouldn't be so welcoming if she knew why this customer was there.

For a second, Thessaly considered asking if Tony was in, but she thought better. 'You know what, I forgot what I came in for.'

The woman grinned. 'Happens to me at least once a day. Take your time.'

Thessaly smiled and the woman went behind the counter

and started tapping on her keyboard. Thessaly moved away and spent a minute examining some engine oil before heading back to the door, not wanting to stick around.

'I'll come back,' she said.

IO

The McDonald's was quiet. School wasn't out yet, so the after-noon clientele was a scattering of senior citizens and a couple of moms with toddlers. There were plenty of seats by the window with a clear view across the street. The last time Thessaly had been in a McDonald's it had been in Berlin. They served you on crockery when you bought coffee or anything from the baked goods section. There were no such bold innovations here. She ordered a soda and nursed the paper cup while she kept a watchful eye on comings and goings from the store.

There wasn't all that much to keep an eye on. Traffic was light on the street outside. In twenty minutes, there was only one customer: a short, dark-haired man in chinos and a short-sleeve shirt driving a Lexus. He parked outside, went into the store, and emerged a couple of minutes later carrying a pack of bulbs.

She was at the bottom of her Coke. She checked the time: it had been forty minutes. Perhaps T. Andrews, Manager, had a hands-off style.

But then a shiny black SUV rounded the corner at the inter-section and slowed on the approach to the store. It was a BMW X7. She was almost positive it was the vehicle she had seen the other night. She took a deep breath and leaned forward.

It pulled into one of the spaces outside and the driver's door opened. A man got out. He had dirty blond hair, was wearing sunglasses. Thessaly felt the hairs rise on the back of her neck. The right height, the right build, roughly the right age. He leaned across to the passenger seat for something and took out a pile of papers. He removed his sunglasses and placed them on the dash above the steering wheel. He straightened and swung the driver's door shut. Only when he came around the hood of the car did she get a good look at his face.

Was it him? She thought so. That it was the man from the diner, at any rate. But could she be certain it was Casper Sturgis?

She ignored the butterflies in her stomach as she watched the man stride toward the entrance of the store. He moved like he owned the place. But then, Thessaly thought, in small businesses like these, the manager oftentimes is the proprietor. Too late, she remembered that she should get a picture. She picked up her phone and opened the camera. She would be ready when he came back out.

The glass frontage of the store let her follow his movements inside. He leaned over the counter, exchanged a few words with the cashier, then slapped his hand down on the counter. Was he angry about something? No, when she saw the cashier throw her head back and laugh, she realized it was a punchline. He turned and went through the door marked Private. Thessaly noticed that the cashier's grin vanished as soon as the door closed behind him.

Thessaly zoomed in with her phone camera and took a few pictures of the BMW, making sure to get the license plate in focus. What now? Should she go in and risk getting a close-up view of him? She felt sick at the thought. She was grateful when the decision was taken out of her hands. He emerged from the back office again, juggling the keys in his hand. He waved absentmindedly at the cashier as he passed. She snapped a few more pictures of him, though the quality of the zoomed image wasn't great.

As he was opening the driver's door, a red car turning out of the McDonald's crossed straight into the path of an oncoming van, which slammed on its brakes just in time to avoid a collision. The man calling himself Tony Andrews stopped and looked up as the van driver leaned on his horn. For the first time, Thessaly was able to get a clear look at his face.

And at that moment, she lost all doubt.

The red car moved out of the way and the van driver pulled away, pausing to loose a stream of invective through his open window. Casper Sturgis shook his head and gave an amused smile, then got into the BMW and backed out of the spot.

As the BMW passed out of her line of sight, it was as though a switch was thrown in Thessaly's brain.

She had found him.

After twenty years, she had found him.

She got to her feet. She walked to the door, not really knowing what she planned to do next, just wanting to be outside. She had her eyes fixed on the front of Atlantic Auto Parts as she stepped out of McDonald's, so she didn't see the approaching figure until it was too late.

II

Thessaly slammed into the person crossing her path and felt an elbow dig into her chest.

She flinched back a step and blinked the sun out of her eyes as the woman she had collided with toppled over with a yelp. She heard a small plastic clatter and looked at the source of the noise to see a set of car keys bounce once on the sidewalk and drop neatly down a drain.

'Oh *shit!*' The tone was more surprised than angry.

Thessaly looked down at the woman, who had landed on her butt with one leg underneath her, steadying herself with her right hand. She was in her mid-thirties. Brown hair, wearing a floral dress underneath a beige overcoat. Her phone was lying face down on the sidewalk.

'Oh God, I'm so sorry,' Thessaly blurted, after the sudden shock had worn off. She crouched down and picked up the phone, then handed it to the woman. The screen was miraculously unmarked. She accepted Thessaly's outstretched hand, and Thessaly leaned back and helped her to her feet. The two of them peered into the drain. There was no sign of the keys, other than a ripple of black rainwater.

'Should we ... call someone?' Thessaly asked.

'Entirely my fault,' she said. She held up her phone as if to say that it was the real culprit. 'Freakin' WhatsApp groups. Should carry a health warning.'

'I wasn't looking where I was going, it was my fault.'

'I think we've all learned a lesson today,' the woman smiled. Then she narrowed her eyes. They were hazel. She glanced down at the drain again and then shook her head in frustration. 'Damn it.'

'Do you have a spare set?'

'In the house. Believe it or not, this isn't the first time this has happened to me.' She looked at the time on her phone and groaned. 'I gotta pick my kid up from school. I'll have to call my husband.' She glanced up and down the street as she held the phone to her ear, shaking her head as the call went unanswered. She left a short message. 'Hi, you're not going to believe this, I lost the car keys. Call me asap, I need you to pick up Aiden.'

'I'm parked right here,' Thessaly said, gesturing at her car in the McDonald's lot. 'Can I give you a ride?'

'Could you? That would be such a help.'

The woman's name was Casey. She had decided to get a latte from McDonald's before picking up her son. 'I was running late as it was, I guess this is my punishment.' Thessaly found herself warming to her immediately. It was good to have a distraction to take the edge off seeing her brother's killer from a few yards away.

'So, you from around here?' Casey asked as they drove.

Thessaly shook her head. 'No, I'm visiting friends.'

The lie slipped out before she had time to think about it. Why had she said that?

'Oh yeah?' Casey asked. 'Maybe I know them. Where do they live?'

'I don't know the street. Over by the park. The Fullers.'

Casey seemed to think about it and for a moment Thessaly had a horrible feeling she was about to say, 'Oh yeah, Joe and

Margaret Fuller, their daughter babysits for us.' But instead she just said 'Hmm,' in polite acknowledgment.

Thessaly decided to pivot to something she could elaborate on more easily if necessary. 'To be honest, they're just the excuse. I needed a change of scene to try to get some work done. I'm going to drop in to say hi and then find a hotel.'

'What do you do?'

'I'm a writer. I just had my deadline brought forward, like two months. Sometimes it helps to get out of the house and go somewhere unfamiliar so I can focus on the book.'

Casey looked interested. 'What do you write?'

'Anything they pay me to. I'm actually working on a book for somebody else right now.'

Before Casey could ask a follow-up question, her cell phone rang.

'Hey,' she answered. 'Yeah, I know, right? No, it's okay, someone's giving me a ride. Yep. Tell me about it. Yeah, that would be great. Okay, love you.'

Something about Casey's accent didn't sound quite local either. It wasn't obvious, and Thessaly couldn't quite place it.

She followed Casey's directions across town. The route took them over a covered bridge that crossed the river, and through the older part of Grenville. They passed picturesque Victorian townhomes and a redbrick church with a tall spire. They made it to the elementary school just in time for the bell. The school was a long symmetrical redbrick building, set back from the road behind a wide grassy space and a row of trees. As Thessaly pulled the parking brake on, the doors opened and kids started to spill out chaotically as an older, bird-like teacher stood at the door attempting to direct the flow.

'You're a life saver,' Casey said as she unbuckled her belt. 'Thanks again.'

'Not at all, it was my fault. Do you need me to give you a ride home to get your spare keys?'

Casey shook her head. 'My husband's dealing with it. Thanks, though.'

'Least I could do,' Thessaly said. 'I'll try to look where I'm going next time.'

Casey grinned. 'That should make two of us. I hope you enjoy your visit. You know where you're going?'

Thessaly assured her that she did. She knew exactly where she was going next.

12

'Oh, you're back.' Detective Washington's words were polite, but her expression needed a little work.

Thessaly closed the door behind her. Washington had happened to be out front as she arrived, and had watched her walk in from the car. Detective Lewis was still on the front desk, his head down, focused on some paperwork.

'I'm sorry to bother you again so soon,' Thessaly said, 'but do you have a second?'

Washington looked past Thessaly to the parking lot. 'I was actually about to knock off.'

'It won't take long, I promise.'

The detective exchanged a meaningful look with Officer Lewis and sighed. 'Five minutes.'

They went back into the tiny interview room with the mold stain. Thessaly took the nearest chair and sat down. She had thought carefully before going back to the station. Perhaps this was a mistake, and Detective Washington would make it more difficult to pursue the man she was looking for. But if she wanted her help, it was better to be upfront. She had only spent a short time in her company, but Washington seemed thorough and conscientious. She didn't seem like the type to be obstructive for the hell of it.

'I found him,' Thessaly said.

Washington blinked. 'What?'

'I found him. Casper Sturgis.'

Washington waited for her to elaborate. Thessaly unlocked her phone. The clearest of the photos she had taken from across the road was already on the screen. Looking at it now, it wasn't that great. The quality reduced by the zoom, everything a little out of focus.

'This is the guy. He's going under the name Tony Andrews, and he manages an auto parts store right here in Grenville.'

'Tony Andrews?' Washington repeated.

'That's the name he's using,' she said.

Thessaly told her how she had criss-crossed Grenville looking for a dark-colored BMW SUV, to no avail. The gas station clerk pointing her in the direction of Atlantic Auto Parts, saying the picture looked a little like the manager.

'How do you know it's the same man?' Washington asked. She glanced down at the picture again. 'Like I said before, this guy wouldn't exactly stick out in a crowd in this state. You'll probably find a hundred in the crowd at any college basketball game.'

'It was him.'

Washington said nothing. She didn't have to, the slight raise of her eyebrow said it all.

'I had a good, unobstructed view, and I saw him get out of his vehicle. It was a black BMW X7, I have the license plate here.' She reached into her bag and took out her notebook. She opened it to the page where she had taken down the details and slid it across the desk. Washington glanced down at it. She folded her arms and looked at Thessaly, and at once, Thessaly noticed that her tone had changed from earlier in the day, when she had been open-minded, keen to help. There had been an element of humoring her, Thessaly thought, but that was better than the concern she saw in Washington's face now. The detective sighed and opened her mouth.

'I know what you're going to say,' Thessaly said quickly, cutting her off.

'Really? What am I going to say?'

'That just because it's the guy I saw the other night, doesn't mean it's him. Doesn't mean it's Casper Sturgis. You think I saw someone who looks like him, and I want it to be him so badly, that I'm making it fit.'

'I didn't say any of that, Ms Hanlon.'

'Call me Thessaly.'

'I didn't say any of that, but it sounds like you've been thinking a lot about it.'

That stopped her cold. She was right. That exact thought had been at the back of her mind for the last two days. No matter how much she told herself it was him, there was always the nagging sensation of doubt. Washington was good. She had gotten her to say it out loud herself first. It was like some kind of Judo move. She wondered how many suspects Washington had interrogated inside this room, and how many of them regretted talking more than they had to.

She sat back and folded her arms. 'I'd have to be pretty arrogant not to consider the possibility that I'm mistaken, yes. But it would be equally wrong to assume that I definitely am.'

Washington didn't respond directly, perhaps conceding the point. 'To tell you the truth,' she said. 'I'm a little concerned about what you're doing here.'

'What do you mean?'

'Searching for this guy on your own. Making inquiries. Taking covert pictures of people. You did the right thing coming to me first, but ...'

'Detective Washington, I don't want you to think I'm some

kind of crazy person. I'm certainly not planning on approaching him, if that's what you're worried about.'

Washington picked up Thessaly's phone again and studied the picture. 'What did you say his name was? Andrews?'

'Tony Andrews. That's it. So do you think there's any way you can …?'

'What? Go and arrest him?'

'Of course not. I know you need more.'

Washington considered before speaking again. 'Look, can we be straight? You seem like a nice person. You had a horrible experience twenty years ago, and you lost someone close to you. But I can't just go around and harass this guy because you think he looks like your brother's killer. He's living hundreds of miles away, minding his own business, and apparently has a completely different name.'

'Not looks like. Is.'

Washington gave her an 'if you say so' look, but didn't vocalize it.

'And anyway,' Thessaly continued. 'I don't want you to go round there right now. If he knows someone recognized him, he might disappear.'

Why did it sound so crazy when she said all this out loud? She knew she wasn't helping herself.

Washington stared at her for a long moment. Thessaly returned her gaze, unblinking. 'Chances are, this is a completely innocent man who just looks like the person you remember. You saw him once, twenty years ago.'

Thessaly felt a flash of irritation. 'You think I could just mistake him for somebody else? This man murdered my brother in front of me. I watched while he shot him twice. I was almost as close as I am to you, and I'm telling you: this is the guy.'

Washington raised an eyebrow at the outburst, and physically pulled back. She straightened in her seat and clasped her hands.

Thessaly winced inwardly. She had reacted before she could tell herself to shut up, that she was jeopardizing the already-fragile chances of Detective Washington being an ally.

'I'm sorry,' Thessaly said. 'It's been a long day. I appreciate you giving me your time, and I know you can't just take my word for it based on no evidence. I just don't know what to do from here.'

Washington scratched an itch behind her ear and considered for a moment. 'I'll tell you what. I'll have a look at this, make a few quiet inquiries. But I want you to really consider the possibility that this may not be the man you think it is.'

'That's all I want.'

'I'm not finished. If I do this, I want your word that you'll back off. No more private investigations. And do not go anywhere near this man. Okay?'

'Okay. Thank you. I really appreciate it.'

'Like I said, don't thank me yet.'

A couple of minutes later, Thessaly was getting back into her car when her phone buzzed. She got into the driver's seat and took her jacket off before checking the screen.

A text message. There was no name, just a number, which meant it had been sent by a contact who wasn't saved in her phone.

And yet, she recognized the number.

13

Thessaly? Did you mean to call?

Thessaly read the short message from Lee Greenwood three times, holding her breath throughout. She tapped out a reply with shaking fingers.

Yes. Can we talk?

She hit send and waited. The seconds drew out. The clock on the dash clicked over to the next minute, and then the one after that. Perhaps she should just have called. She watched cars pass by on the road that ran by the Grenville police station. In the distance, she could see the spire of the church she had passed earlier on, towering above the more modern buildings in view. Eventually, her phone buzzed again.

Okay. I have time at 5:30. Call then.

She tapped out a reply saying she would speak to him then. She sat back in the seat, suddenly aware of how tired she was. It had been a long day. She was as sure as she could be that she had found the person she had come here to find, but she didn't know what to do next. Even if she hadn't promised

Washington she wouldn't approach Sturgis, she couldn't do that anyway. How would it play out? Walk in there and demand that he admit who he really was? That he turn himself in? He would laugh it off. If even a sympathetic cop like Washington was skeptical, how could she hope to convince anyone else to take her seriously?

Then another thought occurred to her: he might very well *not* laugh it off. He might see her as a problem with a very simple solution. In fact, that was the most likely scenario, wasn't it?

The smartest solution was to do what her body was telling her. Go home, get some rest, let Detective Washington make some inquiries, and hope she came up with something. In the meantime, she had a conversation with an old friend to prepare for.

14

Thessaly pulled off the highway at a rest stop just before 5:30, just as it was getting dark. She bought coffee and a raisin Danish and went back to her car. She wound down the window. It was cold out, but the fresh air helped her nascent headache. It was 5:35 by the time she had finished the pastry. She dialed Lee's number and leaned back in her seat while it rang. She massaged an ache in her neck and watched the traffic flash past on the interstate.

Lee answered on the fifth ring. After they had exchanged cautious greetings, she cut to the chase.

'Listen, I would really like to talk to you in person if you have time.'

Hesitation. 'I don't know if that's a good idea.'

That made her wince. She tried to sound as breezy as possible. 'I don't want to cause you any trouble. I just need a half hour. What do you say?'

Long pause. 'Okay, sure.'

'Are you still in Brooklyn?' Last she had heard, Lee had moved to Bay Ridge or Prospect Heights, one of those. A while ago … maybe ten years ago, she had heard he had gotten married. She had been happy for him.

'I'm in Jersey now.' The way he said it gave her the sense

that he didn't want to get too specific. 'I work just outside of West Orange.'

'That's great, I'm headed home now and that's on my way.' It wasn't quite, but it easily could be.

There was a pause. 'Well, okay, sure. Do you want to tell me what this is about, or ...'

Thessaly hesitated. She didn't want to risk saying the wrong thing. 'Would you mind terribly if I waited to talk about it in person?' She wanted to make sure he couldn't hang up on her. And besides, now that she heard his voice, she wanted to see him.

After another long pause, he relented. 'What time?'

'An hour?'

'Sure, I have some things to finish up here. Let me give you an address.'

The place Lee suggested was a bar and grill a little outside West Orange. On the map, it looked like it was on the edge of a small town named Silverwells. She remembered there being farmland there, but things had changed. As Thessaly got within a mile of the destination, the road wound past a long stretch of high walls, finished in clean white stucco. At first she thought it was a golf course or something, but then she started noticing ornate gates. She slowed down to catch glimpses behind the gates. Gargantuan white walled houses, water features, sculptures. Floodlights illuminating everything in the night like a row of art galleries. She noticed security cameras on steel poles at regular intervals. A sign saying MAXX SECURITY PATROLS THIS AREA with a number to call for assistance.

She understood what the walls were now. They call them 'fuck-you' walls in Greenwich, Connecticut, because they're ostentatiously tall and imposing. In other towns, they had brought in stricter planning regulations to limit height, but clearly that hadn't been done here. She thought about stopping to take a closer look at the mansions, but figured if she pulled over then somebody in a Maxx Security car would appear to politely move her along. Was Lee living here? If so then he had certainly come up in the world. She wondered if he had any kids.

The bar and grill was called Horton's. It was low and sprawling, constructed out of brick and solid beams of wood, and the total cost of the vehicles in the lot would have comfortably exceeded the GDP of New Zealand.

Inside there was lots of hardwood and chrome, the appetizing scent of grilling meat in the air. No music, just a low buzz of conversation from the diners. There was a black grand piano in one corner, but no pianist on duty tonight. The waiter who greeted her wore black chinos and a dark red shirt. He had platinum blond hair and a pencil behind his ear. He looked over at occupied tables when she told him she was meeting somebody.

'Are they here already?'

She scanned the tables and the booths on the far wall. The place was about half-full. The clientele all looked well-heeled. Not in any kind of conspicuous way, but their clothes had the ageless look of the excessively comfortable. She wondered if it was her imagination that the waiter was side-eyeing her mid-range pant suit from Century 21. She didn't see any lone men.

'I don't think so, no.'

'Booth okay?' he asked.

She hesitated. 'You mind if I sit at the bar?'

She took one of the green leather upholstered stools and rested her feet on the brass rail along the bottom of the bar. She perused the bound drinks menu and ordered a nine-dollar homemade lemonade, which arrived promptly and with a sprig of mint.

She didn't recognize Lee at first when he arrived ten minutes later. Not because he had changed all that dramatically over the years, but because of how he was dressed. Thessaly had kept one eye on the door as she sipped her fancy lemonade, and had checked out everyone who entered, but she had discounted him at first. *No, just a cop.*

But then she looked closer, because he was the right age and build, and recognized the man she hadn't seen in almost two decades. He wore dark blue chinos with a matching shirt over a blue t-shirt, under a blue jacket. A lot of blue. He spotted her at the bar, seemed to hesitate for a moment, before approaching. As he got closer, she adjusted her initial assessment. All of the blue was there to give exactly the impression she had formed. There was small white lettering on the left breast of the jacket. *Maxx Security.*

She raised a hand to catch his eye and got up off the stool. He had barely changed. Short, dark brown hair, green eyes, a half-inch white scar under his lower lip that she had never gotten around to asking about. The two of them stood awkwardly for a moment, and she swayed, wondering if this was a hug situation, before Lee put that to rest by offering his hand. She took it, saying, 'Thank you for coming. It's great to see you.'

He nodded an acknowledgment, but didn't respond in kind. He took a seat on the stool next to her and rested a baseball cap emblazoned with an M on the bar. He wasn't wearing a wedding ring. A lot of men don't, though.

'Can I get you anything? Are you like ...' she gestured at his uniform. 'On duty?'

He shook his head. 'No, thank you. And no, I just got off.'

'Security, huh?'

His lips stretched for a split second in a perfunctory smile. 'Rent-a-cop. Out at Silverwells.'

'Yeah, I saw the signs. Last time I was out there it was a farm.'

'The Silver farm, yeah. Now it's two hundred acres of McMansions and Sycamore trees.'

'Oh,' she said. 'So, do you like the work?'

'It pays the bills.'

'I drove past. The houses are huge.'

'That they are.'

There was a long silence. She tried to draw him out a little more. 'What are the customers like?'

'Beats me. Half of them don't even live there most of the time. That's what we're here for. You really contacted me after all this time to talk about my shitty job, Thessaly?'

She took a gulp of her lemonade, rattling the ice and the sprig of mint at the bottom of the glass around. 'Cut to the chase, fair enough.' She put her glass down on the bar top hard and looked into Lee's eyes. 'I saw him.'

He blinked, and it took a second for the import of her words to hit him.

'Him? As in …'

'Yes. Casper Sturgis. He's alive.'

He opened his mouth to say something, then stopped and looked away. Thessaly hadn't known exactly what to expect. What he might say when she dropped the bombshell. As it turned out, she had been way off base with any predictions.

'I don't care.'

For a second, she wondered if she had misheard. His voice was as neutral as it had been when he declined a drink.

'What? I don't understand.'

He shrugged. 'What is there to understand? I don't want to know about it. I don't care.'

'You—' She was momentarily lost for words. She hadn't known what to expect, but it certainly wasn't this. 'Don't you want to know … I mean, then why did you agree to meet me?'

'I don't know. I hadn't thought about you or Mitch or any

of that for a long time. I was doing fine. Then I saw that call from you and I couldn't sleep last night. I went ten years not sleeping after what happened, and I don't miss that. So I wanted to tell you I'm not interested in going over all of that. I figured you might listen if I told you face to face.'

'At least hear me out? Otherwise what's the point of either of us being here?'

He took a long breath through his nostrils and then nodded curtly. 'All right. Fine.'

She told him about that first night in the Olympia diner at 2 a.m. The way the sound of the voice from the next booth had felt like a physical weight pushing down on her. Lee seemed unmoved, didn't react. She told him about following the car, losing it outside of Grenville. He spoke only once, when she told him that Detective Hendricks was dead.

'Sorry to hear that,' Lee said. 'He was a good guy.'

She told him that she was too, and continued. Hendricks's partner, Tyler, putting a good word in for her with the police out in Grenville. Her trip to Grenville, looking in vain for the car before finally lucking out with the clerk at the last gas station.

'I watched him from across the street, Lee. It was him. He's alive and he's fucking living a normal life like he's some every-day small-town businessman.'

'Wait a second,' Lee said. 'Backtrack. You said you found him because the guy in the gas station recognized him from your picture.'

'Right, the photofit from 2001, but aged up. It looks exactly like him.'

'And you saw him from across the street. So … fifty feet away, something like that?'

'I saw him up close in the diner. It's him.'

'But you said his name is Tony Andrews. Not Sturgis.'

'That's the name he's going under, yeah. It's him, Lee. It's him.'

He sighed and rubbed his eyelids with his thumb and index finger, and it suddenly dawned on Thessaly that this had been a terrible mistake. When he spoke, it was in the tone of a disengaged father trying to explain why there wasn't really a monster in the closet, it was just a shadow playing tricks on her.

'You weren't that close to him in 2001,' he said. 'Not as close as me and Mitch. You were out of... you were farther away.' He had stopped himself from saying *out of harm's way*, perhaps not wanting to sound bitter about it. 'Neither of us really had time to stare at him. How can you be sure the man you saw in the diner was the same person? I mean... he looks like him, fine. But it was twenty years ago. You can't be sure. A lot of people look like that. What are the odds of you running into him by accident?'

'No, I'm telling you—'

'And he has a name. Tom Andrews. Not Casper Sturgis.'

'*Tony* Andrews. And that's not his real name,' she snapped, slapping her hand down on the bar. The bartender paused polishing a glass at the other end of the bar and gave them a look.

Lee blinked and then looked away from her. 'Okay. I'll tell you what Thessaly, I don't need this shit.'

'I'm sor—'

'You didn't contact me for, what, eighteen years?'

'I didn't think you wanted me to after the... after our argument.'

'Eighteen years, and then you call me out of the blue. I think it must be something important, and deep down I'm hoping it's not about this. You say it's definitely the guy, but how can you be sure? After all this time, how can you be sure? He has a different name.'

'Lee, I would never have bothered you if I didn't think it was him. You have to believe me.'

73

'Thessaly …' he paused and looked as though he was deciding whether to say it. 'You weren't as close as I was.'

She didn't know if he meant as close to his attempted murderer, or as close to being killed. Maybe both. 'I know.'

He picked up his baseball cap from the bar and fitted it over his head. 'I'm sorry, I have to go. It was … you look good. Take care.'

He got off the stool to leave and Thessaly put a hand out to touch his arm. 'It was his voice. It doesn't matter that it was twenty years ago. I hear that voice every night.'

He looked down at her hand on his arm. For a second, they just stayed frozen in that position. Thessaly could see other patrons staring at them out of the corner of her eye. She didn't care.

And then, gently, Lee moved his other hand over and lifted Thessaly's hand from his forearm.

'It was his voice,' she said again, barely louder than a whisper this time. But Lee was already walking back toward the exit.

15

Thessaly arrived home an hour later, taking the Bear Mountain Bridge and following the road as it curved back south, with the Hudson on her right. She knew she should eat, even though it was the last thing she felt like after the encounter with Lee, so she stopped to pick up a couple of slices from Anthony's Pizza. Ham and olives, and they left it in the oven long enough to blacken the edges a little, the way she liked.

She opened the box and left it on the kitchen countertop, taking a napkin and a slice to eat in the study while she logged on to her computer. She was a lot hungrier than she had realized. All she had eaten since lunch was the Danish at the rest stop. She finished it quickly and wiped her hands on the napkin before clicking into her emails.

A flurry of emails from Drake at Graystone. She sent a brief acknowledgment reassuring him that everything was fine, and the new draft would be in his inbox by 9 a.m. on the 19th.

Nothing from Detective Washington. Thessaly would just have to be persistent. Make it more effort for her not to check into the background of 'Tony Andrews'.

Tony Andrews. The name itself was one of the reasons Thessaly didn't think she was mistaken. It sounded utterly generic, one step up from *John Smith.* The kind of name that's easy to spell and pronounce, and gives no real hint of a background. The kind of name you would forget five minutes after being introduced to the bearer. She had interviewed a police sketch artist a couple of years ago for a book. As it turned out, the story went in another direction and she didn't get to use any of it, but she remembered talking through the techniques the artist had to use to get a good likeness of a suspect. The artist was a stocky older guy with a straggly gray beard and a dry sense of humor, and he was extremely knowledgeable about not just the day-to-day reality of his job, but of the history of it. He said the worst result of any session was what he called a ghost.

Sometimes, even with a reliable witness who had gotten a good look at the suspect, the final sketch never takes life. It's a generic type of person, rather than a likeness of one individual person. It may or may not look like the suspect, but it's of no use in picking out one individual from a large suspect pool.

The name Tony Andrews was like that. A nothing. A ghost.

Sturgis would have chosen it deliberately.

She heard the low hiss of tires on the street and looked up. It was after eleven o'clock, and there wasn't much through traffic out there this time of night. She saw the wet road glisten in the wash of approaching headlights. There were cypress trees at either side of Thessaly's front yard, framing the road outside like the stage at a theater. A moment later, a silver SUV appeared from stage left and passed slowly by, probably looking for an address. It reached the end of the road, turned, and went back the way it had come. Thessaly looked back down at her screen.

Despite how low she had felt after the conversations with Washington and then Lee, she had achieved a lot. She had a name and a place of business now. She went through the same searches she had tried the other night, only this time with 'Tony Andrews' instead of 'Casper Sturgis'. She found Atlantic Auto Parts on Maple Avenue. It had a standard Google listing with a phone number and opening times, but there was no website. There didn't appear to be any social media, either. She supposed that wasn't that out of the ordinary. Residents of Grenville would know about it if they needed replacement filters or gaskets or what have you; people not from Grenville would have their own local supplier. It wasn't like you would make a special trip to another town for this kind of business. A local business for local people. Under the radar.

The business was listed, but of Tony Andrews, there was as little sign as there had been of Casper Sturgis. Even scrolling through the Google reviews of Atlantic. They were mostly satisfied customers, but they didn't go into much detail or mention the names of any employees. 'A+ service, would use again' was as in depth as it got.

She dug back a little and found that the store had had a different owner eight years ago, and had been called Pacific Auto Parts. Tony Andrews, or whoever had picked the new name, clearly hadn't felt too creative that day. Just like with his own name, if Thessaly was correct.

Time to see if she could find the man himself. Obvious searches first. Facebook and the other social platforms. There were a number of men by that name in Pennsylvania, but none close to Grenville, and none that looked anything like Casper Sturgis in their profile pictures. He had a good reason not to want to attract attention, of course, but not having any kind of social profile attracts attention in itself, these days. She knew some people who used pseudonyms, or variants of their real name on their social accounts. Some of them were minor celebrities, but not all. Lots of people have reason not to be easily findable. Teachers, cops … murderers.

She browsed through some local pages. Grenville History Page. Friends of Grenville Park. She went through the members of each group, scrolling past endless profile pictures. Sturgis wasn't there. Maybe she should start checking out each of these profiles, look at friends of friends for that familiar face. But she had other things to try first.

She sat back in her chair and considered. Local news, next. Grenville didn't seem to have a local paper. The town Wikipedia page referenced a Grenville *Examiner* which had ceased distribution more than a decade ago. It looked like the paper that covered the area was the Allentown *Observer*. The masthead on the paper's website listed a half dozen other towns including Grenville. She was betting the coverage wouldn't be too detailed, but she tried anyway. No mention of a Tony Andrews. Nothing on Atlantic Auto Parts, either. She tried the general Grenville tag and started plowing through a series of extremely boring town updates.

Thessaly was halfway down an article about a new stop light being installed at the corner of 5th and Main when she heard the hissing of tires on the road again and looked up quickly.

Different car this time. Lucy Page's husband returning late, carefully steering his midlife crisis Mazda MX-5 into their driveway. She shook her head at the way she had jumped. The last couple of days were making her paranoid. It reminded her of how she had felt for months after the Redlands Mall. Flinching at loud noises, quickening her pace when she sensed anyone getting too close to her on the sidewalk, avoiding any interior space without a back exit.

She rubbed the tiredness out of her eyes and looked back at the screen.

What are the odds?

Both Detective Washington and Lee had asked the same rhetorical question. She couldn't blame them, she supposed. She might be asking the same thing if she hadn't seen Sturgis with her own two eyes.

But sometimes the one in a million number comes up. Twice a week, somebody wins the New York Lottery, after all. She remembered a feature that had run in *Inside NY* a couple of years before it closed, about a Holocaust survivor finding himself in the next hospital bed to one of the guards who had been at Belsen, the two men on a different continent, thirty years later.

Compared to that, her chance encounter at the diner probably didn't qualify as a million to one coincidence. But it was striking enough that she couldn't ignore it. It was like God or the universe handing her a chance to do something about what had happened. Her number had come up. She couldn't walk away.

The screen was hurting her eyes now, so she switched it off. She picked up the document folder she used to keep all of her news clippings and notes about Redlands. She went over to the leather couch in the corner of the room and started leafing through the pages.

Newspaper clippings about the murders. The police reports. Articles on the demolition of the mall a few years later. She had the photographs from the disposable camera Mitch had brought with him at the back of the file. She held the picture of the *DEADLANDS* graffiti on the shutter up to the light. The color of the spray paint was like dried blood. Mitch had less than an hour to live when he had taken this picture.

Looking at it now, the word seemed to be a warning they had not heeded. A last chance to turn back.

16

Saturday, February 6

Thessaly woke gasping for breath, her fingers digging into the upholstery of the couch. She was upstairs. The study. The desk lamp still on. The night sky outside.

It took her a minute to catch her breath.

In the dream, she had been back in Redlands. She had had similar dreams many times before, but this one was different. At the end of it, she had found herself in her own kitchen, walking slowly over to the window above the sink. The lights wouldn't go on, no matter how often she called out. And then she had heard that voice behind her.

Not your lucky day.

She shuddered and got to her feet, wincing at a cramp in her leg from the way she had fallen asleep. She tapped her keyboard to wake the screen and check the time. It wasn't yet 6 a.m., but Thessaly didn't think she'd be sleeping anytime soon, not after that.

The nightmares had been a constant presence for the first couple of years after Redlands, but gradually, they had lessened in frequency and intensity. She didn't think there had been one in at least a year. And they had always taken the form of the early part of the dream. She found herself back in the mall, alone, running from the man with the gun. The end of the dream was different. Sturgis had never appeared in the here and now before. She doubted that a psychiatrist would have to spend much time decoding that one.

That made her think about the counseling sessions after Mitch's death. Talking about the dreams helped, even though it was difficult. Her counselor had recommended talking to a close friend about it, or failing that, even talking to herself. She went back into the kitchen and took her small digital voice recorder out of the drawer. She used it to work through plot ideas when she went for walks in the woods, but perhaps it would work just as well for DIY therapy.

She clicked the button and leaned on the kitchen island, looking out at the back yard as she talked through the dream. When she got to the part where she had moved through the dark kitchen toward the sink before hearing that voice in her ear, she physically walked through the steps she had taken in the dream. To her surprise, it seemed to help a little. She felt a notch less anxious.

She put the recorder back in the drawer and told Alexa to play some morning music. After a moment's consideration, Bobbie Gentry's 'Morning Glory' started to play. She made herself a coffee, her hands still shaking, and went over to the glass patio doors. She watched as the sky lightened above the treetops in the woods. The caffeine and the music helped. So did the crisp dawn light seeping in through the glass, changing the house from the scene of her nightmare to a familiar, comfortable home again.

She unlocked the patio door and slid it open. The air was cold, just above freezing, but it felt good to breathe in through her nostrils and then out, watching her breath make a cloud.

She decided to do something she hadn't done in a while: an early morning walk in the woods. She took an old coat from the kitchen cupboard, slipped on the sneakers she had left by the door over her bare feet and went out into the yard.

There was a small paved patio giving way to a fifty-by-fifty-foot square of grass, enclosed by a six-foot wooden fence. Not quite the 'fuck-you' walls she had seen at Silverwells the previous evening. She wondered if those made the inhabitants feel any safer, or if it really was all about the impression. Her fence had a gate set into the northwest corner with a small padlock securing it. She unlocked it and opened the gate.

This had been one of the big reasons she and Josh had bought the house. It was the last house on the street, and the street was the last street on this side of town. It felt like a bonus; a compromise between the suburbs and being somewhere more rural. She liked the idea that she could walk out of her back door and immediately find herself in woods where she could walk for miles without seeing another human being. There were no trails around this way; the trees rose from a thick covering of poison ivy and tangling weeds. The dogwalkers and the joggers stuck to the picturesque walkway down by the river and the park, so she had the woods to herself.

The dream had really rattled her. The part at the end where she had found herself in her own kitchen in particular. It had felt so real, so immediate.

The thought of an intruder in the house had always been one of her baseline fears. It had intensified around the time Josh had moved out, coinciding with a spate of burglaries in Buchanan. She had wasted hours scrolling through updates on social media while obsessing about the house being securely locked at all times. Once, when she couldn't find the key for the patio doors she had gotten a same-day locksmith to replace the lock. Naturally, she found the key underneath the living room couch immediately after the locksmith left. Even at the time, she had known her anxiety wasn't just about the recent break-ins.

In that period, she had gone back to an idea she had always dismissed. She had been firmly against having a gun in the house; on principle and for practical reasons, but the paranoia made her rethink. She reasoned that if she knew how to use and store a gun, it would be safe enough. Perhaps it would help her sleep more soundly, knowing that she could protect herself if necessary.

A block of three sessions with an instructor at the shooting range over in Cortlandt had put paid to that idea. She had test-fired a dozen different weapons. Mostly handguns; Glocks and Rugers. She balked at the offer to try an assault weapon. She learned how to handle a gun safely, how to keep it in good working order, the mechanics of shooting, the best place to aim for on an attacking enemy. She was good on the theory. The problem was, she couldn't shoot for shit. She wasn't just bad, she was so bad that it seemed to baffle her instructor, Enrique.

'I'm not cut out for this, am I?' she had observed toward the end of the third session, after missing the target with every shot at a distance of twenty feet.

Enrique had solemnly considered this and come up with a suggestion. 'If you can get the bad guy to move *very* slowly toward you … down a *very* narrow corridor, you might be okay.' Then he laughed and told her she would improve with practice. She took his word for it, but she didn't persevere. What she hadn't told Enrique was why she had such difficulty with the shooting. Every time she pulled the trigger, she felt physically sick. It didn't matter that she was aiming at paper targets. Each gunshot took her back to Redlands.

After the third session, she realized that she was intensely relieved at the thought she wouldn't have to touch a gun the next day. And so she never went back, and that was that. There wasn't much point keeping a gun in the house if you couldn't hit the broad side of a barn.

The undergrowth in the woods was almost impenetrable, even in the winter. By the spring, there would be no almost about it. She picked her way carefully through the poison ivy and followed the invisible path that only she knew, leading her down to the stream that bounded the woods from the fields beyond. There was a big oak tree that had been blown down across the river in some long-ago storm. The trunk was covered in thick moss, so thick that it felt like a cushion on a dry summer's day. Sometimes Thessaly would bring her laptop down here to work. It was a good thinking place. A complete change of scene from her study, or from the coffee shop in town, her usual workplaces.

The moss was damp from the previous night's rain, so she didn't attempt to sit on the trunk. Instead she went down to the stream and crossed using the stepping stones, avoiding the big rock that had twisted and dropped her into the water the last time she had been down here.

She reached the other side and climbed up to the boundary fence. She stood and listened to the ripple of the stream and looked out over the fields as the sun rose behind the transmission towers on the horizon.

She hoped the nightmare was a one-off, but she feared not. She had unlocked something, like it or not.

Tony Andrews.

How had he managed it? Somehow, Casper Sturgis had just dropped off the map after 2001 and created a whole new life for himself. What had happened in the intervening years? How long had he been Tony Andrews? Had he been anyone else?

She wondered how deep the deception ran. At first she had hoped that it would be easy to prove that he wasn't who he said he was. The more she thought about it, the more optimistic that seemed. He owned a business. Presumably he had a home, maybe a mortgage. That demanded a little more effort and planning than just using a phony name when checking into a hotel. He would have had to fake documents to use as proof of ID: birth certificate, previous addresses. He drove a vehicle, so he probably had a driver's license in his new name.

Even these days, it probably wasn't that difficult to create a false identity that would pass muster under most everyday scenarios. And depending on how long ago he came up with it, it would snowball. Real bank accounts and credit history and employment history would start to accrue over the kernel of falsehood at the core. Unless anyone had cause to dig deep, then after a while it would be as though he had always been Tony Andrews.

She had an advantage though, because after seeing him twice she was positive that Tony Andrews was a fiction; Casper Sturgis the buried truth.

But how to prove it?

Sturgis had changed his name, his location, his official records. What couldn't he change?

17

'A retreat? That sounds like a great idea.' Drake's voice sounded deafening over the Bluetooth connection to Thessaly's car stereo. 'I hope you're going someplace appropriately cinematic and desolate.'

'I found a place that's pretty out of the way. Just need to get out of the house, get my head down.'

'Great. And you're still okay for the nineteenth? If you need anything, just let me know.'

'You know me, Drake, I don't suffer in silence.'

She cut off the call and grimaced at the mild white lie. Maybe it wasn't that much of a lie at all. After all she would try to get some work done in Grenville. She had a plan, but she didn't know exactly how long it would take to execute. And the place she had booked into was cute. Perhaps a change of scene really would help with the book.

She left at ten in the morning, to avoid rush hour, and the drive took her just over two hours. The guest house was close to the river's edge on the south side of Grenville, so she was able to avoid driving anywhere near the police station, only feeling a little guilty as she made the detour. After all, she wasn't doing anything wrong. She had promised Detective Washington that she wouldn't approach Sturgis, yes, but she thought she would be able to keep her word on that, if everything went to plan.

She pulled into the driveway of the guest house just before 1 p.m. It was a sprawling country home with white wood siding. There were three levels, and she knew from the pictures on the booking site that there was an open second floor porch around the back.

A blonde woman in her sixties wearing a purple velour jumpsuit came out to greet her with a welcoming smile.

'Thessaly?' she asked as she got out of the car. 'Hi, I'm Rosemary.'

Thessaly's cell buzzed in her pocket and she took it out and looked at the screen.

'Do you need to get that?' Rosemary asked.

She didn't recognize the number. 'It's okay, I'll call them back.'

The ground floor was a large open plan space with brown floor tiles and white walls. It felt like a boutique hotel reception, with discreet seating areas and nooks dotted around. Rosemary led her up the open tread stairs in the center of the space and along a long corridor with suspended Tiffany lampshades. They climbed a shorter set of stairs to the third floor, and she showed Thessaly to her room. It was an eaves room with a single bed and an old-fashioned rolltop desk by the window and a bookcase stocked with mysteries and romance novels. There was a framed painting of a butterfly on the wall. The window looked out through the bare branches of one of the tall sycamores that surrounded the yard. Thessaly could see the river churning its way north, the sound just audible though the window was closed.

'You're sure you didn't want any of the bigger rooms? They're normally more expensive, but we're off-season, so if you wanted something more roomy...'

'No, this is perfect,' Thessaly said. 'Cozy.'

'If you're sure. We serve dinner at eight, and breakfast is from seven. If you—'

Thessaly's cell buzzed again.

'I'm sorry,' she said, giving Rosemary a pained expression and digging her phone out, meaning to switch it to silent. Her face froze as she saw Detective Washington's name on the screen. Shit. Had Washington seen her driving through town? She felt like she had been caught with her hand in the cookie jar.

'Is everything all right?'

'Yeah, I need to take this, I'm really sorry.'

The call had gone to voicemail by the time Rosemary stepped out of the room with a polite smile and closed the door. Great first impression, now she looked like the big city douchebag in a Hallmark movie who's too busy for the slower pace of life out in the sticks.

But that was the least of her worries. She took a breath, steeled herself, and hit the button to call back.

18

'Hi,' Thessaly said, tentatively, when Detective Washington picked up. 'You called?'

There was a pause. She closed her eyes, waiting for the lecture. Was Washington a yeller? Or would it be worse, like… cold and unamused.

But when Washington spoke, it was neither. She sounded apologetic. 'Is this a bad time?'

Thessaly cleared her throat. 'Uh, no. No this is fine. Hi. How are you?'

'Are you sure? You sounded a little weird there.'

'No, it's just… I hadn't expected you to call back. I mean, so quickly.' *Please don't ask where I am.*

'Well, first thing, you have Storm Dennis to thank. I was all booked in to attend a conference in Augusta this weekend, and my flight got delayed at the airport, and then canceled. I was bored with the book I was reading, and the woman next to me was doing a Sudoku, so I decided to look into another kind of puzzle. I made a couple of calls. I took a closer look into Tony Andrews, and there were no red flags. He isn't known to us. No criminal record, no nine-one-one calls to his address, not so much as a traffic violation. There is absolutely nothing to suggest he isn't who he says he is.'

'But that just means he's been keeping his nose clean,' Thessaly said. 'What if—'

'I'm not finished. I decided to have a look and see if there was anything else I could dig up about him. He doesn't seem to have any social media, which is ...'

'Suspicious.'

'Some people would say that. Others would say it's an entirely healthy approach to modern life. But sure, usually there's *something*. All I had was a name and some records. The DMV photo of him was the only picture on record, and the license was issued in 2014, so the picture is a few years out of date. I wanted to see him in person. I went down to Atlantic Auto Parts. Not in an official capacity. I was in luck, Andrews was on the desk when I went in. I asked him about brake fluid.'

'What was he like?' Thessaly asked, feeling a frisson at the thought of actually speaking to Sturgis.

'He was normal. Most people are normal when they don't know they're speaking to a cop. I made conversation, saying I hadn't been in since the change of owner. He said they'd been here for a few years. I tried to keep the conversation going, but he didn't seem like a talker. Not rude, not dismissive, just not chatty. He sold me my brake fluid and told me to have a good day. I decided to have a look into his history in Grenville. Property records show his home was purchased in 2014.

'The business changed hands around then, too. I called the realtor who sold the house and managed to speak to the guy who sold the house. He remembered it without having to check the records because it was such a smooth deal. One man came by, took a very quick look around the place, and made an offer for ten per cent above the asking price on the spot. The other reason he remembers it is the fact that the guy who viewed the place wasn't the same guy who picked up the keys two weeks later.'

'That sounds pretty weird,' Thessaly said.

'The realtor didn't seem to find it unusual, said it happens a lot when someone is moving from another state. They get somebody local to view the place and give them the okay before they buy. I checked out the records of the sale, because usually they have the previous address. Guess what?'

'No previous address?'

'Nothing. Everything handled through a lawyer in DC. I contacted them to see if I could finesse some more information out of them, but I hit a wall.'

'Can't you get a warrant or something?'

She could hear the amusement in Washington's voice. 'I'm afraid you need a lot more justification than that to get a warrant. No. That was a dead end. Wherever Andrews came from before he bought that house, it was someplace out of state. If there's more information out there, I'm going to need more than you saying the guy is not who he says he is. And even that isn't necessarily a crime.'

Thessaly sat back and considered the new information. This was more than she had really expected Washington to do, deep down. 'So what do you think?'

There was a long pause. 'I think something is a little unusual with this guy. Nothing that you would notice if you weren't looking, but there are a few too many gaps. I don't know if he is who you think he is, but I think he's hiding something.'

'Where in town is this house?' Thessaly asked, trying to make it sound as casual as possible, but Washington was on to her immediately.

'No way. You leave this to me. We made a deal, remember?'

Worth a try, she thought, and said, 'I know, I'm sorry.'

'To tell you the truth, I was just looking to find proof you were wrong. Instead, you got me curious.'

'I really appreciate it, Detective Washington. I have every faith in you.'

As she hung up, Thessaly thought about how her words had been sincere. She really was grateful. She really did have faith in Washington to look into this. But that faith wasn't absolute, and it certainly didn't mean she was about to sit on her hands and hope for the best.

She looked down at her phone and saw that there had been another missed call. This time, there was a text message. When she saw who the short message was from, her eyes widened.

Hi – it's Kayla from the Olympia. I saw that guy you were asking about again.

*

Thessaly pulled into the lot of the Olympia fifteen minutes later. She wondered what could have prompted Sturgis to drop in again, considering he didn't seem to be a regular. Kayla's message had come a little late, of course. She already knew Sturgis's new name and his place of business, but a deal was a deal. And perhaps Kayla would have picked up something else that was useful.

There were a few more cars in the lot than there had been last time, but no black BMW SUVs. She parked in the same spot she had used last time and went inside.

A blonde, bespectacled waitress carrying a coffee pot caught her eye and started approaching, but then Kayla appeared from the kitchen. 'It's okay, Sally, I got this one.'

Sally shrugged and changed course to refill the cups of a couple of truckers at the booth nearest the door.

Kayla showed her to a table and waited until she had sat down.

'Hey, I didn't expect you to be so fast.'

'I was in Grenville,' Thessaly explained. 'I tried calling, but your phone was off, so I thought I would drop by and say thank you.'

'Joe makes us leave them in the locker when we're on shift,' she said with an eyeroll. 'So you got the message? I saw that guy you were looking for.'

'The man with the plaid shirt, yeah. Listen, I already found him, but I really appreciate you letting me know. When did you see him? Today?'

There was a pause, and Kayla shook her head.

'No, not that guy. The other one.'

19

'The other one?' Thessaly asked. She had all but forgotten about the bald man in the gray suit Sturgis had been speaking to that first night. The one she had pegged as a traveling salesman. But Kayla was right. The other day, she had asked her to give her a call if *either* of those guys came in.

'Yeah,' Kayla said. 'I've been looking out for them, like you asked.'

'When was he here?'

'Around one. He didn't stay long.'

'Was he meeting someone?'

'No,' Kayla said. 'But he was looking for someone. The same someone as you. The man in the plaid shirt.'

'But why wouldn't he—' Thessaly had to take a second to catch up with what Kayla was saying. 'You mean, he didn't know him?'

'I'm assuming so, if he was asking me.'

'But they were talking that first night. They were at the same table.'

'Yeah.'

'They were talking to each other.'

'Is this going to take long? And are you going to order something so my boss thinks you're a real customer?'

'Uh ... coffee, apple pie, whatever,' Thessaly said. She closed her eyes and tried to get this straight in her head. 'Okay, you're telling me the bald guy who was meeting the guy in the plaid shirt came in.'

'That's right.'

'And wanted to know if *you* knew the guy in the plaid shirt?'

'Yes,' Kayla said. 'He actually seemed really stressed out. Like he really needed to know.'

Thessaly considered. Once she had picked up Sturgis's trail in Grenville, the man he had been talking to that first night had basically become an afterthought. Inasmuch as she had thought about him at all, she had assumed he was a friend of Sturgis's. But now she knew that wasn't the case, it threw a different light on what she had seen. Maybe this was some kind of business deal.

But if so, what kind of deal was made in the dead of night, between two people who didn't know each other, in a place neither of them were regulars? Something shady? Maybe. But even in that case, why wouldn't he have a way to contact Sturgis?

Kayla reappeared with the coffee pot, placed a cup with the 'O' logo on it in front of Thessaly, and filled it up. 'So, you said you wanted to know if he came in, and he came in.'

Thessaly checked the time. Kayla had said about one, so … just over an hour ago. He could still be in the area.

'Did he say where he was going next?'

Kayla shook her head.

He could be anywhere by now. Thessaly didn't know if this was important, but if he wanted to get in touch with Sturgis and seemed worked up about it, she wanted to know why.

Thessaly suddenly noticed Kayla had a small, anticipatory smirk on her face. Like she was holding something back.

'What is it?'

'Well, he was like you. Really keen to talk to the man from the other night. And he did the same thing as you.'

Again, it took Thessaly a couple of seconds. 'He left his number?'

She nodded. 'Said the same thing. If I see the guy, call him and he would make it worth my while. Although, not as worth my while as you said. He offered twenty bucks.'

'I'll give you two hundred for that number.'

20

Thessaly waited outside in her car. The clouds had darkened overhead, and it looked like rain might be on the way. She had moved her car to the back of the lot so that she could sit and watch the entrance from a distance. She had sent the message from her own phone. Bait.

Hi, it's Kayla from the Olympia, we spoke earlier. That guy you were looking for is in right now. If you want, I can slow down the service?

Thessaly knew the car was his before she saw the driver. The roar of an approaching engine, decreasing speed rapidly, taking the turn into the lot so quickly that one of the front wheels left the ground as it bumped across the hole at the entrance. She had her phone in her hand, ready to go. She steadied it on the curve of her steering wheel and took a series of shots of the car as it pulled in.

It was a silver Ford Taurus. Difficult to know for sure, but she thought it was the other car she had seen here the other night. It looked like it had been recently washed, but the sills had been splashed with mud even more recently. She saw the driver as he swung the car around to park. He wasn't looking in her direction, but she could see it was the man from the early hours of Thursday morning. She zoomed in and took a couple of pictures of him as he got out and cast a glance around the lot. She lowered the phone below the wheel, but even if he noticed her sitting in the car, his gaze didn't linger on her. He was wearing a sports coat, a white shirt and jeans. He locked the car and went inside the diner.

Thessaly got out. She held her phone down by her side and carefully snapped a series of pictures as she approached the Taurus. No distinctive dents or markings. It looked almost new, or maybe a rental. Rhode Island plates.

She could see the man waiting at the 'Please wait to be seated' sign, staring pensively at the almost-empty seats in the diner. Kayla had swapped with Sally to take her break early, so that it wouldn't be her who served him.

Without breaking stride, Thessaly switched to the sound recording app on her phone and hit the red button to start recording. It wouldn't be as good quality as her voice recorder back home, but it didn't need to be. She had no idea what business this guy had with Casper Sturgis, but she wanted a record of the conversation.

As she got inside, she saw Kayla's co-worker Sally show the man to a table in the window. Sally looked up and raised her eyebrows, recognizing Thessaly from a half hour before. Thessaly smiled at her and turned to walk to the table where the man was sitting. He was looking down at his phone as she approached. He only raised his head when she took the seat across from him. He was a little older than Thessaly had guessed from seeing him that first night. He had a fuzz of shaved hair at the sides of his head. His mustache had gray in it too. He gave her a wary look over the rims of his glasses. He didn't seem to recognize her from the brief time they had crossed paths the other night. When she didn't say anything, he spoke.

'I'm sorry, ma'am, this seat's taken. I'm waiting for somebody.'

His voice had the tone of somebody who was used to their suggestions being followed promptly. It had an edge of 'don't push it' under the politeness.

Thessaly positioned her bag on the table, making sure it wasn't too far from her hand.

'I know. Tony sent me to ask what we can do for you.'

The guy blinked, then straightened in the seat. 'Who are you?'

'You first.'

He shook his head. 'This isn't acceptable. Where is he? The deal was with the man.'

'He can't be here right now.'

The man's gaze switched from Thessaly to the register, where Sally was tallying up a check while one of the truckers she had been serving earlier waited. Then his gaze moved to the kitchen door with 'Staff Only' on it. Thessaly knew what he was thinking. She hoped she wasn't causing any trouble for Kayla.

'One of the waitresses told us someone was looking for him,' she said quickly. 'Tony had another engagement, so he asked me to stay here and ask what we could do for you.'

'Tony, huh,' the guy said.

She found it hard to get a read on the reaction. Was the name new information to him? Maybe he knew him as Sturgis. She was starting to regret this course of action. Still, what could he do here, in front of all these witnesses?

'Tell him I need to talk to him. In person.' He handed her a blank card with a cell number written down. The same number he had given Kayla. No name. 'As soon as possible. And tell him it's off.'

'It's off?' Thessaly repeated. He didn't respond. 'So, no deal?'

His eyes narrowed, and immediately she knew she had said the wrong thing.

The man took a look around the other customers, glanced outside at the lot.

'Who the hell are you, lady? You're not with him.'

Thessaly swallowed and started to reach for her bag. 'I think I should go.'

Another mistake. He grabbed the bag out of her hands.

'Hey!' she yelled, taken by surprise.

He dug around in the bag and took out her phone, saw the recording app counting the seconds. A murderous glare flashed in his eyes and he stood up. He took her arm and pulled her up out of her seat. Sally was approaching, one hand on her chest, a nervous look as the man towered over her. 'Everything okay here?'

Reaching into his coat with his free hand, the bald man flashed some sort of ID at Sally. 'Nothing to see here, ma'am, we're going to talk outside.' Sally backed off. Thessaly couldn't see what he had shown her from her position. Was he a cop?

No. There was something furtive about the way he was dragging her outside. A feeling that he was only just keeping himself under control. He took her outside and told her to put her hands on the wall. She looked around the lot. There was nobody close by. The big trucker had paid the check and was climbing up into his rig on the other side of the lot, but he had his back to them. The bald man roughly pushed her around.

'I said hands on the wall.'

She could hear him behind her going through her bag. A creak as he opened the purse that held her driver's license.

'Thessaly Hanlon. Buchanan, New York,' he read. 'What the hell are you doing out here?'

Thessaly started to turn and he roughly pushed her back. 'Who are you?' she asked.

'I'm none of your fucking business, lady. What do you know about him?'

'Who?'

'You know who I'm talking about. The man I'm here to see.'

'I told you, he asked me to take a message from you.'

He grabbed her arm again roughly, spinning her away from the wall. He started pulling her after him as he walked to the car. She felt a stab of panic. He wasn't a cop. He hadn't done the things cops are supposed to do, like identifying himself or reading her her rights.

'Where are we going?'

'We're going for a drive.'

She tried to plant her feet. 'I'm not getting in the car.'

He tugged her arm hard and she almost fell, stumbling forward.

'Is there a problem here?'

The two of them stopped and looked around at the accent that sounded like it hailed from one of the Carolinas. The trucker had gotten back out of his rig and he was walking toward them. He was burly, over six feet. Reddish-brown hair and a bushy mustache. He wore gray overalls and was holding a worn and faded cap in his hand, and Thessaly couldn't remember the last time she had been so pleased to see another person.

'Get lost, Cletus,' the bald man snapped. 'Police.'

The trucker hesitated, glanced at Thessaly.

'I don't want to go with him,' she said clearly.

'If you're a cop, show me your ID,' the trucker said, seeming to draw a measure of confidence from Thessaly's unambiguous statement.

The guy considered for a moment, his fingers tightening on Thessaly's arm. Then he let go.

Without another word, he turned and walked back to the car and got in. He started the engine and tore out of the lot, wheels spinning.

'Thank you,' Thessaly said. 'I don't know who that guy was. He said he was a cop, but…'

'He didn't act like one,' the trucker said. Then reconsidered.

'Actually, maybe he did. Apart from I never had no cop back down when I asked him for ID before. A punch yes, backing down, no.'

Thessaly turned to look along the highway where the silver Taurus had long since vanished. She rubbed her arm. She could see red abrasions in the inside crook of her elbow where he had been gripping her. 'I don't know who he was, but I'm glad he's not here anymore.'

She remembered something and opened her bag. *Shit*. He had kept her phone.

21

'Jesus, are you okay?'

Kayla's eyes were wide as Thessaly stepped back inside the diner. Sally was standing beside her, having evidently brought her coworker up to speed.

'Yeah,' Thessaly said, still feeling a little lightheaded. 'If he comes back, call the police.'

Kayla looked from Thessaly to the window, at the spot outside where the silver Taurus had been parked.

'I don't think he will come back, though,' Thessaly added quickly.

He had seemed panicked, couldn't get out of there fast enough when challenged. Kayla wasn't exactly thrilled at this instruction, but perked up when Thessaly transferred another two hundred dollars to her PayPal as a thank you for sticking her neck out.

'Drop by anytime,' Kayla said. 'Anything else I can do for you?'

'Yes. Give me your Wi-Fi password.'

Thessaly opened her laptop and tried the Google Find My Device link, hoping the man from the diner would be dumb enough to track himself all the way home. As soon as it zeroed in, she saw that whoever this guy was, he wasn't an idiot. The device was already turned off. Last known location, about two miles east along the highway from the diner.

She drove there anyway, ready to take off in a hurry if she saw his car, but just found an empty wide spot at the side of the road. She parked and surveyed the area. After a couple of minutes, she found the mangled remains of her phone, smashed to shit. The SIM and the memory card nowhere to be seen. As she stood by the car, it started to drizzle lightly.

Thessaly was still a little shaken when she got back to the guest house. The bald man couldn't have been a cop, surely. And yet... the way the waitress had immediately backed off. It wasn't just that he had waved ID at her, it was the authority in his voice. That really did sound like a cop. And now that she thought about it, perhaps she had guessed wrong on her original impression. Salesmen looked weary and wore crumpled suits, but so did police officers.

But if he was a cop, what did he have to do with Sturgis? Why had he tried to drag her into his car? And why had he backed down?

The most practical concern following her meeting at the Olympia was that she needed a new phone. She got in touch with her carrier and to her surprise, it was reasonably straightforward to pay for a new one to be couriered to the guest house. She could even get it delivered by 7 a.m. for an extra $4.95.

She logged into her cloud account and saw with satisfaction that her pictures of the bald man had uploaded. The sound recording hadn't, because it wasn't set up to back up automatically. Still, she had a couple of decent shots of him, and the full license plate from his car. Perhaps she could talk to Washington about it, see if she had any ideas about the man. But not yet. She had some other things to do before she was ready to go back to the Grenville PD, and there was no guarantee of success.

She closed the browser window and opened a PDF document she had downloaded back home. She had only gone looking for background information about Atlantic Auto Parts store, to see if any names or dates jumped out. What she had found was a bonus.

The floor plan of the store, from the sale listing years ago.

22

Monday, February 8

The courier buzzed the doorbell of the guest house at 6:28 a.m. Thessaly was already dressed and made it down to open the door before a second ring, but Rosemary had already emerged from her room wearing a purple dressing gown. She smiled politely at Thessaly's apology and went back into her room.

A half hour later, Thessaly was parked across the street from Atlantic Auto Parts as the sun began to rise over the roofs of the buildings on the other side of the street. There was a smattering of birdsong. The thick scent of cheap eggs frying drifted out from the vents of the McDonald's kitchen. She watched through her windshield as the early bird traffic built up, never approaching anything that could be called rush hour, but getting busier. Eventually, she saw the familiar black SUV round the corner and pull into the space marked 'Manager' outside the store.

She caught her breath as Sturgis got out of the driver's seat. She wondered if she would ever get used to seeing him, and decided that maybe she didn't want to. That cold, sick feeling in her stomach kept her on her guard. She thought that was a good thing. She put a hand up to her brow to cover her face. He didn't look in her direction, though. He closed the car door and tapped his fob to lock the doors with a blink of lights, before going into the store.

Thessaly had spent a lot of time scouting out the territory. She had found the expired listing from when the business was sold, which contained interior photographs, and most importantly, a floor plan. It showed the main store area, a stockroom taking up most of the western quarter of the building, a single restroom, and a small office tucked into the northwestern corner at the back. Last night, after the sun had gone down, she had confirmed that the small window in the office was unobstructed by shutters or blinds.

She made herself wait five full minutes after the door of the store had closed behind Sturgis. Just in case he had forgotten something and came back out.

When the five minutes had elapsed, she picked up the baseball cap from the passenger seat and fitted it over her head, pulling the brim down so it shaded her face. She got out, suppressing a shiver as the cold air bit into her after the warmth of the car. She kept her eyes on the front of the store as she opened the rear door and took out the small backpack, swinging one strap over her shoulder. She could see the reception area, the same woman from the other day on the desk. Her head was down, examining something.

Thessaly crossed the road and turned left, hurrying to the end of the block, casting a glance back as she reached the corner to reassure herself the black SUV hadn't moved. She jogged along South Street and turned right again on Acacia, which ran parallel to Maple. There was an alley between the buildings that led to the vacant lot that backed onto Atlantic Auto Parts.

She passed through the alley and found the square of scraggly green space at the back of the store.

There was a beech tree in the corner of the space, its branches bare. She turned around to ensure no one was watching her from any of the overlooking windows, and sat down with her back to the trunk of the tree. She opened her backpack and took out the compact set of binoculars. Josh had bought them on their trip to Florence, for their night at the opera. They had lain unused in a drawer since then. She raised them to her eyes and trained them on the small window at the back of the store. She could see a desk, a computer, shelves lining the wall with document files. What she couldn't yet see was the owner of the store.

She adjusted the focus and shifted position to try to take in as much of the room as she could see through the small window. She checked off the visible items that might be suitable. The keyboard wouldn't do. The mouse might, although its absence would be noticed immediately. There were no documents lying on the desk.

The shadows in the room changed. A door had opened. A second later, Sturgis passed by the window. He sat down at the desk and she saw that he was carrying a sheaf of envelopes. The morning mail delivery. That could be her opening.

Fingerprints.

You can change a name, a credit history, but − short of going to work on yourself with acid or a belt sander − there's nothing you can do about your fingerprints.

When Sturgis initially came up as a suspect in 2001, Detective Hendricks told her he had been arrested three years before in Jersey on a simple assault charge. His prints were on record. If Thessaly could get a sample of his prints and convince Washington to check them against the '98 arrest, she would be able to prove who he really was. She tried not to think about how she could convince Washington to go along with it, but she would cross that bridge when she came to it. The bridge in front of her was challenge enough for the moment.

He had a mug of coffee, holding it by the handle. That was

no good. He lifted it and took a sip, and then started opening the mail. Thessaly heard the whine of a motorcycle from Maple Avenue and lowered the binoculars to watch as it passed between the buildings.

Thessaly raised the binoculars to her eyes again. Sturgis was sitting at his desk now, opening the mail. He was wearing a light blue shirt, open collar. He looked every inch the upstanding local businessman. She wondered if anyone around here knew who he really was.

If this morning's gamble paid off, they soon would.

She watched as he opened the envelopes, pausing to study the contents of each for a second before depositing in a pile on the desk. He opened the final envelope and examined it for a little longer. He put it down on the desk on top of the others.

Jackpot. If she could only get into the office somehow, there would be fingerprints all over that stack of opened mail. If even one could be matched to the set on record for Casper Sturgis's arrest in '98, it would be enough to prove her story to Washington once and for all.

She stayed in position for another forty minutes, grateful she had thought to bring gloves. She only wished she had thought to bring a flask of hot chocolate. She watched as Sturgis carried out what looked like admin tasks. Replying to some emails, making two phone calls. She wondered who he was speaking to. The binoculars were good enough to read text on the screen, but his body blocked most of what was there. At one point, he switched to a different screen.

Thessaly noticed the blacked-out frame of an incognito window. It looked like another email inbox, separate from the standard Outlook window he had open. She adjusted the binoculars and tried to make out anything on the small patch of the screen that wasn't blocked by his head and right shoulder.

There were only a couple of messages in the inbox, one in bold signifying it was unread.

She adjusted the focus, trying to see if she could make anything out from the text on screen. She saw the word *Urgent* in the subject line. Before she could make out anything else, he changed windows to an Excel worksheet.

Thessaly's face felt numb from the cold by the time she had been watching for an hour. She wondered if she should head back to the car. Sturgis didn't look like he'd be moving anytime soon, and she thought she had seen as much as she was going to.

But then she heard a distant ringing noise, and Sturgis moved in reaction. He reached over to the phone on the desk and picked it up.

There would be good prints on the phone too, but like the mouse it wasn't the sort of thing that might plausibly go missing of its own accord. The mail, on the other hand? Mail goes missing all the time, and nine times out of ten, it doesn't even matter. Everything important is backed up electronically. The mail could disappear and it might not even be missed. Most likely it would be forgotten as a minor irritation. She hoped she could make it a major irritation.

Sturgis turned just enough so that she could see his lips move. His brow was knotted. Whatever he was being told, he didn't like it. She didn't need to be able to lip-read to tell he was ending the conversation. He put the phone down and stood up.

He moved out of the frame of the window, and a moment later reappeared, pulling his jacket on.

She felt a rush of excitement. He was going somewhere.

The mail was still lying on the desk.

He hit a couple of keys and his screen locked, the image of a clifftop castle against a pink sunset replacing the spreadsheet. He turned abruptly and faced the window and Thessaly hunched down, worried he would see her. But he wasn't looking at her.

He dug in his pocket, found his car key and bounced it in his hand, then turned toward the door.

And then hesitated. He turned around and walked back to the desk. He reached out and moved his mug from the top of the sheaf of mail and picked the letters up.

'No,' she said through her teeth. He was going to take it with him.

And then she saw it was worse than that. He stepped around the desk and slid them into a shredder that was positioned against the back wall.

Thessaly swore out loud as she watched him switch the shredder off and walk out of the room. The sheaf of papers and the fingerprints covering them slid slowly down until they were gone, transformed to useless ribbons.

The light changed a little again as the door opened and closed. She shook her head in frustration as she waited for the sound of an engine starting up. After a moment she heard Sturgis's vehicle rumble to life and reverse out onto the road, before driving off.

Goddamn it. He would have left plenty of other prints in there, all over the furniture and the door handles. But not on anything portable. She didn't have the first clue of how to lift fingerprints from a surface, even if she had the equipment. She needed something she could take, and the mail would have been perfect. She would have to wait for another chance. Sighing, she raised her binoculars and took one more look into the office. The window was like a framed painting of a rather boring still life: the monitor screen and the keyboard and the empty coffee mug.

And the empty coffee mug.

23

Sturgis had drunk out of the mug while Thessaly had been watching. She had discounted it as a possibility for getting his prints early on because she knew the handle wouldn't work. Not enough surface area for a full print, and even partial prints would be smeared.

But when he lifted the mug off the pile of mail, he hadn't used the handle. He had gripped it around its circumference with all five fingers. Potentially a perfect sample, and it was sitting there on the desk waiting for her. All she needed to do was get in there. And that was the other reason she had to wait until there was only one member of staff in the building.

She stuffed the binoculars inside her backpack and walked quickly back around to Maple Avenue. The parking spaces out front of Atlantic Auto Parts were all empty. That was good. She got into her car and drove across the street, parking in one of the spaces outside the store. Before she got out, she popped the glovebox and took out the leather-bound owner's manual. She didn't think she had opened the thing in the two years she had owned the car. Her local garage took care of everything for her.

The electronic buzzer sounded as she entered and the clerk behind the desk looked up. Same one as last time. Small business, probably not a lot of staff on the payroll. Thessaly wondered if she had any idea of who her boss really was.

'Good morning,' she said, smiling. She showed no sign of remembering Thessaly from Friday.

Thessaly tried not to look directly at the door she knew led into the office. She was less than twenty feet from her objective. All she needed was a distraction of a few seconds. But she would only get one shot at this.

'Hey, this is probably a stupid question, but you sell headlight bulbs, right?'

'Of course, what size are you looking for?'

She examined the page she had opened the manual to. 'Uh ... H11?' she said uncertainly. 'Does that sound right?' The uncertainty came easily.

The clerk went up on her tiptoes and craned her neck so she could see past Thessaly to the spot out front where the Subaru was parked. 'Yeah, that sounds right.' She moved a short distance to a rack of blister packs. Thessaly glanced at the office door. She had hoped the bulbs would be deeper into the store. Perhaps she should have asked for something more unusual.

The clerk came back to the register, holding a pack of two bulbs in her right hand. She scanned the barcode.

'I don't suppose I could ask you a big favor?' Thessaly began.

The clerk nodded as though she had been expecting this. 'You need some help fitting it?'

'I have no clue. I had a look at the manual and it's all Greek to me. But then, I can only just about work out where to put the gas in.'

The clerk glanced at the sign on the wall that said, '*We offer a bulb-fitting service, please ask for details.*'

'It's normally nine ninety-nine.'

'That's no problem at all,' Thessaly said, producing her credit card, then changing her mind and taking cash out of her purse.

'Ah it's fine, we're quiet.' Then added, 'Just don't tell the boss,' with a wink.

'Hardass, huh?' Thessaly asked.

'He has his moments.'

She took the jacket from the back of her chair and started pulling it on.

'Do you have a restroom I can use?' Thessaly said quickly.

The clerk gestured at the door on the opposite side of the counter from the office. A sign on the door showing both male and female stick figures. *Restrooms are for customer use only.* She reached behind the desk and produced a key, holding it out. 'Swap you.'

Thessaly handed her the keys, telling her the blown bulb was on the driver's side. She let the clerk pass her before starting to move toward the restroom, doubling back the moment she was out of her line of sight. She bent over the low part of the desk and looked at the spot where the clerk had retrieved the restroom key.

How long did it take to change a headlight bulb? Thessaly had no idea, but she suspected it wouldn't be long for someone who knew what they were doing. As she angled herself over the desk, she heard the sound of her locks disengaging outside.

'Come on, come on, come on...' she whispered to herself, then felt a surge of relief when she saw what she wanted.

There were three other sets of keys hanging from a small rack. Two of them had multiple keys, and looked like they would fit exterior doors and shutters. The third had only one key. She took it, and after a split second's hesitation, replaced the restroom key on the hook, then made for the office.

From outside, she heard the thunk as the catch on her hood disengaged. She was burning time.

Thessaly slid the key into the lock of the door marked Private and tried to turn it. It didn't move. She glanced behind her and tried again, jiggling it in the lock. This time it turned, and the door opened.

After watching the office through the small, rectangular

window for the last hour, physically stepping into it felt a little like walking onto the set of a familiar TV show. The desk, the monitor screen with the screensaver of the clifftop castle. The mug on the desk.

She reached for it and then froze, her fingers an inch from picking it up. She couldn't pick it up like that. She would smudge the prints.

From behind her she heard the sound of her hood slamming shut. The clerk couldn't be done already, could she? It had been seconds.

Thessaly made her fingers into a shape like she was manipulating a glove puppet and slid them into the mouth of the mug, then opened them, bracing them against the inside of the mug. She lifted it from the desk and dropped it into her bag. She started to move away and then stopped.

The mug had been left on top of a small pile of magazines on one side of the desk. Now she had moved it, she could see there was a small sticker at the corner of the copy of *Newsweek* on top. The sticker was a printed address label; for postage to subscribers.

T. Andrews, 222 Elm Street, Grenville.

She backed out of the doorway, pulling the door closed. The key stuck in the lock again. She jiggled it and got it to move, hurrying back to the desk. She slipped it onto the hook and straightened just as the door opened, accompanied by the buzzer.

'Good news,' the woman said, holding Thessaly's keys by the fob. 'I didn't have to change it, they're all working now.'

Thessaly frowned and hoped the woman wouldn't notice she had broken out into a sweat in the last couple minutes. 'That's weird.'

'Just come back in if it goes again. You want me to refund these?'

Thessaly shook her head. 'No thanks, I'll just take them anyway. I have somewhere I need to be.'

24

Thessaly got back into the car and drove around the corner. She didn't want to risk Sturgis coming back and seeing her car, particularly if he noticed his mug had disappeared and started asking questions. Perhaps it was just paranoia, but she couldn't help thinking the woman had suspected something when she came back in.

Her new phone was unfamiliar. It took her a minute to find Maps and add it to the home screen. Once she was in, she typed in the address she had seen on the magazine from memory. She had been reciting it in her head ever since she hurried out of the store. 222 Elm Street.

Easy to remember. *A Nightmare on Elm Street* had been the first horror movie she had ever seen, on a fuzzy old VHS tape at a sleepover at Carol Langford's house in sixth grade. She hadn't slept soundly for a month after that. It would be a few more years before she discovered that real life monsters looked nothing like Freddy Krueger.

She knew she should hold off on checking out the address. She had already accomplished way more than she expected to today. Potentially a full set of the prints from Casper Sturgis's right hand. If she could convince Washington to put them through the system, it would be enough to prove to her that there was a killer living in this unsuspecting community.

Her phone said 222 Elm Street was an eight-minute drive, taking her across the covered bridge and through the older part of town. Thessaly decided to take a circuitous route and park a couple of streets down from Elm itself. She had no idea how much attention the locals paid to strange vehicles. Or strange people.

Better to be safe than sorry. She parked on Pine Avenue and decided to leave the hat in the car this time and wear sunglasses, just to slightly change her look again. She took her backpack, although she had no intention of staking this place out. She just wanted to take a look at where Sturgis lived. Where the killer hung his hat.

Elm Street was located to the east of the larger of the two rivers that flowed through Grenville; one of the nicer neighborhoods Thessaly had seen in her driving tour of town the other day. Wide lawns, mature trees, well-maintained 1950s homes. Definitely the more upscale side of Grenville. If Casper Sturgis had traded in his old life for a completely new one, he seemed to have done okay out of the deal. Something was bothering her about the street, just the same. These weren't quite the kind of surroundings she would have expected. The large homes on generous plots reminded her a little of her own too-big house. Maybe she had something else in common with Sturgis. Maybe he liked space too.

She stayed on the odd-numbered side of the road, and tried not to look conspicuous. There were only a few signs of life. A silver-haired man in his seventies was sweeping the pathway that led to his front door with a wooden broom, and paid Thessaly no notice as she passed. Two little boys were tossing a football back and forth in another yard. A Labrador in the yard of number 244 growled at her from behind the picket fence at the edge of his domain. Aside from that, the street was quiet.

As she approached the house she was interested in, she saw

that there was no vehicle in the driveway. She could risk getting in close. Take a glance through the windows, maybe even go around to the back yard. She could say she was a courier, looking for somewhere to leave a package. She wished she had thought of that earlier. She could have brought something to use as a plausible prop.

She got closer, and at first glance, 222 appeared pretty much the same as every other house on the street. A wide two-story with white wood siding. As she got closer, she noticed it had a couple of features that set it apart. The plots on this street were wide, with a generous amount of space in between each one, so most had open space on either side of the building. Sometimes trees or bushes.

222 was completely closed off on both sides of the house. Nothing that looked too obtrusive, but there was a wood fence on either side, maybe seven feet high, painted a dark green that blended in with the grass in the front yard and the trees on either side of the house. The fencing extended all the way from the walls of the house to the boundary fences on either side, completely filling the gaps that existed on the other plots. The fence on the left-hand side was unbroken; the one on the right-hand side had a gate built into it. Not quite a fuck-you wall. Much more subtle than that.

Thessaly couldn't see if there was a lock on the gate, but she was pretty sure there would be. The effect was interesting. The house really didn't stand out from the rest of the neighborhood unless you were really looking. If you were driving past, it wouldn't be noticeable at all. The style and color of the fence helped it to look classy and elegant, rather than what it was, which was an unusual extra layer of security for a quiet residential street in a mid-size town with low crime rates compared to the national average.

She hadn't known exactly what she was looking for when

she decided to recon the house, but already she was glad she had done it. It was just one more question mark hanging over Tony Andrews. A person who seemed to fit into Grenville just fine, until you decided to look a little closer.

Thessaly slowed her pace as she heard a vehicle approach on the cross street and held her breath, wondering what she would do if Sturgis's black SUV rounded the corner. But it was just a delivery van. It rounded the corner a little too quickly and accelerated past her, slowing when it reached the next intersection and continuing onward on Elm.

She was only one house from 222 now, still diagonally across the street, and she could see another thing that wasn't a standard feature. There was a small camera above the door, positioned to cover the approach to the house and the street outside. She picked out two other cameras quickly: one on the right-hand side of the fence, another on the south-facing slope of the roof. She supposed there would be others round the back, perhaps even some more out front that she couldn't see. The shrubs along the front of the yard could be concealing another. That put one idea out of the question. Even if that gate in the fence was unlocked, she wouldn't be walking up the path to try it, much less peering through the living-room windows. Which, now she was directly across from the house, she could see were lined with white wooden venetian blinds, fully closed. Again, very tasteful, very subtle. The set-up achieved the same levels of security and privacy that a high chain link fence and blacked-out windows would achieve, but without calling attention to itself in the same way.

She could hear Detective Washington's counter-arguments already. So Tony Andrews liked to keep his property private and secure. What did that prove? Absolutely nothing. But it suggested he had something he wanted to protect, or something he wanted to hide.

Thessaly picked up her pace after she passed the house, deciding to turn right at the intersection and complete the circuit of the block to retrieve her car. And then she heard the sound of another car approaching. This one was coming from behind her. She kept going, not risking a look back in case it was Sturgis's SUV.

But then she heard the vehicle slowing. It sounded like it was turning, entering one of the driveways behind her. She stopped and bent down, pretending to tie her shoelace. She looked behind her in time to see a blue car swing into the driveway of number 222. It wasn't a black BMW SUV, but the driver was familiar, and she had seen the car before too. She just hadn't thought to put the two together

She blinked, but the car had already passed out of her line of sight, going behind the thick trunk of the Sycamore tree in the yard of 218. She moved quickly back along the road until she had reached the tree and could see the driveway of 222.

She hadn't imagined it. A blue Honda Accord. A woman with long brown hair was getting out of the driver's side, on the opposite side from Thessaly. A Tigger sunshade on the rear window. She was carrying something. She used her hip to bump the door shut and then she addressed someone in the back of the car.

This was why the street felt wrong.

'Come on, Aiden, we don't have all day.'

Thessaly bit her lip as something she hadn't even considered hit her like a lead weight. There was no response from whoever was in the backseat. The rear window was obscured by that Tigger sun shade.

Thessaly hunched back behind the tree, but Casey wasn't looking anywhere near her, she was bending down to hurry up the occupant of the backseat.

'Get your butt out here *this minute*. Don't make me tell you a third time, Aiden Jonathan Andrews.'

25

A family.

The bastard didn't just have a new life, he had a fucking wife and kid.

Thessaly was so stunned that she unconsciously walked three paces toward number 222 before she realized what she was doing. She drew back into the shadows and watched as Casey helped a young boy – Aiden Jonathan Andrews, apparently – from the back of the car and closed the door. The kid looked five or six years old. He was dressed in jeans, a puffy green jacket and a baseball hat. She could see blond hair under the hat. Light blond hair.

Lighter than his father's.

She was close enough to catch the conversation as they approached the door.

'Can I play with the Switch before dinner?'

'Clear up the Lego on the floor of your room and we'll talk about it.'

Casey put down the box she was carrying and tapped a code into the keypad on the door. The light on the panel went from red to green and started beeping a rapid, urgent tone. She took out a key and unlocked the door, pushing it open. She pushed Aiden in ahead of her and followed.

Thessaly stepped forward again, hoping to get a glimpse

of the interior of the house before the door swung closed, and then froze as Casey reappeared at the door. She pointed a hand at the car and the lights blinked as the lock engaged. She stepped back inside the house and the door swung shut with a heavy click, and the street was quiet again.

Thessaly started to walk slowly back around to where her car was parked. She felt lightheaded.

A wife and kid. A fucking wife and kid.

Her first thought: Casey was on to her. She had seen her staking out Atlantic Auto Parts and had deliberately bumped into her. What if she had spotted her just now, and was playing it cool so that she could call her husband as soon as she got inside?

Thessaly was already running as the fear began to set in. She stopped thinking coherently, just ran flat out, throwing the occasional glance behind her until she reached her car. She flung the door open, got in, and started the engine. She had to stop for an oncoming car at the cross street, and then took off, taking a series of turns until she had put a safe distance between herself and Elm Street.

She pulled to a stop outside the park, leaving the engine running and checking in the rear-view mirror to make sure no one had followed her.

She took a deep breath and the panic began to ebb away. She turned the key to shut off the engine and closed her eyes for a moment, gripping the steering wheel and feeling the rubbery surface material flex a little beneath her fingers.

It was okay. Or at least, it probably was.

Tony Andrews ran Atlantic Auto Parts. Casey Andrews had been parked there the other day because her husband owned the place. Not because she was keeping watch on Thessaly.

Thessaly adjusted the rear-view mirror to take a look at herself. Her eyes seemed unusually red around the edges, or perhaps that was just because her face had turned pale. Either way, she looked unhinged. Maybe she had been, for the last five minutes. She hadn't given any thought to how this whole thing might be affecting her on a deeper level than she was aware of. Up until now, it had felt like she was working on a puzzle. But at that moment when she had decided she was in immediate danger, she had started to fall to pieces.

She thought of Lee's words. *I don't need this shit.*

He was right. Neither of them needed it. Maybe it was exactly what they didn't need. But there's a funny thing about the things that are bad for you. Sometimes you can't stop doing them anyway.

A half hour later, she was back in the little bedroom in the big guest house on the outskirts of Grenville. She sat at the charming old rolltop desk and opened her bag. The mug was still there, resting on top of her balled-up hat and gloves.

She repeated the same maneuver she had used to take the mug earlier, with less haste this time; spreading her fingers and using the pressure to lift the mug from the bag and place it gently on the surface of the desk. She hunched down and inspected it in the light. She could see loops and whorls in the shine from the light on the lacquer.

She had watched enough cop shows and true crime documentaries to know that the police were often able to identify a suspect from a single print, or even a partial. In one case she dimly remembered – she couldn't remember if it was fact or fiction – usable prints had been recovered from a gun that had been lying at the bottom of a lake for an indeterminate period. Surely there would be enough here to match with the prints on Sturgis's record.

She kept her eyes on the mug as she took her phone out. The call was answered by the exact person she was looking for.

'Grenville PD, Washington.'

'Hi,' Thessaly said, surprised. She had anticipated having to negotiate some suspicious desk sergeant, and after that, probably having to leave a message, best case.

'Hello?' Washington prompted.

'Sorry. It's Thessaly Hanlon again. I was just calling to ask—'

'If I've dug anything up on Tony Andrews? You're not a fan of delayed gratification, I see.'

'I wasn't calling to nag you, Detective,' she began, 'I just...'

'As a matter of fact, I was about to call you.'

'You were?' Thessaly was taken aback.

'I've been looking into this a little, and I'd really like to discuss your inquiry in person. Is there any chance you can come to Grenville? I was thinking in the next couple days, even?'

She thought about admitting where she was. That she could be there in fifteen minutes. Decided to play it safe. 'I can be there this afternoon. When suits?'

Washington paused before answering. 'I have some other business this afternoon. How about tomorrow? Noon give you enough time?'

'Noon is perfect.'

They exchanged goodbyes and Thessaly hung up.

All of a sudden, she forgot about the tiredness and the way she had managed to scare the hell out of herself earlier on. She lay back on the bed and smiled up at the beamed ceiling. Finally, it felt like everything was starting to go to plan.

It would be the last time she would have that feeling.

26

Thessaly woke up almost an hour before her 7 a.m. alarm, opening her eyes to see a razor of watery gray daylight along the gap between the curtains and the windowsill. She could hear birds singing in the woods that lined the river outside. There had been no nightmares, just a long night of broken sleep and a series of dreams where she had been walking the empty streets of Grenville, never seeing a soul.

She sat up in bed and reassured herself that the mug was still on the desk, and then reached for her phone. No new messages from Detective Washington.

It had taken her a long time to fall asleep, even though she had made sure to turn in early. Part of her was regretting not coming clean with Washington and telling her she was already in town. She hadn't expected the detective to beat her to the request for another meeting. It had to mean she had found something.

As she brushed her teeth in front of the oval, rose-tinted mirror in the en-suite bathroom, she thought about the best way to bring up the mug with the fingerprints. It was a delicate balance. She would have to be vague about exactly how she had come into possession of the prints. No, that wouldn't work, would it? Washington was a cop, she wouldn't be satisfied with vague, she would want to know the exact circumstances.

She spat and rinsed and stared into her own eyes for a minute, wondering just how convincing she would need to be.

Technically, she had broken the law. Made an illegal entry, stolen some property. But surely that wouldn't matter if the prints proved he was Sturgis? Thessaly wasn't a police officer making an official search that could be ruled inadmissible. They wouldn't be building a case on the prints, just using them to establish his identity. She hoped that with the confirmation, they could find a route to nailing him.

No, she couldn't lie. It wasn't fair. She would fess up and hope that Washington's curiosity about Sturgis would overrule her misgivings.

Thessaly stepped into the shower, which was hotter and more powerful than it looked. After drying off, she dressed in shorts and a hoodie and a pair of running shoes that she hadn't used since the previous summer. She had packed them without much expectation of using them, but running was a good way to think, whether about the book, or what she was really here for. This morning, they would serve a different purpose: camouflage.

Washington's voice in her head: *Don't approach him.*

She wasn't approaching him, she told herself, she was approaching his house. Washington hadn't said anything about that. She wasn't going to do anything anyway. She just wanted to take a look at the place again. To see his home again before she started the ball rolling.

She drove back into town, making sure to take a route that took her past Atlantic Auto Parts. Sturgis's black SUV was in the lot. Good. She drove east toward Elm and parked on the adjacent street again. As she got out of the car, the air was still cold enough that she could see her breath.

She started jogging before she reached the corner of Elm.

She found it hard going almost immediately, which shouldn't have come as a surprise after a long winter of sitting on her ass typing. The cold air wasn't helping, either. As soon as this was all over, she had to get into shape again. She couldn't help smiling at that. Of all the excuses to avoid exercise. *Yeah, I'm going to start on healthy living just as soon as I catch this murderer.*

She rounded the corner onto Elm. The street was as peaceful and quiet as it had been yesterday. A Grenville Public Works street sweeper was trundling down the street, clearing dead leaves from the curbside, leaving freshly brushed asphalt in its wake. A cat waited for the sweeper to pass, then darted across the road. It seemed obscene that Casper Sturgis could just settle down here with no one noticing. And what about Casey? She had to know something. But how much? Did she know that her husband had murdered innocent people in cold blood?

She knew that was why she was really here. To see Casey. She wouldn't actually do it, but she wanted to knock on the door. Tell Casey that she knew who and what her husband was. Ask her how she could be with this man.

222 was up ahead. She started to slow.

She saw another jogger on the opposite sidewalk. An older guy in sweat pants and a hoodie. His pace was impressive considering he must have had thirty years on Thessaly. He called out a hello as they passed, and she responded with a friendly wave.

As she turned her head back, a small blur darted out from 222 onto the sidewalk, stopping just shy of the curb. She recognized Aiden. She slowed down a little more as Casey appeared. She was in blue jeans and the same coat as she had been wearing on Friday, when the two of them had collided outside McDonald's. She looked up and saw Thessaly, recognition in her eyes after a second.

'Oh, hello again.'

Thessaly stopped and smiled. 'Hey. Casey, right?'

'That's right,' she said, looking a little bemused.

'And this must be your little boy.'

Thessaly looked down at Aiden. His fair hair was long, almost getting in the way of his eyes.

'I'm Aiden, I'm six.'

'I'm Thessaly, and I'm ... a little older than six.'

'Keeping fit, huh?' Casey asked, eyeing Thessaly's running shoes.

'It's as good a way as any of avoiding work,' Thessaly said, then turned her eyes to the house. 'This your place?'

Casey nodded. 'Home sweet home.'

'Nice.'

'It is. Roomy. Did you find someplace to stay?'

'Yeah, the uh ...' she stopped short of saying the name of the guest house. 'Just an Airbnb, it's nice. I'm actually getting some work done.'

'Well,' Casey said, looking down at her kid. 'We are on our way to the park before school.'

'To do homework,' Aiden said. 'I have to find six types of leaves.'

'That sounds like more fun than my homework,' Thessaly said.

'Do you want a glass of water or anything?' Casey asked, glancing back at the house.

A chance to look inside the house? Thessaly opened her mouth to say yes, but Casey's gaze had moved from her face to something beyond her.

'Oh, hi, you're back.'

There was a weird look in Casey's eyes as she spoke, one that was in opposition to the breezy tone of her words.

Thessaly turned and saw him.

Less than three paces from her, as though he had appeared out of thin air. Six feet, over two hundred pounds. Dirty blond hair with a sprinkling of gray. The blue, empty eyes. He looked unreal up close. It was like seeing a famous actor in real life. Or a monster from a bad dream.

'Oh,' Thessaly said, putting a hand to her mouth.

She had only seen Casper Sturgis from a distance before now. The impossible-to-forget moments in the Redlands Mall. Looking out of the cracked window as the car cruised to a stop. Then from her hiding place under the tables in the food court.

Or more recently, from across the street as he entered his store, then hiding in the lot that backed onto it. In each case, she had observed him without his knowledge. That was the only reason she was alive.

Up close, he seemed taller than she had expected. Bigger, too. His hands were clasped in front of him, like a preacher holding his hat in front of him before entering the home of one of his flock.

'I forgot my laptop,' he said. The deep, unmistakable voice. 'Nice morning for a walk, so ...' he moved past Thessaly, slid an arm around Casey's waist and kissed her on the cheek before looking at Thessaly. 'Hello.'

A question, more than a greeting.

'I'm ...' she hesitated for a moment before remembering she had already given Casey her real name the other day. 'I'm Thessaly.'

'Nice to meet you,' he said, smiling.

She fought back the urge to vomit and returned the smile.

Sturgis ... *Andrews* ... glanced at his wife, waiting for her to explain.

'I ran into Thessaly the other day,' Casey said. 'She gave me a ride when I lost the keys.'

It wasn't her imagination. Casey seemed weird now. Did they know? Or was it just because Thessaly herself looked so obviously uncomfortable? She felt a sheen of sweat gather in the nape of her neck. Fresh sweat, not from the running. It felt like they'd been caught in some kind of infidelity. Sturgis had noticed something too. The smile was in place, but his brow had creased a little. This had been a big mistake.

Thessaly cleared her throat. 'It's a small world. Running into you here and the other day.'

'Not really,' Sturgis said.

She felt her mouth go dry in the pause between him saying that and elaborating.

'It's a small *town*.'

'Right, yeah.'

'You're not from round here, though?'

'It's that obvious? No, I'm from New York.'

'The city?'

'Ossining.' Close enough. Probably too close. She should have said Albany.

Another silence. Even more awkward this time.

'Well, I guess I should let you two get to the park,' Thessaly said. 'It was nice to see you again.'

'Oh, did you want that glass of water?' Casey said, suddenly remembering.

'You know what, I'm fine, just needed a rest.'

'Take care,' Sturgis said. 'People in Grenville drive around with their eyes closed, it seems like.'

Thessaly tried a laugh in response. It came out like a strangled 'aahhh'. 'I'll see you around,' she said and jogged away from them.

She resisted the urge to look back. She knew they were standing there, watching her, perhaps already whispering about who she was and why she was acting so weird. Before she knew it, she was running. Her previous fatigue gone.

If things went the way she hoped at the meeting with Washington, she would never have to be that close to Casper Sturgis again.

27

Officer Lewis wasn't on the desk this time. Instead, Thessaly was greeted by a female officer, in her early twenties. Thessaly told her she was here for a noon meeting with Detective Washington, and the officer asked her to take a seat.

It had been a matter of hours since she had spoken to Washington, but there was so much she had to tell her. The guy at the Olympia. The prints. She thought both of those would likely land her in hot water, considering Washington's instruction to keep a distance, so perhaps it would be better not to mention that she had been face to face with Sturgis himself this morning.

She wondered what Washington had found that had made her so keen to meet. It had to be something important. As far as Washington knew, Thessaly had had to drive all the way from Buchanan just to be here today.

'Thessaly?'

Washington had appeared at the door. Thessaly was struck by how different the detective looked from the other day. Not the way she was dressed. It was her body language, the look in her eye as she shook Thessaly's hand. The other day she had had a kind of weary resignation about her. She hadn't been unkind or dismissive, but she had clearly wanted to get the meeting over with and move on to the rest of her list. Now she looked like she had her game face on. Whatever she was about to tell her, she meant business.

'Come on in.'

She followed Washington down the corridor and into a larger meeting room than the one in which Thessaly had first met Washington the other day. This one had a long boardroom table, large enough to seat a dozen people. Thessaly noticed that she hadn't been offered a drink this time. Washington's whole demeanor was different. She had been prickly and skeptical at first, but much warmer on the phone, when she realized there really was something buried in the patch of ground where Thessaly was digging. But now it was like someone had hit a reset button, and they were back to the first meeting.

Thessaly took a seat. Before Washington could say anything, she reached into her bag and took out the Ziploc bag with the mug in it. She held it by the top of the bag and gently placed it on the table. Just before she had entered the station, she had made her decision. She would present it as a fait accompli, and hope Washington was feeling receptive.

Washington looked confused. 'What's that?'

Thessaly took a deep breath. 'It's a sample of Tony Andrews's fingerprints.'

The detective opened her mouth. Then closed it again.

'I know what you're going to say,' Thessaly said quickly.

'I'm pretty sure you don't, Thessaly.'

'If the prints on this match Casper Sturgis, that's all you need, right? It proves it's him. Or anyway, it proves that the man who's calling himself Tony Andrews is the same one who was suspected of two murders.'

Washington sighed. 'How did you get this?'

'I took it from his desk at the auto parts store. If you want to arrest me for that, go ahead, but all I'm asking is that you check the prints. If I'm wrong, you can forget you ever met me.'

Washington slid her elbows forward on the table and put her head in her hands. 'Believe me, forgetting I met you is not an option,' she said.

'What do you mean?' Thessaly asked, confused. She thought she had prepared herself for every reaction along the spectrum, from a grudging acceptance of what she had done to being read her rights, but she hadn't been prepared for this. Washington looked defeated somehow. But that didn't make sense.

There was a sharp knock on the door.

Washington told whoever it was to come in. A heavy-set man in his fifties wearing a gray suit opened the door and leaned in, glancing at Thessaly and then at Washington. 'Your one o'clock is here.'

'He's early,' Washington said, not sounding best pleased about it. Then she sighed again. 'Send him in.'

Thessaly looked from the man at the door to Washington, questioning.

'There's somebody I'd like you to meet,' Washington said.

Somebody else? This wasn't going according to plan.

The door opened again and another man stepped in. He wore a neat black suit, white shirt, dark tie with a paisley pattern. He was probably in his late forties. Had short salt-and-pepper hair and spectacles with frames that were thicker than the modern style. He looked as though he had stepped out of a movie that was set in the early sixties. Like he had hung up his fedora and trench coat before entering the room. That he was law enforcement of some kind wasn't in doubt.

Washington stood up as he entered. 'Thessaly, this is David Volcker, of the United States Marshals service.'

'Hi,' Thessaly said, wondering what the US Marshals had to do with this. This was a murder investigation, wasn't it? The cops and the FBI handled that. US Marshals were ... well, actually, she wasn't sure what they were for. Pretty much the only thing she knew about them was that Tommy Lee Jones had played one in *The Fugitive*. Was that what this was? He was already on Sturgis's trail?

Washington stayed standing. Volcker seemed to size up Thessaly for a moment, then his eyes moved to the Ziploc bag and the mug. He walked around the long table. He reached for the bag. Thessaly flinched, had to stop herself from snatching it away from him. Volcker paused, absorbing her reaction with interest, and then lifted the bag up, holding the mug through the bag, making no effort to avoid touching it.

'Prints?' he asked. He looked at Washington and then Thessaly. She hesitated, then nodded.

'I'll save us all some time,' Volcker said, sitting down in the chair across the table. His accent had a little southern in it, but only a little. Like he had been born in the south but lived elsewhere most of his life. Or perhaps that he had picked up that slight intonation in the military. 'You accessed private property and took this because you believe it bears the prints of one Casper Sturgis, who you believe to have murdered your brother, Mitch Hanlon, in New Jersey in 2001. Is that correct?'

Thessaly swallowed. Looked at Washington. No help there, she was standing in the corner, arms folded, her gaze fixed on the carpet.

'Yes,' Thessaly said.

'I don't know how you got this, but in all likelihood, this mug does carry Casper Sturgis's prints,' Volcker said, leaving a pause for her to say something. She didn't, waiting for him to get to the catch. 'Furthermore, in all likelihood, he was responsible for your brother's death, along with several other serious crimes. You're absolutely right about all of it, Ms Hanlon.'

She said nothing, waiting for the other shoe to drop. She felt nauseous. Whatever was coming next wouldn't be good. Volcker leaned forward, holding her gaze.

'But I'm here to tell you that there is no way on God's green earth that Casper Sturgis will be arrested for any of those crimes.'

PART 2

Thessaly

28

It took a moment for Volcker's words to hit home.

'What ...?' Thessaly began, and then realized she didn't know how to finish that question at this moment. Volcker's face was impassive, his unblinking gaze locked on her face. He had come here to deliver a message, and he had done it, and now he was waiting for the response. She looked over to Washington, who met her eyes this time. She wasn't happy about this at all.

'If ... If he ... What do you mean? If you know he's really Sturgis, then ...'

Thessaly's voice dropped out, as though she was a caller to a radio show and a producer had faded her out.

Washington cleared her throat. 'All right, I think you owe her an explanation, at the very least.'

Volcker hesitated, then gave a grudging nod.

'Casper Sturgis doesn't exist anymore, not really. He ceased to exist more than fifteen years ago. There have been a couple of other names between then and now, but he really is Tony Andrews.'

'I don't understand.'

Washington spoke, an impatient edge to her voice. 'Marshal Volcker works for the United States Witness Protection Program. He contacted me last night and asked for an urgent meeting. He particularly wanted to speak to you.'

It was like feeling your way around a dark room, and suddenly someone turns the lights on and you can see. Only, what you can see is that you're in a giant warehouse, and there's a hell of a lot more to this place than you thought there was when you were feeling around in the dark.

'Oh my God,' Thessaly said quietly.

Volcker seemed almost relieved. Like he wasn't used to dealing with civilians and was just happy somebody else had gotten through to the moron in front of him. Washington was watching her with sympathy.

'You're saying he's …'

'Untouchable. Sadly,' Washington confirmed.

'Immune from prosecution,' Volcker clarified, glancing at Washington. 'For any crimes committed before June 23rd, 2004. And yes, that would include the alleged killing of your brother.'

'Witness *protection*?' Thessaly repeated. 'Who the hell was he a witness for?'

'The US government,' Volcker said, deadpan, then even had the nerve to add a sardonic smirk. 'Hence, witness protection.'

'You know perfectly well what I meant,' Thessaly said, standing up and leaning forward over the table. Volcker didn't flinch or move back. He was completely at ease. 'Who was he testifying against? What was so goddamn important that you would give this animal a free pass for murder, and God knows what else?'

'I can't go into details about that,' Volcker said. 'For obvious reasons. When you've had a chance to calm down—'

Washington cut in. 'Marshal Volcker, I don't think Thessaly wants to hear you telling her to calm down right now.'

He turned to issue a rejoinder, then changed his mind when he saw the look on her face.

'I don't think I want to, either.'

He cleared his throat and looked back at Thessaly. 'I apologize. I understand this isn't easy to hear.' He almost sounded sincere.

Thessaly felt a swell of gratitude toward Washington. She sat down again and put her hands in her lap, waiting for Volcker to continue.

'Look. The reality of the world is that sometimes, we have to make deals with bad guys to put away even worse guys. That's what happened here. You don't need to know the details. Sturgis assisted in putting some very dangerous people away, and in return, we put him in the program.'

'And you came all the way out here from ...' *From where?* She wondered *D.C.? California?* 'Wherever, just to tell me this?'

'No,' Volcker said. 'I came all the way out here to make sure you fully understood the situation.'

'What situation?'

'I understand this isn't what you wanted to hear. But the last thing anyone wants is for you to do something rash.'

'Rash,' she repeated, looking from Volcker to Washington. 'Rash.'

'Rash like calling the *New York Times* and telling them tax-payers are picking up the tab for a multiple murderer to live in a five-bedroom house in fucking Picket Fence, USA, you mean?'

'That's exactly the kind of thing I'm talking about, and I wanted you to understand it would be a very, *very* unwise thing for you to do. First off, compromising a federal witness means putting lives at risk. Innocent lives. Like I said, I'm not at liberty to go into detail, but any attempt to go public with any of the information you have or think you have right now, would create major problems. It would jeopardize ongoing court cases. It would put people in danger.' He paused and moved closer, perching on the edge of the table. 'And worse than all of that, it would piss me off.'

Thessaly stared back at him, not saying anything, but unable and unwilling to keep the contempt out of her gaze. She wasn't going to give him the satisfaction of arguing. She just wanted him to finish his speech and get the hell out of here so she could think about what to do next.

'You want to know why it would piss me off?' he said after waiting ten seconds or so. He looked disappointed that she hadn't asked. 'It would piss me off because I would have to fix it. If I get the first hint that anyone or anything threatens to compromise the security of one of my witnesses...' he snapped his fingers. 'I put a very well-rehearsed operation into motion. My witness will be picked up within thirty minutes and taken to a secure location. Tony Andrews will cease to exist. He'll be transferred somewhere at least a thousand miles away from this town, and he'll have a whole new life. You think I like that? I don't like that. I know what he's done, I know more than you about what he's done. But I also know that we need people like him to keep everyone else safe. It's for the greater good, Thessaly.'

He looked down for a moment and shook his head.

'I'm very close to pulling the trigger on this anyway, but Detective Washington here thinks you'll listen to reason. Is she right?'

Thessaly's gaze met Washington's.

'I'm sorry, Thessaly, he's right. We can't go any further here, and even if we did...' she shrugged and looked over at Volcker. 'It wouldn't do any good.'

Volcker gave an approving smile and slowly repeated Washington's last words, like a teacher reinforcing the lesson. 'It wouldn't do any good. But it would do some bad. It would do a lot of bad for you.'

'What do you mean?'

'A hell of a fine for starters. Imprisonment for at least five years. Depending on how good your lawyer is.'

She blinked at that; up until now, she had been fully occupied with the shock of not being able to bring Sturgis to justice. It hadn't even occurred to her that she could be in trouble.

'That's right,' Volcker continued. Thessaly couldn't help thinking that he was enjoying this a little. 'Andrews goes to some nice new neighborhood, gets a new car, new job, and you go to the New York Metropolitan Correction Center and sit in a six-by-eight cell for the next half decade.'

She closed her eyes. 'Not much of a choice, is it?'

'It is not.' He put his hands on the table and leaned back in his chair. His expression softened. 'I don't like this any more than you do. But if you do anything to jeopardize the program, I'm not going to have any choice. Do you believe me?'

'This is so fucked.'

The corner of his mouth cracked into a smile. The first genuine one of the meeting. 'No argument there. Welcome to my world, Thessaly.'

29

After that, it was just a matter of nailing down the details.

Volcker went back over all of the reasons why Thessaly couldn't go anywhere near Tony Andrews, and then reiterated the severe penalties, as well as ultimate futility, of doing so. Thessaly was grateful for Detective Washington's continued presence in the room. She was pretty sure Volcker would have preferred to have spoken to her alone.

Finally, he stopped lecturing her and summed up with what he probably thought was sensitivity. 'We know it's not easy. The US government is grateful for your cooperation.'

Thessaly didn't want the gratitude of the US government. She wanted Casper Sturgis put away for good. She knew it would do her no good to say that out loud.

Washington came to her rescue again, suggesting that it had been a difficult meeting for everyone. She kept talking and very smoothly made it clear to Volcker that he had achieved everything he came here to do, reassured him that there would be no further investigation into his witness, and got him to agree to leave. He did so, but only after giving Thessaly his card, so she could call him if she had anything else to tell him. The look that he gave her as he did so suggested that she had better not have anything else to tell him.

When the door closed, Washington backed against it and blew a stray lock of hair out of the way of her eye.

'Not what you wanted to hear. Not what I wanted to hear, either.'

'I just can't … all this time the question was, was I nuts? But it was really him. I wasn't crazy. And it doesn't matter.'

Washington put her hands on the table, leaning forward. 'You look like you could use a drink.'

Washington's shift had officially finished forty minutes before the meeting with Volcker concluded, and she decided her paperwork could wait until tomorrow. There was a bar along the street. Or a pub, to be exact. Kelly's Pub & Restaurant. The place had parquet flooring and exposed brick walls and a dark wood bar with about a million craft beer taps along it. An array of different whiskeys arranged on a shelf behind the bar above a wide mirror. They sat at the bar and Washington ordered Thessaly a gin sling and herself a beer.

'Only one,' she said. 'It would be embarrassing if you got pulled over on the way back to your hotel and they asked who you were drinking with.'

Thessaly laughed and took a drink. Washington had been right. She definitely needed it.

'How did he find out?' she asked.

'It was probably unavoidable,' Washington replied. 'I made a few calls, mentioned Casper Sturgis's name to some contacts in other jurisdictions. When I called you yesterday, I was already pretty much convinced you were right about who this guy was. While I was doing that, I guess somebody in the know worked out what was happening, and all the alarm bells went off at WITSEC HQ. Volcker called me last night to shut me down.'

Thessaly closed her eyes and rubbed her temple.

'I just can't believe it. How can it be that he can just ... just literally get away with murder?'

'It's bullshit,' Washington agreed.

'So we have to do what he says? Just back down.'

Washington took a sip of her beer before answering. 'Not much else we can do. It's not about Volcker. I can't go over his head, seek a higher authority. Sturgis cut a deal. They'll honor the deal, there's no choice.'

'Just because he helped put some other douchebag away?'

'Yes. And more than that. Look at it from Volcker's point of view.' She put her hand up to ward off Thessaly's protests. 'I know, I know. The last thing you want to be doing right now. But look at the bigger picture. If the government doesn't follow through on its promises, if it lets harm come to witnesses in the program, the whole thing falls apart.'

'So we need to take one for the team. The greater good. You sound like him.'

'That's because unfortunately, he's right.'

She shook her head. 'He was such an asshole about it.'

'He was. But he doesn't like it any more than we do. Helping scumbags, giving them a break.'

'You think? I don't think he cares. I think he just saw me as an unnecessary problem that had to be dealt with.'

'Does it make any difference that you were right? That you found the man who killed your brother?'

'I don't know.'

'And at least you have some kind of certainty now. Yes, you know he's still out there, but he's not a danger. He's neutered. He can't put a foot wrong without putting himself in danger. If he's kicked out of the program ... well, I don't know the details, but I'm assuming it won't do wonders for his life expectancy.'

If he's kicked out of the program. Thessaly had forgotten about the most important hanging question from the conversation with Volcker. The one he had made sure not to go anywhere near answering.

'Who would be coming after him, though? Who did he testify against?'

Washington put her bottle down and wagged her finger. 'No. We're not going down this road. I don't know and I don't want to know. You heard Volcker – you keep nosing around and there will be problems. For me too. He had to play nice today because he was on my patch, but I have no doubt he could pull some strings and drop me in deep shit if need be. I told him you would understand once you had had a chance to absorb it. To get used to it.'

'I didn't give you my permission to do that.'

'No?' The look in Washington's eyes hardened. 'Well maybe you should be thankful that someone was looking out for you.'

Thessaly looked down at her drink. 'Look, I got the message okay? Even if I try something, it wouldn't do any good. He would just spirit him away to Cincinnati or Peoria or wherever. But I want to know, for me.'

Washington took another drink, eyeing her suspiciously.

'You're curious too,' Thessaly said. 'Has to be the mob, right? That or terrorism.'

'We're not having this conversation.'

'Come on. After this, I'm going to go back to my guest house ...' she lifted her almost-empty glass. 'Probably have a couple more of these, and get some sleep. Tomorrow morning, I'm going to drive home and try to forget any of this ever happened. I'm just making conversation.'

Washington shrugged a concession. 'Mob or terrorism, probably. They don't spend hundreds of thousands of dollars protecting you and changing your identity if you testify against someone for insurance fraud.'

'What about the wife and kid, then? Are they part of the cover?'

Washington narrowed her eyes. 'How do you know he has a wife and kid?'

'I happened to meet her when I was checking out the auto parts store the other day.' Not the whole story. It wasn't a lie, Thessaly told herself, it was… editing.

Washington shook her head. 'I'm not an expert on witness protection or anything, but no, I don't think that's a thing. If he's married, it's probably legit.'

'And he probably met her after he was in the program.'

'Not necessarily. I think if you have a spouse, they bring them in too. For obvious reasons.'

That made Thessaly think a little about another repercussion for pushing any more. Did Casey even know about her husband's past? Chances were she knew something, but that didn't mean she deserved to be put in harm's way. And her kid certainly didn't. She sighed and knuckled her eyelid.

'Shit.'

'I know.'

There was a pause in conversation. They sat cradling their drinks, looking at their reflections looking back at them in the mirror behind the bar.

'Listen,' Thessaly said. 'There's something else I was meaning to tell you.'

Washington took a long drink. 'Of course there is. Spit it out.'

She told her about how she had left her number with Kayla, the waitress at the Olympia, and how she had gotten back in touch to say she had seen the second man from that first night. Washington listened, not interrupting, her amusement morphing to concern as Thessaly got to the part where the bald man said he was a cop and tried to force her into the car.

'Doesn't sound like he was a real cop,' Washington said. 'You get a look at the ID he showed the waitress?'

'No, it was pointed away from me.' She took out her brand new phone and found the images on her cloud account. 'This is him, I take it you don't recognize him?'

Washington didn't. She scrolled through the short series of pictures and got to the close-up of the license plate. She took a pen and copied down the number on the back of her receipt. 'Send me these and I'll see what we can do.'

Washington finished her drink and left a pair of tens on the bar as she got up from her stool. 'You're going to be okay, Thessaly. You're a tough cookie.'

She snorted. 'I've never thought of myself that way. But thanks for trying to make me feel better, and thanks for believing me, even though it didn't work out.'

'I'm not trying to make you feel better, just calling it as I see it. I've been a cop for fifteen years and I've seen a lot of people go through some bad things. Some have it better than you, some worse. What happened to you was horrific, but you got through it. You made yourself a life. You'll get through this, too.'

After Washington left, Thessaly stayed another ten minutes, sipping a water and waiting for the buzz from the gin to fade a little before she got back in the car. She watched the news on the screen above the bar. The sound was off, but she could follow everything thanks to the onscreen text. One of the former president's lackeys was defending the pardon he had received for federal crimes that would have sent less well-connected people to prison for years.

'Bullshit, isn't it?'

She looked up to see the bartender shaking his head at the screen.

'Way of the world,' she said. 'It's all about who you know. And what you can do for them.'

149

★

She drove back to the guest house, half-expecting to see Detective Washington's gray Ford Taurus tailing her. But the road in her rear-view mirror stayed almost empty for the whole ten-minute drive.

She pulled into the parking area outside the guest house and sat there with the engine running. Slow season. A single light was on. It could have been the early hours of the morning, not mid-evening. She reached for the keys to shut off the engine and then hesitated.

Tomorrow she would go home and try to put all this behind her. So where was the harm in one more visit to Elm Street?

30

Elm Street was as static as a still life painting. The cars were all tucked away in their driveways, the windows of the homes lit up as the residents settled in for dinner or an evening in front of the tube. The temperature had dropped again, and frost was starting to form on the lawns and the sidewalk, glittering in the street light.

Thessaly made one slow circuit of the block first. The windows of the upper floor of the Andrews' house were in darkness, only one light burned on the lower level. The BMW and the Honda were both parked in the driveway. Everybody home. She parked at the end of the street and walked back to the house.

She slowed her pace as she got close. The night sky was clear and the roof was a black triangle against the deep blue of the night sky. Venus glinted above the house, almost exactly in alignment with the apex of the roof. It reminded her of an image from a Christmas card. She stood at the edge of the property, where the lawn met the sidewalk. She could see movement in the living room, in between the wooden venetian blinds, which had been opened since the last time she had visited. Low lighting. Flickering blue on the walls from the television. She heard the scrape of a chair moving inside. An exchange of voices from inside, too muffled to hear. She could smell something cooking.

A sweet smell of tomatoes and onions with an undercurrent of basil. Spaghetti sauce.

She saw a light wink on in the kitchen, and a moment later the little boy passed by the window. Aiden. He dragged out a stool from beside the breakfast island that was as tall as he was, and somehow climbed up on top of it. Thessaly held her breath until he made it.

And then Casey appeared and ruffled the boy's head. She disappeared from view and Thessaly heard a pot clanking off a stove. A moment later, she slid a bowl piled high with pasta and sauce in front of the kid, making an exaggerated 'bon appetit' gesture, like a cartoon French waiter. The kid needed no encouragement, digging in. Casey stepped out of view again, and back a moment later, carrying another bowl. She put it down at the spot across from her son and sat down.

Just the two of them. Where was the man of the house?

Thessaly felt a shiver and looked behind her. The street was still empty. The dog in the yard a few doors down growled halfheartedly at something, but he had stopped scratching at the fence.

She took a step onto the path up to the front door, feeling that she was crossing more than a property threshold. She took another three steps toward the house. The cameras would pick her up, if anybody bothered to go back and review the footage for this evening, but it was too late to worry about that now. She had already stood outside the house for long enough to be suspicious.

Another step down the path. She could see that there was a name plate on the right-hand side of the door, saying *Andrews*. Instead of a doorbell, there was an intercom with what appeared to be a camera built into it. 'Tony Andrews' was certainly taking security seriously. She knew exactly why, now. The fence on either side of the building looked solid. She stopped and tried to see if she could see anything in the other windows now she was closer, but the blinds were closed and the lights were off.

The mother and son were still eating in the kitchen. Perhaps she should buzz the doorbell, see if Casey would talk to her.

But that was the stupidest idea she had had in a week of stupid ideas. What would she even say? *Hey, did you know your husband is a murderer? Ooh that spaghetti looks good, enough for one more?*

No. She took a step back.

She walked away, forcing one foot in front of the other. When she had made it ten paces, she stopped and looked back.

There was a figure in the window. Looking right at her.

She turned and quickened her pace. After a minute, she noticed she was running.

31

Stupid, stupid, stupid.

Thessaly kept seeing the glimpse of the figure in the window in her mind's eye as she drove back to the guest house. She had seen only a glimpse, not enough to tell if it was Casey or Sturgis. What the hell had she been thinking?

She parked and made her way quickly up to her room, grateful that Rosemary wasn't around to initiate any small talk. She locked the door of her room and lay down on the bed, looking up at the ceiling. She didn't know what to do next. Go home, she supposed. That was the only thing to do. Anything else was futile. Even if she did contact the media, it would do no good. Maybe they wouldn't even want to run the story.

But she wanted to know more. She wanted to know who Sturgis had put away with his testimony. Who was so bad that stopping them required doing a deal with the devil?

She pulled on a sweater, took her laptop downstairs and sat outside on the balcony overlooking the woods. It was cold, but the fresh air was bracing. She could hear the rush of the river through the trees.

She opened her laptop and gazed at the screen as it woke up, thinking. Casper Sturgis was out of reach, but maybe it would help if she could satisfy her curiosity. Maybe Volcker was right. Maybe against the odds, she could understand if she could discover the greater evil he had been recruited against.

After an hour of searching, she was no further forward. It turned out finding information about specific trials was a lot more difficult than she had thought. She tried everything she could think of. 'Organized crime trials', 'Terrorism trial', 'Key witness'. No shortage of results every time, but that was the problem. The trial could have taken place anywhere, any time over the past couple of decades. She didn't have any of the important details.

Then she remembered that wasn't quite true. Volcker had said Sturgis was immune from prosecution for any crime committed before ... before ... damn it. She closed her eyes and tried to bring it back. Remembering the layout of the room. Volcker's paisley tie. Washington's sympathetic, silent stare.

'For any crimes committed before ... And that includes the murder of your brother.'

Before June 23rd, 2004.

Quickly she scribbled it down on her pad. June 23rd, 2004. That was what he had said. She was sure of it, assuming she could trust her memory.

She tried that date first. With and without Sturgis's name. She tried the date with keywords like 'trial' and 'witness' and 'prosecution'. She tried with 'immunity'. Nothing that was any use. She decided that the witness wasn't the angle the press would approach the story from. Unless the witness is a big name, they focus on the defendant.

From the context, she guessed that June 23rd was probably the date of the agreement with Sturgis, not the trial itself. She needed to widen the focus. She searched for high profile trials in 2004. Her searches threw up a surprising number of familiar names, like Robert Blake and Michael Jackson, and the NBA player Jayson Williams. It appeared to have been a big year for celebrity trials. There was nothing that looked like it fit what she was looking for.

What if the deal was made a year or more in advance? Big trials took a lot of time from start to finish. And come to think of it, maybe she was making a wrong assumption by assuming this trial was 'big' in terms of media attention.

She sat back and looked out at the trees and the road. She needed something else. She couldn't go back and ask Washington.

Her phone lit up on the table in front of her. When she examined the screen, the number was the last one she expected.

32

Thessaly answered with a tentative, 'Hello?'

'Hey.' Lee cleared his throat. 'Um, is this a good time? I'm not interrupting dinner or anything?'

'No, not at all,' Thessaly said quickly. There was an awkward pause. She reached for something to fill the silence. 'How are you doing?'

'Good. I'm good, thank you.'

Another long pause. She wanted to let him take the initiative this time. Eventually, he did.

'I just wanted to apologize about the other night.'

She smiled. A friendly voice, coming just when she needed it most. 'You really don't have to. I didn't think about how you would feel, you were right. I shouldn't have called.'

'No, you should have. I had some time to think about it and ... I want to help. I was thinking, maybe I could go down there with you, see if we can do anything.'

She let out an involuntary laugh.

'What's funny?'

'I'm sorry, it's just ... Your timing, it's impeccable. Look, how long have you got?'

'I'm all ears.'

Thessaly laid it all out. Everything from the last few days. Going back to Grenville, staking out the auto parts store, getting

Sturgis's fingerprints, the discovery that he had a family, the unceremonious shutdown from Volcker. She explained that she had been trying to find out why Sturgis was in the witness protection program, but without success. Lee listened, expressing the same disbelief as Thessaly when she got to the punchline. But he was intrigued, too. He wanted to know why the government had made a deal with Sturgis.

Lee said he could make a couple of calls, no promises. Thessaly tried not to get her hopes up, but her heart skipped a beat when her phone buzzed again an hour later.

'What is it? Did you find something?'

She was back in her room, lying on the bed and aimlessly skipping through channels in a futile attempt to find something that might take her mind off the day. She hadn't expected Lee to call back tonight.

There was a silence long enough that she said Lee's name again, sure he'd been cut off. But then she heard a sigh.

'I don't even know if I should tell you.'

'Well, clearly you have to now.'

'I think I found something that might... I mean, this isn't definite, but—'

'Come on. I have to know.'

'Well, it's like this guy Volcker said. You need to make deals with bad people to stop worse people.'

'Who are the worse people?'

Another pause. Gathering his thoughts. 'Do you know the name Ernesto Vicente?'

She considered. 'I don't think so. Should I? Who is he?'

'He isn't anybody anymore, he died of a stroke a couple years ago. He was the leader of one of the bigger factions of the Gulf Cartel.'

'A cartel? Sturgis was into drug running?'

'I don't think so. I mean, not directly. A couple of the other guys at Maxx are ex-cops. I called in a couple of favors which put me on this track. Vicente's faction was a major force throughout the nineties and into the aughts. If he was American, you would have heard of him. He would have been bigger than Gotti, Whitey Bulger, any of those guys.'

'So he was big time.'

'Big time,' Lee confirmed. 'He had a reputation for being particularly vicious in carrying out his work. Do you have any idea how extreme you need to be to get a reputation for being vicious by the standards of the cartels?'

Thessaly assumed it was a rhetorical question. Even if it wasn't, she wasn't sure she wanted to know the details.

'Pretty bad.'

'Vicente was a monster. Rivals, cops, people who worked with him, their families... no one was off limits. He built up a reputation as the guy no one fucked with. Around 2000, he started flooding the southern US states with heroin. That entailed working with local contractors.'

'So, Casper Sturgis was one of his dealers? Something like that?'

'I don't think so. I think Sturgis was his right hand in the States. Vicente was moving north. He was worried that people might start to get complacent, feel like they were out of his reach. He needed to make sure that didn't happen. He recruited local enforcers. People who knew the territory, who wouldn't stick out. This was all reported on during the trial. Some of his enforcers were indicted. I went through and looked for gaps. The murders that were linked to Vicente, but that didn't result in a conviction. I found eighteen murders across the east coast and the Midwest. Could be more, could be less. They're all technically unsolved. They have similar MOs. They're all suspected to be connected to Vicente's trade. First one was a smalltime dealer in Atlantic City in '96, last one was a nightclub owner in Ohio in 2003.'

He stopped again and Thessaly heard the sound of liquid sloshing in a container. The soft puck noise of a bottle neck withdrawing from lips.

'Lee, are you drunk?'

'Not yet.'

She hesitated before she asked, 'Is somebody with you? I mean, your wife or something?'

He laughed. 'No. Suzanne moved on four years ago. Wait, five. Time flies when you're having fun.'

Thessaly heard the hollowness in his voice. 'I'm sorry.'

'You can stop saying that. Anyway, the list ...'

'I know what you're going to tell me. The other guy Sturgis killed at Redlands. Ammerman. He's on the list.'

'Yes. John Ammerman. He owed a lot of money to one of Vicente's intermediaries. He came up with the money, but too late. Looks like Sturgis arranged to meet him at the Redlands Mall because there would be no witnesses.'

Thessaly had grabbed the little notebook from the nightstand and had scribbled down the main keywords with the pencil.

Vicente
Cartel
~~Drugs?~~ Hits
Redlands

She circled *Redlands* with the pencil as she absorbed everything Lee had said.

'So Sturgis is working for the cartel, bumping off people that this Vicente guy doesn't like. One of those people is John Ammerman. They arrange to meet at Redlands, and everything else is…' she was about to say 'bad luck'. But it was more than that.

She heard Sturgis's mocking words to Mitch in her head. *Not your lucky day.*

'The timings all fit,' Lee continued. 'The killings of people connected with Vicente that are unsolved. The unnamed witness whose testimony put Vicente away for a hundred and twenty years. This has to be what happened. Somehow the feds caught Sturgis, and they cut a deal. McKinley Hills PD would have been deliberately left out of the loop. Hendricks probably didn't know. Even if he knew, he wouldn't have been able to tell us.'

'Shit,' Thessaly said. She felt like punching the wall. On a practical level, she understood it. Deals like this were made all the time. All of those mobsters in based-on-real-life TV movies about the witness protection program had probably done terrible things to other people's families too. But it seemed so goddamn unfair. The fact that Vicente wasn't even rotting in jail for the rest of his life, that a stroke had given him a premature exit, somehow seemed to make it worse. Like the government had let Sturgis off scot free just to put another scumbag behind bars for a couple of years.

'Vicente was arrested in Brownsville, Texas in June 2004. He was given up by one of his own men.'

Thessaly swallowed. 'June 2004 is when Sturgis's immunity dates from. This is it.'

Lee's voice was still unsteady when he spoke again. 'Thessaly, I think you should back off now.'

She swallowed. 'Okay.'

'There's no good outcome from here. Like the marshal said, we can't touch him. And if you think what the government can do is scary… well, it's nothing compared to the people Sturgis used to work for. You need to drop it.'

'I know. Thank you for calling me, and for, for everything.'

Lee didn't respond, and she realized that this must be hitting him hard too, and with an extra dimension. For all that she had gone through twenty years ago, she hadn't been physically harmed at Redlands.

'Are you okay?' she prompted.

She heard him taking a long inhalation, and then the sound of the liquid swirling in the bottle again. 'Yeah, I'll be okay,' he said. 'I just wish... listen, I'll call you in a week or two, just to touch base, okay?'

'Sure, let's do that. And Lee ... I'm sorry, okay?'

There was a final five-second span of silence, and the line went dead.

I just wish... She knew exactly what he wished. That she had never called him.

She sat on the edge of the bed, unable to focus on anything but the thought of Casper Sturgis's perfect second life. She knew Lee was right. She knew Volcker meant what he said with his warning.

She knew she should let this go, at least for a while. But instead, she opened her laptop and started looking up news articles about the Ernesto Vicente trial.

33

Wednesday, February 10

Thessaly checked out of the guest house first thing in the morning. Rosemary persuaded her to stay for breakfast, and she relented. Although Rosemary's French toast was delicious, Thessaly regretted the decision after having to spend the best part of an hour deflecting Rosemary's questions about how much she had enjoyed Grenville. She lied and said she had gotten a lot of work done, and would love to come back some day. In reality, she decided that if she ever came within fifty miles of this place, it would be because she was being marched at gunpoint.

As she drove east and then north toward home, she kept the radio turned up too loud, trying to block out her thoughts with familiar noise from the classic rock station she had found.

It was cold but clear, the sky a deep blue. Lee's warnings had been an understatement. She really hadn't wanted to know the details. She started off with the news reports of the Ernesto Vicente trial. Court updates from the case in Texas. All of the stories covering the verdict in the nationals. A feature on Vicente in the *New Yorker* following his sentence to a hundred and twenty years without possibility of parole. As she immersed herself in the case, she recalled that she had been dimly aware of the case at the time, but had paid it as little attention as every other story about bad things happening in a bad world.

The obituaries from a couple of years ago were notably brief. Not all of the major news sources had even bothered to cover it. Away from his empire, Vicente had cut a diminished figure. Some of the epitaphs noted that the fragmentation of the wider Gulf Cartel had accelerated following the imprisonment of Vicente and his top men.

But not all of his top men.

Through gritted teeth, Thessaly had to admit that they were right. Volcker, Washington … even Lee, for Christ's sake. The greater good had been served by making a deal with the devil. And yet …

She stopped at a gas station on the 287 to fill up the tank and buy a sandwich. She tried to put her mind to work on something where she could actually make a difference. The book. Graystone were expecting delivery on the 19th, which was getting closer. It was the last thing she felt like doing.

Her GPS told her traffic was unusually bad north of Pomona, so she took the Cuomo Bridge instead. She had already taken a couple of turns away from the most direct route home before she realized what she was doing. She stopped at the lights at the bottom of Martins Hill and made her mind up by the time they went green, taking the turn up the hill.

She always felt low level guilt when she was in this part of town. Her visits had been very infrequent for the last few years. Then again, it wasn't as though the person she was visiting would mind.

She pulled into the lot outside the gates and a couple of minutes later she was walking the winding path toward the plots at the top of the hill. Kingstown Cemetery was built on a steep hill. On a clear day, you could see for twenty miles. Thessaly hadn't picked the spot, but she liked the idea of Mitch's final resting place being somewhere with a view.

She stood at the foot of the plot and read the engravings on the two gravestones, like they might have somehow changed in the time since she was last here. How long was it, anyway? Two years? God, she thought it was even longer than that.

Mitch Hanlon – 1979 – 2001, beloved son and brother

And then two names on the second marker

Richard L Hanlon 1952 – 2004

Greta Miller Hanlon 1955 – 2006

Cancer had gotten Mom. That was one she supposed she couldn't lay at Sturgis's door, but Dad had been another story. He never got over his son's murder. The death certificate said a heart attack, but his health had taken a sudden and precipitous downturn after July of 2001. He stopped sleeping, started drinking all the time. Thessaly knew he had never gotten over it. Not just Mitch's death, but the fact that the trail was cold and that Mitch's killer had gotten away with it.

When 9/11 happened six weeks after Mitch's death, it was a weird, disorienting feeling. All of a sudden, everybody else was walking around in a shocked daze, trying to adjust to how life had suddenly and violently changed. It was like the rest of the world had abruptly caught up with the way they had been feeling for weeks.

A bank of clouds drifted in front of the sun and cast the hill into shadow, dropping the temperature noticeably. Thessaly wrapped her arms around herself. She looked back at the two gravestones. The layout was asymmetrical, because there was space for a fourth marker on the right-hand side. Perhaps that was one of the reasons she didn't make the trip here so often. She didn't like such a blunt reminder of her own mortality.

She never knew what she was supposed to do here, either. The first few times she had visited Mitch's grave, and then Dad's, she had brought flowers. On one of their final trips together, her mom had made her promise not to bother for her.

'Such a waste, Thessaly,' she had said, casting a glance at the shriveled and browning bouquet slowly rotting in its cellophane wrapper on the next plot. 'And it's not like I'm going to be able to smell them when they're fresh, anyhow.'

Thessaly had lied and told her they didn't need to worry about that for a long time, and Mom had smiled sadly, and it wasn't six months before she was being lowered into that grave, the stone with its fresh engraving waiting to be reset.

'Now it's just me,' Thessaly said out loud.

The sun was already going down by the time she reached Buchanan. It was only late afternoon, but the February days were so short. She hated this time of year; the way the sense of time flying seemed more acute. Darkness fell and then it lingered.

As she turned the corner onto her street, she saw that she had company.

There was a black Chevy Tahoe parked right outside her house. The man behind the wheel wore glasses with thick black rims and a paisley tie. A different color from the one he had worn yesterday.

She considered turning back and driving around until he got bored, and then wondered how long he had been there. But the driver's door was already opening. Which meant he recognized her car.

Volcker stepped out onto the sidewalk and stood with his hands braced on his belt, stretching his sports coat enough to reveal the shoulder rig and gun strapped beneath. As she passed by and pulled into her driveway she wondered if that was something he did habitually, or just for her benefit.

A few different opening lines floated through her head as

she put the car in park and switched off the engine, from the righteously indignant *What the hell are you doing at my home?* To the playing-it-cool. *Hello, Marshal Volcker, what brings you out on this fine evening?*

In the event, she didn't get to use either, because the opening line was Volcker's.

'You're skating on some very thin ice, Miss Hanlon, and you're not wearing a life preserver,' he said as she was still getting out of her car.

'What are you talking about?'

'You know exactly what I'm talking about.'

Don't let him rattle you, she told herself. She took her time getting out of the car, closed the door, then leaned back against it, folding her arms. 'You made yourself very clear yesterday. Your pet murderer has to be protected at all costs. Fine. Message received. In case you didn't notice, I'm back home now, not in Grenville.' She put one finger to her lips, pantomiming a revelation. 'Oh wait, you do know I'm back home, because you looked up my address to come here and check up on me.'

'Quit playing cute, Thessaly.' First-name terms now, she noted. 'I know what you did last night.'

She met his gaze and kept her lips buttoned. She wanted him to tell her exactly what he knew, rather than letting him rely on her blurting out a confession. The longer this exchange went on, the less sure she was he was bluffing. He had a mixture of anger and satisfaction in his eyes. He knew, somehow. Had Sturgis called him? Or Casey, perhaps?

She was sure now that he was waiting for her to confess or deny. When she didn't say anything, he gave her a look that held a hint of admiration.

'What the hell were you doing at the Andrews' house? I thought I made myself very clear yesterday. Any attempt by you to jeopardize the safety and security of a federal witness will—'

'Get me placed on the naughty step for five years. Yes, I got it.'

'Then what the hell are you playing at?'

'Does Sturgis know? Don't look at me like that, Volcker, you can tell me that much. Did you tell him about me? Maybe where I live?'

'Don't be ridiculous, Thessaly. As it happens, no, I didn't tell him who you were. He contacted me last night, said a young lady had appeared in front of their house and claimed to know his wife. He was a little suspicious, which is good, because nine tenths of my job is drumming into these people that they need to be suspicious all the time. He said his cameras caught the same woman outside the house at around six-thirty last night. I said I would look into it, and to let me know if you showed up again. Do you know what's going to happen if I get that call?'

'Yes. You won't get that call.'

'Good. So why were you out there?'

'I don't know. Closure or … something. After I saw him, for a while I wondered if I had imagined it or if I just wanted it to be him. Then you show up and tell me I'm exactly right, but I can't do anything about it. It just, takes some adjustment. I wanted another look.' She looked up at him and met his gaze. 'I'll drop it now.'

He was watching her as she spoke. She knew he was trying to decide if she was telling the truth. Was she? She didn't entirely know. It would be difficult to move on from this. Perhaps impossible. But on the other hand, she remembered the raw fear when she had turned to see Sturgis within arms' reach of her. If forgetting all about Grenville meant she never had to be that close to him again, perhaps that was a price worth paying.

Volcker's gaze had softened. 'I would rather none of this had happened. I know this isn't easy. But it isn't just about the law. It's better for you if you move on.'

Thessaly thought he was looking for some kind of acknow-ledgment of the wisdom of what he was saying. She didn't want to give it to him. Instead she looked away from him, around the quiet street. The street that wasn't so different from that other street, a hundred or so miles away.

'So you came all the way out here just to tell me this. You couldn't have called?'

'I like to talk to people in person, where possible. I like to see the look in their eyes up close,' he said. He took a moment to glance at Thessaly's house.

Was that deliberate, she wondered? Making it clear that he knew where she lived?

He looked back at her. 'And besides, I'm based in the city. This isn't that "all the way out".'

'So we're done?'

'If you say we're done, I'm happy with that. I'll check in with Andrews and tell him you were just who you said you were. But if I hear—'

'You made yourself clear the first time.'

He nodded slowly. 'Okay. Well, have a good evening.'

He turned to walk back to the Tahoe. She called his name. 'Yes?'

'Don't tell him about me, okay?'

He took a step back towards her. 'You have nothing to worry about. If you don't give me a reason to bring you up, he'll have forgotten you exist this time next week.'

Thessaly stood at the front of her house and watched as Volcker drove off, waiting there long after his taillights had gone out of view. She wished there was some way she could do the same: forget about everything that had happened by this time next week.

34

Thessaly spent all day Thursday and most of Friday working flat out on the book. She was pleasantly surprised when she looked at the clock to find over two hours had passed without her thinking of Grenville or Casper Sturgis or Mitch. But of course, that reset the clock again. She saw a picture in her head of herself changing the number on one of those signs they have outside construction sites.

We have gone o minutes without thinking of our suppressed trauma at this workplace.

She used it as fuel. Threw herself into the job, with none of her usual procrastination or self-doubt. Just kept getting the words down. Writing, rewriting, moving scenes around, cutting a subplot here, amalgamating a couple of characters there. She ran out of steam sometime after ten on Friday, when she realized she had deleted and retyped the same line of dialogue three times. She rubbed the tiredness out of her eyes and sent the latest version of the chapter to the printer while she topped up on coffee.

She stood outside the patio door with the steaming cup, breathing in the cool air from her nostrils while the coughs and stutters of the long-suffering printer drifted down to her from upstairs. The night was quiet, disturbed only by the occasional hoot of an owl from somewhere in the woods, and farther away, the rattle of the night train as it pushed north to Poughkeepsie. She hadn't dreamed since coming home. Exhaustion seemed to be an effective defense against nightmares.

Her mind returned to Grenville and the house on Elm Street. Of course it did. But she noted that for the first time, she could think about it with a measure of detachment. It was as though the stupidly grueling work schedule of the past couple of days had deadened her senses. She could think about the events in Grenville almost like something that had happened to someone else. Lee had been right; letting things be was the right thing to do. Thank God one of them had decided that. If he had wanted to disregard the warnings of Volcker and Washington, she wouldn't have needed any more encouragement. She would happily have done something rash, something that couldn't have been taken back.

Taking a few days had made everything clearer. She couldn't touch Sturgis. The absolute worst she could hope to do would be to cause him some inconvenience. A different name and a different house in a different town. The only person who would see the inside of a prison would be her. Would it really have come to that? She didn't know. Surely any court would be sympathetic to her. But then again, she could see why it would be important to ensure there was a strong deterrent against outing witnesses.

She had read up on the program in between scaring herself half to death with Mexican crime reports and cartel execution videos. The Federal Witness Protection Program – or WITSEC, as it seemed to be commonly referred to by those involved – had become a necessity when the federal government realized in the late sixties that it had to find a reliable way to prevent organized criminals from murdering witnesses and their families.

In the decades since, it had worked pretty well, on the whole. The website for the program proudly boasted that none of their witnesses who followed procedure had yet been harmed. That caveat made Thessaly wonder how many didn't follow procedure, and what had happened to them.

It looked like Casper Sturgis was one of the good boys. Most witnesses were grateful for the protection, because they knew better than anyone what would happen to them if they were left out in the cold. The website trumpeted a series of positive stories of rehabilitation. Former criminals who had seized the second chance, mended their ways, become productive members of society. She supposed Casper Sturgis was one of the success stories. A quiet life in a small town, nice house, business, family.

She felt the anger rise in her again and forced it back down. Maybe she had been overly optimistic a minute ago. Maybe it would take a little longer than she had thought to get past everything that had happened in Grenville. Even the possibility of tracking down the other man from the diner as a consolation prize had fizzled out. Washington had left a message on her voicemail the day after she got back to let her know that line of inquiry had hit a dead end too. The cell was a burner, as expected, and the license plate was fake.

Thessaly went back into the kitchen and slid the patio door closed. The printer was still stuttering away upstairs. It would be going for a while yet unless it hit a jam.

Out of force of habit, she put the empty cup under the coffee machine and then stopped herself. The last thing she needed was more caffeine. What she needed was to go to bed and hope that she was once again tired enough not to dream.

She poured a glass of water instead, trying not to think about the nightmare from the other night as she stood by the sink, and climbed the stairs to the study. Something was niggling at her. A thought she had had a minute ago. As soon as she sat down at her desk, she worked out what it was. The mob witnesses. *They knew better than anyone what would happen to them.*

Suddenly, she felt entirely awake again. It was like somebody had turned up the lights. This was what her brain had been trying not to think for the last few days. Sturgis was untouchable by the law. But what about other angles? She knew Ernesto Vicente's branch of the cartel had all but died out since his incarceration and death, but surely he would still have associates, people who had a professional interest in making an example of snitches?

She wondered how hard it would be. To find a contact in the cartels, somehow let slip that she knew the whereabouts of one of their most wanted. She would have to make sure she kept herself anonymous, of course. And nothing could happen right away. At least a few months' distance so that it wouldn't be too obvious. That would be a good thing: it would give her time to plan, to make sure there was no way the leak could be traced back to her. Volcker would suspect, of course. Hell, more than suspect, he would *know*. But knowing isn't proof. She could do it.

Before she knew it, she was dialing Lee's number on her phone. Just before it connected, she cut it off.

Lee wouldn't help. She knew he wouldn't. He'd talk her out of it.

She looked at her reflection in the window and she could hear his voice running through the reasons she couldn't do this.

It'll be obvious it was you, Volcker will know, and he'll find a way to prove it.

Or

These people are psychopaths. You do this and you become part of that world. You're fair game.

Or maybe, just plain

It's wrong.

She watched her reflection and knew that all of these reasons Lee would give her – that she was giving herself – were true. But they weren't what made her mind up; not even the last one.

Because now she was looking through her reflection, at the Page house across the street. There was a trampoline visible in the back yard, because there weren't any eight-foot security fences in this street. She saw toys strewn around the grass out front. An old school Radio Flyer wagon, a basketball, some dolls.

That was the real reason Casper Sturgis was untouchable. Because he wasn't just Casper Sturgis anymore. Like it or not, he had a family. An innocent wife and child.

The printer finally spit out the last page. The silence filled the house like oil spilling into a sump.

Thessaly looked up at the clock. Almost eleven p.m., but she didn't feel a bit tired anymore. She took the manuscript, tapped it square on the table, and got back to work.

35

'Nice place,' Lee said.

The afternoon had passed with surprising speed. It was the longest unbroken period Thessaly had spent awake and away from her computer in days. She and Lee had eaten lunch at the River Outpost Brewing Co., and Lee still had a half hour before he had to leave to make it back in time for his shift to start, so she had suggested a walk along the water's edge toward Indian Point. They had stopped to sit on a bench facing the river. Small boats skimmed the surface, the low hum of the motors just audible from a half mile away.

'It's nicer in the spring,' Thessaly said. 'I guess everything is.'

Catching up had been Lee's idea, and she had worried about it right up until they met outside the Outpost. They had gotten the obvious out of the way first. How they were feeling about what had happened – both shitty – and then, miraculously, they had managed to move on to more pleasant topics of conversation. Reminiscing about school, trading stories about Mitch. Filling in the years in between. It started to feel like at least one good thing had come out of that rainy night at the Olympia Diner.

'So you never had kids?' Thessaly asked, once they had loosened up a little.

He shook his head. 'I was married for five years.' He stopped and corrected himself. 'No, only four. It seemed longer. Probably for both of us. We talked about it, the first year, but it never happened. Probably for the best, considering how the marriage turned out. You?'

'No. Pretty much the same, except for the marriage. I got close a couple of times, but it didn't happen. Josh was a good guy, but I don't think we ever really understood each other. He always said I was too closed off.'

Lee was looking out across the Hudson as she spoke. Low winter sun was glinting off the traffic on the 202 on the opposite shore. Thessaly's mind roamed back to an old question. Josh had been right about her being closed off. How much of that had been naturally her, and how much had been what had happened to her?

Lee bent to pick up a smooth rock and skimmed it across the surface of the water. 'Did you talk to him about Mitch? About Redlands?'

She considered before answering. 'Yes and no.'

He turned to look at her.

'I know,' she said. 'That doesn't make a whole lot of sense, but...'

Lee shook his head firmly. 'It makes perfect sense. You can tell people about it... but you can't really talk to them. Right?'

'Right.'

'Do you ever wonder...' he paused and Thessaly wondered what he was going to say. 'Do you ever wonder how things would have turned out if it hadn't happened? I don't mean you and me, or—'

'Oh I know,' Thessaly said, too quickly.

'It's just, everyone has these divergence points. Which college they went to, who they ended up dating at the right moment.

176

With us, it was Redlands. Sometimes I lie awake at night and wonder who I would have been without that.'

'Same.'

Lee stared across the water for a moment before changing the subject.

'You're doing okay, though. You're an author now?'

She nodded. 'You won't see my name on any of the books, but it pays the bills.'

'I read your first one. That had your name on it.'

She looked at him in surprise. 'Seriously? Did you hire an intrepid archaeologist to find a copy?'

'I got the ebook. I really enjoyed it.'

'Oh, thanks.'

'You ought to write another one for you,' he said. 'I'd get a kick out of going into a bookstore and seeing one of my friends on the shelves.'

She glanced away from him to hide her smile at 'one of my friends'. She straightened her face before she looked back and shrugged. 'I don't know, it's a job now. I don't think I can still do it for fun. After I get done with this one, I don't want to look at a Word document for at least a couple months.'

They talked a little more about his job. Thessaly thought about what Lee had said about Redlands shaping them, warping the course of their lives like the branches of a tree altered by a bad storm. She wondered how it had affected their choice of careers. Him working in security. Keeping people safe. Her, staying behind the scenes, a ghost. There was a break in conversation. Lee stopped to look at the power plant in the distance. The twin concrete-clad domes covering the reactors rose above the surrounding trees. Thessaly found herself remembering a conversation with one of her more elderly neighbors, who had told her there had been an amusement park on that spot, long ago.

'What was it like?' Lee asked. 'When you saw him that night?'

Thessaly took a deep breath. She had been dreading this, but now that he asked the question, it felt okay. Like that long-ago counselor had said, it helped to talk about it. And particularly to the one person in the world who could understand.

She talked about hearing the voice. How suddenly she was right back in 2001, reliving the worst day of her life. About calling the police, trying to follow Sturgis as he left. When she finished, Lee had a question she hadn't expected.

'So who was the other guy?'

The other guy. She had almost forgotten all about him.

She told him about the encounter a few days later at the Olympia. How he had called her bluff that she was working for Sturgis, tried to force her into his car.

'I gave Washington the license plate and his cell number. She wanted to know why he was impersonating a cop, but the trail was cold. Didn't seem much point thinking about it after what happened with Sturgis.'

Lee was quiet for a moment.

'What if he wasn't?'

'Wasn't what?'

'What if he wasn't impersonating a cop. You didn't get a look at the ID?'

'No. But he didn't act like a cop.'

'The way you describe it, sounds like he acted like a cop who wasn't supposed to be there,' Lee said. 'Why was he meeting Sturgis in the middle of the night?'

'I don't know,' Thessaly said. She had barely thought about the man at the Olympia since the meeting with Washington and Volcker, and she had gladly let work dominate her mind for the few days afterward. Now that the fog had cleared, she decided that that was a very good question indeed.

36

The next couple of days were so busy that Thessaly barely had
a moment to think about Casper Sturgis, or Grenville, or the
bald man from the Olympia.

She polished the draft and emailed it over to Drake at 8:55
on the morning of the 19th, copying in her agent. She felt
pretty good about it. Better than she ought to have done, really,
considering she had rewritten fifty thousand words in a week.
But then again, she had always been more able to throw herself
into work when her personal life was challenging. And boy, had
the last few weeks provided challenges in spades.

Her usual practice after going flat-out to meet a deadline
was to crash on the couch for a couple of days, catching up on
Netflix and eating takeout. But this time she knew she needed
something to occupy her mind. She thought about what she
had said to Lee the other day, that she couldn't write for fun
anymore. Maybe that was true, but perhaps she could write for
another reason. To keep herself occupied; to fill her mind so
that it didn't have a chance to wander. There was a story she
had had in mind for a while, but had put off tackling because
there had never been enough space between the ghost jobs.

It was a mystery, she guessed, but a world away from the pair of novels she had written after leaving the magazine. The story interspersed chapters from the autobiography of an illusionist growing up in New York City in the 80s, with present-day chapters focusing on a diamond heist the illusionist was involved in, having fallen on hard times somewhere along the way. There was a twist, naturally. The set-up and the twist were the only real things she knew about the story, and she was enjoying the unusual feeling of discovery. It was all hers. It reminded her of how much fun writing used to be, before it was a job.

She was enjoying it more than any project she could remember, and she thought that was partly to do with the fact that it was fresh, and nobody had weighed in to tweak the synopsis or suggest adding in a sardonic sidekick. Partly, of course, it was because she knew it was better to focus on this than the other thing.

Drake got back to her on the Friday evening saying that he loved it (standard), but had a few suggestions he and Megan wanted to talk over (also standard), and they set up a meeting for the following week.

She kept working on the new book, astonished when she hit fifteen thousand words in two days. On Sunday afternoon, she was working on her laptop at the kitchen island when her phone lit up with an incoming call from a private number. She thought about letting it ring out, uneasy about who it might be, and then decided to answer. It was Detective Washington.

'I'm sorry I didn't have time to call before,' she said. 'Thanks for sending me the pictures.'

'I thought you said the license plate was a dead end. Did you find something else?'

'We are not using this as a way of getting at Tony Andrews,' Washington said firmly. 'That ship has sailed.'

'I know that. I just want to know why that guy was meeting with him, and why he wanted to find him.'

'Could be totally innocent.'

'So why did he act the way he did when I met him?'

Washington said nothing, conceding the point.

'Anyway, I just wanted to ask you – do you think you could identify this guy if you saw him again?'

'In a heartbeat,' Thessaly said. 'Kayla, the waitress at the Olympia can back me up too. Why, did you find somebody?'

Thessaly had assumed that Washington had given up after striking out on the phone number and the license plate. Now she knew that she had in fact been doing the same thing Thessaly had done with Tony Andrews's true identity. Quietly looking into it. It sounded like a part of Washington was as reluctant to give up on this as she was.

'No, not yet. I'm just shaking a few trees. Might come to nothing. I just wanted to check you were still interested in pursuing this.'

'Absolutely.'

There was a long pause. An idea came back to Thessaly. One she had had after talking to Lee the other day about the man from the diner. She could set up some Google Alerts, like the ones she had for news stories about Redlands. This time, she could filter for any stories involving drugs or murders in Rhode Island. Sometimes the news carried pictures of the police officers involved. She might get lucky.

'I'm curious about this too,' Washington said after a moment. 'If we can find him, we can probably charge him with assault, maybe even attempted kidnapping if you want to push it.'

'What about impersonating a police officer?'

'Did anyone one else hear him claim he was a police officer?'

'Yes, he showed his ID to the other waitress when he was hustling me out of there. Not Kayla, her name was ...' she tried to recall the name of the blonde waitress.

'Sally Chandler. I spoke to her the other day after I met Kayla

Novak. She remembers the encounter, gave me a description of the guy, but she said she didn't get a good look at the ID. Couldn't swear that what he showed her was a police badge. And she said he didn't actually say who he was.'

'Seriously?'

Thessaly could hear amusement in Washington's voice when she replied. 'Hardly anybody actually looks at the ID. Mine could say I'm Daisy Duck for all the difference it would make. I'm just saying it would be good to have corroboration if we do find him.'

'The trucker, though. He told him he was police.'

'And do you know where we can get a hold of the trucker?'

Thessaly didn't have an answer for that.

'I just want you to be prepared,' Washington said. 'On the face of it, there's not much we can do, even if we find the guy. And even if we find out why he was meeting Sturgis, chances are that's where we have to drop it. Volcker wasn't kidding around.'

'I really appreciate you doing this. I guess the federal guys can make your life difficult for getting too close to Sturgis. I wouldn't have blamed you for putting all of this in the circular file, you know?'

'Yeah. Someone else might have, it's just...'

'Just what?'

Washington hesitated, and then continued. 'The Sturgis thing. It's still bugging me. I mean, not like it must be for you. I can't know how that must have felt. But me? It pissed me off. On a professional level, as well as personal. Usually the way it works is, you find the bad guy and you put him away. I feel like I let you down.'

'You didn't. At all.'

'That's the way it feels though. I don't know, maybe if we find this other man who threatened you, it'll make up for it a little.'

Thessaly found herself smiling. She wasn't the only one

looking for ways to stop thinking about a frustrating dead end. 'Thank you.'

'Say it with me...'

She wanted to laugh at Washington's weary tone. '*Don't thank me yet*, I know.'

'That's right. If it's okay I'll give you a call in a couple...'

Thessaly didn't hear the rest of the sentence. A popup had appeared on the screen of her laptop, and she had to blink to make sure she hadn't misread, that she hadn't somehow projected the name onto one that just looked similar. But no. She read it again. Still the same.

'Thessaly?'

'Hmmm?' she murmured.

'Everything okay?'

'Sorry, I just got an email from my agent. He has a... kind of abrupt style of communication.'

'Oh. I was just saying, I have a couple of ideas and I'll give you a call in a week or two to let you know how I get on.'

Thessaly thanked her and said that she had to make another call, hoping that Washington wouldn't think she was uninterested. They exchanged goodbyes and she ended the call.

The popup had long since faded from the screen. It had signaled a Facebook message request. She opened a new browser and clicked through to her account, holding her breath while she waited to see if she had really seen the name she thought she had.

Message request from: Casey Andrews

PART 3

Casey

37

Casey Andrews had always thought herself lucky to have a husband as attentive, as dependable and as just plain down-to-earth as Tony.

It seemed like a year never passed without one of her friends from back home getting divorced, or discovering some long-standing infidelity. Casey couldn't help feeling relief – tinged with a little self-satisfaction, she had to admit – when she heard another of these tales of woe.

She clearly remembered the moment all that changed abruptly. The night in October the previous year, in a hotel room in Cleveland, kneeling on the floor with blood on her hands.

Before that, it had been an everyday, normal marriage. A good marriage. More than that: a family.

She had met Tony six years prior to that night. When they met, it had been less than a month since she had finally broken it off for good with Marc, her boyfriend of two years. Casey had been working as a paralegal at one of St Louis's larger law firms and Marc was one of the firm's rising stars. He was a different person away from the job, and not in a good way. Needy, manipulative, jealous. It had taken her months to disentangle herself. He still messaged her late at night, occasionally making oblique references to not being able to carry on without her.

The guilt trips had kept her in the relationship a lot longer than she wanted. Eventually she had forced herself to go through with the breakup.

Less than a week later, she met Tony. The occasion was the afterparty for the Lawyers' Association annual Award of Honor dinner at the Chase Park Plaza. Marc wasn't at the party that night, which was the reason she hadn't tried to get out of it. It was the usual work thing: lukewarm white wine and over-cooked chicken. The clientele was the usual lawyer gaggle, but Tony had stood out from the crowd. For one thing, he wasn't wearing a suit or a tie. He wore jeans and a tennis shirt. He didn't feel the need to posture like the other guys, but he didn't seem like he felt out of place. He *wasn't* out of place. The alpha males seemed to get on great with him, to accept him despite the fact he wasn't one of them and wasn't wearing a three-thousand-dollar suit.

He fit in with them, but he wasn't like them. There was something about him. A confidence. He didn't need to impress.

He was a little older than anyone Casey had ever dated before, but perhaps that was part of the problem with the men she had dated before. And he wasn't *old* old, after all. Handsome, too, but not in a pretty boy way. With the dirty blond hair and the blue eyes, he reminded her a little of a kind of mixture of Robert Redford and Willem Dafoe. And the voice. Deep and dark, like melted chocolate.

They got serious fast. Tony was reserved. Never showed excess emotion, never wanted to talk about himself. Which all made him the exact opposite of her last couple of boyfriends. He started staying over at her apartment most nights. She only saw his place a couple of times. It was small and he said he didn't spend that much time there. He'd had some problems, a couple of break-ins and trouble in the neighborhood.

Tony was an auto parts dealer. Most of the business came

from making connections, he told her. He was at the party because he played golf with one of the partners at the firm.

Marc, unsurprisingly, wasn't happy when he found out that Casey had a new boyfriend. He made a point of reminding her that she had said she wasn't looking for a relationship right now. The late-night messages increased in frequency again. Alternating pleading with abuse.

He just wanted her back.

She was a whore.

He couldn't wait for this new guy to trade her in for a younger model.

It would be different this time, if she gave him another chance.

Tony awoke one night to see her staring at her phone. He asked her what was wrong, and she told him. She had mentioned Marc before, of course, but she hadn't told him about the messages. He asked if he could read them. Reluctantly, she showed him. He read through the list of messages. She expected him to react with anger, but his expression stayed impassive. At the end, he handed the phone back to her.

'I know,' she said. 'You're going to tell me I should call the police.'

He seemed to consider that as if it hadn't occurred to him, and then shook his head. 'I'll have a word with him.'

She told him he didn't have to, that Marc would get bored sooner or later, but he told her he would have a quiet talk with Marc anyway. He didn't ask for his address or his number, and Casey wondered if he actually planned to follow through.

The next day, her phone rang in the evening. She saw Marc's name on the caller ID and hesitated. Tony glanced at the name and said, 'You should take it.'

She answered. Marc sounded like a different person. He apologized and said that he wouldn't contact her again, then hung up. She looked over at Tony. He didn't raise his head from the magazine he was reading. 'I just asked him to back off.'

Marc never contacted her again. Two days later, she went into work and found out he had abruptly quit the firm the previous afternoon. It was the talk of the office for a couple of weeks, and then everyone gradually forgot about Marc. Nobody made the link to her.

She and Tony had only been an item for five months or so when Casey realized she hadn't had her period in six weeks. The little line on the pregnancy test had made her stomach drop through the floor. She didn't know how Tony would take it. She didn't know if he would be happy, or if she would never see him again. She wondered what she would do if he just bolted. He wasn't a native St Louisan, and he didn't seem to have much in the way of roots in the city. He mentioned living in New Jersey a few years before, but that was all she knew of his background. It seemed like a strange thing to focus on, among all the other worst-case scenarios, but she was suddenly certain that he would just disappear. And when he did, she knew that she would never find him.

But that wasn't what happened. It was the opposite of the worst-case scenario. It was pretty damn close to the fairytale scenario.

Tony was over the moon when she told him. He said that she had pre-empted his news, that he had been offered a business opportunity in some town in eastern Pennsylvania. A store to take over. That brought back a little of the trepidation again before he said that it was perfect.

'Marry me. We'll move to Pennsylvania and we'll buy a big old house, and we'll raise this kid.'

And that had been pretty much what had happened.

He disappeared for a week, and she had convinced herself that he wasn't coming back, but then she got a phone call from him. He apologized for the radio silence, said he had been working on closing the deal, but everything was done. He was sending a friend to pick her up. And so, five months pregnant, she moved almost a thousand miles east to live in a town she had never heard of with a man she hadn't known a year before. And the crazy thing was, she was deliriously happy about it.

Tony's friend was a guy in a suit who said his name was Ray. Ray wasn't much of a talker. He asked a few questions about her family and then was quiet for most of the trip. He seemed a little antsy, like he didn't want to be there.

When they pulled off the highway for Grenville, a part of her was still thinking this was some hoax, that she would get there and Tony would have disappeared. But he was there, standing in front of the gorgeous house on Elm Street holding a bouquet of white roses.

In that moment, she felt like the luckiest woman on the planet.

They married two weeks later, just a simple ceremony at the county courthouse. Casey's mother had passed ten years ago and she hadn't seen her father in a lot longer than that. Tony had looked almost relieved when she told him that. He said he didn't get on with his folks. So it was just the two of them and a couple who were there to arrange their own wedding as witnesses.

Aiden was born the following January. Seven pounds, twelve ounces.

The next couple of years were a blur. Tony opened the store. He still had to make road trips to line up contracts. Not every week or anything, maybe once every couple of months. Casey hadn't given it a second thought until Karen Anderson, one of the other moms at sing and sign class, mentioned that she made a point of calling the hotel every time her husband was away to make sure he was booked in at the place he had told her, and that there was only one person in the room. 'Don't you do the same, honey?'

Of course she didn't. She trusted him. So why did she feel herself going a little red, feeling a little stupid as those words came out of her mouth?

That night, Casey actually had the phone in her hand, the number of the Holiday Inn Raleigh Downtown in front of her, before she decided she was being ridiculous and put the phone down. Tony had given her no reason to distrust him. And without trust, what was a marriage? She remembered Marc, and the way he would scroll through her messages when she left her phone unattended. She didn't want to be anything like Marc.

And so they built a life in Grenville. The business seemed to take off fine, going well enough for her to be at home full time with the baby. She settled unexpectedly well into the role of homemaker. Tony never quibbled with any of her interior design choices. He didn't seem to care about things like wallpaper and tiling and drapes. What he took an interest in was security. She didn't suppose she could blame him, after his bad experience in the apartment in St Louis, even if she did feel some of the precautions were a little over the top. The security cameras front and back. The top-of-the-range alarm system. The keypad entry as well as the standard door key. The only thing she tried to fight was the fence. She saw no reason why they had to seal the back yard off like a prison yard, and she thought the high fence would look ugly. But on this, Tony was unwilling to bend. She went along with it. Once the fence was painted, it didn't look so bad after all. She supposed it was a first world problem. A husband overly committed to the safety of his family.

If there was one thing that was missing, it was close friends. She kept in loose contact with her circle back in St Louis, but it was difficult to find people like herself in Grenville. She developed the normal acquaintances with neighbors and other moms with children around Aiden's age, but no real friendships. Nobody she could talk to about anything deeper than watercooler television or parenting hacks. She couldn't decide if it was Grenville itself, or just the natural tradeoff you make when you become a parent. And she didn't mind, really. Tony and Aiden were her circle now.

Aiden grew into a happy ball of energy, and before she knew it, he was starting kindergarten at Grenville Elementary. Casey shed a tear or two at the school gates, but felt guiltily happy about the freedom. She started volunteering, reading the newspaper to some of Grenville's blind and partially sighted residents.

Her favorite customer was Marcie Englehart, a sprightly octogenarian who was in her own way as energetic as Aiden was at the other end of life. Her husband, Charles, was a short, gray man who communicated mostly in grunts.

Marcie died the previous September. Right before what happened in Cleveland. Looking back, Casey remembered the drinks after the funeral as a joyous occasion. Marcie's friends had rented space at Kelly's bar and given her a proper send-off. Her husband had had one beer and left early, his duty done. Casey spent a happy evening among women forty and fifty years her senior, recounting anecdotes about Marcie, learning things about her friend that happily astonished her.

Thinking about it, that night was the last time she had been happy.

38

It started with a broken leg.

At the beginning of October, Casey's Aunt Barbara had tripped over a trailing cable from the vacuum cleaner and had plunged down the stairs of her small home in Toledo. Fortunately, she had been able to call for help and had been fixed up and was being sent back home from the hospital. Barbara was seventy-nine and had no children, and she didn't like to impose, but... Casey told her it was no problem at all, she would be happy to come and stay with her for a few days until she felt more comfortable around the house.

She told Tony, and he was fine about it. Maybe not over the moon, but he understood. He said that she should go, that he could hold the fort for a few days. It reminded her again, she was a lucky woman.

So she drove to Toledo, and her aunt was in a pretty bad way. She was bedridden, dehydrated. Hadn't had so much as a glass of water since the ambulance had dropped her back at her house. Casey helped her change and made sure she had her meds and something to eat and drink. When her aunt had gone back to sleep, she went down to the small kitchen and called Tony to tell him she would have to stay a few more days than planned. He would be fine about it, she was sure.

Tony told her that wouldn't work. He had been called to

meet a new contractor at short notice, and he needed Casey back to look after Aiden. It had caught her by surprise, the uncompromising tone of his voice. It was as though he expected her to just drop her aunt and come back immediately. They had one of their rare arguments, terminated by her hanging up the phone.

Tony had called back ten minutes later. He told her that if her aunt really needed her, he could take Aiden on his trip, it would be okay. Casey didn't want that. It would mean Aiden missing two days of school. She told him fine, she would just have to come home. He said it was okay. Aiden would love it.

'Are you sure?' Casey asked. 'What about when you go to your meeting?'

'The place has a nanny service. The kid'll love it, he's always asking to go away with me, isn't he?'

That was true. But Casey still wasn't sure. She asked for the name of the hotel. Had she imagined the moment's hesitation before he answered? Probably.

'It's the Seabreeze, on West 10th Street.'

She was still concerned, but as soon as she finished the call, she googled the hotel. It did have a nanny service. Plus a pool and a kids activity club. And Tony was right, Aiden always wanted to go away with his daddy. Perhaps it would be good for them.

The next day, Aunt Barbara's friend Dina showed up. It turned out she had contacted more people than just Casey. It was as though she had sent out a series of distress beacons, and two of them had been picked up. Dina had traveled even farther than Casey had, all the way from Pasadena. She was about the same age as Aunt Barbara, with dyed red hair and what could be charitably described as an outgoing personality. She certainly brought a lot of energy with her. Casey got a brief hello, and then she was recommending wrinkle creams for around her eyes.

Barbara apologized for the double-booking, said she had been out of her gourd on painkillers and had clean forgotten she had asked them both for help. Casey wondered when the next ring of the doorbell would come. As soon as Barbara hinted that Casey didn't need to be sticking around, she gladly took her at her word.

Casey wasn't looking forward to repeating the long drive so soon after coming all the way to Toledo. And then she thought, Cleveland wasn't so far away. Practically on the way. Why not surprise Tony and Aiden?

So she drove east on I-80. Traffic started to slow down at about the halfway point, before grinding to a halt. Her GPS flashed up an accident near the exit for Elyria. Casey watched the minutes tick away as she sat in stationary traffic, knowing she was going to miss Aiden's bedtime. Still, she would be there for him waking up in the morning. She made it to the Seabreeze at around ten, leaving the car in the parking garage across the street. She didn't know Tony's room number, of course, but she thought it would be fun to knock on the door and surprise him.

The lobby of the Seabreeze was neat but a little tired looking. The carpet looked like it had been laid in the nineties, and the uplighters on the wall were of about the same vintage. The twenty-something male receptionist looked up as she approached. He had jet black hair and a carefully sculpted soul patch below his bottom lip.

Casey said good evening and explained, a little sheepishly, that she was surprising her husband. As she said it, she could see the guy raising an eyebrow. She knew what he was thinking. That she was a suspicious wife, checking up on her husband. That wasn't what this was, of course … was it?

Hurriedly, she took out her purse and showed him her driver's license, so that he could see it was the same address.

She could tell he felt weird about it. She said he could come up with her and knock on the door if he wanted.

'Uh … just give me a second,' he said, watching her warily.

She was regretting the whole thing by that point. Suddenly, the whole idea seemed a little silly.

He started tapping away at his keyboard, glancing up from time to time as though he expected her to do something crazy. And then he stopped and examined what was on the screen, before looking up again.

'I'm afraid there's a problem here, ma'am.'

'What problem?'

'We don't have a Tony Andrews staying with us.'

'Are you sure?'

'I'm sure.'

'Did you try Anthony?'

'There are no Andrewses staying with us this evening, ma'am. Could you … perhaps have gotten the wrong hotel?' He was looking at Casey like he couldn't quite work out what the scam was, but he knew there had to be one.

'No,' Casey said, shaking her head. 'Seabreeze Hotel, West 10th Street. You have a nanny service. I looked it up.'

'Yes, we do,' he said, looking confused.

'I didn't get the wrong hotel. The Seabreeze. There's only one. Tony sent me the link to your website, said he was already booked in.'

The guy behind the desk looked around for help somewhere in the foyer. None was forthcoming. 'I … don't know what to suggest.'

'Could you just check if you have any rooms with one adult and one child staying in them?'

He glanced at the screen. 'I'm afraid I can't divulge that information.'

'Why the hell not?' Casey threw up her hands and walked

away from the desk. She took her phone out to call Tony. It went straight to voicemail. Tony wasn't at the Seabreeze, at least not under his own name. Where the hell was he, and where the hell was Aiden?

She tried to suppress the wave of rising panic. Maybe there was a simple explanation some kind of a mix-up. Or Tony had changed his mind about the hotel. Or, Jesus … what if they were in an accident on the way there? What if that car wreck on the 80 was them? All of a sudden, she was convinced that something was wrong, that they were hurt, or worse. She tried Tony's cell again. Nothing. She was tapping out 911 with shaking fingers when she heard her name.

Casey looked around and there he was. Standing in the lobby, just inside the electronic doors as they closed smoothly behind him. He was wearing jeans and a shirt and a navy blue jacket that she didn't recognize. He didn't look happy to see her.

She didn't really register it in the moment, but thinking about it later, she realized it wasn't just the jacket that was unfamiliar. She hadn't seen any of those clothes before.

At that moment though, she was so relieved that she didn't stop to question it.

'Where's Aiden?'

'He's … he's up in the room. What are you doing here?'

'But … I asked at the desk and they said you weren't staying here.' She looked back at the desk, where the guy from earlier was leaning over the desk, drawing a route on one of the tear-off paper maps on the desk for another customer.

Tony glanced around. 'Come upstairs, Aiden's fine.'

They rode up in the elevator and went to the room. The carpet in the corridor was the same as the one downstairs, and it was more evident on this floor that the building needed some TLC. The wallpaper was torn at the joins here and there, and two of the spotlights along the ceiling were out. Tony opened the door to his room and Aiden was sitting on the bed playing Animal Crossing.

'Mommy!' he yelled, practically diving off the bed and running in for a hug.

Casey hugged him back and told him she loved him. 'Can you stay here for a second? Mommy and Daddy have to talk outside.'

They went back out in the corridor and Casey closed the door firmly and deliberately.

'Look, I know what you're going to say ...' Tony began.

She cut him off, so furious she could barely get the words out. 'Where the hell were you, Tony? What the hell were you thinking, leaving our child alone in a strange hotel room? Anything could have happened.'

'I'm sorry, you're right. I had to do some follow-up with the client. Aiden was fine, he knew I was only going to be twenty minutes.'

'Fine? What if there had been a fire, Tony? What if someone had fucking abducted him?'

'Twenty minutes, Casey, it's not like ...'

'Who meets a client at ten o'clock at night anyway? What kind of ... oh God, you were seeing somebody, weren't you?'

Even as she said the words, she knew that that wasn't it. There was something very wrong here, but it wasn't that.

There was a momentary look in Tony's eyes that said he couldn't believe she had suggested that. And then he just changed. He put his hands on Casey's shoulders and moved her along from the room into an alcove. They were beneath one of the blown bulbs, where the corridor was in deeper shadow. He looked up and down the corridor, and for the first time in Tony's company, Casey felt something like fear. His voice was very quiet, but very deliberate.

'There isn't anyone else, Casey. I told you, I had to deal with a work thing, and actually I've had a really, really shitty day.'

Up close, she noticed that his hair was messed up, and there was a sheen of sweat on his forehead. If she didn't know better, she would say he had been in a fight.

Casey had never seen him like that before. She was a little scared. But somehow, she also believed him, about it not being a woman. And then, as he stepped back from her and removed his hands from her shoulders, she saw something on the cuff of his shirt. Wet and dark and shining in the hallway light. It looked like blood.

She didn't ask him about it then. Thinking about it later, she wasn't entirely sure why. An instinct that it would have been a big mistake, perhaps. Instead she just backed off, stepped out of the alcove.

'I was worried about you, about both of you. When I got here and you weren't checked in ... then when I saw you had left Aiden all alone. He's *six*, Tony.'

He nodded. 'I'm sorry I worried you.'

They went back into the room and Casey read Aiden a story in the bed while Tony showered. As soon as she heard the sound of the water change, the drops bouncing off a body instead of flowing into the tray without obstruction, she told Aiden to try reading by himself for a moment.

She went over to the door and looked at the clothes where he had left them on the floor and saw that she was right. They weren't his clothes. Touching them, they felt brand new. She kneeled and examined the shirt. There was blood on the cuff of the shirt. More than she had thought. It was still tacky.

The shower shut off and she dropped the shirt hurriedly. The blood smudged on her dress, and she slid the shirt back under the jacket before scrambling to her feet. The door started to open before she had time to get back to the bed, so she stopped at the window, pretending she had been looking out.

'Not much of a view here,' she said, gazing out at the lot where her car was parked.

'If I had known it was going to be a family trip, I'd have gotten us one with a view of Lake Erie.'

He was standing in the doorway, a towel wrapped around his waist. He stepped forward and something made her want to flinch as he raised his hand and touched her cheek. He glanced at Aiden, who had discarded the book and was lying back, his eyes already closed.

'He'll sleep tonight,' he said.

'It's three hours past his bedtime,' she said reprovingly. She was still pissed off at him, and she was grateful for it. It gave her something to focus on. Something easier to process than the blood.

'I'm sorry I left him. You were right.' He kept talking, saying he was so glad Casey had come to surprise them both. He told her he had instructed the desk not to release his name to anyone. He had some salesman doorstop him at a hotel one time. It all sounded very plausible.

Casey showered after him, waiting until she got into the bathroom to undress. There was a little blood under her fingernails. When she came out, the shirt was gone, so were the jeans. The jacket was hung over the chair. She asked him if it was new. He said he had had it for a while, he left it in his bag for trips.

They climbed into the too-small bed on either side of Aiden. She slept fitfully. She kept hearing sirens. The city at night was very different to the silence she had gotten used to over the years in Grenville. The room was too warm, and every time she dropped off she saw visions of wrecked cars and blood circling a shower drain. Eventually she drifted into an uneasy sleep.

When she woke up in the morning, Tony was in the shower again. There was no sign of the jacket or of the jeans he had been wearing. She didn't ask about it again.

39

They decided to go to the zoo before heading home to Grenville. It was the last thing Casey was feeling like, but Aiden had seen it on one of the 'nearby attractions' flyers left in the hotel room and would not be dissuaded. They took Casey's car, leaving Tony's in the lot beneath the hotel.

Tony seemed different on the drive, and once they got into the zoo. Not distant or preoccupied, like Casey felt, but the exact opposite. He was so present. He seemed to be making sure the three of them were always talking about something.

Aiden reacted well to it, positively glowing in his father's presence. Casey realized it was the best family day they had had in a long time. Maybe Tony knew he had screwed up the previous night, and was making up for it. It was heading into the offseason, so the zoo wasn't overly crowded. They got good seats for the wildlife show at the Savanna Theater.

Aiden loved the show, and Tony was occupied asking his son about the different animals. Casey tuned out a little, tired after her night of broken sleep. She took out her phone to look for somewhere to get lunch when they went back to pick up Tony's car. When she Googled for restaurants around the hotel, she saw a series of local news stories.

There had been a homicide last night in the area. She tapped on the top story and saw a picture of a cop manning a taped-off perimeter. There was a map showing the location of the incident, with the curve of the shore along the top of the screen. She zoomed in closer and saw that the victim had been found right around the corner from their hotel. She felt a chill, thinking that somebody could have been murdered outside while they slept.

She turned in her seat to show Tony, but he was lifting Aiden up to give him a better view at a thirteen-foot African rock python that was held across the outstretched hands of a half dozen audience volunteers.

She didn't really think much of it at that moment. Or perhaps she didn't want to connect any more dots.

Casey didn't mention the news report when the show finished. They went to the gift shop, where they sold Star Wars toys and Lego as well as the expected wildlife-themed lunchboxes and stuffed animals. Aiden persuaded Tony to buy him an expensive Boba Fett action figure, over Casey's objections that it wasn't very zoo-related. They drove back to the hotel and Tony picked up his car. Casey took Aiden in the Honda. Tony had wanted to take Aiden, but he didn't fight her on it when Casey insisted it was her turn for mother-son quality time.

The drive took a little under four hours. Casey asked her son questions about the last couple of days and nights. She drew the questions out over the trip, interspersing them with questions about the best Ninja Turtle or the scariest dinosaur. She didn't want him to sense that he was being interrogated.

Did you have a nice time?

Aiden had had an awesome time. He wished there were a zoo in Grenville. He asked if all cities were as big as Cleveland.

The road is pretty busy, isn't it? How was the drive over on Wednesday?

Aiden said Daddy seemed kind of grumpy on the drive out to Cleveland, and he thought he didn't want him to be there.

Casey told him his father was just worried about work and had told her that he had loved taking Aiden along.

Which is the best Avengers movie?

The first one, obviously.

What did you guys do last night?

Aiden said they got to the hotel and it did have a pool. And they ate dinner at Chuck E. Cheese, and then they went to a store and Daddy bought some new clothes, then they went back up to the room and he watched a Pixar movie while Daddy talked on the phone to someone at work.

What's the name of that YouTube kid you like, the unboxing guy?

Aiden said it was a kid called Ryan.

What happened last night when Daddy went out?

Aiden said Daddy took a shower and put his new clothes on and told him he had to go out but he would be back soon. It must have been a while, because Aiden watched two episodes of *Mandalorian* and then played on his Switch. And then you came back, Mommy.

Casey stopped for gas before they reached Grenville. After she finished filling up, she called the Seabreeze on her cell phone and said she thought she had left a pair of her sunglasses in room 1802. They checked the log and they hadn't found anything. They said, 'I'm sorry, Mrs Womack.'

Tony arrived home ahead of them. He greeted his wife and son with a kiss on the lips and a ruffle of the hair respectively. Casey ran Aiden a bath and read him his story and tucked him into bed, and then she came downstairs. Tony was waiting for her in the living room. He said he was sorry he had left Aiden alone, and it wouldn't happen again. It was a key client, he had needed to talk to him right then. She wanted to ask him about the clothes, but something stopped her. Instead, she said she was tired and it was fine, and she went up to bed. She couldn't fall asleep. She kept thinking about the blood, the new clothes that disappeared. Hesitantly, she reached for her phone on the nightstand.

There was a little more information about the murder now. Still no arrests. The victim was a man named Oswald Kinderman. Forty-eight years old. He had been stabbed. The police were appealing for witnesses who had been in the vicinity of Frankfort Avenue between 10 p.m. and 10:30. Right about the time Tony had come back to the hotel with blood on him.

They were looking for a suspect. Caucasian, six feet, wearing a blue jacket.

Casey didn't sleep that night. When Tony climbed quietly into bed she murmured and rolled over, pretending to be asleep. She kept going back and forward in her mind. Should she wake him up and ask him straight out? What if there was some innocent explanation? The suspect was a man who had been seen in the area, but that didn't mean he had anything to do with the death of the man on the news. Perhaps Tony had just been in the wrong place at the wrong time.

But he had said the meeting was across town.

And there was the blood.

40

In the days after Cleveland, there was a palpable tension in the air. A feeling that had never been part of their house before. One night Casey was putting Aiden to bed and he started crying quietly as she was turning his lights out. She asked him what the matter was, and he said, 'Are you and Daddy sick?' When he said it, it was like he had articulated something she had been trying to put into words for days. They were sick, that was the truth in some way. And unless there was some kind of acknowledgment of the problem, it was going to kill them.

She didn't know what to do. She checked the website of the Cleveland Division of Police again. It had been a few weeks by then, so the unsolved Kinderman case was old news. The *Plain Dealer* website had one follow-up story, focused on the victim. Oswald Kinderman had some gang history. He had gotten off on a technicality with some big drug bust the previous year. She knew it was cold-blooded, but that information made her feel better. Like she knew that whatever had happened that night, the person who died had not been some pillar of the community. There was a picture of Kinderman's mugshot from his arrest. He had a gray complexion and short, scraggy brown hair. His eyes were avoiding the camera.

Still, she told herself she was being ridiculous. A series of weird coincidences, that was all it was. After all, what possible reason could there be for her husband to ... No. It had to be her overactive imagination. Seeing crazy things where there was nothing. But then she realized it wasn't just her. Tony was different, too. Quicker tempered, even with Aiden. Spending more evenings working late at the store. Everything had changed. It was as though one of the family was seriously ill, and that it had knocked the whole dynamic off. Like there was a sickness in the house.

And that was why she couldn't forget about it.

One evening after dinner, she casually mentioned that she had seen something on the news about a murder in Cleveland that must have happened while they were there. She wanted to see how Tony reacted. He changed the subject. He was smooth about it, made the quick change of subject seem natural, but it was obvious. She started asking him again about that night in Cleveland. If he had seen anything when he was out.

Tony shut down. He started coming home from work later. It was like she was married to a different man. Like an old science fiction movie where the husband is replaced by a doppelganger, and no one else can see it. Around everyone else, he was the same old Tony. Garrulous, generous, funny. Inside the house, it was gone. It was as though he had taken off a mask.

Christmas and New Year's passed. To Casey, it was the coldest, darkest winter she could remember. The three of them seemed to retreat to different corners of the house. There were more business trips for Tony, and he stayed away longer. Aiden stopped running around the house as much, started spending more time with his Nintendo Switch and lining up his toy cars.

Once, she tried talking to one of the other moms at the park. Mary-Anne was the mother of Connor, one of Aiden's closest friends. Mary-Anne had been good naturedly complaining about her husband and somehow Casey had found herself asking if she ever felt that she didn't really know her life partner. If she had ever found out something about him that made her feel differently. She hadn't been planning to tell her anything in detail, of course, but just for a moment she wondered if she could connect with someone else about how she was feeling. But a funny thing happened. Mary-Anne seemed to turn cold. She changed the subject and within a couple of minutes remembered a vague reason why she and Connor had to get home. Had Casey struck a nerve? Or had she seen something in Casey at that moment that she didn't want to explore further?

Either way, the message was clear: keep it light. Casey didn't bother trying to talk to anybody else after that.

Slowly, reluctantly, she came to a decision. If things went on like this, she and Aiden would have to leave. It would be difficult, but she would do it. She started making preparations, telling herself she wouldn't need to go through with it. Toward the end of January, she called her cousin Francine back in St Louis and mentioned that she had thought about coming over to stay for a while, would that be a problem? It was only after making the call that she realized why she had settled on asking Francine. It was because Tony had never met her, and didn't know where she lived.

She was a little scared that he might not let her go.

Again, she told herself she was being ridiculous. It felt hollower with every repetition.

Better safe than sorry.

She pulled an old suitcase out of the basement and packed it. Changes of clothes for her and Aiden. Some of Aiden's toys and books, the ones he wouldn't immediately miss. A couple of other items she might need if her suspicions were correct. She took the case over to Marcie Englehart's house, waiting until her husband's car was gone from the driveway. She went into the yard and took the key for the little potting shed from under the ornamental rock next to the door. Marcie used the shed to store her roses for the winter. Casey had helped her move them in just before Marcie became ill. She opened the shed and slid the case under the bench at the back.

All the way home she thought about the case, sitting waiting there. She didn't know if she could go through with it.

A couple of nights later, there was a storm. She came downstairs from reading Aiden his story and tucking him in. He was nervous because of the lightning outside, but he eventually settled. When she walked into the kitchen, her tablet was lying on the kitchen island. She had left it on the living room couch, and now it was in the kitchen. It wasn't like she could have moved it and forgotten about it, either. It was positioned, like someone would display an expensive painting or a sculpture after long, careful thought. And then she remembered what she had been looking at earlier that day, and she couldn't remember if she had closed the browser window. It was like a punch in the gut. She tapped the screen to wake it up, and it was showing the last website she had looked at. It was the last update on the Kinderman story, from just before Christmas.

So now there was no ambiguity. He knew that she knew.

She jumped as she heard Tony's deep voice from behind her. Quiet, and chillingly calm.

'Sit down.'

Casey turned to face him. She sat down on one of the stools, saying nothing. Tony took the next stool and sat down, his eyes meeting hers.

'Talk to me. I know this is about Cleveland. You haven't been the same since that night.'

Her voice came out steadier than she expected. 'I know you lied about where you were.'

'Talk to me,' he said again. A command. He looked down at the newspaper article on the screen.

She did as she was told. She talked, told him she had seen the news report about the murder. She said he had been wearing new clothes, and he had gotten rid of them. She kept waiting for him to say something: a denial or a confession, or even laughing and telling her she was nuts, but it was worse than that.

He just kept letting her talk, staring at her like he was taking her confession. And the craziest thing was, that was exactly what it felt like. It felt like she was in the wrong. Keeping secrets, making plans. She wished she could go back to worrying, rather than having it all out like this. She had been sure that it would feel better, but it was the opposite.

After she had finished talking, Tony just stared at her. Then he leaned in close, reached up and brushed some hair off her face. It was all she could do not to flinch away, because the touch of his fingers felt like someone else, too.

He looked at her. And again, it was like somebody else's eyes. When he started talking, it was like he had read her mind. She had a moment of clarity. This wasn't a new Tony. This had always been him. It just felt like he was different because she had never really crossed him before. Suddenly, she knew why Marc had never bothered her again.

'Casey, it's been a little … fractious around the house the last few weeks. I don't like it that way, and I know you don't like it that way. Would you like for it to stop?'

And she just nodded, almost without hesitation. And not because she was scared, although she was, but because in that moment all she wanted was for it to stop. And he was offering that to her.

He kept looking in her eyes, as though he could tell if she really meant it, and then he just smiled and said, 'Good, because

I'd like it to stop too. But the only one who can really stop it is you. Stop dwelling on things that can't be changed and things that can't do anybody any good. Tomorrow, we're taking Aiden out to lunch, and I'm going to apologize to him and you're going to apologize to him for the way things have been, and we're going to eat lunch and we're going to move on, and everything's going to be okay. I'll make sure work doesn't come between us again.'

Looking back on it, it would have been impossible to explain to someone else how logical, how easy it had seemed in that moment. The sound of the rain on the grass in the yard. Distant thunder. And his voice. The voice that was Tony but wasn't Tony. And Casey just nodded again and said, 'Okay.' And she wanted it to be over, even though deep down she knew it couldn't be.

And the craziest thing? It worked.

She climbed the stairs and got into bed and fell asleep as soon as she lay her head down. She slept the whole night for the first time in months. The next morning, the storm had broken. They had left the drapes open and the bedroom was flooded with golden light. Aiden came through and Tony told him they were going to Steak 'n' Shake. It worked out just like Tony had said. They had a family talk and they told Aiden they were going to try harder and be a proper family.

Things seemed to go right back to normal.

Tony came home at the regular time. He played with Aiden in the yard. He made bad jokes and complimented Casey on her cooking, like he had before. It was like the sickness had left the house. Whenever she thought about those dark winter weeks after Cleveland, she started to think that it seemed so silly. What was done was done, after all. You can't bring people back. So what was the point of poisoning your life over something you couldn't change?

Tony had offered her a deal – forget about this, and everything goes back to normal. And she had taken the deal.

Later, thinking about it, she wondered if maybe that made her as guilty as he was.

41

Things were almost normal for the next few weeks. Still, there was always something that Casey couldn't ignore just beneath the surface. The man she was married to was not who she thought he was. He was loving and attentive and a good father, but there was something underneath all of that. She had pulled back the curtain a little and seen, not everything, but enough to ruin the illusion.

She wondered if her inability to completely come to terms with it made her naive. After all, he had provided for his family for years. How many spouses truly know everything their partner does to put food on the table? She didn't think the wives of investment bankers lay awake at night worrying about the people their husbands had harmed in the course of their jobs. She couldn't stop speculating about what could have happened that night. And there were all the other nights he had been away over the course of their marriage. Was it something to do with drugs? The dead man in Cleveland had been involved with drugs. Or could it be something even worse?

But she knew what would happen if she picked at the scab, if she started to ask questions again. Nothing was worth going back to that, not while Tony was keeping his end of the bargain. And if that changed?

Well, the suitcase she had packed was still in the potting shed at Marcie Englehart's house.

Casey fell back into the routine of daily life. Taking Aiden to school, keeping house, putting dinner on the table, like a perfect housewife. She had never resented that before, back when everything had seemed more real.

Something changed the second time she ran into the woman from New York on the sidewalk outside the house.

'Oh, hello again.'

Thessaly stopped and gave a smile that almost looked natural. 'Hey. Casey, right?' She was dressed in sweatpants, sneakers and a t-shirt. She was a little red, but she wasn't sweating much. Perhaps she was still warming up.

'That's right,' Casey said.

'And this must be your little boy.'

They exchanged pleasantries. Aiden snapped into his charm-the-grown-ups mode. Casey had been grateful for Thessaly's help the other day when she had lost her keys, but there had been something... odd about her. She had wondered about it afterwards. And now she was showing up all the way across town, right outside...

'This your place?'

'Home sweet home.'

'Nice.'

'It is. Roomy. Did you find someplace to stay?'

'Yeah, the uh...' Thessaly started and then seemed to change her mind about what she was going to say. 'Just an Airbnb, it's nice. I'm actually getting some work done.'

What was Thessaly doing here? She was acting strangely. There were no vacation rentals around this neighborhood, so far as Casey knew. All big family homes. Thessaly would have had to run from the White Cart Guest House, or the new apartment block over on Sullivan. Both were far enough away to work up a little more of a sweat.

She told Thessaly that they were going to the park before school, wondering if Thessaly might find some excuse to tag along. Aiden cut in to proudly tell her about his homework. Six types of leaves.

'That sounds like more fun than my homework,' Thessaly said, smiling down at Aiden.

'Do you want a glass of water or anything?' Casey asked, curious to see if Thessaly would want to come into the house.

Before Thessaly could answer, she saw there was someone approaching on foot from behind her. She waved at Tony and said hi.

Thessaly followed her gaze and turned around. And that was when something weird happened. She said, 'Oh,' and put a hand to her mouth.

Casey's suspicion crystallized in that moment. This was about Tony. Did they know each other, somehow? There was an awkward pause. Tony glanced at the woman in front of him, and then over her head at Casey.

'I forgot my laptop,' he said, an unspoken question in his eyes. *Who is this?* 'Nice morning for a walk, so...' he stepped around Thessaly. Casey noticed that the other woman took a preemptive step back. He put his arm around Casey's waist and kissed her on the cheek. 'Hello,' he said, addressing the other woman.

'I'm... I'm Thessaly.' Again, a hesitation. As though she had wanted to say something else. Was Thessaly her real name?

'Nice to meet you,' Tony said.

Again, a hesitation, but she smiled thinly in acknowledgment.

'I ran into Thessaly the other day,' Casey explained when Tony's eyes turned in her direction. 'She gave me a ride when I lost my keys.'

'It's a small world. Running into you here and the other day.'

'Not really,' Tony said. 'It's a small *town*.'

It was, Casey thought. Not that small, though.

Tony asked where she was from, noticing that she didn't seem from around here. Thessaly said she was from Ossining, New York. Casey got the feeling she was lying.

There was another long silence. This one was so awkward that even Aiden registered it, squeezing Casey's hand and looking up at her with unease in his blue eyes.

Thessaly said she had better let them get to the park. Casey offered her the glass of water again, and she turned it down. And then she took off running again, picking up the pace quickly.

'What's her deal?' Tony asked, an edge of suspicion in his voice.

'I think she's just awkward,' Casey said. 'Not a people person.'

Tony didn't say anything. He watched Thessaly as she ran away, a preoccupied look on his face.

'You want to skip work and come to the park with us?' Casey asked quickly, hoping to change the subject.

'Would love to, but duty calls.'

She kissed him again and he went into the house. They started walking away. There was something strange about Thessaly, she was sure of that. But she was sure of something else, too. She had only started acting *really* strange when Tony showed up.

It was on her mind all day. She went through the motions. The park with Aiden, a visit to the grocery store because they were out of spaghetti for dinner. Tony came home early. He seemed preoccupied. He went into the study and spoke to someone on the phone for a while. She served dinner and heard her own phone buzzing. She remembered she had left it in the living room. She didn't bother to switch the lights on, the screen was lit up on the couch. If she had put the light on, she wouldn't have seen the figure outside.

Casey forgot about the phone and walked to the window. There was someone there; a woman. As she watched the woman turned and started to walk away from the house. Then she stopped and looked back, looking straight at Casey in the window. The woman flinched and turned away again, quickening her pace.

Thessaly. She was sure it was Thessaly.

'Something wrong?'

She jumped and turned to see Tony at the doorway. 'You scared me.'

Tony moved forward, looking beyond her out at the now-empty street. 'What was it?'

'Nothing, I thought I saw a raccoon.' She turned and smiled. 'You boys save any dinner for me?'

42

'I'll see you tomorrow night,' Tony said, appearing from the basement door. He always had the same preparation routine for the overnight trips. He packed a couple of changes of clothes, a toilet bag and so on into a suitcase. Then, just before he went, he would go down to the basement and come back up with a small backpack.

Casey had never really paid attention to the routine before Cleveland. If she had thought about it at all, she probably just assumed the basement was where he kept the files or whatever he needed for business trips. Now, she was looking at everything in a new light.

For instance, she knew there was a locked cabinet down there where Tony kept his gun. Casey didn't like the thought of it in the house, but she knew he had had trouble back in St Louis. She was relieved that he was so responsible about keeping it locked up.

While he was at work one day, she had gone down to the basement. The cabinet was larger than she remembered. Big enough to contain more than a handgun. The door was secure. She couldn't see a key anywhere around, and none of the ones on the hooks in the kitchen would fit it. It occurred to her that she had never seen the cabinet open.

Tony closed the door to the basement and carried the small backpack he had brought up from the basement through to the hallway, to where he had left the suitcase. He put them side by side and looked back at Casey.

'Say, you ever see that woman again? Tracy?'

She knew exactly who he meant. Was he pretending not to remember her name? She affected confusion. 'Who?'

'You know, the one who came over a couple of weeks back, we met her out there.' He nodded his head in the direction of the front of the house.

'No, I only saw her that time and... and in town.' Two lies of omission. Leaving out the third time she had seen her, and the specific location where they had crossed paths in town. Right outside the store. 'She was only in Grenville to visit with friends, I think.'

He left a long silence, watching her. 'All right. If you see her again, let me know, okay?'

'Sure,' Casey said. 'How come?'

He shrugged, as though to say 'no reason'. 'Just let me know.'

She kissed him goodbye at the door. He gathered Aiden up in his arms and gave him a tight hug.

Before Cleveland there would have been some conversation about where he was going. He would have complained about the number of meetings that had been lined up, or about the hotel he was booked into. There had been four trips since Cleveland, and they hadn't discussed them. Each time, he had simply informed her that he was going away, and she had told him that was fine. Each time when he got back, she asked him how his trip was and he said, 'It was okay,' and that was the last it would be mentioned.

What was he doing? Something that allowed them to live

here in a house with a mortgage that exceeded the monthly takings from the auto parts store. She had known that from before Cleveland, of course, but it was easy not to think too much about it, to assume Tony was just really good at budgeting or playing the stock market or something. She didn't ask questions. Doing that was a lot harder since Cleveland, and the truce had started to break down since the morning they had seen Thessaly outside.

She stood at the door and watched as Tony reversed the BMW out of the driveway, turned in the road and drove off.

Aiden looked up at her as she closed the door. 'Mommy? I'm bored.'

She watched the car until it was out of sight. Who was he? She had convinced herself that she didn't need to know. Didn't need to know that he was a drug dealer, or some organized crime boss, or whatever the hell he was. She had been lying to herself. She needed to know.

'Mommy?'

She looked down at Aiden. 'Go play your videogame.'

'But I haven't finished tidying my room yet, and you said ...'

'Tell you what, this once, I'll let you skip to the game. If you promise to finish your room afterwards.'

Aiden didn't wait around for her to change her mind, racing up the stairs to his room.

She closed the door and took the laptop through to the living room. She turned the armchair around so that she could see out of the window and sat down in it, keeping her eyes on the road as she logged in. Tony had a habit of showing up unexpectedly, or coming back after he had left. She used to think he was just forgetful, now she wasn't so sure about that.

She hoped her confusion about Tony's question had been more convincing than it felt. She had been thinking about Thessaly a lot over the past couple of weeks. At first, she had started to think she had something to do with her husband's trips. But that didn't seem quite right. She had been so uneasy when Tony had appeared unexpectedly. She couldn't put her finger on it, but she thought that Thessaly knew something. Tony's parting words this morning had made her sure of it. He wouldn't have asked about her if he knew who she was.

'Thessaly' was an unusual name. So unusual that Casey had wondered if it was her real name. A few days after seeing her from the living room window, she had waited until she knew Tony was at work and had started looking into how rare it was. The name came from a region of Greece that appeared in the *Odyssey* as the kingdom of Aeolus. There were a few Thessalys in the United States on Facebook. Only one of them on the east coast, as far as she could see.

Thessaly Hanlon
Lives in Buchanan, NY

The profile picture wasn't that good, but it looked like the woman she had met. Thessaly had said Ossining. A quick look at the map showed that Buchanan was less than ten miles north of Ossining. She clicked on the profile, but it was almost completely locked down. Just the profile pic and the location.

She found the profile page again and took another look at the picture. It was definitely her.

Casey raised her head to look out of the window. The driveway was still empty, the street outside quiet. From upstairs, she heard the bleeps from Aiden's game. She bit her lip and thought carefully before committing. She clicked 'Send message'.

43

Hi – is this the Thessaly who was in Grenville 2 weeks ago?

Casey hit send and waited. She knew she could be waiting a long time. Thessaly would get a message request and would have to accept in order to read it. She might never see the request, or might have a policy of not responding to unsolicited messages from strangers.

But almost immediately, the check mark next to her message changed to a tiny version of Thessaly's profile picture, denoting that it had been seen.

Ellipses appeared. She was typing a message. They appeared and disappeared five or six times. The respondent was either typing a very long message, or kept changing her mind about what she wanted to say.

After a couple of minutes of this and a long pause, a message appeared.

Thessaly: Yes.

Well, that answered one question. Casey started typing immediately.

Casey: Hi – would like to catch up for a coffee if you're free?

Long pause, then the ellipses.

Thessaly: Hey. Um, sure. I can give you a call? What about?

Now it was Casey's turn to hesitate. She thought through some responses. Maybe she should ask to talk on the phone. No, too easy to dismiss, too easy to hang up if things went wrong. She wanted to do this in person, and Tony had handed her an opportunity. He wouldn't be back from his trip until tomorrow evening.

Casey: Rather talk about it in person. Can come to NYC.

She hit send and held her breath. No pretense now. This wasn't a request for casual chit-chat. If Thessaly really had no idea that there was something wrong about Tony Andrews, she would respond either with confusion or a polite refusal.

The longest pause yet. Ellipses appeared and disappeared a few times.

Thessaly: Friday?
Casey: What about tomorrow? Noon?

Immediate reply.

Thessaly: Works for me.

She had agreed right away. Meaning she wanted to talk to Casey as much as Casey wanted to talk to her.

Casey: I'll be coming into Penn, so anywhere nearby.

A link to a coffee shop on 42nd Street appeared within fifteen seconds, followed by a question mark.

Casey: Looks great, tomorrow at noon.
Thessaly: See you then.

Casey went back through the message trail, deleting all of her messages. She wondered if Thessaly would notice, and what she would think about that. Then she closed the laptop and looked out at the street, thinking about what they would have to talk about tomorrow at noon.

44

Monday, February 22

Casey left straight from dropping Aiden at kindergarten and drove as far as Secaucus, where she paid thirty dollars to leave her car at the station before taking the Northeast Corridor line to Penn Station. She had never attempted to drive in Manhattan and didn't intend to start now. She supposed she could have suggested meeting Thessaly nearer her home, but the city seemed more neutral. Her train pulled in two minutes late, but she was in plenty of time.

She hadn't been in New York for three years. The last time was when she had managed to organize an overnight babysitter for Tony's birthday. That was no mean feat in Grenville. The other parents in Aiden's peer group were happy to make polite small talk with Casey at bake sales and at the park, but she had never really shaken the outsider tag since moving to town. On this occasion, it had been a straight quid pro quo. Melissa Halford, who lived five houses down on Elm Street had been desperate when her arrangements fell through with an hour's notice. She had turned up at the house and offered to take Aiden whenever Casey wanted in exchange for her babysitting Melissa's twin daughters for the night. Casey had offered to repeat the arrangement anytime, but Melissa hadn't offered again and didn't seem to catch any of her periodic hints.

That one night in New York had been fun, though. Dinner and a show and a pricey one-night stay at the Waldorf Astoria. She didn't recall much about the show, but she remembered it had been nice just to be alone with Tony. Now it felt like those memories belonged to a different person.

Every time she came to New York she was taken aback by the sheer scale of everything. The way the buildings towered, the wide streets always running away in four directions, seemingly infinite. If anything, the feeling of being dwarfed seemed more pronounced this time. Without her really noticing, her world had gotten a lot smaller since she had moved to Grenville. In every respect.

She made her way north and west to the coffee shop Thessaly had suggested. She still had well over an hour before the rendezvous, but her intention was to check the place out before Thessaly arrived. The more she thought about this, the warier she got.

She stopped at the crosswalk at 5th and 42nd and saw the sign outside the coffee shop just across the road. The walk sign lit up and the pedestrians on either side of her crossed, not waiting for the traffic to come to a full stop. She hesitated, her eyes on the sign in front of the coffee shop. She could go round in circles about this all day. In the end, she only had two options: go ahead with the meeting, or turn around and go back home. It wasn't really a decision. There was only one way to find out why Thessaly seemed to be so interested in her husband. She had to know.

She crossed just as the lights started counting down and quickened her pace to reach the opposite sidewalk before an impatient yellow cab mowed her down. She ignored the blare of the horn and scanned the sidewalk outside the coffee shop.

No one hanging around, just lunchtime crowds heading east and west clutching bagged sandwiches and go-cups.

There were a lot of customers inside, but still some tables and spaces at the lunch counter along the window. She took a seat at the window, close to the door, placing her purse on the adjacent stool. A good spot. She could see anyone familiar approaching from either direction. She ordered a latte and waited.

She had been waiting around a half hour when she switched from looking west to east and flinched as she saw Thessaly outside on the sidewalk, staring in at her. After a second, she lifted a hand, a redundant gesture as there was no doubt she had seen her. Thessaly returned the wave, equally redundantly, and walked the last few paces to the entrance.

'Hello,' Casey said. 'You're early.'

'Not as early as you.'

She reached over to the next stool and lifted her purse. 'I saved you a seat.'

Thessaly sat down and looked up as a waiter appeared. He wore a black shirt and his hair was unkempt. He projected a hung-over air. 'Something to eat, or just drinks?'

She shook her head. 'Just a coffee, please.'

He pointed at Casey's latte. 'Same?'

'No milk, just straight up.'

'Thank you for coming,' Casey said, when the waiter had moved out of earshot. 'I wasn't sure if you would.'

Thessaly's eyes narrowed. She seemed to be considering her reply, not wanting to give too much away.

'I was curious. You went to some effort to find me.'

Casey took a drink of her latte, cold now, and wondered if Thessaly noticed that her hands were shaking a little. 'I ... I wanted to ask you something. You're interested in my husband.'

Thessaly broke out into a grin, as though she had told a joke. 'Casey, I think you have the wrong idea. I—'

'I don't mean that way. You were at the store. And then later you came by the house. You lied about why you were there. And then you were out there at night. I saw you.'

Thessaly's grin drained away. She said nothing.

'You don't know me. You didn't have any reason to be in Grenville. I checked, there are no Fullers in the whole town.'

Thessaly took a moment to think about that. 'It's a free country. I can be wherever I want.'

'Our business and our house? You were there because of us. And since you and I don't know each other, that means you were there for my husband.'

The waiter arrived with Thessaly's coffee, reaching in between them to put it down and breaking the tension for a second. Steam swirled upwards in narrow ribbons from the cup.

Thessaly picked up the cup and blew on it. Took a sip. Took her time. She put it down and gazed out at the traffic on 42nd.

'Are you denying it?' Casey said. 'It's not a coincidence. You knew where we lived. How did you get the address?'

Thessaly turned back to her. 'You asked me to meet. Why?'

'I just told you why. I want to know why you're stalking my husband.'

'Stalking?'

'What would you call it? You come all the way to our town, to our business, to our home. And that's just what I know about.'

Thessaly looked a little guilty for a second, and Casey wondered what she didn't know about. And then her features hardened and she straightened on her seat.

'What's that big old fence around your house for, Casey? To keep something in, or to keep something out?'

Casey looked away from her. She swallowed and fought back the tears that suddenly threatened. She picked up a sugar pourer and weighed it in her hand. It was time to stop dancing around the reason they were both here.

'I think my husband might have killed someone,' she said, her voice only slightly unsteady. Then she turned to look at Thessaly. 'And I think you know something about it.'

Thessaly sat back. She glanced around, maybe to check if any of the other customers were listening in.

She closed her eyes and then opened them again. 'Casey…' She stopped.

Casey followed her gaze to see the waiter was looming over her.

'What?' Thessaly snapped.

'I just wanted to ask if everything was okay with your order. *Sorry.*'

'We're fine, thank you.'

He moved away, openly rolling his eyes.

Thessaly leaned in, her voice just above a whisper. 'How much do you know about it?'

Confirmation. She knew. Casey started toying with the sugar pourer again, turning it this way and that, watching the sugar settle like the sand in an hourglass.

'How much did he tell you?' Thessaly pressed.

Casey sighed. Where to begin? At the beginning, she supposed.

She told Thessaly about the party after the Award of Honor dinner in St Louis, about how Tony didn't seem like the other guys in the room, the immediate mutual attraction.

'You know, the funny thing is, I really don't think he was looking for a relationship either. He was new in town, doing some kind of contract work, and if anything I got the impression he was, you know, a player. I was okay with that. We dated. Started seeing each other every day, and the next thing I know, I was pregnant with Aiden and, well, things just kind of went from there.'

Casey lifted her cup to take a drink and found it was empty.

It had been almost full when Thessaly arrived, she must have taken a lot of nervous sips unconsciously.

'You want another?' Thessaly said quickly, but she shook her head. Thessaly ignored her. Picked up the cup and looked beyond her at the waiter, raising her eyebrows.

'I was scared. As soon as I saw that pregnancy test. I just didn't know what was going to happen. I didn't know how he was going to react. But when I told him, he ...' she breathed out. 'God, I've never talked to anybody about this.'

She told her about driving to Pennsylvania with Tony's friend Ray. A friend she had never seen again. About the big house and the bouquet of roses.

The waiter appeared with another cup, sliding it in front of Casey and removing the empty one. Casey didn't seem to notice it. Thessaly told him thank you. He said they were very welcome in an exaggerated way.

'I know what you're thinking. White roses, so cheesy, but at that moment ...' she stopped and cleared her throat, remembering where she was and who she was talking to. She took a sip of the coffee and shrugged, embarrassed as she said it. 'It was all I wanted.'

Thessaly nodded and put a hand on her forearm.

'I get it.'

There was something about Thessaly that Casey didn't trust. Or maybe not so much Thessaly herself, but her intentions here. She wanted something. This was personal to her, somehow. But she had gone this far, she might as well finish the story.

'We moved in, and we got the place just the way we wanted, and Tony was working hard at opening the business, and it seemed impossible, but somehow we kept going and we got there. And then Aiden was born. Do you have kids?'

Thessaly took a second before answering. 'No.'

'Okay, well, ask any parent. It's kind of a blur. Especially those first six months. But we got through it, even though it seemed impossible. Things were great for years. The business seemed to be going well, Aiden started school ... And then last October. That's when it happened. Cleveland. Oswald Kinderman.'

Thessaly's hand moved from her forearm then, and she looked thoughtful. No, she looked confused. She looked like she had never heard the name before this moment.

Suddenly, Casey felt a swell of rising panic.

'Thessaly? That's what you're here to talk to me about, isn't it? About Oswald Kinderman?'

45

As Casey looked on, she saw the realization dawn in Thessaly's eyes. A moment after Casey had come to the same conclusion: they weren't talking about the same thing. And perhaps that meant this meeting was a big mistake.

'You don't know what I'm talking about,' Casey said. 'Oh my God.'

Thessaly blinked. 'Casey...'

But she was already moving. Stuffing her phone into her purse, looking around for her coat, shuffling off the stool.

'Casey, wait.'

She avoided Thessaly's gaze. 'Please don't tell anyone about this. Just, just forget any of this happened. I can't... He can't find out about this. That I talked to you.'

'Casey, you have nothing to worry about,' she said, putting a hand on her shoulder. Casey flinched, and Thessaly dropped her hand immediately.

Casey turned for the door and then turned back, unexpected anger rising in her. 'Who the hell are you anyway? What is this? Do you just stalk people, try to dig into their secrets?'

'No, I thought... I thought you wanted to talk,' Thessaly said, lowering her voice, and making Casey aware that she was practically shouting. Some of the other customers were paying attention to them now. Nothing like somebody else having an argument to provide a welcome distraction.

'Forget you met me,' she said quietly. 'You don't know who you're dealing with.'

Casey moved quickly toward the door, not looking back.

She turned west, heading back toward Penn Station. She started moving faster, almost running.

She cast a backward glance and saw Thessaly following, an anxious look on her face. Casey kept going, weaving between the streams of pedestrians, brushing by some of them to grunts of disapproval. A guy wearing a backwards baseball hat and a Giants jersey, staring down at his phone, suddenly stepped unexpectedly into her path and she wasn't able to course-correct in time, catching him on the shoulder and knocking the phone out of his hand.

'Hey!'

She ignored him, kept running. She rounded the corner onto 5th. Thessaly caught up to her as she tried to cross in front of the New York Public Library and put a hand on her shoulder. Casey spun around and swung her right hand, slapping Thessaly across the face. Thessaly looked more surprised than hurt.

Still, Casey flinched back from what she had done. She hadn't planned to hit her, had just reacted on instinct. She opened her mouth to apologize automatically, and then closed it.

Thessaly held her hands up in front of her in what Casey guessed was intended to be a calming gesture. 'Casey, you're right, I didn't know about Oswald Kinderman. But I do know about Mitch Hanlon. Do you know that name?'

Casey raised her hand gingerly to check the damage she had inflicted on Thessaly's face, but she caught herself and lowered it again.

She shook her head. 'No.'

'Mitch was my brother. Your husband killed him twenty years ago.'

They didn't go back to the coffee shop. Instead, they crossed 5th and walked along 40th to Bryant Park. They sat at opposite ends of a bench at the south of the park. They didn't say anything for a minute, sizing each other up like sparring partners on opposite sides of the ring. Waiting for the bout to begin, waiting to discover everything about an opponent they thought they had prepared for, only to discover they knew nothing.

'I'll go first,' Thessaly said.

She started talking. Her voice was calm and clear, like she had been telling this story all of her life. Maybe she had. Or for half of her life, anyhow. She talked about her twin brother Mitch, about the house in Connecticut where they had grown up. She talked about a road trip they made after graduation to see some band, with Mitch's friend Lee. About hearing about a dead mall outside of some town in Jersey.

'I don't remember all that much about getting in there,' Thessaly said. 'We can't have been there longer than a half hour when... when the men showed up.'

Casey took a breath. She knew who one of 'the men' had to be.

'We had split up to explore. I was on the upper level, close to a window that looked onto the parking lot. At first I thought they were security guards or something. We had parked around back, so I hoped they wouldn't see our car. There were two of them. They came inside. I tried to call Mitch, but the signal was too weak. Lee didn't even have a phone. A lot of people didn't, back then.

'I went down to the ground level to find them but before I could, I heard the shutter opening. I was caught out in the open, so I ran for the only hiding place I could see, under some broken-up tables and chairs and junk that was stacked at the edge of the food court. I knocked over a half-full can of paint as I was climbing underneath and then I saw they were close. I just froze and prayed they wouldn't see me. The paint was probably what saved me. He walked around the spill, it stopped him getting close enough to see me under the tables.'

Thessaly had been staring into the middle distance, absently watching some kids play on the grass in the center of the park, but her eyes found Casey's now.

'It was your husband, Casey.'

'Tony.'

'Tony, that's who you think he is. *Tony*.' She said the name with a mocking tone. 'He was talking to the other man. The police told me later he was a car dealer, his name was John Ammerman. It was some kind of arranged meeting, and the other one, Ammerman, was intimidated by him. He had a briefcase. Your husband looked in it. Ammerman said it was the best he could do.

'We never found out what was in the case, or what the meeting was about. Maybe, if Lee hadn't appeared, they might have done whatever they had to do and left.'

'What happened?' Casey asked quietly. She didn't want to know. She had to know.

Thessaly swallowed, seemed to summon an extra reserve of will for the next part.

'Lee was looking for us. We had split up and he had been in another part of the mall. When he came back they saw him. He said he didn't want any trouble. Stur... your husband. He pulled a gun. He asked the other guy if this was some kind of set-up. Ammerman started babbling, and all of a sudden...' she stopped and rubbed the side of her head. It was like relating the story was causing her physical pain.

'All of a sudden?' Casey prompted after a minute.

She took a deep breath. 'He just started shooting. Lee ran and he shot him in the back. I thought he was dead. He shot

Ammerman in the head. Then he saw Mitch trying to make a run and shot him in the leg. He fell right in front of me. We saw each other. He didn't want me to give myself away. St... your husband walked over to where we were. Mitch had fallen in the pool of white paint. I remember the white paint on the dirty floor and the blood mixing with it.

'Mitch was terrified, but he tried to keep him talking. Said it was just the two of them and he swore he wouldn't tell anyone what he had seen. Your husband just... I mean he acted like it was nothing. What he was about to do was nothing. He said something to Lee about being in the wrong place at the wrong time, and that it just wasn't his lucky day. And then he said that waiting for luck is like waiting for death. I always remembered that. That and his voice. And then... then he shot him.'

Casey put her hand over her mouth. She didn't say anything. She felt a tear run down her cheek and over her knuckles where they crossed its path.

Thessaly kept talking. The killer taking the briefcase the other man had brought, and leaving. Discovering that Lee was alive. And then the police and the media and a suspect. A hundred leads that dried up like spilled soda on a hot pavement, and then nothing, for twenty years.

Thessaly cleared her throat. 'And then, a couple of weeks ago, I happened to stop just outside of Grenville in the middle of the night, at the Olympia Diner.'

'That's where you saw him. After all those years.'

Thessaly stared back at her for a moment. Casey wondered if she expected her to deny it. To protest that her husband couldn't have done these things, couldn't be this person. Or even say that it could be a case of mistaken identity. A year ago, she would have been saying all that, of course. But even though this was all new information to her, it wasn't coming as a surprise, not after Cleveland.

'I didn't even look at the two men in there at first. I was tired and I just wanted to eat and get out of there. But his voice. I never forgot that voice.'

Casey knew what she meant. That deep, intense voice had been one of the things that attracted her to Tony. More recently, she had come to fear it. She remembered Tony's voice in the kitchen that night, telling her the way things were going to be. Strong, uncompromising, hypnotic.

Thessaly continued with the rest of her story. How she had tried to follow Tony, losing him outside of Grenville. And then the days of investigation, trying to get help, going to the police, eventually finding the auto parts store, right up until the moment she and Casey had met.

Casey put her hand to her face, lowering her head. When she looked up, Thessaly was watching her. She wiped at her eyes with the heel of her hand.

'I am so sorry,' she said. It seemed hopelessly inadequate, but she had to say something.

'You believe me?' Thessaly's voice was incredulous. Like she had expected another slap, or at least for Casey to get up and walk away.

'Of course I believe you. Why would you make something like this up?'

'I don't know. Most people ...' she stopped and thought about it. 'Most people would give their husband the benefit of the doubt over a complete stranger.'

'Most people aren't married to my husband.'

Thessaly leaned closer. 'Who is Oswald Kinderman?'

46

'I know what you're thinking,' Casey said after she had finished talking about Cleveland and her suspicions and finally, the talk with Tony in the kitchen.

'I didn't—' Thessaly began.

Casey raised a hand to cut off the protest.

'You are thinking it. I would be too. You're thinking he brainwashed me. Or gaslit me, or whatever you call it these days. And shit, maybe that's exactly what happened. But I don't think so. I think he was offering me a deal – forget about this, and everything goes back to normal. And I took the deal. And the craziest thing is, it was working. Right up until you showed up.'

She sat back on the end of the bench and put her hands on her lap.

'That's what I thought you were there for. I thought you were investigating the Kinderman murder. Or maybe you weren't a cop, maybe a private investigator or something. Anyway, it brought everything to the surface again. It made me wonder if maybe … maybe keeping quiet makes me as bad as he is.'

Thessaly took a breath. 'Casey, there's something I haven't told you yet.'

She felt a shiver as she saw the look in Thessaly's eyes. There was *more*? What could possibly be worse than what had already been said?

'Something else about Tony?'

She took a deep breath. 'His name isn't Tony. Your husband's real name is Casper Sturgis.'

'What?'

'Casper Sturgis. That's his real name. He's the man who killed Mitch.'

Casey shook her head. None of this made sense. 'No, he's Tony. I've seen his birth certificate. The business is in his name.'

'That night you saw me outside the house. I left Grenville right after that. I had given up.'

'But … why?'

'I told you I had spoken to the local police. Detective Washington, she was nice, she gave me the benefit of the doubt when a lot of people in her position wouldn't have. She took me seriously.'

'But …'

'But as soon as it looked like we could prove that Tony Andrews wasn't who he said he was, that's when we ran into trouble.'

'I don't understand …'

'I went to meet Washington. There was someone else there. A guy from the US Marshals Service named Volcker. He said he knew what I thought and I was right, but it didn't matter. Tony Andrews is Casper Sturgis, but we can't touch him. He's out of reach.'

Casey waited for her to drop the bombshell. At the back of her mind, she already had an idea. The moving around. The way he never talked about his past. The fact that his name wasn't really Tony Andrews. The fence. The cameras.

'Your husband is in the federal witness protection program. He testified against some drug lord years ago and they set him up with a new identity. The reason no one could find him was because he didn't exist anymore. The government was protecting him.'

'Jesus,' Casey said. A million questions flooded her mind.

'Casey, I know this is a lot to take in, but it's the truth.'

'No ... I mean, it's crazy, but suddenly everything makes sense.'

'I'm sorry, I thought you knew. I thought you would have *had* to know.'

She put her face in her hands. 'Shit, all of the security. The fence. The door alarms. The gun. He told me someone broke into his apartment when he lived in St Louis. That you can't be too careful. All of that stuff... I was glad about it. It made me feel secure. I liked that he wanted to make sure we were safe. But now that you tell me this... I mean, I'm in witness protection and I didn't even know it? How is that even possible?'

'I'm guessing because your relationship post-dates him going into the program. You're not a dependent who was inducted in, you're somebody he met as Tony Andrews. I don't know if there are official guidelines, but maybe he didn't have to tell you. Maybe he was even encouraged not to tell you. Either way, what are they going to do, show up and tell you your husband is a reformed contract killer and a government witness? How do they know how you're going to react to that? What if you left him and told everybody?'

Casey considered that for a moment, imagining how that conversation would have gone. Wondering what her reaction would have been.

'Somebody probably decided it was safer not to,' Thessaly continued. 'To all intents and purposes, in the eyes of the law, he's not that person anymore.'

It was as though somebody had erased her entire history for the last few years, and replaced it with something that looked superficially the same, but was completely different.

'I've been trying not to think about what he's really doing on those trips for months. And now you show up and drop this ... this whatever it is on me and ...'

Thessaly looked down at her hands, clasped in her lap. 'I'm sorry. I can't imagine.'

'I'm the one who should be sorry. I mean your brother, I ...' Casey stopped and took a breath. 'He hasn't stopped whatever he was doing, has he?'

Thessaly said nothing.

'Jesus. I just don't know what to do. I was scared of him already, and now I find out I didn't know the half of it. What do I do now? And Aiden ...'

Thessaly leant forward and put her hand on top of Casey's for the first time. 'You need to get away from him. Both of you.'

'I've thought about it. I got close to doing it. But ... I'm really afraid he won't let us.'

'Then we don't give him the option,' Thessaly said. 'Because I think you've just given us both a way to get what we want.'

47

They walked to a pizzeria on West 39th, more for the warmth than the food. It was half-full, but the customers had gravitated toward window seats, so the tables at the back were mostly unoccupied. The lighting was dim in the back. Small, circular tables with red and white check tablecloths and a candle in the center. A Dean Martin greatest hits collection playing a little too loudly on the speakers. Thessaly ordered a large pepperoni to share, having to raise her voice above 'Little Old Wine Drinker Me' for the waiter to hear her.

'I'm not hungry,' Casey said.

'You're going to eat something,' Thessaly said seriously. 'You look so pale you're practically blue.'

Casey took another look around the area of the restaurant as the waiter made his way back to the kitchen. The nearest diners were twenty feet away, and they wouldn't hear any conversation over the music, but she lowered her voice anyway.

'He'll kill me. I know you want me to help me, but I can't do it.'

'Listen to me ...' Thessaly paused, choosing her words with care. 'It's not without risk.'

Casey snorted in laughter and then caught herself and straightened her face. '"Not without risk", God, you certainly know how to understate.'

'Look. You want to leave him. You told me that. You were planning to, until ... until he talked to you in the kitchen. And I understand exactly why that made you change your mind. But you still want to, don't you? You want to get yourself and your son out of harm's way.'

'That's it though, Thessaly. There is no "out of harm's way". He'll find us. He's smart, he's resourceful. How the hell could I possibly be sure that he wouldn't find us wherever we ran to? And how am I supposed to just ... just disappear? That's not the world we live in. Aiden's little now, but he'll grow up. He'll be on social media. He'll be findable, because Tony wouldn't ever stop looking. Whatever he's done, he loves Aiden. I would be looking over my shoulder until the day I die. I can't live like that. Even ... the way things are now, even the way they were before we talked. It's not the life I want, but it's better than that.'

'That's what I'm talking about,' Thessaly said. 'We don't put you out of harm's way, we put *him* out of harm's way.'

She blinked in surprise. Did she mean ... 'What are you talking about? Like *killing* him?'

'No!' Thessaly exclaimed. 'I mean ... I don't even know if I would want to do that even if we could be certain of finishing the job. But if we could make it so he goes away, so he never gets out ...'

'Wait a second, you said he was untouchable. Because of this cartel guy, the witness protection program. I thought you said that was airtight, the government made a deal.'

'It is airtight. That bastard will never do a minute of jail time for Mitch or for any of the other people he killed before 2004.'

It took Casey a moment to catch up. 'But Oswald Kinderman was after the deal.'

'Exactly. I looked this up. I went over all of it after I found out about the witness protection thing. He has immunity for all crimes committed before he cut the deal. But any crimes he commits afterwards?' She shook her head. 'He's out of the program. And this isn't a parking ticket or wire fraud; if he murdered somebody, they won't just kick him out. They'll put him away for good.'

'But you need me.'

'I need you,' Thessaly agreed. 'If you go to the police and tell them what you know, I think they'll be able to put together a case. You said the police in Cleveland don't have a suspect. You can give them their suspect.'

Based on her word? Casey wasn't so sure about that. But what if it wasn't just based on her word?

She opened her mouth to say something, but then decided to wait. She needed time to think this through. All of it. Thessaly Hanlon wasn't some kind of impartial party here. She didn't have to think about what was best for her child.

'Wait a minute. I've barely even been able to catch up with all of this. I mean, apart from your brother and the cartel stuff. I'm finding out now, today, that I'm in witness protection. What if the people he worked for...' She stopped. Didn't even want to start imagining further horrors, when she had plenty to deal with as it was.

Thessaly leaned forward, across the table. The candlelight threw angular shadows on her face. 'I don't think the cartel would be interested in you. From what I hear, that faction is pretty much out of business anyway. But still, if Sturgis's cover was blown and he was out of the program, I was worried you could be collateral damage if someone came looking for him. This way, even if someone does get to him, he'll be in jail. Away from you and Aiden.'

'And you would be just fine if that happens, right?'

Thessaly didn't blink. 'I wouldn't shed any tears, no.'

Casey looked down at the table. She knew she couldn't blame her for that answer. 'This is... I need time to think about this.'

Thessaly sat back from the table, put her hands up. 'Absolutely. I can't imagine what it's like to hear all of this, even though it sounds like where you were wasn't a picnic.'

'I'm picking Aiden up at six. Tony will be back home at seven. Oh God, I was planning on roasting a chicken tonight.' She laughed, incongruously. 'A chicken dinner, that's the first thing I have to think about tonight, right? A fucking chicken dinner.'

Thessaly made an effort at a reassuring smile. It looked brittle. She was worried. Didn't want to lose this opportunity. Casey couldn't help but hate her a little for it. 'You got this, go home, focus on dinner, read your kid a bedtime story. Have a stiff drink. Sleep on it. We don't need to do anything this minute. We don't want to, in fact. If we're going to go down this road, we need to do it right. And if you don't want to ...' she hesitated, and it looked like she wanted to choke on the next words. She got them out anyway. 'I'll understand.'

Casey wasn't sure that she believed that. She avoided Thessaly's eyes by looking down at the screen of her phone to check the time. They had been talking for longer than she had thought. 'I'll call you tonight. After Aiden goes down.'

Thessaly nodded. 'Only if you're ready, take some time.' She reached into her bag and took out a cheap prepay phone, placing it in the middle of the table. 'And call me on this, not from your regular phone. My number's programmed in.'

48

On the train back to Secaucus, Casey looked up the shootings at the Redlands Mall in 2001. She used the burner to do it. After Tony finding her search history on the tablet, she wasn't taking any chances.

There wasn't much there. If the shootings had happened now, or even ten years ago, there would be a lot more on the internet. Hell, there would probably be a twelve-part podcast about the case. But it had happened twenty years ago, so all she was able to find was an article in the *Star-Ledger* saying that two people had been killed and one critically injured in a shooting at the abandoned Redlands Mall. Police were looking for anyone with information.

She checked the address of the mall. It had been razed to the ground in 2007 and replaced with housing. There were a few pictures of the deserted mall on an urban exploration blog and a reference to the killings, but no other information.

The murder of Thessaly's brother had basically been forgotten about. Casey supposed that was the rule, rather than the exception. How many homicides were there in the United States every year? How many ended up unsolved?

Every year, there were probably thousands of people just like Thessaly, forced to go on with their lives knowing that the person responsible for the death of their loved one will likely never see justice. The only difference was, this time she had happened to cross paths with the killer, years later.

Thinking about it, she knew what night it had to have been. She remembered the rain coming down hard, so hard she could hear it hammering off the roof. She had gone to bed early with a migraine, leaving Tony watching the news downstairs. She had dosed up on Advil and fallen fast asleep, so if he had taken the car out, she hadn't heard it. But she remembered him sliding into bed a little after the rain stopped. The alarm clock said it was after four.

Thessaly had mentioned another man in the diner. A bald man in a suit. Who was this person that Tony had been meeting?

When Casey got to Secaucus she picked up the car and drove back to Grenville, making it back in time to collect Aiden from school. They got home and she put the chicken in the oven and peeled some potatoes. It seemed ridiculous, that she and Aiden were unknowingly in the witness protection program. Perhaps that explained how they were able to afford the house. Maybe the government paid toward it, or there was some kind of relocation grant. She wondered what the program would do if she contacted them, asked them if she could leave. What had Thessaly said the US Marshal's name was?

She was taking the chicken out of the oven when there was a soft ping from the screen on the kitchen wall. Aiden heard it from the living room and ran through to the kitchen, in time to see his father's car pull into the driveway on the camera feed from outside. Casey had always thought it was cute how excited Aiden was reacting to the alert that heralded a visitor. Before last year, she had never stopped to wonder why Tony liked to have advance warning of guests.

Aiden hugged him as soon as the door was open. He laughed and said it was nice to be missed.

'Did you bring me something?'

Tony sucked his teeth and said, 'I was pretty busy on this trip...' He waited for the disappointed look from Aiden before smiling and reaching into his coat pocket. 'But I did pick up a little something.'

He handed Aiden a box. Aiden squealed in delight and ran over to show his mother. It was some kind of action figure. Casey made the expected interested noises and said sure he could open it, but after dinner.

They ate without much in the way of conversation other than exchanging pleasantries about their days and Aiden's questions about exactly how many days it was until his birthday.

Nothing was really different from when they had eaten dinner together last night, or the night before. Except that everything was different. As she watched him act like he was a normal father, she felt consumed with rage. How dare Tony do this to her? To both of them? How dare he act as if this was a real life, rather than a sick illusion?

'You okay, honey?' Tony asked after a particularly long pause in conversation.

'Fine. Why do you ask?'

'You've been real quiet all night. Bad day?'

'Not really.'

'What did you get up to today?'

'Usual, I guess.'

'Laundry's still in the basket, I noticed.'

She blinked. 'What?'

Tony grinned and glanced at Aiden. 'Oh, I'm in trouble now. Sorry, I didn't mean it that way. It's just unusual. You're usually on top of everything. I don't know what us boys would do without you.'

'I went for a drive,' she said.

'Oh yeah? Where?'

'Nowhere in particular. Just had to get out, you know?'

Tony considered the idea for a moment. 'Sure. Most days I'd kill to have a day in the house by myself, but maybe that's just me.'

'Maybe it is,' she said. She wondered if his choice of words had been deliberate. He'd *kill* for it. Was that an inside joke? Did he enjoy the deception?

They cleared the plates and stacked the dishwasher. That uncomfortable silence still hanging over them. Casey forced herself to make small talk. He couldn't think that anything had changed.

As Tony was wiping down the surfaces, he seemed to think of something and turned to Casey. 'Oh, I forgot to say, I have to go away again tomorrow.'

Casey folded her arms. 'So soon? Anywhere nice?'

'Not really. Atlantic City, I'll be back Wednesday.'

She had long since stopped being disappointed when Tony went away, but she thought she better disguise the relief.

'Aiden will miss you. He likes it when you read him a story.'

'I'll bring him back something nice.' He leaned in and kissed her on the cheek. 'I'll be home before you know it.'

'I know.'

Tony took a beer from the fridge and went through to the living room to watch the tail end of a basketball game. That last thing he had said, probably without thinking about it, had flicked a switch within her. *I'll bring him back something nice.* He always did. A toy, a comic book, a snow globe, an action figure. What did these offerings represent? What were they intended to make up for?

She pictured the shelf above Aiden's bed, the one that was a pain to dust because it was where he lined up all of his action figures. How many of the damn things were there? Two dozen? More? And Aiden had positioned his Boba Fett figure in the dead center of the shelf, pride of place. The toy his father had bought him in Cleveland.

She gave him a couple of minutes to get comfortable, and then she took the burner from her purse and opened the back door. She went out into the yard and texted a short message to Thessaly Hanlon.

I'm in.

49

Thessaly texted back within thirty seconds: **Okay to talk?**

Casey went out back to take the call, down to the rattan love seat in the corner of the yard. She often came out here in the warmer months to read. She answered Thessaly's call on the first ring.

'How do we do this?' she asked, not bothering with hello. 'Do we go to the police?'

'Well, I'm still trying to work that out,' Thessaly answered. 'But you have no idea how good it is to have somebody else to talk to about it.'

'Actually, I have a very good idea.'

'Of course. Are you somewhere safe to talk now?'

'Yeah. Aiden's playing upstairs. I'm out in the yard. I don't know if Tony could have some way of listening in in the house. It sounds paranoid, but...'

'It doesn't sound paranoid at all,' Thessaly said.

Casey felt like she was seeing the world through new eyes since speaking to Thessaly. It was weird, but just the experience of speaking to someone else who knew what her husband was had almost rewired her brain. She was considering possibilities that would have seemed laughable a few months ago. She was sitting in the corner of the yard, the fence towering over her. The height of it had always made her feel a little boxed in.

Tonight it felt like a prison. She thought about all the visible defenses: the fence, the cameras, the keypad lock, and wondered what others there might be that she couldn't see.

'Are there any cameras in the yard?' Thessaly asked.

'Yes,' Casey said, glancing at the camera that covered a wide arc of the yard. 'But I'm in the blind spot.'

'Good,' Thessaly said. 'So, first thing we need to do is lay out exactly what we need to do. It isn't going to be easy. Volcker is ready to yank the three of you out of there at the first sign I'm still poking around at this. Whatever we do, we can't tip your husband off.'

'So who do we go to? The cop you were talking to?'

'Detective Washington. I think we can trust her. If we go to her and you tell her everything, maybe she can reach out to the cops in Cleveland and maybe they can get something concrete. DNA, prints. Maybe if you can get a sample of his hair or something they can—'

'What if she doesn't believe me? What if she tells this Volcker guy?'

'I don't think she will. But we need to make her believe your story, and I think we can do it. I don't think she can ignore it if it's coming from his wife.'

Casey hesitated. As soon as she said this, it would mean no backing out. Before she could change her mind, she spoke.

'I think there might be something else we can do.'

'What do you mean?'

Casey caught movement out of the corner of her eye as Thessaly spoke and looked back at the house to see the door from the kitchen opening.

'Honey?'

She hurriedly whispered, 'He's here,' and hung up, tossing the phone in the flower bed just as Tony appeared and started walking toward her.

'Little cold to be outside, isn't it?'

She shrugged. 'It's not that cold. I needed some fresh air.'

Tony approached, a smile on his face. Had he seen the phone before she tossed it? She stood up, taking a couple of steps away from the seat and the rose bed. He drew her in for an embrace, running his hands down her side in a way that felt uncomfortably like a subtle frisk.

'You don't mind me going away?' he asked.

'Of course not. Will I see you in the morning?'

He made a pained expression. 'I have to be on the road by five. Want me to put Aiden to bed?'

'Sure,' she said.

She ran the bath and when Tony was reading Aiden his story, she came back downstairs and into the yard. She had to root around in the flower bed for a minute before she found the burner. There were a half dozen anxious messages from Thessaly. She replied with a short message.

He's going away again tomorrow. Can you come to Grenville?

50

Casey had driven by the public park a few times when she first moved to Grenville, hardly noticing it. The first time she passed on foot, she had decided to see if she could cut through toward Main Street. She discovered that she could, but also that the park was deceptively large. Sixty acres according to the noticeboard at the south entrance. There was a pond and a play area for kids, and some winding woodland paths. She brought Aiden here often. She had always found it a calming place. She felt that more than ever now, and decided it was because she could be sure there were no cameras or locks. She had thought of the park immediately when Thessaly asked where she wanted to meet.

School was closed for the morning, a teacher training event that she had forgotten to add to the calendar on the fridge, so she had had to bring Aiden along. She was watching him play; another activity that always calmed her. He was wearing a bright red raincoat and a blue wool hat. He was halfway up the rigging on a little wooden pirate ship, anchored in a sea of wood chippings. Another kid in jeans and a green jacket was at the top, bracing himself with the flagpole, below a fluttering skull and crossbones. Aiden had no idea his life might be about to change forever.

Casey had stood up to issue another of her regular 'be careful' reminders when she saw Thessaly appear from the direction of the south gate. She wore a long coat and a wool hat. The day was cold but cloudless, so she didn't look out of place in sunglasses.

She took a seat at the other end of the bench. The same formation as back in Bryant Park in New York.

'So, how are you?' Thessaly said quietly, not looking directly at Casey.

Casey didn't take her eyes off the pirate ship. Aiden had scaled the rigging and was triumphantly standing in the crow's nest, the other kid having relinquished his position.

'I've been better. I didn't sleep last night. I told Tony I was ill. He offered to call his trip off, but I told him he should go.'

'What a sweetheart.'

'He is, sometimes,' Casey said, turning to look at her for the first time. 'That's what makes this difficult. I wanted to believe that that's the real Tony, not ...'

Thessaly bit her lip. After a moment, she said, 'I'm sorry. I know this is hard for you.'

'I've been thinking a lot about everything you told me the other day. It sounds insane, unbelievable. I really want to believe this is all some big misunderstanding, but ...' She shook her head. 'It isn't just the Cleveland thing, or the ... or what you talked about. It's lots of things, ever since I met him. I know him better than anyone, or I thought I did. I've been with him for seven years. There should be a hundred ways I could poke holes in your theory. I should be able to say he can't have been shooting your brother in New Jersey in 2001 because he was working in a bar in Australia or something.

'But instead, it's the opposite. It all fills in the blanks. It explains things I never had an answer for before. It explains the fence, the cameras, the paranoia. It explains those business trips. I thought maybe he was having an affair. God, I wish he was just having an affair.'

She laughed. Thessaly didn't join in. She straightened her face and continued.

'It explains why he's so quiet about his past. He knows everything about me, but I only know the basics about him. He grew up in Jersey, didn't go to college, worked as a truck driver for years. He always acted like it was too boring to talk about. But seven years is a long time to live with someone. The thing that really nailed it, the moment I knew you couldn't be making it up, was when you told me about your brother, about where it happened.'

'We went to Philadelphia Mills a couple of years back. It's one of those gigantic megamalls. Tony hates being places with too many people, but he *really* hated that place. We talked about malls for a little bit, just the kind of random conversation you forget about. But he said he liked dead malls better. He talked about this place he'd been once where it was all closed up. Out in Jersey. He said it was peaceful. Not a living thing in sight.'

'He was talking about the Redlands Mall,' Thessaly said quietly.

'I mean it has to be, right? He was always so reserved about his past, and I guess I noticed it at first and then just accepted it. Some people are like that. You know, closed off.'

'Sure,' Thessaly said, looking a little uneasy.

'But he couldn't help let some things slip through, and it seems like all of those little things back up what you're saying about who he really is. It's like I had this jigsaw puzzle with some missing pieces all this time, and you've given them to me.'

'I wish they made a better picture.'

'Me too,' Casey said, and then remembered another piece she wanted to ask about. 'The night you saw him at the Olympia, you said he was meeting another man.'

'That's right. I actually tracked him down briefly. Before I found…' she paused before saying the name, like it was an effort. 'Before I found Tony, I asked the waitress to call me if she saw either of the two men from that night. He left a number and I got him to come back.'

'So you saw him?'

Thessaly nodded. 'Spoke to him too. Turned out to be one of my dumber decisions.'

'Stop talking.'

'What?'

Thessaly followed her gaze and saw that Aiden was barreling toward them. She put her head down and started to look at her phone, acting like a stranger sitting on the same bench. Casey wondered if Aiden would recognize her from up close. Kids were observant, he might remember her from a couple of weeks ago, even in the sunglasses and with her hair hidden by the hat.

But he ran up to the bench at full tilt, braking his forward motion with both hands on the armrest nearest his mother. He didn't glance at the other lady on the bench, just breathlessly said, 'How much longer to play?'

Casey pushed his hair out of his eyes. 'Another ten minutes, sweetie.'

'Okay.' He turned and ran back.

'I'm dropping him off at school at noon,' she said when he had gone. 'Then we can get started.'

'I think the two of us should go together and see Detective Washington, tell her everything,' Thessaly said. 'But before we do that, I'd like to see the house.'

Casey had been half-expecting this. She knew Thessaly would want to see if she could find out more about what Tony had been doing, but she knew there was more to it than that. She wanted to see what his life was like.

'Okay,' she said after a minute. 'But there's somewhere else we need to go first.'

51

After hugging Aiden at the school entrance and telling him she would see him soon, Casey walked around the corner and saw Thessaly's car parked a hundred yards down the street, away from all the other parents' vehicles. She recognized the burgundy Subaru from a couple of weeks ago. As she approached, she glanced around to see if anyone was paying attention to her. Satisfied, she opened the passenger door and got in.

'Where to?' Thessaly asked.

'To visit a friend.'

Thessaly talked as they drove across town to Sycamore Road. She told her the rest of the story about meeting the second man at the Olympia.

'What did he look like?' Casey asked when she had finished.

'He was older. Bald with a mustache. Maybe five-ten, two hundred pounds. Sound familiar?'

Casey shook her head.

'I didn't think so,' Thessaly said. 'He didn't seem to know anything about your husband. When I tried to bluff, calling him Tony, it was news to him.'

'What do you think he meant, about "Tell him it's off"?' Casey asked, thinking about the conversation as Thessaly had related it.

'I don't know. All I do know is, there was something wrong

about the whole thing. Washington tried to track the guy down, but by that time the trail was cold, if it was ever warm to begin with.'

They parked outside Marcie Englehart's house. It was a long ranch house with a low-pitched roof and gray brick walls. Casey felt a tug of sadness as she saw the pair of terracotta pots flanking the door had been moved and stacked carelessly in the corner. There had been roses in those pots. Casey had hoped they would see another spring.

'Who lives here?' Thessaly asked.

'Someone I used to like a lot.'

The door opened and Mr Englehart appeared. He wore slacks and a sky-blue sweater over a shirt with a collar. He peered over the rims of his spectacles at the two women on his doorstep, not seeming to find Casey any more familiar than he did Thessaly.

'Mr Englehart? It's Casey, I was a friend of Marcie?'

He didn't answer, unless you counted the lines between his eyebrows deepening further.

'I used to come by with my little boy and read the newspaper to her?'

'Oh yeah,' Englehart said, Casey's words triggering a dim memory. 'She's dead.'

'I know, Mr Englehart, we spoke briefly at the funeral. Such a beautiful service.'

He paused and then said, 'Okay,' starting to close the door. Casey put a hand on it, pairing the action with a wide smile.

'I just dropped by because I had stored a couple of things in her potting shed out back. Would you mind if we got them?'

Mr Englehart grunted and took a moment to look at the two women, sizing them up. Evidently he decided agreeing to the request would be the line of least resistance, because he turned away from them and started rummaging with something hidden by the door frame. Casey heard the tinkle of keys jingling together. A moment later, he reappeared with a small brass key. The twin of the spare beneath the rock.

'You know where your stuff is?' he asked.

'Yes, there's no need to—'

'Good. Just leave it on the doorstep when you're done.'

The door swung closed. Not quite a slam.

Casey led Thessaly around the side of the house and into a back yard that, like the front, had seen better days.

'Marcie loved her roses,' she said.

'What's in the shed?' Thessaly asked.

Casey stopped and looked at the shed for a moment. The wood was painted green, and it had a peaked roof and a brass padlock on the door.

'Last year, after Cleveland, I thought a lot about leaving Tony. I hadn't really decided, didn't know if I really wanted to, but I started thinking through the logistics. Even before I really worked it all out, I knew it would be difficult. I might need to leave in a hurry.'

She led Thessaly toward the shed. She brushed some cobwebs off the padlock and slid the key in.

'So I put together a go-bag. You know, some money, a credit card, ID. Change of underwear, toothbrush, all of that stuff. The only problem was, a go-bag looks like a go-bag. If I had left it in the house, Tony might have found it and he would have known.'

She pushed the door open.

'I put some other stuff in the bag too. Something else I didn't want him to know that I had. I wasn't really thinking about why I was doing it, but I guess I knew, deep down.'

The interior of the shed was neat, but tightly packed with shelves on both sides and a small workbench at the back. It had plainly not been used since Marcie had passed away. Casey bent down and moved a sack of compost that was underneath the table out of the way. She pulled out the small case. She unzipped it. It hadn't been touched since she had slid it under there. Five hundred dollars in fifties, two changes of clothing for both of them, a couple of toilet bags. The *Star Wars* pajamas probably wouldn't even fit Aiden anymore, he had sprouted in the last couple of months.

Casey dug underneath the clothes and pulled out a cream-colored canvas tote bag. Carefully, she opened the bag and showed Thessaly what was inside.

The blue dress she had been wearing that night in Cleveland. She turned it over in her hands until she found the stain on the hem. A small reddish-brown circle, about the size of a quarter.

261

52

They left the go-bag in the trunk of Thessaly's car when they got to the house. Thessaly parked a safe distance along Elm Street and turned off the engine. Casey took out her phone and opened the app that controlled the cameras. She brought up the one showing the front of the house. It displayed the empty driveway and the grass and a little of the sidewalk. She tapped to pause the recording and the picture went blank.

Thessaly was looking at the screen. 'Won't he notice?'

She shook her head. 'Only if he happens to check it in the next couple minutes.'

They got out of the car and walked along to the house. Casey paused on the way to the door to get her keys out of her purse and noticed that Thessaly had stopped a couple of paces behind her, just inside the gate. She took a step back and put a hand on her forearm.

'Are you okay?'

'Yeah, just … Are you sure?' her gaze traveled over the front of the house. Casey turned and, for a moment, saw the house not as her familiar home of almost seven years, but as Thessaly saw it. The blinded windows, the black lens of the security camera staring back at her like a cyclops.

Casey nodded. 'It's off. As far as I know he never checks it.' A moment later she caught herself and grimaced. *As far as I know.*

Still, he would have to run through the whole day's footage to find the small gap, one that could plausibly have been caused by a system glitch.

She tapped the code in on the security panel on the door and then put her key in the lock. She opened the door onto the hallway and turned to face Thessaly.

'You don't have to come in if you don't want to. We can just take the dress to Detective Washington now.'

'No.' Her voice cracked a little. She cleared her throat and said it again, more firmly. 'No. I'm coming in. I want to see the place first.'

She led Thessaly through the house. First, she went into the kitchen and touched the small screen on the wall to wake it. The screen was divided into six squares, showing different camera feeds from the front and rear of the house. She tapped on the single blank square and restarted the camera that showed the front of the house.

'Does he have a home office? A computer?' Thessaly asked.

Casey led her through to the office. The window looked out onto the back yard. Not much to see other than the stretch of grass and the love seat and the too-tall fence. Thessaly glanced out at the yard for a moment and then turned to scan the spines of the books on the bookcase. Casey could have told her there was nothing remarkable there. Sports autobiographies. A DIY manual. A biography of LBJ. The same kind of suburban dad selection you would see in a million other homes like this. Nothing to give a hint of who the man really was.

Thessaly turned away from the bookcase and went over to the computer on the desk by the window and tapped on a key to wake the screen.

'You have separate accounts?' she asked.

'Yeah. I used to know his password, but he changed it after Cleveland. He left it unlocked one afternoon and I had a quick look at his emails. There was nothing, he deletes his inbox and his trash.'

Thessaly scanned the items on the surface of the desk. It was relatively neat. Keyboard, mouse, desk tidy, a set of keys, a block of Post-its.

She looked under the desk and reached down to pick up the trash can. The two of them peered into it. A browned apple core, a couple of opened bill envelopes, an empty soda can. As Thessaly bent to replace the can, she stopped. She put it down and reached under the desk. There was a scrunched-up square of pink paper where the trash can had been. Like it had bounced off the rim and been forgotten about. Thessaly picked it up and uncrumpled it on the surface of the desk. It was a Post-it note, with something scribbled down and circled a couple of times, like Tony had taken it down while on the phone.

138 Main.

'What's 138 Main?' she asked. 'An address? This anywhere you know?'

Casey thought about it. 'Doesn't ring a bell.'

Thessaly started to put the note in her pocket, stopped when Casey opened her mouth to object. Instead, she put it back on the desk and took a picture of the Post-it on her phone, then recrumpled it into an approximation of the size of ball it had been before, and dropped it back into the trash, replacing the receptacle under the desk.

'If it is an address, we're going to have our work cut out narrowing that one down.'

They went back through to the kitchen and Casey put on a pot of coffee while Thessaly sat on one of the stools at the island and looked up 138 Main Street in a few different locations.

'138 Main Street in Grenville is a sandwich place, apparently,' she called over as Casey took out a couple of mugs from the cupboard.

'That's Teddy's,' Casey said. 'They do a mean Reuben. It doesn't mean anything to Tony, so far as I know. What about in Cleveland?'

Thessaly was quiet for a moment, then shook her head. 'There are main streets all over the metropolitan area. None of them near where you were.'

'Atlantic City, check that. That's where he went today.'

She tapped on her phone again. 'No. Nearest Main Street is Pleasantville, New Jersey.'

'How many main streets are there in America anyway?' Casey asked as she poured the coffee.

There was a brief pause. 'Seven thousand, six hundred forty-four,' Thessaly read.

'Seven thousand Main Streets,' Casey said as she put the cup of coffee on the marble worktop. Her hands were shaking a little, and she could see that Thessaly had noticed. 'Kind of a challenge, huh?'

She offered Thessaly cream and sugar, but she declined. She sipped the coffee and looked around the kitchen again. Casey wondered what kind of a place Thessaly lived in. She didn't have kids and hadn't mentioned a partner. Everything about her said apartment, but she had mentioned a house.

'How much do you know about your husband's income?' Thessaly asked, looking at the cooker. Casey followed her gaze. That had cost eight thousand dollars when they remodeled last year. Thessaly put her cup down and seemed to notice the marble worktop for the first time. Two hundred bucks per square foot for the marble. Casey remembered seeing the bill.

'It's a nice house, isn't it?' Casey said. What she was really saying was, *It's too good to be true, isn't it?*

'Have you ever seen the books for the store? Do you know how well it's doing?'

'Not in detail, no. Tony said we were doing okay.'

'And if there are no money worries, it's not been a priority for you to dig deeper.'

'No money worries,' Casey said. 'My family was, well, I don't know if we were exactly on the poverty line, but it was tight, you know? We didn't go on big vacations every year. We only had one TV. I was so worried about money when I found out I was pregnant. When we got here and I saw the house, I did think ... well, I wondered what the catch was. But time went on, and the bills got paid, and I guess I got used to it. Or maybe not used to it. Part of me always wondered. I don't know, maybe I thought asking too many questions would be tempting fate. God, I sound like an idiot.'

'You don't,' Thessaly said. 'And unfortunately you were right. There was a catch.'

'That's an understatement.'

Thessaly looked around her again, taking in the surroundings. 'I read a lot about the witness protection program. They give you a budget for relocating, but once you're established, particularly if you're settled in with a job and everything, you're on your own. This place tells me there's another income stream coming in.'

Casey's eyes were on the marble worktop. 'It's drugs, isn't it?'

Thessaly shrugged, but didn't offer any other suggestion.

'I keep thinking about that man he was meeting that night in the Olympia. Do you think that was part of it?'

'I think so,' Thessaly said. 'But I don't know about drugs. I actually said, "deal's off" and he looked at me like ... well, like he knew I didn't know what I was talking about.'

'Oswald Kinderman, though,' Casey said. 'He was definitely involved in drugs. He had literally just gotten away with some huge bust, on a technicality. You think that was what happened? Tony was involved in some kind of deal that went wrong?'

'Could be.'

'And what you said he was involved in before, the cartel stuff. He must know all about it from that.'

'Maybe. My contact says he did some strong-arm work, up to and including hits. I don't know how much he was involved with the actual buying and selling. Maybe he's brokering deals or something. Maybe something went wrong with Kinderman and they got into a fight.'

Casey put her face in her hands. 'Shit. I could have told somebody, I could have ...'

'Hey, I told you. This is not your fault. You didn't make him like this. And you did tell someone, me. And you are doing something about it.'

Casey took her hands from her face and rubbed the heel of her hand against her right eye. 'I know, I just ...'

A soft ping noise emitted from the screen on the kitchen wall and she took a sharp breath. It couldn't be ...

Thessaly's brow furrowed. 'What's wrong?'

Casey ran over to the screen and tapped it. 'Oh fuck.'

She heard Thessaly gasp behind her as the screen awoke to show Tony's BMW in the driveway outside. The driver's door was opening.

53

'You're back.'

Tony stopped in the doorway and smiled. 'What a welcome.' He had one strap of his backpack over his shoulder, his phone in his hand.

She moved toward him and embraced him rigidly. 'Sorry, you surprised me. I thought you were coming back tomorrow?'

He put the bag down, then closed the door. 'I got done early.'

'I was just going to pick Aiden up from school.'

Tony glanced at his phone to look at the time. 'I'll take a shower and I'll come with you.'

'He'll like that,' Casey said quickly.

Tony smiled and started to move past her along the hallway, stopping when Casey didn't move out of his way. He looked at her questioningly.

'I thought you were going to take a shower?' she said.

'Yeah, I'm just going to dump my clothes in the machine.'

'I can do it for you,' Casey said, reaching for the sports bag he was carrying in his right hand. Her hand closed around the handle, but he didn't move to release it.

'It's okay,' he said. 'I'll do it.'

Reluctantly, she stepped aside and he walked quickly toward the kitchen.

'So it was a good trip?' She tried to keep her voice breezy. He had already noticed she was acting a little strangely.

'Same old, same old.' He gave her a curious look again. She never asked about his trips anymore, not since Cleveland.

'Aiden and I were going to order pizza for dinner, unless...'

'Pizza's good,' he said. He opened the door of the utility room. Casey tensed. He stepped inside and pulled some crumpled laundry out of the bag, tossing it in the machine. No bloodstains this time, so far as she could see.

He came back out and glanced at the coffee mug Thessaly had left on the worktop. He looked back at it a second later, his brow furrowing.

'You start drinking it black?'

'Milk smelled a little funky,' she said quickly. She picked the mug up and poured it out in the sink. She should have done that as soon as she had come into the kitchen. She needed to stop screwing around and commit to the role if she was going to get through this.

She dropped the mug in the sink and turned, wrapped her arms around him. He smiled and moved his hand up to brush her hair off her face.

'I like it when you take short trips,' she said, while running her hands up his chest to push his jacket off. He broke the embrace to let her push the jacket off him. She brought it around and folded it in half across her arm. 'If you're fast in the shower, we might have time for a proper welcome before it's time to pick up Aiden.'

He looked a little surprised, but pleasantly so. She hadn't exactly been taking the initiative lately.

'I like your thinking.'

They kissed. 'I'll see you in a minute,' he said, making for the stairs. Casey watched him go. As soon as he rounded the corner and started climbing the stairs, the smile vanished from her face. She stepped quietly into the hall and listened as his footsteps crossed the landing and a minute later, the shower started running. She ran back to the kitchen and opened the door to the small storage area. It was a cramped space that extended out from the corner of the kitchen into the void underneath the stairs. Coats hung from hooks along the wall on the left-hand side. Thessaly was crouching at the back. She looked like a cornered animal.

'He's in the shower,' Casey whispered. 'Give me thirty seconds. I'll turn the camera out front off again. As soon as you hear me climbing the stairs, get out of the front door and go. I'll keep him busy.'

54

There was no sign of Thessaly when Casey came downstairs. The door to the storage space was closed, as was the front door. If Tony checked the feed from the cameras over the past day, he would see that it had cut out at two points in the afternoon. But that would be all he would see. They drove to the school in Tony's car and Casey risked checking the burner phone while he waited outside to pick up Aiden. There was a message from Thessaly.

Call me when you can.

Tony was at the gate, watching as the class surged out from the doors toward the waiting parents. She called Thessaly, keeping the phone below the window, and put it on speaker so she could talk without holding it to her ear.

'Are you okay?' Thessaly asked, without bothering with hello.

Casey cleared her throat and put her hand in front of her mouth so that Tony wouldn't see her lips moving if he happened to glance back. 'Yeah, I'm fine.'

'What did he say?'

'I think he was suspicious. He saw your coffee. Thessaly, I think he's starting to suspect me. I mean, he can't know what we're doing, but he suspects something.'

Aiden had appeared at the door. Tony raised a hand to attract his attention.

Thessaly spoke again. 'Look, stay calm. Can you get away from the house?'

'No. I'm at the school. Tony's collecting Aiden. He'll be suspicious if I go out again, and I'm not leaving Aiden with him. Where did you go?'

There was a pause. 'I'm at the police station just now. I talked to Detective Washington.'

'What? But if she—'

'It's okay, she's not going to do anything yet, I swear.'

Aiden had reached Tony now, arms outstretched for a hug. They would be back at the car in a minute.

'You told her?'

'Yes. Everything we've got so far. And I showed her the dress.'

'So what does she think?'

'She wants to speak to you asap.'

Tony and Aiden were turning to walk to the car. They were ten seconds away.

'Casey? Are you still—?'

'Look, I'll take Aiden out for a walk after we get home. We often do that, it won't look suspicious.'

'What about the park?'

She sighed. 'I guess it's too late to back out now. Okay, meet me at the park in an hour.'

She hung up before Thessaly could reply and stuffed the phone into her jeans pocket as Aiden ran up to the car window.

55

Thessaly was waiting with a dark-haired woman that had to be Detective Washington in a gray Ford in the lot at the park. Casey made eye contact with both of them as she walked past with Aiden. As she and Aiden passed through the gates, she heard the sounds of two car doors opening and closing.

She saw Mary-Anne and Connor standing by the pond. They were usually here at this time, and she was glad today was not an exception. She wouldn't have wanted to leave Aiden playing on his own, but she didn't want to risk him telling his father about the people Mommy stopped to speak to. Casey exchanged pleasantries with Mary-Anne before she got to it.

'Listen, I have to call somebody about our washing machine. I hate to ask, but would you mind keeping an eye on Aiden for ten minutes?'

'Of course not, take all the time you need.'

'Thank you. I feel like I'm always dumping him on you.'

'It all balances out over time,' Mary-Anne said, smiling.

Casey turned to tell Aiden she would just be a few minutes, but he was already deep in conversation with Connor. She thanked Mary-Anne again and walked back to the parking lot. She got in the back of the Ford and sat down. Detective Washington turned around to face her. She was in her mid-thirties, with dark hair and brown eyes.

'Pleased to meet you, Casey,' she said.

'I wish I could say the same.'

Washington held her gaze, seemed to be sizing her up. She wondered how much this stranger already knew about her. 'I'd like to hear everything from you.'

Casey glanced back in the direction of the playground. 'I only have ten minutes, but I'll give you the short version.'

When she was done, Washington glanced at Thessaly, who had kept entirely silent the whole time, letting Casey tell her story. Then she looked back at Casey and nodded slowly. She reached down and took something from the footwell. When she straightened up, Casey saw that she was holding a clear plastic bag, sealed at the top. Inside was her folded blue dress.

'This is the dress you were wearing in Cleveland?'

'Yes.'

'I'll be honest, I don't know if this will be admissible. There's no chain of custody, nothing to say that the blood got on your dress the way you said it did. If this goes to trial, his defense can argue the blood got there some other way.'

Casey took a sharp breath. 'You mean we can't—'

'Hold on, I'm not finished. The most important thing we have here is you, Casey. If the blood on this matches Oswald Kinderman, then it lends credence to your account. It means we have a credible witness putting your husband in the area when the murder took place. My counterparts in Cleveland also have a witness who saw a man who matches your husband's description. I think if we give CDP a named suspect, they'll be able to find more.'

Thessaly let out a sigh of relief. 'That's great. So what's the next step?'

'Don't get ahead of yourself. There are a lot of ifs and buts here. But the most important one is all about you, Casey. Are you sure?'

Casey took her time answering. 'If you can guarantee Aiden's safety,' she said slowly, 'then I'm sure.'

Washington looked pained. 'I'll do everything I can to keep you safe. But nothing is a hundred per cent, so I'm going to ask a second time. Are you sure?'

She hesitated, then said 'Yes. I want out. I want the both of us out.'

'All right,' Washington said. 'I'll speak to the PD in Cleveland and tell them we might have information on a suspect for the Kinderman murder, and we'll see how fast we can get DNA on this bloodstain. And then I think the next step is to talk to Volcker.'

'Volcker?' Casey said, looking at Thessaly. 'The FBI guy?'

'He's with the US Marshals,' Washington said. 'But yes.'

'You can't talk to him until we're set. If Tony finds out about this ...'

'I know. Casey, we're going to do this right, I promise. We're going to make a plan, and we're going to get you out of there.' Washington's phone buzzed with a message as she finished speaking. She held eye contact with Casey for a moment before reaching for her phone.

'Casey, trust me. This has to happen,' Thessaly said as Washington read the message.

'You would say that, wouldn't you?'

Thessaly looked momentarily stung. She opened her mouth to say something: perhaps a retort, perhaps an apology, but she stopped when she noticed that Washington was still staring intently at her screen.

'What's wrong?'

It took Washington a second to react. She looked up and then turned the screen of her phone so they could see it. It showed a man in his fifties, bald, with a mustache and thin-rimmed glasses.

'That's him,' Thessaly said at once.

It took Casey a moment to put it together. 'Is that the man from the Olympia? The one Tony was meeting?'

'That's him,' Thessaly said firmly.

Washington's eyes moved from Thessaly to Casey. 'How about you, you recognize this guy?'

She shook her head. 'I've never seen him before. Who is he?'

Washington thought it over for a second before answering. 'Not the priority right now. Keeping you safe is what we're doing now. This gentleman can wait.'

'I've been thinking about a place to go,' Casey began. 'My cousin has—'

'No,' Washington said. 'It can't be a relative. Can't be anywhere he could find you if this goes south.'

'He doesn't know about Francine, I don't think I've ever mentioned her to him.'

'You don't think?' Thessaly cut in. 'You're going to stake your life on "don't think"? You think it's going to be impossible for your husband to track a blood relative down?'

'I'm afraid she's right,' Washington said.

'Definitely I'm right,' Thessaly said. 'I read everything I could find about the witness protection program after I found out about your husband. And the first rule is, they don't put you anywhere you have a connection to. That's what we have to do with you, Casey. We have to hide you until he's behind bars.'

Casey bit her lip and turned around so she could look through the rear window of the car. She could see Aiden playing with his friend as Mary-Anne looked on. His life was about to completely change. There was a good chance he would never see his friend again.

She spoke without looking back at Washington.

'Where are you going to put us?'

276

56

Wednesday, February 24

The result came back a lot faster than Washington had predicted. She had warned Thessaly and Casey to prepare for a wait of at least seventy-two hours. It came back in under twenty-four. The blood that had transferred from Tony's clothing to Casey's dress was a match to Oswald Kinderman. Washington called Thessaly with the news just after two that afternoon, and Thessaly called Casey. A half hour later, they were both sitting in Casey's car at the side of the road by the river when Washington's Ford pulled up behind them.

Washington got out and walked over to where they were parked, talking on the phone as she approached. As she opened the rear door, Casey caught the end of the conversation.

'...you and me both. All right. See you in a few hours.' She ended the call and put her elbows on the front headrests and leaned forward to talk to Casey and Thessaly. 'I just spoke to Mike Hatherley, the primary on the Kinderman case at CDP. He's on his way, going to be here tonight.'

'Tonight?' Casey repeated, glancing at Thessaly, who looked as surprised as she was. In a little over twenty-four hours, things had started moving at a pace she hadn't expected, or prepared for.

Washington nodded. 'I think I made his year. It means it wasn't one of his own men.'

'What do you mean?' Thessaly asked.

'With Kinderman's background, a lot of cops wanted him out of the picture. Professional Standards were sniffing around somebody in narcotics for killing Kinderman as payback for skating on the bust. We just handed Hatherley a great suspect who couldn't be further from being a cop.'

'You think that's why the DNA results came back so quickly?' Thessaly asked.

'I think it didn't hurt.'

Casey took a deep breath. 'So what next?'

'As of now, the plan is we're going to arrest your husband first thing in the morning.'

'What about Volcker?' Thessaly asked.

'You can't tell him,' Casey blurted out. 'I need time. I don't think we can...'

Washington held a hand up. 'It's okay, Casey, we're going to make this work. First off, I'm not speaking to Volcker yet. It's too much of a risk. I think there's a chance he'll be able to pull rank and take Sturgis out of there before we move. In this case, I'm more comfortable asking for forgiveness than permission. I'll wait until we've got Sturgis in custody, then I'll give Volcker a heads-up immediately. He won't be happy about it.'

'Are you okay with that?' Thessaly asked.

'Into every life a little rain must fall. Don't worry, I can handle Volcker. He'll understand.'

'Are you sure about that?'

She shrugged. 'Hopefully it won't matter. Cleveland has blood from the Kinderman scene that didn't match the victim. They think it came from the killer. If we have that, and Casey's testimony – which will count for a *lot*, believe me – it's going to be very difficult for them to ignore all of that.'

'What if the blood at the scene doesn't match Tony?' Casey said.

'I'm taking the gamble,' Washington said. 'But worst-case scenario, if it doesn't match, we still have you. The witness who saw the male in the blue jacket fleeing the scene already identified your husband from a six pack. And I think we'll find more.'

'A six pack?'

'A photo line-up,' Washington explained. 'The suspect plus five fillers.'

'What about Volcker? You think he'll make trouble about this?' Thessaly asked.

'I don't see why he should, when he knows the facts. Sturgis made a deal. Uncle Sam got what he wanted out of it. Sturgis has broken the deal, so there's no reason to play nice with him.'

'So how do we get Casey and Aiden out safely?' Thessaly asked.

'Do we need to go tonight?' Casey added, before Washington could answer.

Washington shook her head. 'No way. Tonight you have to do whatever you were going to do if this wasn't happening. That's very important. He can't suspect a thing.'

'But...'

'This is all about the timing,' Washington continued. 'We need to get you both out of harm's way before your husband knows what's up, but we can't tip him off, either. We need to make sure you're safe and then we'll make a move.'

'Where? You already said I can't go to my cousin's place, and there's nowhere else.'

'We have a safe house in Patchway.'

'Not far enough,' Casey said. Patchway was the next town, only five or six miles away.

'Let me finish. For one thing, it's not how far away it is, it's how secret it is. This place fits the bill. It's an apartment. I've used it before. It's not on any databases, and it's secure. Rent's paid through general expenses, only I know about it.'

'I don't know about this...' Thessaly said.

'Listen, you've done very impressively so far, for amateurs. But I'm a professional, and from the looks of it, so is Casper Sturgis. I'm playing catch-up on this guy, but one thing I know for sure, he's connected. If we put Casey and Aiden in a hotel somewhere, then he might be able to get to them. So the best thing to do is put them nowhere. A place that isn't on any lists. We're keeping this simple. The only people who will know where you're going are the three of us, plus Officer Lewis. He'll drive you there tomorrow morning. The place in Patchway is secure. We can get you there from the house inside of a half hour. Lewis and I will take turns watching the building. All we have to do is keep Casey and Aiden safe until Sturgis is locked up.'

'I want to go with them tomorrow,' Thessaly said quickly.

Washington opened her mouth, but before she could say anything, Casey said, 'I want you there too.'

'All right,' Washington said after a pause to weigh it up. 'Like I said, it's going to be the safest place to be.'

'Whose case will it be once he's in custody?' Thessaly asked. 'The cops in Cleveland?'

'For the Kinderman murder, yes. But the WITSEC thing complicates it, not to mention if he's involved in something bigger. Narcotics, or whatever it is. From what you've told me about all those business trips, drugs sounds right. More likely than not that crosses state lines. Anyway, I'm not going to be precious about it. I don't care who gets the credit. He needs to be put away, and we need to keep Casey and Aiden safe. Nothing else matters.'

57

Later that night, Casey went out into the back yard and called Detective Washington at the appointed time.

'I've got you on the speaker, Casey,' Washington said. 'It's just me and Detective Hatherley from the homicide unit at Cleveland Division of Police. We're in the interview room, nobody else.' She paused. 'How you doing?'

'I've been better,' she said.

'I hear you,' Washington said.

A male voice joined in. 'Hi, Casey. I just wanted to thank you for your cooperation. It's an important thing you're doing here.' Hatherley sounded gruff. He sounded like his comfort zone was yelling out orders, not soothing a scared witness.

'Kind of seems like it's the only option at this point,' Casey said. 'Where's Thessaly?'

'She's staying in town tonight,' Washington answered. 'I told her to get some sleep ahead of tomorrow.'

Casey wanted to laugh. 'You think anyone's going to sleep tonight?'

'No use worrying about it. Nothing to do now but focus on the play. Let's go through it again.'

They had planned tomorrow morning out in detail, leaving as little to chance as possible, because they were only going to get one shot at this. Everything had to appear to be entirely routine until the trap closed on Tony. The way the timing had worked out with the DNA results and Detective Hatherley was in their favor, because Tony usually worked from home on a Thursday morning.

The plan was for Casey to go through the morning routine as normal. Six-thirty alarm. Shower, breakfast, chit-chat. Then at around 7:20, she would kiss her husband goodbye, and she and Aiden would leave the house for the short walk to school. Only at that point would the morning divert from the routine.

Casey would walk toward school, but instead, an unmarked car would be waiting for her at the corner of Pine. She and Aiden would get in the car and the driver would call in to Detective Washington. As soon as Washington got confirmation that the two of them were in the car, the arrest would take place.

Given Sturgis's background, they weren't taking any chances. Four cars. Two would circle the block, ready to give chase to a suspect on foot if necessary. Washington and Detective Hatherley would knock on the door and make the arrest. All going to plan, he would go quietly. They would read him his rights and cuff him and put him in the car and take him down to the station.

'And meantime, Aiden and I are in Patchway.'

'Correct. You're going straight to the safe house. All being well, you won't be there long. I don't think we'll have a problem keeping him in custody.'

'But what if you're wrong? What if he gets out?'

'That's why we're taking care. Like I said, I'm not expecting you to have to hide out longer than a day or so. But it's there if we need you to be kept safe for longer.'

'Okay. I haven't packed anything, like we said.'

'That's good. Nothing to tip him off. Have you said anything to Aiden?'

'No. I'll tell him … shit. I don't know what I'll tell him.' In her mind, Casey had been playing different versions of the inevitable conversation with her son ever since it became clear what was going to happen. There wasn't a parenting guide for this situation.

'Don't worry about that now, Casey,' Washington said. 'We can talk about that together once the hard part's over.'

'Easy to say,' Casey said. In truth, she couldn't see any time in the near future where the hard part would be over. It was all hard from here on in.

'I've worked with a lot of kids as part of my job,' Washington said. 'At that age, they're resilient. They cope with sudden change a hell of a lot better than adults.'

'Losing his dad forever? Because that's what we're doing to him, Detective Washington.'

Hatherley's voice started to chip in for the first time in a while. 'Look, Casey, I don't—' he stopped abruptly, and Casey could imagine that Washington had shot him a shut-the-fuck-up look. Maybe even kicked him under the table. There was silence on the line for a long moment.

When Washington spoke again, her voice was sympathetic, yet utterly firm. 'You didn't make him who he is, Casey. Tony is doing this to his family, not you.'

'No,' she said after a moment. 'It's Casper Sturgis who's doing it.' It had been a struggle up to now even to think the name. This was the first time she had said it out loud.

There was another long pause before Washington spoke again. 'That's a good way of putting it, I guess.'

They went over the order of events three or four times. Casey kept her eyes on the house while Washington spoke and she asked occasional clarifying questions. Hatherley didn't say much other than murmurs of agreement. There weren't that many moving parts. Casey hoped that meant there wasn't much to go wrong. When they had gone through it enough times,

Washington asked if there was anything else Casey wanted to ask.

'No.'

'Then we'll see you in the safe house tomorrow,' Washington said. 'And by that time, this will all be over.'

'I hope you're right,' Casey said, and hung up.

She slid the burner into her back pocket and went into the house. The sounds of a basketball game echoed out from the den. She went upstairs and took a last look around her home.

58

Thursday, February 25

06:29

Lying on her side, eyes wide open, Casey watched as the digits finally clicked over to the half-hour and the soft chimes of the alarm clock sounded. Outside, she could hear the hiss of rain on the lawn. Tony leaned over her and hit snooze.

'Time to get up.'

'Hmmmm,' she murmured, as though she had got any sleep whatsoever.

Tony got out of bed and went into the en suite and a second later she heard water running and the buzzing of Tony's electric toothbrush. He had always been more of a morning person than her.

The last morning.

Whatever happened in the next few hours, it surely would be, wouldn't it? She thought through her usual routine. She would gently wake Aiden while Tony was in the shower, then she would hop in after him, and whoever was downstairs first would fix breakfast. Nothing fancy on a weekday. Cereal or toaster waffles.

Cereal or toaster waffles?

Another ten minutes to wash her hair, or just wear a hat?

It seemed utterly surreal that choices as mundane as these would have to be made today. But she remembered what Detective Washington had said.

Nothing can be different. As far as your husband knows, this is just a normal Thursday morning. Nothing out of the ordinary. Do whatever you usually do and leave. Don't rush, unless it's always a rush, in which case do. Don't be too quiet, unless you're always quiet in the morning.

Act exactly like yourself.

Why did that seem nigh-on impossible right now?

She forced herself to move. The toilet flushed and she heard the shower cubicle door squeak open. She got out of bed and guided her feet into her slippers. The hard floor surfaces downstairs were always cold this time of year, no matter how early you set the heating to come on. She crossed the landing and opened Aiden's door. He was on his back, mouth slightly open. On a weekend, of course, he would be up already. But never on a school day. Never when it might actually be convenient.

She bent down and caressed his brow, brushing the hair aside. And suddenly, she wished more than anything that she could go back and erase the last few days. Stop herself from talking to Thessaly, to agreeing to pressing the self-destruct button on their lives. But it was too late for all of that. The train was already in motion. All there was left to do was act normally.

'Wake up, sleepy head.'

Aiden's blue eyes slowly opened. He blinked a couple of times and sat up, opening his arms to hug his mother. She loved that about him. After settling into a routine when he was a baby, he had always been a great sleeper. You kissed him goodnight and that was it, like powering down. And when you woke him up, he was always pleased to see you.

''s for breakfast?' he asked, rubbing his eyes.

'Your choice, kiddo.'

He swallowed and opened his eyes fully. 'Pancakes.'

Not quite routine for a school day, but she said, 'I think we can manage that.'

She told Aiden to get dressed while she went downstairs to the kitchen and cooked up a short stack. Every move she made, she thought 'Last time.' Last time cracking an egg in this kitchen. Last time using the skillet.

Of course, it might not be. She didn't know exactly what would happen. Perhaps it would all go smoothly and she and Aiden would be allowed to return to their home. But would it still be their home? She thought about Thessaly's skeptical glances around. Wondering how they could afford the place. If it had been secured by ill-gotten gains, what then? To whom would the house belong?

She had barely begun to think about the logistics. How did you divorce somebody in prison? What if they didn't consent?

'Pancakes? This a special occasion?'

She turned to see Tony in the kitchen doorway, buttoning up his shirt. He was smiling, but he looked like something was on his mind.

'By request of you-know-who. It doesn't really take any longer than cereal, when you come down to it.'

'I'm not complaining.'

Aiden squeezed past him and raced to the table. He wasn't ordinarily so fast at getting himself dressed when it was cereal for breakfast. Abnormal behavior all over the place this morning; she wasn't doing a great job.

'You going in to the store today?' she asked as she poured syrup over Aiden's pancakes.

'It's Thursday. I'll go in after lunch. Oh ... I forgot to say, I might be going away again next week.'

'Again?' she asked. She had to force herself to sound a little displeased. That would be normal, after all.

'Sorry, couldn't be helped. This is the last one for a while.'

'Okay.'

She put Tony's pancakes down on the marble worktop and instructed Aiden to put his plate in the dishwasher when he was done.

'You're not eating?'

'Not in a pancake mood,' she said. 'I'll get something after drop-off.'

She showered quickly and dressed. In the tote bag she often took out with her, she had stuffed a change of underwear and another outfit for Aiden. Thessaly told her they could pick up anything else they needed once they got to the safe house. *The safe house*, Jesus. None of it seemed real.

7:15. She was running a little late, but that was normal enough.

She descended the stairs. Aiden was still in the kitchen, lining up some of his racecars on the table.

'I put my plate in the dishwasher.'

'Good job.'

'He reminded me,' Tony said, slapping the kid lightly on the back and smiling.

She reciprocated the smile without thinking about it. Could this be real? How could this man who, despite his flaws, had built them a happy home, be the monster she now knew he was?

'You be back here after drop-off?'

She had a line ready. 'I'm meeting Mary-Anne for coffee afterward, she's having issues with Paul again.'

'Okay, I thought I could make an early lunch before I go out.'

'Sounds good,' she said. 'I shouldn't be too long.'

Why did she feel so guilty? What would happen if she told him right now what was going to happen as soon as she left the house?

'Great, I thought—'

His phone buzzed in his pocket. He took it out and glanced at the screen. 'Just a second.'

He went out in the hall. She could hear his voice moving farther away as he answered the call. He lowered his voice and said something she couldn't quite hear.

'How come you guys get to have lunch?' Aiden asked, not looking up from his cars. 'Can't I stay home?'

'Sorry, you have to go to school. It's the law.'

'The law is dumb.'

She was looking out at the hallway. Tony had been gone a couple of minutes now. She wondered who was on the phone. A client?

She glanced at the clock on the wall. 'Oh my gosh, we have to go.'

She helped Aiden struggle into his coat and grabbed hers from the hook in the storage space where Thessaly had hidden two days before.

When she closed the door, Tony was back in the kitchen. The phone in his hand. There was a strange look on his face, like he had been given bad news.

'You okay?'

He nodded after a moment. 'Sure.'

'Who was it?'

He shook his head. 'No one. Just a supplier.'

'We're running late,' she said, eyeing the clock. 'So, I'll see you in an hour or so?'

'Yeah. Love you.'

'You too,' she said quickly, and leaned in for the kiss. The routine kiss before they parted each morning.

Last time.

She was pulling Aiden's hand gently behind her and halfway out of the door when Tony said her name.

She turned, hearing something strange in the tone of his voice.

'Yes?'

'You forgot something.'

Her mouth went dry and she felt her stomach lurch. Did he know? Could he sense something was wrong?

He reached down and lifted up Aiden's backpack.

'Oh Jeez, thanks,' she said. He threw the bag to her and she caught it.

'I'll see you soon,' he said.

59

Casey walked quickly, holding Aiden's hand. It was raining harder now, a large puddle forming in the spot where the sidewalk dipped outside the neighbor's house. She pulled up Aiden's hood as they walked, but left her own hood down. She didn't want anything obstructing her sight or hearing.

'Too fast,' Aiden complained.

'Sorry, we're running a little late.'

He started talking about something to do with *Jurassic World*, but it was as though she was listening to him from underwater. The words were vague, shapeless. She allowed herself to glance back when she had passed the next two houses on the street, half-expecting to see Tony standing out on the sidewalk, that same odd look on his face like just after he had taken the phone call.

She saw a car parked facing away from them. A man and a woman in front, wearing suits. Washington's people? She forced herself not to glance at the car as they passed. They really were running late. She was supposed to be at the pickup point on Pine Avenue two minutes ago.

They rounded the corner and she picked up the pace again. Aiden took a break from his monologue to protest.

What if the car wasn't there? What if something had gone wrong and she had been left to twist in the wind?

She turned the corner and saw the gray Ford Taurus. Engine on, wipers working. She felt something that wasn't exactly relief. As she got closer, she could see Thessaly in the passenger seat, craned around to look out at her. There was a man in the driver's seat. Dark hair with a little premature gray at the sides. Officer Lewis, that was his name.

She cast a glance behind her at the corner and then increased the pace again, practically dragging Aiden along behind her. Suddenly, she had a crazy certainty that Tony knew. He knew and he was running after her.

But he couldn't know, could he? Because in that case, he wouldn't have let her leave.

'Mommy, you're hurting me!'

'Sorry, baby,' she said as they reached the car and fumbled for the rear handle, quickly pushing Aiden in.

'Mommy, where are we going?' Aiden said, his expression brightening as he saw Thessaly, remembering her from two weeks ago. 'Oh, hi, Thessaly.'

'Hi, Aiden,' she smiled. 'No school today. We're going on a trip.'

Casey hurriedly climbed in after her son. 'Drive.'

Officer Lewis was already pulling away from the curb as the door slammed shut. He tapped the radio again. 'Kanga and Roo in the vehicle, repeat, in the vehicle and we're rolling.'

'Kanga and Roo?' Thessaly repeated. Lewis shrugged sheepishly.

A female voice on the radio. 'Copy that, now get out of here.'

Lewis turned onto the main road out of town and the speedometer jumped up to fifty.

'Mommy, I'll get in trouble.'

'You won't, I promise,' Casey said, hoping Aiden couldn't hear the anxiety in her voice.

'But it's the law.'

'Everything's going to be fine,' she said, trying to make herself believe it. 'Everything's going to be fine.'

The same voice again from the radio. 'Okay, we're going in now.'

'Is that Washington?' Casey asked.

Thessaly nodded. 'All going to be over soon.'

'What's happening, Mommy?'

'Nothing, sweetheart. We're taking a day off today.'

Lewis increased his speed yet again as they joined the interstate. Sixty miles an hour. Seventy. The car shook as it hit each bump in the surface. He switched the wipers on to fast, and they were only just keeping up with the rain.

Thessaly's phone pinged and she looked down at the screen, her brow furrowed.

'Is that Washington?' Casey asked.

Thessaly didn't answer. She had to tap her on the shoulder to get her to respond. 'No, it's just ... just a news notification.' She put the phone down and looked at the radio. 'Why hasn't she called yet?'

'She'll call,' Lewis said, his voice artificially nonchalant. 'It hasn't been that long.'

It had been almost ten minutes. Long enough.

Casey pointed out some cows to Aiden in a field they were passing. They were huddling together against the rain. Her eyes met Thessaly's in the rear-view mirror. Thessaly looked tense as all hell. She looked down at her phone again and started to scroll through whatever was on the screen.

'Shit,' she breathed under her breath.

'What is it?' Lewis asked, not taking his eyes from the road. They were in the fast lane, the needle nudging ninety as they blew past the slower cars.

'Mommy, she said the S-word.'

Casey shushed Aiden, her eyes on Thessaly in the front seat.

She was reading something on her phone. Something that seemed important enough to distract her from the eerie silence from the radio.

Thessaly put her phone in her pocket. 'I need to talk to Washington, can you try her again?' Lewis was slowing for the exit to Patchway. As soon as they were off the ramp, he pulled to the side of the road and tried the radio again.

'Sarah, do you read me? Do you have an update?'

Silence. The little bars on the display stayed stubbornly flat.

'Oh, God,' Casey said quietly.

Lewis looked pained. He glanced back in the direction of the highway, as though weighing up turning back around and heading straight back to Grenville. He exchanged a glance with Thessaly, not bothering to mask the concern now. It had been twenty minutes. All three of them were thinking the same thing. There was simply no way Washington would have forgotten to check back in, no matter what had happened.

He put the car in drive and started out on the road again. Nobody spoke, other than Aiden's occasional observations on the things he saw as they passed. Thessaly kept her eyes fixed on the radio on the dash.

As they pulled into the lot outside an ugly three-story apartment building, Lewis's phone chirped with an incoming call. He hurriedly brought the car to a premature stop and fumbled in his pocket.

He glanced at the screen and answered with his name.

Casey was close enough to hear the voice on the other end of the call. But it wasn't Washington's voice. Whoever was on the other end of the call was male, and he sounded panicked.

Lewis listened. He took an intake of breath a couple of times, like he wanted to say something, but then kept listening. Finally he spoke. Just two words.

'Oh, God.'

PART 4

Sturgis

60

Tony Andrews was a real person.

That revelation had been as much of a surprise to him as to anyone else. The other names had felt like what they were: convincing yet false identities. But this name, this life, was different.

After the trial in 2005, he had been Ed Barker for two years, a warehouse handler in Palm Springs, California. The city had been chosen for a variety of reasons, not least because it was on the opposite coast from his old stomping grounds. The population of Palm Springs triples in the summer, making it a great location for the program. You can come in with the crowd and be blended in by winter.

He had to admit he had enjoyed it for a few months. It really was like the 'welcome to the program' materials had promised. A new start, a chance to put his old life behind him and become a productive member of society. It was a radical change from the years of slowly building stress: working for Vicente, getting pinched by the feds, the constant looking over his shoulder while everything was still up in the air. And then the stress of the trial itself. Standing across a courtroom from Vicente and spilling his guts while the old man tried to burn holes in him with his eyes. He didn't feel guilt, exactly. He had to look out for number one. Vicente wouldn't have hesitated to do the same thing to him if their positions had been reversed.

But after his testimony was done and his handlers were satisfied, it was a weight off his shoulders. Ceasing being Casper Sturgis was like quitting a job you once loved but had grown to hate. He enjoyed the vacation for months. The little apartment, getting used to answering to the name Ed. Even the work. It was physically hard, but mentally undemanding. He lost weight, noticed that his upper body was becoming as toned as it had been in his twenties. It was like a government-funded life-coaching service. A whole new you. It was a pity it wasn't available to the general populace. The only downside was the money. Or to be exact, the relative lack of it.

He drank with some of the guys in a bar next to the warehouse after work. A couple of them asked him where he had lived and worked before, but they were as incurious about those things as men usually are. They were more interested in his opinions on sports and politics, and that he bought his round. He socialized enough not to stick out, just as the program advised. There was one man who recognized something in him, though. A supervisor at the warehouse named Rick. He said there was a little money to be made on the side for a man who knew what he was doing. He thanked Rick but said it didn't sound like his kind of thing. He meant it, in a way. It might have been Casper Sturgis's kind of thing, but it wasn't Ed Barker's.

In general, he felt good. There were things about his old life he missed, of course, but in those early days, he didn't think about it often. He suspected it wouldn't last. After a while he had been proved right.

The novelty wore off. The relocation money was exhausted after six months, and he was down to living on the minimum wage plus overtime that Ed Barker, warehouse drone, brought in. His contact officer at the program in those days had been a skinny, balding Boston native named Jeffrey Grant. Grant was satisfied that things were going smoothly, that the new Ed

298

Barker had settled perfectly into anonymous civilian life, that he would be one of the success stories. He signed off on the one-year review and the relationship moved into the hands-off stage. A twice-yearly check-in from then on, but no regular contact unless there was a problem.

For weeks ahead of the review, he knew that he was going to take advantage of the scaled-down contact. The next time he saw Rick he asked him if his offer of money on the side was still open. It was.

The requirements were simple. He would carry in small packages provided by one of Rick's contacts and pack them in the boxes that were marked with a non-standard code on the label. As long as he did that, there would be an envelope with some money waiting for him on a Friday. He had a pretty good idea what the packages contained. It amused him to think how much more experience he had in the movement of such goods than Rick, who viewed him as a competent but simple-minded worker bee. The money was good, double what he was making legitimately.

But he knew it couldn't last, and it didn't. Rick was sloppy. He talked big, but his mistakes were frequent, his willingness to take unnecessary risks a red flag. He made sure to distance himself enough that when the bust came, none of it could be tied to him.

Grant was suspicious, of course he was. More than suspicious, the asshole actually had the nerve to look *disappointed* in him when he was less than satisfied with the answers to his questions. Grant was easy to maneuver around. In the end, he did the only thing he could do – moved his charge to another posting and warned that a closer eye would be kept on him.

After that, he was Kevin Rusterson for three years. Grant was as good as his word. The leash was tighter this time. He was relocated to a small town. Dyersville, Iowa. Another shitty manual job. It was tougher to supplement his income out in the sticks, which was probably the main reason he had been placed there. His Jersey accent stuck out. The rural types were a little more nosey, quicker to ask questions. When he was moved on from there, it wasn't his fault. One of Vicente's men had shown up asking questions. He called Grant's boss, said that he had been put in danger with this relocation. It was basically true. The program yanked him out of there and Grant was reassigned.

None of the small-town bullshit this time. It had been a near miss in Dyersville. He wanted somewhere bigger, and he wanted to be set up with a decent job. His own business. To his surprise, he got everything he asked for.

St Louis. A Goldilocks city: not too big, not too small. His new contact at the program had noted that he had worked in automotive repair after leaving high school, and set him up with an auto parts business. The name Tony Andrews. It went smoothly for a year or so, and then his new contact officer mentioned they might need to transfer him again. Nothing specific to him, something to do with them having too many witnesses clustered in that part of the Midwest. They offered to sweeten the deal with a bricks and mortar business to take over.

He was thinking it over when he got the invite to the lawyer dinner. He almost ducked it. If he had, he might still be in St Louis. But on that night he had met Casey, and everything had changed.

He had had his share of women, but Casey wasn't like anybody he had known before.

She was beautiful, yes. That was what had caught his attention at first. But she was more than that.

After a couple of weeks, he was in love. He had been married briefly in his old life, and the experience hadn't made him want to rush back to that. Casey was different, though. Different from anyone else he had met. She seemed to like the things about him that put other people off. He told the program he didn't want to take the transfer to Pennsylvania. He wanted to stick around in St Louis, be Tony Andrews from now on. They said they couldn't guarantee his safety. He didn't care.

But then that day Casey called him, her voice shaking a little. She wanted to meet. She had news.

He called his contact officer that afternoon and said that he had changed his mind. He would take the transfer to Grenville. But he wanted a house, not another apartment. He had a family now.

And for a couple of years, he really had been Tony Andrews. But the relocation money dried up again, and it was tougher to make legit money with the store in Grenville than it had been in St Louis. And not just that. He missed the life. He was doing work that he could get by in, but he wasn't doing the thing he was good at, the thing he had been made for.

When the next offer came, this time from a wholly un-expected source, it was easy to say yes.

No small-time shit. Clearly defined jobs for good money. He went back to work.

It was easy to cover. The business took him out of town from time to time, so Casey didn't question it when he had to go someplace on short notice. The money rolled in as the jobs were notched up. The mortgage arrears were cleared in months. He decided he didn't have to choose. He had the best of both worlds. He could be two people.

And he was. He balanced it perfectly. Everything went like a dream, until Cleveland.

Casey's Aunt fucking Betty, or whatever the hell her name was. If she had looked where she was going when coming down those stairs, none of it would ever have happened.

The Kinderman job had gone south. He hadn't expected the other man to go on the offensive, and had let him get too close. Instead of a nice, clean double tap to the back of the head, there had been a struggle for Kinderman's knife. He hadn't killed anyone with a blade for a long time. He had very nearly lost the fight.

When he saw Casey in the lobby of the Seabreeze, for the first time he could remember, he was utterly unprepared. She knew something was wrong, and there was nothing he could say that would convincingly explain everything away. When he was disposing of the clothes, he noticed that some of Kinderman's blood had gotten on him. He wondered if Casey had seen it.

She was quiet for the next few days, and he began to hope she would just forget all about it. But soon he came to accept that it was a vain hope. She had changed. Knowledge was a curse. Not that she really knew anything, of course, but for the first time, she knew there was a side to her husband that he had kept hidden.

Still, he was almost impressed when he discovered just how much of it she had uncovered. He knew she had made the link with Kinderman, but it was a shock to go through her online activity and discover how much she had put together. There was one good thing, though. She hadn't told anybody. She was thinking about it, but she didn't know who she could go to. A line in her notes jumped out.

I just want it to stop.

He knew what he had to do. He hoped she would go along with it. If not, he didn't want to think about what would have to happen.

It had almost gone back to normal. It wasn't quite like it was before, but it was close enough. He imagined it must be something like a marriage that carries on after an affair. Both sides working at it, but with something else always in the room. It wasn't perfect, but it was good enough.

Something had changed again in the last couple of weeks,

though. She had tried to hide it, but he knew. She had said nothing about Cleveland, asked him no unusual questions. He had checked her laptop thoroughly. The one thing that had stuck out was the woman who had been outside their house that day. The runner. The way Casey had acted so weirdly around her, and the way the woman herself had acted. Then he saw Casey looking out of the window that night, jumping when she realized he was behind her. He checked the camera later and sure enough, she had been out there. The same woman.

Something was up. Whatever it was had simmered away over the last couple of weeks. And something had changed very recently. Something was going to happen.

When the phone rang on Thursday morning it was a shock, but it wasn't a surprise.

61

'Who was it?'

Casey looked back at him from the kitchen as he stood in the doorway, gripping the phone so tight that his knuckles were white. Her hazel eyes seemed like the eyes of a stranger now. Someone who's been caught doing something she shouldn't. It would have been harder to deal with the betrayal a year ago. Now it just felt like an inevitable next step in a journey neither of them had wanted to take.

The voice on the phone had been economical with the details, but had been very clear as to what was about to happen and what he should do now.

Let her leave, we know where she's going. We can talk to her, don't worry about it. When they get there, just go with them. Do not say anything. Sit tight and wait.

'No one,' he said. 'Just a supplier.'

'We're running late,' she said, glancing at the kitchen clock. She *was* running late. She had been acting a little strange all morning. All week, really. 'So, I'll see you in an hour or so?'

'Yeah. Love you.' The words sounded like someone else was speaking them.

'You too.' They kissed, and she was rushing away. So quickly that she forgot Aiden's backpack. She never did that.

They weren't going to school.

Let her leave.

What the hell was happening? He had an inkling. He had been on his guard for days now. But everything was moving so fast. He went to the window in the living room. Casey and Aiden were already out of sight. It was raining harder than it had been, the sky as dark as late afternoon.

When they get there, just go with them.

No. If this was moving too fast for him, it was moving too fast for his employer too. That phone call hadn't been part of a careful strategy. Clearly, they had only just been tipped off. They wanted to warn him not to do anything stupid. But was that to protect him, or them? There had been no real details in the brief phone call, but the instructions were enough to tell him a lot.

Let her leave.

She was working with the cops or the feds. They needed her, which meant she must have agreed to testify. But what did she know? Really know? She knew he had killed Kinderman in Cleveland, but she had no proof. Or did she? Suddenly, the fact he hadn't been able to find any evidence that she had continued to investigate him was in itself suspicious.

Go with them.

They were coming to arrest him. This was coordinated. He was expected to be caught unawares.

We know where she's going.

The police station? No, it sounded like they were talking about a safe house.

Do not say anything. Sit tight and wait.

For them to come to the rescue? Or for them to cut him loose and make sure he couldn't implicate them?

No. Fuck the instructions. He was changing the script.

He descended the stairs to the basement and took the key from his pocket to open the steel cabinet. He took out the Glock, checked the load, put it in his jacket. There was a small canvas bag with two thousand dollars in it. He took that. Lastly, he lifted out the AR-15. He wanted to be out of here by the time they knocked on the door, but he knew they would come after him. If they had Casey, they were on their way to knowing everything.

He would take the BMW and put some miles between himself and Grenville. He could find someplace to hole up. Then he would make them tell him where Casey was hiding with his son. It was his own fault, really. He should have taken action a month ago, once he was sure. He should have known the marriage was dead from that point. Sentimentality had never been one of his vices before. Seven years of marriage had obviously brought it out in him.

He had left the BMW in the garage overnight. He took out his phone as he climbed the steps from the basement, accessing the app to control the garage door. As he reached the ground floor, he heard the sound of an engine from outside on the street, a car slowing, stopping. *Already?*

He went to the side of the window and looked out between the blinds. A silver Ford Taurus, parked deliberately to block the driveway. A woman and a man getting out of either side. Cops. He thought he recognized the woman. He had seen her around town. He started moving toward the back door and then stopped. He switched apps on his phone and brought up the feed from the cameras out back. There were two other cops stationed just beyond the back fence, guns drawn, alert, waiting for him to run.

Surrounded.

But the two out front didn't have their guns drawn. They were expecting to be the first sign of trouble.

They were a little late.

The two of them walked up the path and a second later, he heard the bell ring and a knock on the door. They didn't announce themselves.

He hesitated for a second, sorting through the dwindling options now available to him. Then he switched back to the other app on his phone and tapped on the button to open the garage door. He heard the low bleep from outside and the electronic hum as the door started to swing slowly up.

He heard a raised voice from outside. The two of them stepped back into view, guns drawn now, eyes on the garage door.

Now that they were closer, he could see that they were both wearing vests under their raincoats. He was glad he had taken the AR-15.

The two cops started to approach the garage door, guns aiming at the widening gap. He raised the AR-15 and trained it on the male cop, planning to take the bigger target out first. But the woman must have caught movement from the window out of the corner of her eye. She yelled out to her partner as she turned, raising her gun. He pulled the trigger and sprayed them both with automatic fire. He aimed above and then below the vests. He saw both jerk with the impact of the bullets. The woman got two wild shots off before going down.

He ran for the door.

The cops were lying motionless on the lawn. The shattered glass from the living-room windows sprayed out over them. They were both hit in the head and legs. The man had an entrance wound in his left temple, eyes open, definitely dead. The woman was face down, but didn't look in much better shape. He glanced at the Taurus blocking the driveway, and remembered that it had been the man who had gotten out of the driver's side. He kneeled beside the body, dug in his hip pockets and found his car keys. He ran for the Taurus as he heard raised voices from somewhere out of his line of sight. The two around the back scrambling to get around the front, perhaps. Or maybe others he couldn't see.

He heard the blare of a siren and saw a marked police car accelerate toward him. No hesitation. He raised the AR-15 and sprayed the windshield with bullets. The car swerved, mounted the sidewalk and crashed through a perimeter hedge before coming to a stop. He fired another burst through the passenger window and then got behind the wheel of the Taurus.

He turned the key in the ignition and put the car into drive. Another police car rounded the corner at speed, approaching from the opposite direction. He put his foot down and took off from the curb, aiming to blow right by them. They swerved in the road and turned side-on, trying to block his path. But this was a wide road. Even perfectly positioned in the middle, there was a gap at both sides. A uniformed cop leaned out of the window, aiming his gun as the car accelerated forward.

A bullet smacked through the windshield on the passenger side. He put his foot down and aimed at the rear of the police car. Easier to shunt from the rear, no engine. There was almost enough space to pass without touching the car once he had mounted the pavement. The edge of the bumper clipped the rear of the police car and he smashed past. The Taurus bumped and skidded and found purchase again, gaining speed as he blew past the police car and across the intersection.

Four dead cops, and he was just getting started. One thing was for sure. Tony Andrews was no more after today. Casper Sturgis gripped the wheel and put his foot down.

62

The sky lightened and the rain eased off as he headed out of town. A couple of miles later, he saw his next mode of transportation. Before that, he saw the people. There were two of them. A man and a woman, maybe mid-twenties. She was standing by the passenger door of the black Ford Mustang while he stood at the hood and peered inside. She wore slacks and a green raincoat. He was coatless, dressed in jeans and a black tennis shirt that was drenched with rain.

Sturgis pulled the stolen Taurus to the side of the road in front of them and got out.

'Having problems?'

The woman didn't respond, eyeing him warily. The guy straightened up and smiled broadly. 'I think we're okay, thank you.'

Sturgis kept approaching, gestured at the engine. 'What was it?'

'Running a little rough. Looks like the distributor cap came loose.' He gestured at the cap. Sturgis was impressed despite himself, not many men under fifty would know a distributor cap from the fuel cap these days.

The kid walked around to the driver's side and started the ignition. It was one of those push-button jobs. The engine purred to life and he grinned, showing a set of perfect teeth. 'There we go, Stacey, told you.'

'Let's get out of here,' Stacey said, coming around to the passenger side.

'Appreciate you stopping, mister,' the kid said, wiping his hands on his jeans.

'Anytime,' Sturgis said. 'This is a nice vehicle.'

'It is. Rental unfortunately.'

'I think I'll take it.'

'What?'

Sturgis reached behind him and took out the Glock, pointing it at the kid. He looked perplexed, then slowly raised his hands. His girlfriend screamed. He visualized it. The kid, then the girl. He barely had to think about it at this point.

Sturgis's finger tightened on the trigger, then loosened. He just needed the car. Killing these two would make no difference either way at this point. He glanced up and down the quiet highway. Had to be at least five miles to anywhere, in either direction.

'Give me your phones,' he said.

Driving away in the Mustang, he decided he really was getting sentimental. He would be making up for that later today.

'What the fuck did you do? I told you not to—'

The voice on the other end of the phone was frantic, angry too. But Sturgis was angrier.

'Shut up,' he said. 'You gave me five seconds of a head start. I could have used a little more finesse with more notice. I wouldn't have had to shoot anybody, or get shot at. This is on you.'

'This is *not* fucking on me! I told you to sit tight.'

'If they've got Casey, they've got me,' he said. 'I know some of what she knows. She might have more. Where is she?'

'You killed cops. You think we can sweep this under the rug?'

'I don't give a shit what you can sweep under the rug. You told me you knew where she was going. Where is it?'

'Don't make this worse.'

'You have no idea how much worse I can make this. She has my son. Tell me where the fuck she is.'

There was a long pause and a resigned sigh. 'I take it you're going to kill her?'

Sturgis said nothing.

'Either way, we do need to deal with her. Her friend too. So if you insist … the police have her in a safe house in Patchway. I can make sure the cop is out of there if you give me a half hour. You got a pen?'

'I can remember an address.'

63

Patchway wasn't far. If the cop was out of there, all well and good. If he wasn't, Sturgis didn't intend to let him stand in the way.

Seven years. Seven years of marriage. In all honesty, this morning had just crystalized the decision. The Cleveland situation had broken them. If it hadn't been for Aiden, he would have made a decision before now.

Aiden. It was funny, he had never really cared about anybody before. But Casey hadn't just decided to betray him, working with the cops. She had betrayed all of them. Sold out her family. She was planning to take Aiden away from him for good. He wasn't going to allow that to happen. In a way it was his own fault. He had hoped she would be able to move past the unfortunate knowledge she had gained in Cleveland. It had been a stupid hope.

Patchway was the lower-rent twin of Grenville. It was the place you settled for if you couldn't afford better. He had tossed his phone on the way out of Grenville, but there was a map in the glove box of the rented Mustang. He wondered where the young couple were from, where they had been going before they had the bad fortune to run into him.

He found Salem Street quickly. According to the voice on the phone, Casey and Aiden were in an apartment building at the north end of the street. They were with the woman, Thessaly. She was the one who had caused this. He didn't know how, but somehow she had brought all this down on them.

He found it easily. An ugly stucco building, three floors. The kind of place that blends into overcast skies. There were only two vehicles in the lot outside, and neither of them looked like they could conceivably belong to the police. That was good. Maybe they had been left alone. Two women and a kid. He hoped the apartment was big enough for him to move Aiden to another room.

Life was going to be very difficult for a while. Probably a long while. Thanks to the actions of his wife and this other woman, Aiden's life was going to be turned upside down. He would never be able to go home. Would never be able to see his friends again. He would grow up without a mother. But he would have his father. The one person in the world who would do anything for him.

Sturgis parked around the corner. He took the Glock out of the bag and put it in his jacket pocket. He hadn't thought about the logistics yet. From the look of the building, he knew the apartments would be small and mean. He didn't have a suppressor, so he would have to kill the women with his hands or with a blade. But how could he make sure Aiden didn't see anything? It was going to be hard enough explaining why Mommy had gone away without traumatizing the kid.

He might have to take them someplace else, or lock them in while he took Aiden down to the car. Yes, that was the way to do it. Get in, take their phones, lock them inside and take Aiden down to the car. Tell the kid he would be back in five minutes. He could make as much noise as he wanted after that.

He regarded the building. The safe house was apartment 2-B. Looked like two apartments to a floor. On one side the windows were all covered by blinds. On the other, he could see an older woman with red hair framed in one of the windows as she scrubbed the inside of the glass with a sponge. She gave Sturgis a suspicious look as she saw him staring.

One flight of stairs. It was neat and well-kept. A pot-plant on the landing. The apartment opposite had an expensive-looking red door and a nameplate that said, *Carlton, 2-A*.

2-B looked like all the others in the building, and there was no nameplate. There was no doorbell, either. He flattened his palm over the peep hole and knocked hard on the door, putting his ear to it to listen.

A second later, he took his ear away as he heard the door behind him open.

'Can I help you?' It was the woman he had seen cleaning the window. She was wearing sweatpants and a blue smock, and had rubber gloves on. In contrast to her words, she didn't look like she wanted to help him in any way. She was squinting at him through the tinted lenses of her glasses.

'Just visiting,' he said. There hadn't been a sound from inside, or if there had been, it had been drowned out by this woman.

'It's against the building rules, you know.'

'I'm sorry, I'm not sure I ...'

'Airbnb. I know what's going on. That place lies empty for weeks at a time and then some weirdos show up for a few days. They're not supposed to have that in here. I don't know who the owner is, but ...'

'Someone ... checked in here today, right?'

'Yes. Two women and a little boy. At least they're probably not going to be having a party, but ...'

He was tiring of this conversation. Clearly, this was the right apartment. He turned as the woman was speaking and banged harder on the door. He didn't bother to cover the peep hole this time. Let them see him. There wasn't any other way out, unless they climbed out of a window, and he would hear that.

314

'Excuse me, sir, I was *speaking* to you.'

He didn't turn around. Banged again, harder.

'Obviously they're not in. I'm going to have to ask you to leave.'

He turned around, stepped forward. 'Did they get here in a car?'

She flinched back. 'Yes, I think so. There was a man with them but he left almost immediately. In quite a hurry.'

'What about the women and the boy? You see them go anywhere?'

'No, but I was watching *Murder, She Wrote*, so ...'

He turned around and eyed up the lock. The door didn't look too strong. He was glad he wouldn't have to try breaking down a sturdy one like the neighbor's.

'Now if you'll please—'

He raised his foot and smashed it into the door. He heard a crack and it bent in a little. The woman emitted a shocked gasp behind him as he slammed his foot into the door below the handle a second time, a third time. Finally, it cracked open on the third kick, the door swinging back and hitting the wall.

He heard the neighbor's door slam shut behind him, followed by a lock slotting home and the rattle of a chain. He wondered how long he had before the police got here. Long enough. He went through the small apartment, kicking open doors, opening closets, upending furniture.

They were gone. In the bedroom, the bed was stripped for a new occupant, new sheets still in their packaging on top of the mattress. He saw something shiny and colorful in the corner and bent to pick it up. One of Aiden's Ninja Turtle buttons. He clenched it in his fist and stood up.

Gone. But where?

PART 5

Thessaly

64

Thessaly looked out at the tall white walls and the ornate gates as they rolled by the tinted passenger-side window of the black Toyota Tacoma. Eighty or so miles from Patchway, but it felt like the same charcoal color clouds had been their companion the whole way. It wasn't raining anymore, at least.

'Where are we?' Casey asked from the backseat.

Lee answered from the driver's seat as he slowed for the next turn. 'Still in Jersey, about ten miles south of the state line.'

'Thank you for this,' Thessaly said.

Lee looked over at her for a second, and then back to the road. 'If you were right, if you were even halfway right ... well, you can't be too careful.'

Everything had changed during that twenty-minute drive from Grenville to Patchway, starting with the notification Thessaly had received as they were leaving.

A week ago, long before Washington had showed her the picture of the man from the Olympia, she had set up Google Alerts for Rhode Island news stories including certain keywords. She knew there had to be a connection between what Sturgis was involved in and the meeting with the man who claimed to be a cop on that first night, the man who drove a car with Rhode Island plates. The alert that came through while Lewis was driving the three of them out of Grenville had been the one she had been waiting for.

It was a breaking news story about a police officer at the Rhode Island State Police being arrested on suspicion of murder. There was a photograph of the officer accompanying the story. It was the bald man from the Olympia. The man whose picture Washington had shown her the night before.

The story identified him as Sergeant Jonathan Markham. The details were scant. The victim was unnamed, but the story said the body had lain undiscovered for several weeks at a building on Main Street, Pawtucket. It didn't give the exact address, but Thessaly would have put her next advance on it being number 138.

There hadn't been time to look for more at that moment, because there were more pressing things to worry about: first the unnerving radio silence from Washington, and then the news that something had gone very wrong with the arrest. Officer Lewis left them at the apartment in Patchway, not saying anything, but leaving them in no doubt that something catastrophic had happened.

Thessaly told Casey about the report as the two of them stood in shock in the galley kitchen of the small apartment in Patchway. As they were speaking, more news started to filter through. Not from Rhode Island, but from Grenville. Several police officers shot in some kind of spree, at least one confirmed dead.

Thessaly's head spun trying to process all the new information. She knew one thing. This morning's plan had been blown. Sturgis had to have been tipped off, and that meant somebody had inside knowledge. Knowledge that might well include the location of this supposed safe house.

To her relief, Lee answered her call on the first ring. He listened as she told him everything. The botched arrest on

Sturgis, the link to the killing in Rhode Island, the unshakeable suspicion that as bad as things had gone, they were about to get a whole lot worse. He agreed, and told her to get out of the apartment right away.

While they waited, she and Casey put together what had to have happened. This was why Washington had been hesitant to discuss the man from the Olympia after she had shown them both his picture. He really was a cop. But like Lee had guessed: he was a cop who wasn't supposed to be there.

The timing was no coincidence, she knew that. Washington must have made inquiries about Markham while they were waiting for the DNA result. Thessaly didn't know exactly what had happened, but something Washington had done must have precipitated Markham's arrest this morning. Maybe it had led directly to the discovery of the body at 138 Main Street, or perhaps Washington's interest panicked Markham into doing something that showed his hand.

Thinking about it, that sounded more like it. The fact that the body had lain undiscovered for several weeks. Whoever the victim was, she knew that the killer was likely Casper Sturgis. That had been the job. Not a deal, a hit. And that meant perhaps Oswald Kinderman hadn't been a deal gone wrong either. Casper Sturgis was still doing his old job: murder for hire.

But who was he doing it for? Not the cartel, that was for sure.

An hour later, Lee met them at the Gulf station on the eastern edge of Patchway. On the drive back to Jersey, more news reports about the massacre in Grenville fed through on the radio. Three dead, three injured, one critical. Thessaly didn't know if Washington was one of the dead, but she had no doubt she would have been one of the officers to knock on the door.

Lee had come up with the same solution she had, before she had had a chance to suggest it. Relocation. A real relocation, one that nobody could know of, outside of their small group. If there was a mole in the Grenville Police Department, then she had to assume the safe house was compromised. They had no choice but to abandon the apartment. But for the same reason, she couldn't simply drive Casey and Aiden back to her own house in Buchanan. Luckily, they had a third option.

They passed the sign for Silverwells with the Maxx Security logo in the corner of the sign.

'You sure this will be okay?' Casey asked. 'I mean, do these places get … inspected or anything?'

'Yeah. Luckily, I know the inspector,' Lee said, and then glanced back at her and smiled. 'Me. There's a cleaning and maintenance rotation, each house gets a visit every eight weeks. This one was serviced two weeks ago, so it'll be a while before anybody checks it. In the meantime, it's safe. The owner's in the Azores for the winter.'

They turned into the main entrance to the gated community and Lee slowed to a sedate twenty miles an hour as they passed orderly spaced rows of white-walled mansions with sprawling grounds. Thessaly knew it was a good thing, but she couldn't help but feel unnerved by how empty it was. No residents tending their flower beds, no dogs snapping at yard fences.

Lee turned off the main drag and down a smaller road, and then along a narrow service lane running between the backs of two plots, slowing and finally stopping when they came to a particular gate. The top floors of a three-story mansion were visible above the gate. The roof had terracotta tiles, and there was a turret at one side.

'Is this a castle?'

'Next best thing,' Lee said, winking at Aiden in the mirror. He fumbled in the glove box for a remote and clicked the button, opening the gate so they could drive through into a wide car port at the rear of the building. He parked with the bumper to the wall and looked around at Casey and Aiden. Aiden was engrossed in his Switch game.

'Welcome to the Silverwells Witness Protection Program,' he said quietly.

Casey let out a breath that sounded like she'd been holding it the whole trip. 'Nobody knows we're here? You're sure?'

Lee shook his head. 'Nobody outside of this car.'

He took out a small tablet from the door pocket and opened it up. He navigated to a website that showed what looked like a still black-and-white image of the lane they had just driven down. It took Thessaly a moment to work out that it was a live video feed; the only hint being the clock in the bottom corner. He tapped a couple of buttons and the time jumped back two minutes. As they watched, Lee's black Toyota rounded the corner, the Maxx security logo obvious on the hood.

She started to feel her chest tighten, and realized why after a second. It reminded her of the screen in Casey's kitchen, showing her husband's car returning. She pushed the memory out of her mind and tried to concentrate on what Lee was saying.

'This would probably be fine even if anybody else checked it, which they won't,' Lee continued. 'They can see it's a company car. All this shows is that I was here, which is fine. Still...' he pinched the screen to mark a two-minute section on the timeline and hit a button. A prompt came up asking if he was sure he wanted to delete this segment. 'Yes, I do,' he said as he tapped the link.

'Any cameras inside the house?' Thessaly asked.

'Exterior only,' Lee said. 'Covering the front and the back. We don't get auto alerts or anything. The only reason we ever access these is if somebody reports an issue.'

'What about the neighbors?' Casey asked. 'Won't they notice somebody's at home?'

'For one thing, half of these places aren't occupied. For

another, everybody minds their own business here. This isn't a town. Every house is its own little self-contained island.'

Casey looked unsure. She glanced at Aiden, still playing his game.

'If you're worried about it, stick to the back of the house. Ground floor at nighttime. The walls are high enough that nobody could see a light on there.'

The interior of the house was massive. You could practically fit Thessaly's entire house inside of the foyer. There were eight bedrooms, a grand staircase, a chandelier, a basement level with a floodlit indoor pool and a home movie theater with a dozen felt-upholstered seats.

'Lee, we couldn't have designed a better safe house, thank you,' Thessaly said when Casey went to help Aiden get unpacked.

He nodded seriously. 'The only thing is, it can't be forever. We need to make sure they're safe long term.'

'I know. And they won't be safe while Sturgis is still out there.'

'The cops will be looking for the two of them too,' Lee said. 'And I'm not saying it's consideration number one, but you and I could be in trouble.'

'We can't call the police,' Thessaly said. 'We don't know who tipped off Sturgis. The only one I trust is Washington, and ...'

'I know,' Lee said.

Thessaly thought it over. They couldn't stay here forever.

'We sure have some problems,' she said. 'So how do we fix them?'

65

Hours later, the sun was sinking below the rooftops and glinting through the tree branches as Thessaly returned to her home for the first time in two days. She felt a chill as she pulled the rented Nissan Versa into her driveway, the falling sun reflecting in a furnace of red and orange on the unlit windows of the second floor.

She hit the button on the remote on her key chain and waited for the garage to open. As the door slowly rose, she looked up at the house. It felt like she had lost something in the last twenty-four hours. Entering a doorway, even in her own home, now took an effort of will, a steeling of herself. Every building was an enemy fortress to be approached with trepidation.

And then she wondered if it wasn't a loss. If it was, rather, regaining something that she had gotten rid of over the long, painful passage of years, and had no wish to take back. Because now she thought about it, this feeling wasn't new. It was the same anxiety she had battled for years after the Redlands Mall. The ever-present unease of being inside. Confined. Cornered.

But unless she wanted to stay in the car for the rest of her life, she had no choice.

Part of her had expected some kind of police welcome. Were they looking for her? She wasn't sure. Technically, she had removed a witness from protective custody without permission. But then again, Casey had gone willingly, more than willingly, and there was no reason to suggest otherwise. She had no idea if they had tried to contact her, ask her where the hell she was. She had turned her phone off as soon as they had left Patchway.

The garage door was fully open now. She pulled the Nissan inside and waited for the door to close automatically behind her. She popped the trunk and got out from behind the wheel.

A few minutes later, Thessaly sat down at her desk in her study, looking out over the street. She opened her laptop and looked for the latest updates of the two major news stories in which she was involved. Two stories unfolding hundreds of miles apart, and for now, apparently unconnected.

Grenville first. Detective Washington had survived the shooting, barely. She had undergone emergency surgery and was now stable in the hospital. Thessaly would have given anything to be able to pick up the phone to her and compare notes, find out for sure if her hunch was correct. That wouldn't be happening for a long time, though.

And then, Rhode Island. The victim had a name, now. Alan Shepherd, like the Mercury astronaut, but spelled differently. He had been suspected of murdering his wife, and hadn't been seen since February 6. His body had been concealed within an apartment at 138 Main Street, Pawtucket for days. From her own experience in the Olympia and checking with Casey, she was pretty sure she could give the authorities an accurate window for a time of death. The evening of February 7, a few hours after Thessaly had met the man she now knew was Sergeant Jonathan Markham at the Olympia, and on a night Casey's husband had been making one of his business trips.

Tell him it's off.

She thought she knew why Markham had been so desperate

to get in touch with the man he didn't know that day. For whatever reason, he had decided not to go through with it. But it had been too late.

She and Lee and Casey had talked it over. It was the only thing that made sense. But the only person who knew exactly what had happened was Casper Sturgis. Sturgis, and perhaps one other person.

She didn't have to make the call. She could simply lock the doors and go to bed and most likely, everything would stay in a holding pattern until the morning. Everything could wait until tomorrow.

But she knew that wasn't really an option. There was only one person who might be able to help her end this. She lifted the receiver of her phone and dialed the number from the business card that had lain at the bottom of her purse for the last two weeks.

It rang three times and was answered with a cautious 'Hello?' She could hear noise in the background. Somewhere outside. Cross-cutting conversations, someone yelling orders, a beeping sound like a truck backing up.

'Is this Volcker? This is Thessaly Hanlon speaking.'

She heard a sharp intake of breath before he replied. 'Thessaly? Jesus Christ, where are you? Where's Casey?'

'We're safe, we're all safe. After what happened, I just thought we had to get out of there. How's Detective Washington? I saw on the news that she was stable.'

'Stable and conscious. I talked to her. She explained the whole thing.'

'Then you know about Cleveland and all of it.'

'Yeah. We're working on the assumption that Sturgis had some kind of deal with this guy Kinderman and it went south. It'll probably take some time to unpick it.' There was a silence.

'We've been looking for you. Everyone's been worried, what with Sturgis still out there. We'll find him, but...'

'I was hoping you guys would have caught him by now,' Thessaly said, cutting in. 'I guess we screwed up your whole witness protection thing.'

There was a pause and she wondered how he was going to take that comment. But then he said, 'Don't worry about that. When Washington explained what they were arresting Sturgis for, when I looked at the evidence... well, I told you we had a deal, right? Sturgis broke that deal. Am I angry? No, I'm goddamn furious. But I'm furious with him, not you or Casey.'

'That's good to know,' she said. 'Listen, I called you because I don't know who else to talk to.'

'You did the right thing. I can help you.'

'It's going to sound nuts, I don't even want to say it.'

'Trust me, when you've been doing my job long enough, nothing sounds nuts.'

'I think...' Thessaly sighed and left a moment's pause. 'Are you alone?'

'Just a second.' She heard him say something to someone else, then there was the sound of a car door opening and closing, and the background noise disappeared. 'Okay, I'm in the car outside the scene at Sturgis's house. Nobody else can hear you.'

She took a deep breath. 'I think somebody told Sturgis what was happening, and I think it was somebody on the inside.'

There was a pause before he answered. 'You mean somebody in Washington's team?'

'Yes. Officer Lewis. The one who took us to the safe house. I think it had to be him.'

'Lewis,' Volcker repeated, like he was writing it down. 'Little guy, buzz cut?'

'You've met him?'

'Not for long. He was at the hospital when I got there.

Seemed agitated, although I suppose that's understandable. What makes you think it's him?'

'It had to be. I think he made sure he was the one driving us so he wouldn't be in the firing line. I think his job was to babysit us until Sturgis could get there, but we screwed up his plan by leaving before he came back.'

'So he was the only one who knew about the operation but wasn't involved in the actual arrest?' Volcker asked.

'Exactly. And there was something… there was just something about him, you know? The way he reacted to everything. It's like it was a performance to him.'

'I think you could be on to something. Somebody tipped Sturgis off, and you're right, it had to be someone in the know. Do you know if Washington told anyone else?'

'I don't think so,' Thessaly said. 'She was really careful about that, she knew we had to keep a lid on it to give Casey and Aiden the best chance of getting out of there. It was just the officers making the arrest, plus Detective Hatherley and one of his men from Cleveland. She didn't want to tell you until after the arrest. That's how I know I can talk to you.'

'Thank you,' Volcker said after a minute. 'I appreciate you trusting me on this. And don't worry, this won't go any further. We're coordinating with the Grenville cops and the FBI on this, but I'll personally take a look at this Lewis guy. If you're right about him, we'll come down on him like the wrath of God.'

'I'm just worried he could still be helping Sturgis find us, I guess.'

'And you're right to be,' he said. 'Thessaly, we need to talk about that.'

'I know. Casey was wondering… she's scared of him, like really scared. She wants to know if you could make her disappear, the way you did with Sturgis.'

'I'm going to be completely up front with you, Thessaly, that isn't up to me. Maybe it can happen if this goes to trial, I don't know. But I promise you, we can keep you all safe.'

'I was hoping you would say that. I just... I feel so responsible. I got them into this. If I hadn't seen Sturgis that night, if I hadn't pulled on the loose thread...'

'It's not your fault,' Volcker said. He was sounding like an almost completely different person to the stern authority figure Thessaly had first encountered in Washington's interview room two weeks ago. 'You did the right thing by reaching out to Washington when Casey came to you. He killed someone. I'm not saying we don't look the other way on some of the small-time shit that our charges get up to in the program, but not something like this. No way. And that was before he killed three cops this morning. You think you want this bastard bad? I want him more.'

Thessaly wanted to point out that she still had a much more personal reason for her animosity toward Sturgis, but she let it go. 'Thank you.'

'Thessaly, we need to know where they are. You know that, right?'

She hesitated before answering. 'They're safe.'

'Are they somewhere near Grenville? If she's with anyone who her husband could tie her to...'

'She's not anywhere in Grenville, she's safe.'

Volcker cleared his throat, and she could hear him making an effort to keep the frustration out of his voice. 'I don't want to labor the obvious here, but I've been doing this job a while, and I know a little about protecting a witness. I've never lost one yet.'

You lost one today, Thessaly wanted to say, but kept it to herself.

'I also know all the mistakes people have made in all the years leading up to this. You don't have that advantage. You need to let me help you.'

Thessaly let the pause draw out before speaking. 'I promised I wouldn't tell. Tell *anyone*, not even Washington.'

'I understand that. Sometimes you have to make a hard decision between keeping your word and doing what's in the best interests of the person you want to help.'

She let the silence spin out. Volcker didn't say anything, giving her space.

'Look, let me talk to Casey first. Give me until tomorrow.'

The tone of his voice grew softer. 'Thessaly, she could be in danger the longer we don't know where she is. God forbid he finds her ... how would you feel if I could have helped you and you didn't let me?'

'How about I meet you tomorrow? If Casey says it's okay, I'll tell you where they are.'

He sighed, perhaps knowing that this was as far as he could push her for now. 'Fair enough. I can be there at noon, good enough? The house at the end of the street next to the woods, right?'

'No, don't come to the house,' she said quickly. 'There's a coffee shop in town.' She gave him the address, making sure he wrote it down.

'You're not giving me much choice,' Volcker said. 'Okay, I'll see you there.'

'Thank you. And tell Detective Washington I was asking for her.'

'I will do.'

'See you soon.'

'Yes, soon.'

Thessaly hung up and stared out of the window at the world outside for a long time. The streetlights winked on. The last remaining light bled out of the sky.

Darkness fell.

66

The full moon rose over the tops of the trees, casting an icy white beam across the tiled kitchen floor. It was bright enough that Thessaly didn't have to switch on the lights. She preferred not to, anyway. She wanted to be able to see out in the back yard.

She flipped over the final cards and finished the game of solitaire. By her count, that was the sixth game. She had won three, had to give up on three.

Standing up from the stool, she stretched, rubbing an ache in her neck. The digital clock on the display of her microwave said it was just after eight o'clock. She started to lay out the cards again on the surface of the island. Best of seven. Perhaps nothing would happen. Perhaps she would still be here considering a best of ninety-one when the sun came up.

There was a soft creak from directly above her. She stopped, one card held in her hand. A floorboard. She cleared her throat loudly. There was no further sound. She resumed laying the cards on the worktop.

She finished laying out the seventh game and considered the first move. She had two aces right off the deal. She moved them to the corner and a king to the left-most position. Flipping the next available card exposed another ace.

'My lucky night,' she said to herself.

And then the doorbell rang softly. She looked through the open kitchen door, down the hall to the front door. She could see the silhouette of a man through the stained-glass panel.

Taking a deep breath, she opened the drawer beside her. She gathered up the cards and squared them, took a moment to organize things and closed the drawer. She took her time, but the man at the door was patient. He didn't ring the bell again or follow up with a knock.

She moved slowly down the hall, her sneakers slapping lightly on the tile. When she got within a couple of feet of the door, she called out, 'Who is it?'

'It's me, Thessaly. Volcker. Can I come in?'

She opened the door, leaving the chain on. Volcker stood there, his tie loosened and the top button of his shirt undone.

'I thought you would still be down in Grenville?'

'Forensics guys are all over the house, FBI are taking witness statements. I was kind of a third wheel after a while. I'm sorry to bother you this late, but there's some new information I think you need to be aware of.'

Thessaly bit her bottom lip and angled her head so she could peer out past him. Volcker was alone. No car parked outside that she could see.

'Just a minute.'

She closed the door, took the chain off and opened it again, standing back to let him in.

'What is it?' Thessaly asked. 'Is everything all right?'

'Thank you,' Volcker said, stepping inside. 'And I don't know, is the honest answer to your question.'

Thessaly gestured down the hall toward the kitchen. 'Come on in, you look like you could use a coffee.'

She locked the door again and led him into the kitchen, telling Alexa to turn the lights on. The room lit up brightly, turning the glass doors looking onto the yard into a mirror.

She took a mug from the cupboard and glanced at the clock. 'Decaf?'

He looked amused by the suggestion. 'I don't think I'll be doing much sleeping tonight, so full strength is fine by me.'

She smiled and turned to work the machine. 'To be honest, I drink so much of the stuff that it doesn't make much difference to me getting to sleep. I need two or three in the morning just to get to baseline, you know?'

'There are worse addictions, right?' Volcker said.

'You have a point,' she said, placing the cup under the jet and touching the button. The aggressive grinding noise filled the air as she turned to him. She waited for the noise to finish before she spoke. 'So what's up?'

Volcker folded his arms and gave her an appraising look, like he wasn't totally sold on saying more. 'I'm telling you this in confidence, Thessaly, and only because I trust you. But I think you're dead right about Officer Lewis. I think he warned Andrews... warned *Sturgis* about what was going to happen.'

'Wow,' Thessaly said, taking a deep breath. 'What did you find out?'

'He was still at the scene after I spoke to you, so I talked to him. He acted upset, like the rest of them, but I got that same feeling you talked about, Thessaly. Something was off about him.'

'After we spoke, I thought maybe I was nuts,' Thessaly said. 'Imagining things. But if you think so too...' She put Volcker's cup down on the island, where she had been playing solitaire.

He sat down on the stool, taking a sip of the coffee. He licked his lips. 'That's good. I needed this, thank you.'

'No problem.'

'I asked around discreetly. It turns out Lewis and Sturgis are members of the same gym. I went down there and talked to the owner. He says they're buddies, they work out together and he's seen them in the same crowd in the bar some nights.'

Thessaly put a hand to her mouth. 'My God. So you think he saw his friend was in trouble and decided to help him out? I mean... that's some favor to do a buddy.'

Volcker nodded. 'I think it goes beyond that. I think Lewis is in deep with whatever Sturgis has been involved in. I can't prove it yet, but I think he was part of what happened in Cleveland.'

Thessaly shook her head in wonder. 'Jesus, we opened a can of worms.'

'That you did,' Volcker said. 'Anyway, it's been a long day. Lewis isn't going anywhere, and he has no reason to think I suspect anything. If we get lucky, he might lead us right to Sturgis. In the meantime, I need to look into Sturgis's activities over the past year, and I'm counting on you to help me. But we have a priority more important than any of that stuff. We need to get Casey and Aiden into the program.'

Thessaly frowned. 'Into witness protection? I thought you said that might not be doable?'

Volcker gave her a modest smile. 'I pulled some strings. It wasn't easy, but the deal's done. We can pick them up and they'll be safe and sound within a couple of hours. We have a secure facility in Newark for tonight, and we can have them in a new location in two days. I don't know where you've got them stashed, but trust me, Sturgis will be able to find it. He won't be able to find our place.'

'I have to say I'm impressed,' Thessaly said, after a long moment. 'I call you a few hours ago and you've already checked out Lewis and got us everything we asked for. It's... unbelievable.'

Volcker shrugged modestly. 'Hey, sometimes things fall into place. I can't take all the credit.'

'Unbelievable,' Thessaly repeated. She took a long sip of her own coffee. 'I wondered if you would come tonight,' she said after a moment.

'You did?'

'I did. You didn't sound like you wanted to take no for an answer earlier. Even though we were going to meet tomorrow.'

Volcker said nothing, his face betraying nothing. Or maybe not nothing. Was there a hint of amusement in his eyes?

'You don't think they're here, do you?' she asked after a moment.

He smiled slyly and widened his hands. His jacket opened with the motion, giving her a glimpse of his gun in its holster. 'Guilty as charged, your honor.'

'I thought so.'

'You can't blame me for trying. And you seemed a little too keen for me not to come here.'

'I prefer not to have people visit my house. It's a thing I have. Particularly when they come in under false pretenses.'

He looked wounded. 'Oh, now what I said was true. No false pretenses. I am worried about who tipped off Sturgis, and I do need you to tell me where Casey is. For her own safety. And yours.'

'And mine?'

He nodded slowly. He smiled again, but this time it didn't come anywhere near his eyes. He was no longer amused.

'I don't think I should tell you,' she said. 'I'd like you to leave now.'

He made no move to leave. After a moment, he put the coffee cup down. 'It's like you said earlier, Thessaly. I'm not taking no for an answer.'

She held his gaze for a few seconds. 'You going to threaten me with a fine again?'

'A fine?' He shook his head slowly. 'No.'

'Do you want to know what I think?' Thessaly asked after a pause. 'I think you're right. I think somebody on the inside warned that bastard. And I think they're helping him now. But it wasn't Officer Lewis.'

'I have to admit, I'm a little confused, here.' Volcker's tone was even, but there was a cold look in his eye.

'We know Sturgis killed Oswald Kinderman last year in Cleveland. All this time, we thought it was some kind of drug deal gone wrong. Kinderman was a dealer, and, well, we know Sturgis's background gives him all the experience he needs to get involved in that line of work. But I don't think that was it at all. I don't think it was a drug deal, and I don't think it went wrong.'

'We don't have all night, Thessaly. You're going to tell me where Casey is, one way or another.'

She ignored the interjection. He had affected a bored tone, but she could tell it was a front. He was intrigued to see whether she had actually worked it out.

'The first night I saw Sturgis, he was meeting somebody. It turns out that somebody was Sergeant Jonathan Markham of the Rhode Island State Police.'

Finally, a real reaction. Volcker's eyes narrowed. But he didn't say anything. He wanted to know how she knew, though, she could tell. He didn't speak this time, didn't taunt her or ask again about Casey's whereabouts.

'Markham had a problem. A man named Alan Shepherd. He wasn't the same kind of problem as Oswald Kinderman. He wasn't a drug dealer or anything. Markham thought Shepherd had gotten away with killing his wife. He decided to do something about it. He couldn't do it personally, though. He heard about a service that was offered. Seamless. A man who could take care of his problems and disappear. A man who would never be connected to a random killing. A man who, to all intents and purposes, didn't exist.'

All trace of humor had faded from Volcker's face.

'How long have you been doing it, Volcker? What's the split? I mean, Sturgis is doing all the work on these hits, you're just finding him the customers.'

Volcker's voice took on an angry edge. 'I don't know how you came up with this, but listen to yourself. You sound ridiculous.'

'He's not the only one, is he? You have a whole stable of these guys.' She shook her head. 'David Volcker, Deputy US Marshal by day, hit coordinator by night. Pretty sweet deal. No wonder you got antsy about me poking my nose in.'

'*Chief* Deputy,' Volcker corrected mildly. He took his gun out and cocked it. It looked like one of the Glocks Thessaly had fired that disastrous day on the gun range all those years ago. She didn't doubt Volcker's marksmanship was better than hers. He laid it down on the surface of the island. An implied threat. He didn't think he needed to do anything more.

She kept talking, hoping the nerves weren't audible in her voice. 'It took me a while to work out how I could possibly confirm it, though. And then I wondered if I could get you to do it for me. So I did what I'm good at. I came up with a story. I mixed in a little truth and I made it plausible, and I waited to see what you would do with it. If you were innocent, you would have checked Lewis out and found nothing, but you jumped in with both feet. I mean, is he even a member of a gym?'

Volcker looked on with amused contempt, saying nothing, letting her talk.

'The only thing I'm not sure of – do you exclusively hire Sturgis out to law enforcement, or is it anything goes?'

For the first time, Volcker looked slightly impressed. 'How do you mean?'

'Kinderman was let off on a technicality, so I'm guessing that pissed off somebody in the Cleveland police enough to want him dead. Washington told us professional standards were looking at somebody in the narcotics unit before we came up with Sturgis as a suspect. I'm betting they had the right person after all, they just didn't know he had contracted the job out. Hatherley wasn't involved, otherwise he wouldn't have cooperated with us, and he would be alive right now. Markham was a cop too. He contacted you because he wanted to get to someone he thought was guilty. I met Markham, you know. I think he had a change of heart. Discovered his conscience at the last minute.'

Volcker smirked. 'Hypothetically speaking, that wasn't it.'

'No?'

'Hypothetically, maybe new evidence came out and Markham discovered his suspect was innocent. Too late though. Hypothetically.'

Thessaly blinked. It was worse than she had thought. She understood why Markham had been so desperate that day at the Olympia.

'You killed an innocent man.'

'Me? I didn't kill anybody.' Volcker straightened up and rubbed the back of his neck. 'It's a great story, Thessaly. You ought to be a writer. Now tell me another story. Where are they?'

'You're not going to tell me I'm wrong? I want to hear you say it first. You heard about Markham's arrest and you knew what was going to happen, so you tipped off your boy Sturgis.'

'You want to hear me …' Volcker blinked, and at once Thessaly knew she had overplayed her hand.

He stepped forward and grabbed her by the shoulders.

'Are you wearing a wire, you fucking bitch?'

She took a sharp intake of breath as he roughly started to pat her down. She didn't cry out though. She wanted him to say it.

He found nothing and roughly pushed her backward. She slammed into the refrigerator. She heard liquid slosh and the sound of something made of glass breaking inside.

He looked around and then his eyes alighted on the cup of coffee. And the drawer beneath. He yanked it open and found Thessaly's digital voice recorder, the little red light blinking steadily. He took it out and picked up the gun with his other hand. He walked over to her, holding up the recorder.

'What did you think? I was going to blab my mouth off on tape and just walk away?' His voice rose, real anger in it now. 'Is that what you thought? Are you actually that fucking stupid?'

She shook her head. 'Not exactly.'

And that was when a figure moved from the shadows of the hallway into the light of the kitchen.

67

Lee said, 'Drop the gun.'

Volcker looked from Thessaly to Lee, evaluating the situation. His body was angled away from Lee, who was standing just inside the doorway. He had his gun pointed straight at Volcker's chest from five feet away. He couldn't miss at that range, and Volcker couldn't hope to get his gun into position to fire on Lee first.

'What the hell is this?'

'This is her backup,' Lee said. 'Now do what I told you.'

Slowly, Volcker turned. He laid the gun on the island and lifted his hands.

He glanced from Lee to Thessaly and back again. 'We can talk about this,' he said. 'I think there's been a big misunderstanding here.'

'Really? That's what you're going with?' Thessaly asked.

Volcker smiled thinly and kept addressing Lee. 'I don't think you want to shoot a Chief Deputy US Marshal, son, and I definitely don't want to get shot. Think about it. You kill me in her kitchen, unarmed? Going to be a *lot* of questions.'

Lee said nothing. His aim didn't waver.

'Maybe we can make a deal. I walk out of here, and I won't bother either of you again.'

'Not much of a deal,' Thessaly said. 'We know why you came here tonight. We have you on the recording, Volcker.'

He glanced down at the recorder, still on the floor where he had dropped it. He gave a theatrical sigh. 'Thessaly, if you had spent as much time as I have inside courtrooms, you would know you've got nothing. Less than nothing. You've got you, spinning some ... fucking wild conspiracy story and me listening, out of politeness. All you have, is a recording of you trying to con me into saying I did something I didn't do.' He cast a wary eye at Lee and the gun before lowering his head a little, speaking directly at the recorder. 'Here's a good line for the recording. *Inadmissible.* You get that okay?'

'I have a good friend out in Rhode Island,' Lee said. 'He's the one who gave us the background on the Markham arrest. It wasn't difficult to put it all together once we knew the details. My friend thinks Markham will talk. And Markham can identify Sturgis. Can he identify you too?'

Volcker thought for a moment, lowering his hands a little. 'Okay. Hard bargain. Without giving any sort of credence to your theory, maybe we can come to a financial settlement.'

'You want to bribe us now?' Thessaly asked. She looked at Lee and shrugged. 'Sounds completely like the actions of an innocent man, right?'

'I want to walk out of here in one piece. I'm willing to pay for the privilege.'

'Why don't we call the police instead and let them decide?' Thessaly asked.

Volcker started to say something and then shut his mouth. He raised his eyes to the ceiling, as though trying to recall something. 'Buchanan. That's not under the state police, is it? You have your own local PD.'

Thessaly didn't answer. All of a sudden, she had a bad feeling she knew where this was going.

'Chief Gorman up here, isn't it?' Volcker continued, his voice teasing.

Was that the name of the chief of police? Thessaly had no idea. She had spent a lot of her time talking to cops since 2001, but none locally. She had never so much as had a speeding ticket in Buchanan. The name Gorman did sound a little familiar. Was that because it was really the name of the police chief, or was it just the power of suggestion?

Thessaly shot a glance at Lee. His expression had softened a little. He looked back at her, a little unsure all of a sudden. The kernel of doubt threatening to grow into something bigger.

'That's right, Chief Benjamin Gorman,' Volcker continued. 'Ben. We know Ben.' He looked over at Thessaly. 'Call them. They have, what, a dozen officers? Doesn't matter who they send out. We'll talk to Ben, the three of us.'

'Thessaly, maybe we should ...' Lee began.

'Keep that fucking gun on him,' she snapped. 'You're dirty, Volcker. You're not going to walk away from this.'

As though to immediately disprove her words, he took a cautious step backward. Lee didn't move. Slowly, Volcker turned around. He walked over to the glass doors, being careful not to make any sudden moves. The kitchen lights turned the doors into mirrors against the blackness outside.

'Volcker, stay the fuck where you are.' Thessaly said.

He stopped, three feet away from the patio doors, as though admiring his reflection in the glass. And then he did something that didn't seem to make sense. He nodded.

Thessaly had time to say, 'What ...' before Volcker's reflection rippled crazily and a black patch of night appeared in the glass door. A moment later, she heard the gunshot, and then another. She heard a cry from beside her and turned to see that two patches of dark red had appeared on Lee's white shirt. He looked down at the stains uncomprehendingly, and then back up at Volcker, who had turned around and was making a move in Thessaly's direction, grabbing the gun on the island.

Lee slumped to the floor, his gun firing three times. One of the bullets caught Volcker just below his right eye. He stopped halfway to Thessaly, a surprised look on his face. Dark blood spilled out of the hole, like someone had turned on a faucet. He pitched forward, sprawling on the floor, falling with his gun hand beneath him. Thessaly ran to Lee and crouched beside him, looking at the rapidly spreading patches of blood on his shirt, the two stains already meeting at the edges. His eyes weren't on her. They were looking straight ahead. It took her a second to realize what he was looking at.

Who he was looking at.

His mouth formed a one-syllable word that came out like a groan of agony.

'Run.'

68

Thessaly ran into the hallway, just ahead of the bullet that splintered the wood of the door frame.

She had caught a glimpse of Casper Sturgis just before she turned. Looming at the glass door, reaching through the broken glass for the latch. Fuck. She had expected Volcker to show up, but both of them? As she reached for the key in the front door, she flinched as another bullet smashed into the glass an inch from her hand. She would be dead before she could turn the key. She gave up on the door, turned to run up the stairs. Another thing on her mind: she didn't know how badly Lee was hurt, but she needed to lure Sturgis as far as she could from him.

She barreled up the stairs, seeing a flash of movement as Sturgis passed by in the hallway, hot on her heels. She reached the upper floor and kicked the door of her study open, hoping it would be enough to give him a moment's pause, to stick his head in and turn the light on, at least. She turned and headed straight down the corridor on the landing to the window at the far end. She pushed the window up and lifted one leg out, then the other, swinging around and gripping the ledge, extending to her full height before dropping. She hit the soft grass ten feet below and rolled. The grass was brittle from frost. The cold bit into her. She could see her breath.

Decision time. No point trying to get to her car, even if it wasn't in the garage. The keys were in the kitchen drawer. Run to a neighbor's house? Sturgis would only follow her there. They might have time to call the police, but even if Volcker had been bluffing about his reach, it would take them ten minutes to get here, minimum. Long before that, she would be forced to face Sturgis. Doing it at a neighbor's house would only risk another life.

Ignoring every instinct, she ran in the opposite direction. Away from civilization. Away from help.

She crossed the grass and unlatched the gate into the woods. Casting a glance back as she heard the thump of two hundred pounds of human being impacting the ground, she saw there was no use in closing the gate behind her. Sturgis was already out of the window and on the ground, picking himself up and raising his gun.

'Stay there!' he yelled. She wondered if he had really expected her to obey as she ducked through the gate, taking comfort from the fact he hadn't fired again. The first two shots had been wide deliberately. He wanted to make her reveal Casey's whereabouts. That was her one advantage: he didn't want to kill her before she talked.

She moved as fast as she could through the undergrowth. She had never ventured into the woods at night, and she was losing her bearings. The moon overhead through the trees provided her only reference point. She kept running, hearing the sound of Sturgis tearing through the woods behind her. Her own progress was loud enough; snapping fallen twigs with seemingly every step. Maybe he couldn't see her, but he would definitely hear her as long as she kept moving.

His voice sounded, terrifyingly close. 'Don't make it more difficult, Thessaly. You'll only piss me off.'

The son of a bitch sounded calm.

She heard the rush of water off to her left and paused just a second to orient herself. There was the big, moss-covered fallen tree that she recognized. She clambered over it and down the slope.

She found the crossing place. If she could make it across the stream and over the fence, she could hunker down. He didn't know these woods. Perhaps he would give up eventually. She could just make out the black shapes of the stepping-stones. As she was putting her weight down on the third stone, she suddenly remembered it was loose. Too late. It turned and she slipped into the freezing water. It wasn't deep, only came up to her calves, but the splash broke the silence of the night. She put her foot on the next stone and tried to go faster, heedless of the noise of the splashing now. She had almost made it to the bank when she heard the voice. Close.

That voice. The voice of a bad dream come to life.

'That's far enough.'

69

Slowly, Thessaly turned around.

Sturgis was at the edge of the water. He had caught up while she maneuvered her way across the stream. He moved quietly, for a big man.

'Where are they?' he asked. He wasn't even out of breath.

She shook her head. She shivered, her feet and ankles numb from the water. 'Far away from you.'

'They're my family. You can't take my family away.'

'How many people have you taken from their families, Sturgis? Dozens, isn't it? Do you even keep count?'

In the moonlight, she saw the smile spread across his face as he came to a realization. 'So that's it. I should have known. Who was it? Husband? Daddy?'

'Brother.'

'Well, I apologize for any inconvenience. Whoever it was, it wasn't personal.'

'Redlands Mall, 2001. I was there too. Hiding from you. I saw you kill him.'

He considered it and nodded. 'Then you had a lucky escape. You should have quit while you were ahead.' He glanced behind him for a second. The house was out of sight behind the rise of the hill and the trees. 'Get over here.'

No other option. She did what she was told, but she took

her time. Stepped onto the first rock and then the second. She hesitated before she got to the loose rock. She would need to hop over it onto the next secure stone. Unless…

'Out of interest, how did you find me?' Sturgis asked, breaking her train of thought.

'Does it matter? You're going to kill me anyway.'

'Maybe, maybe not. You tell me what I want to know, I have no reason to kill you. I can't go back to being Tony Andrews anyway. So before you tell me where my kid is, tell me that.'

'The Olympia Diner, three weeks ago. I was driving home, stopped to get out of the rain, you were there.'

Sturgis whistled, momentarily impressed, despite himself. 'You want to know something crazy? That was the first time I had ever set foot inside that shithole. You're telling me if I had told that cop to meet me in the next truck stop along, none of this would have happened?'

'Some of it would. Casey and Aiden would have left you sooner or later. She knows what you are now.'

'Well, she and I are going to have a conversation about that. Maybe she'll see the light.'

See the light. Thessaly had the beginnings of a plan already, but that gave her another idea.

'I'm not going to tell you where they are.'

'Then you'll die. Your friend back there will tell me, if he's still alive. He's not going anywhere. And I'll find them anyway. I'm not going to hurt Aiden. I would never hurt him.'

'And Casey?'

He considered the question. Perhaps he decided it wouldn't help him to lie. 'I'll make it quick.'

'If you promise to let her go, I'll tell you.'

He didn't agree right away. 'I don't know. She knows a lot about me. Harder to disappear if she's helping them.'

'You'll manage.'

He considered for a moment. 'Okay, deal. But if you bullshit me ...'

'You'll be back,' Thessaly said. 'I know that.' Was he planning to honor the deal? She could almost believe it. But whatever happened next, it would be academic. She wasn't telling him where Casey and Aiden were. She would die first.

She looked down, squinted her eyes as though she wasn't sure of the next step. She held out her right hand. 'Help me?'

He glanced down at the stones, wary. He kept his gun on her, turned his body a little so he could reach out his left hand for her. But he couldn't quite reach. He glanced down again and then back at her, watching her for any sudden moves as he extended his right foot to step on the third rock.

Their fingers met as his foot planted on the stone and it started to turn. She gripped his hand and yanked as hard as she could, pulling him in the direction she knew the stone would turn. In a split second, his weight advantage turned into a liability. He muttered a curse and brought the gun up, but she had already started lunging in the other direction.

There was a bang as the gun went off, followed by a splash that sounded almost as loud as Sturgis tumbled into the stream. Thessaly jumped, landed on the bank and took off at a run, back toward the house.

Up the muddy slope, over the fallen tree, through the tangling weeds. She could hear him behind her, crashing through the undergrowth, gaining on her. He wasn't yelling or cursing, but she knew he wouldn't be in a mood to show mercy now. If this didn't work, she was dead.

She made it through the gate and swung it shut behind her, hearing the latch catch on the inside. Buying her another five seconds, maybe. She sprinted across the familiar grass of her yard. Ahead of her, the sliding patio door leading into the kitchen was still open, the rectangle of artificial light almost blinding her after the dark of the woods. Like a portal in the darkness. She could see the bullet holes in the glass. She could see Lee, still propped against the wall where she had left him. He wasn't moving. She could see Volcker, still sprawled on the ground, also unmoving.

She heard another two gunshots and the sound of wood and metal splintering as Sturgis took the easy route through the gate. She reached the kitchen door and yelled out, 'Alexa, lights off!' Every light in the house winked out. The rectangle of the doorway changed from bright white to pitch black. As she passed through the doorway she blinked the afterimage out of her eyes, still able to make out the shapes. Lee by the wall, Volcker on the floor.

She skidded to her knees on the tile floor, dug underneath Volcker's body. He weighed a ton. She couldn't feel anything. She could hear the thump of Sturgis's boots on the grass outside, getting closer. And then...

Her fingers found the hard metal of Volcker's Glock. She closed her hand around it, pulled it out from under him. Turned as Sturgis's frame filled the doorway. He looked bigger than God. Bigger than the world.

Too big to miss.

She pulled the trigger again and again, lighting up the kitchen with the muzzle flash. She heard the bullets impact bricks and aluminum frame and glass and flesh and bone. She saw the silhouette jerk and then trip on the edge of the door frame and fall backward. She got to her feet and walked forward, not breaking stride as she took the gun in both hands and fired again and again into the motionless form on the grass. She stopped only when the gun wouldn't fire any more.

She took a cautious step forward, then another. Part of her waiting for him to lunge up from his supine position like a movie monster. But as she got closer, she could see he was entirely motionless. His gun had fallen a couple of feet from his hand.

She stepped over him and picked it up.

'Alexa, lights on.'

The cool tinted kitchen lights spilled out onto the backyard grass, lighting up the body. Not a movie monster. Not a nightmare. Just a man.

One eye stared sightlessly up, the full moon glinting in it. There was nothing to reflect the moon on the other side. One of her bullets had gone in that way. From the dark mass beneath his head, she could see that it had exited out of the back, taking most of the contents of Casper Sturgis's head with it.

'I guess it wasn't your lucky day, fucker.'

She heard a low groan from the kitchen and glanced back to see Lee had slumped over. He was conscious.

70

Six weeks later

Volcker had been bluffing.

There was no Chief Benjamin Gorman. The Buchanan Chief of Police was Elizabeth Child, a short, serious woman with dark hair swept back into a tight bun.

Thessaly wondered if it would have mattered, even if he hadn't been bluffing. Two dead men: a relapsed contract killer and his federal handler. Even without Thessaly and Lee as witnesses, it immediately suggested all kinds of scenarios, none of which a small-town police chief would particularly want to attach herself to.

The cops and the paramedics had responded a little quicker than she had expected. Seven minutes from her call, not ten. In the meantime, she had followed the dispatcher's calm instructions, keeping pressure on Lee's wounds and talking to him, keeping him conscious.

Later, the surgeon at New York-Presbyterian Hudson Valley Hospital told her how lucky Lee had been. He had collapsed with his full weight on the gunshot wounds, cutting down the blood loss just enough to let him hang on. Very lucky indeed.

'How are they?' Lee asked.

They were sitting at one of the tables outside of the hospital cafeteria, watching the early-spring afternoon sun dip toward the treetops in the park. Lee in his dressing gown, looking thinner and paler and more ragged around the edges than he had in February, but aside from that, pretty good, considering. Thessaly didn't have to ask him who he meant.

'They're okay. Better than I would be.'

Lee took a drink from the opaque steel water bottle Thessaly had brought for him. He had had only one request for her visit, and she thought it was an entirely reasonable one, even if the hospital might not agree.

'Jesus, that's good,' he said with feeling, licking a line of foam off his top lip. 'I've missed that.'

'Shhh,' she said, raising her eyebrows. 'No one is that happy about Gatorade.'

He laughed and took another long drink. She wished she had thought to bring some gum or something to cover the smell of beer on his breath when he went back to the ward.

'Thanks for the reading material, too,' he said, tapping his good hand on the bound manuscript Thessaly had brought. She had finished the book over weeks of days and nights where sleep was elusive, but work was a lifesaver. The title page said:

The City Sleeps
by Thessaly Hanlon

'I hope you like it,' she said.

'It has your name on it,' Lee commented with approval.

He winced at the movement as he turned his head to look across the road at the park. It was a warm day. A group of kids were playing on the swings.

'What did Casey tell the kid?'

'Some of the truth. What will do the least harm, I hope.'

Lee shook his head. 'It should have been me.'

Thessaly regarded him with confusion over the rim of her coffee cup. 'I should have shot you?'

'No. It shouldn't have gotten that far. I was there to protect you. I should have seen him coming.'

'We were only expecting Volcker. We didn't know Sturgis would be there too.'

'I should have. What did Washington say?'

'That we were incredibly stupid and we're lucky to be alive.'

'She's probably right.'

'I know. I think she understood though. I told her I knew they would be coming sooner or later, and I decided I wanted it to be on my terms.'

Lee finished the last of the beer and screwed the top back on the bottle, wincing as the movement aggravated his bad arm. 'Anyway, how are you?'

Thessaly put the bottle into her bag and shrugged. She thought about Lee's injuries. The doctors didn't think he would fully regain the use of his right arm. Washington was out of danger, but she had painful months and years of recuperation ahead. Three other officers were dead. And then there were the wounds that didn't show. Casey, having to deal with the fact her husband was dead and their whole marriage had been a lie. But maybe not all a lie. Thessaly wondered if that made it better or worse. And Aiden. It was seven years of Casey's life, but his existence in its entirety. And he knew nothing of the context. All he knew was that he didn't have a father anymore.

'I got off pretty lightly, I'd say.'

'You did good. I thought you told me you couldn't hit the broad side of a barn.'

Thessaly shook her head. She thought about the way the gap had forced Sturgis to slow down, to put a hand up to brace himself against the door as he entered. 'Close range. He couldn't dodge in the doorway, I couldn't miss.'

Lee was silent for a moment. 'You think about it?'

She knew what he was asking. How she felt about killing Sturgis. About taking a life.

'Sometimes.'

Thessaly thought about it often. There were few nights she hadn't found herself back in that moment while lying in bed in the darkness, trying to drop off. Visualizing it. The doorway. The deep blue night sky behind the ragged outlines of the treetops. The black shape filling it. The up-close target that she could not miss. The strange calm that had descended on her in the split second between aiming and firing. And then the blinding lightning strikes of the muzzle flash in the dark. Again and again. She had been utterly steady. Now, she flinched with each shot as she remembered it.

She had given a lot of thought to it, and not just because of the counseling sessions. She had crossed a threshold, taken another human life. People had told her that it was okay to feel guilt. That it didn't matter that it was self-defense, it was natural to be conflicted. Then they reassured her that she had the best reasons in the world for doing what she did.

But the truth was, she was shocked by how little that part of it affected her. Killing Sturgis hadn't felt like a transgression. It had felt like ... like exorcising a demon. Like cutting out a cancer.

Lee was watching her. The unspoken question in his eyes.

How did she feel about herself? To know that she was a killer?

She couldn't have told him, not in general terms. But killing Sturgis? For her, it felt like laying down a heavy weight. It felt like breaking the surface of a calm lake after diving for too long. It felt like walking out of the darkness into the light.

It felt like an ending.

Acknowledgements

2020 was a tough year to be trying to focus on anything, so it was a great benefit to have so many wonderful people to draw on for support and advice, even if for the most part, it had to be done at a minimum six-foot distance.

All of my books change quite a bit from the initial roughly sketched out plot, but this one did so more than most. I suspect lockdown is responsible for the fact the climax went from being set in a bustling Grand Central Station to being set in a version of my kitchen and back yard, with Alexa as a supporting character.

Anyway, first of all, thanks go to Laura, Ava, Scarlett and Max for giving me space and time to work. Writing aside, it's been cool to spend more time with you all in our bubble.

My agent, Luigi Bonomi, and Alison Bonomi were as brilliant as always, helping out at all the crucial stages of hammering a book into shape.

Thanks also to my editor, Francesca Pathak, who always has great instincts for those extra touches to really improve a book, even once the author has got past the point of being sick of the sight of it. Thanks to everyone else at Orion, especially Lucy Frederick, Alex Layt, Emad Akhtar and Francine Brody for always being so collaborative and fun to work with.

Hopefully, by the time this novel is published, the world

will be getting back to something approaching normality. More than anything else last year, I missed going to book festivals and author events and hanging out at the bar with bloggers, booksellers, readers, publishers and other authors. Let's make up for lost time soon.

Credits

Alex Knight and Orion Fiction would like to thank everyone at Orion who worked on the publication of *Darkness Falls* in the UK.

Editorial
Francesca Pathak
Lucy Frederick

Copy editor
Francine Brody

Proof reader
Linda Joyce

Audio
Paul Stark
Amber Bates

Finance
Jasdip Nandra
Afeera Ahmed
Elizabeth Beaumont
Sue Baker

Contracts
Anne Goddard
Jake Alderson

Design
Debbie Holmes
Joanna Ridley
Nick May

Production
Ruth Sharvell

Editorial Management
Charlie Panayiotou
Jane Hughes

Marketing
Folayemi Adebayo